MEILA'S
TRIUMPH

JAKAYLA TWITCHELL

ISBN 978-1-68526-407-9 (Paperback)
ISBN 978-1-68526-408-6 (Digital)

Covenant Books
11661 Hwy 707
Murrells Inlet, SC 29576
www.covenantbooks.com

CHAPTER 1

Willowsville, Washington. Late fall, 2001

Meila checked the neighborhood before closing her blinds. She was only thirteen, and her father had left to go drinking again. Some nights, like tonight, he came back so drunk that he had to be carried home. Most nights, he would go out to drink for a few hours and then return and would beat her. He was usually home by now. She wished for an escape, had planned many, but each one had been foiled by the time he got home.

She continually watched the dangerous streets hoping for no out of the ordinary activity. Maybe tonight, she can sleep peacefully. She threw her long, wavy black hair over her shoulder. No one had been on the other rooftops tonight or out on the streets. Many had waited on her father to settle debts with him. Meila had been held for ransom more times than she cared to admit. Her father had either found a way to get her out or paid for her.

She turned off her bedroom light and climbed in between the few blankets she had. Meila had just turned over when she heard a crunch outside. How had someone escaped her notice?

She silently moved over to the window. She saw a figure back away and then run toward her. Meila moved to the corner of her room, slipping under her bed, just as the window came crashing down. The strange man ripped open her door and moved to the front of the apartment. She waited for the footsteps to fade away before leaving her safe spot, grabbing her already-packed backpack, and clambering out of the broken window.

She had nowhere to go but took off running away from her apartment. She had to get away. She knew the price that was on her head and on her father's head. She also knew that if the right price came along, her father would have exchanged *her* for something or something better.

She turned a corner, tucking herself into an alleyway. She was breathing heavily, trying to collect her thoughts. *What was happening back at her apartment? Was her father dead? Arrested!* As long as she was away from that awful place, it didn't matter what happened to him.

Meila looked up, observing her surroundings. She was down by the Old Mill. She had used it many times in the past few years as a hiding place. She pulled open the side door. The man who owned the building didn't like her very much, but she would be quick.

She had snuck into this building often enough, so she knew how to get around it in the dark. She knew of a lookout place on the roof. The Old Mill was only a few streets away from the apartment her father had hid them in. That would give her the perfect vantage point that she would need.

Multiple brick-covered columns filled the warehouse, holding the concrete roof up. A few windows lined the walls, but they were high up. The walls were covered with brick until they hit the window line. Boxes and crates filled the rest of the room. The second floor was much smaller. It was more of just a lookout into the rest of the building. It contained two small offices and a landing that joined them. Only one set of stairs led up to the second floor.

She quickly managed her way through the dark, maneuvering to the stairs and up the rope ladder. She threw open the door to the roof.

A light breeze met her when she pushed the trapdoor open. Meila climbed out. She walked close to the edge of the building. There were many different colored lights coming from her father's apartment—blue and red. *So it was the police that found him first this time.* She sat down on the roof and watched the lights, grateful that she was not there.

Meila looked around again, pausing to look at all of the buildings around her. The night was quiet. She wished that it could be this quiet more often. She wrapped her oversized, black leather closely around her, wishing she would have thought of bringing something that would have kept her warmer. There was no way that she could attempt to get one now.

Meila sighed. She knew that she should not stay at the Old Mill for long. She knew that the cops would start to search for her. The police would know that Old Man Manning had a daughter; he had been arrested before. He had told them so. She needed to get moving. Besides, if Mr. Narch found her up here, he would be angry. She didn't need another issue in her life right now.

Meila stood and turned away from the flashing of the red-and-blue lights. She moved away from them and back toward the trapdoor in the roof.

A noise behind her made her jump. She swung her head back out toward the lights. She scanned the silhouettes of the building, the flashing of the red and blue lights allowing her to look for anything out of the ordinary. Her nerves were startled; the hairs on the back of her neck stood on end. She knew that someone was there.

Meila dared not blink as she moved slowly and lowered herself closer to the roof. If someone was outside, they would probably see her. She heard the noise again. More distinct this time. She scanned the street below her. No one.

She checked the buildings around her. Very few lights were on, but no one was out tonight. Meila looked back toward the lights. Then she saw it—a figure. He was scaling the neighboring building.

Meila stood up a little bit taller. She checked behind herself again, making sure that the door to the roof was still open just in case she needed an escape. It was just as she left it.

She turned back to the man. He had disappeared. Meila scanned the houses and roofs around her. She saw a figure dashing on the roof kitty-corner to hers, running toward her building.

3

As he got closer, she moved to the edge. Something about this man was different. He jumped off of the three-story store to the building next to hers. He started to scale it, moving as if he was a spider. He had no difficulty at all.

A hand clamped over her mouth, a deep accented voice whispered in her ear. "I thought that I told ye not to be coming up here anymore, Wilma." Meila felt the mill owner's hot breath on her neck. Mr. Narch had pinned her arms with one of his beefy hands. "Get away from my building. 'Ve heard the bad that your pops has done. I know right who to turn you over to. Besides, I hear that there is a pretty price for the most wanted man's daughter. Manny's only living relative, the one who knows everything about his business."

Meila bit the man's finger. He released her, letting out a string of curses as he did so. Meila stepped away from Mr. Narch and turned.

"Wilma? Okay, dude. Now it's just getting worse. Last time it was Mylee. But my name is Meila. Just a simple me and a la. It's so simple."

All of a sudden, a figure came from nowhere and took down Mr. Narch. They both hit the ground with a thud. Mr. Narch didn't even try to get up. The other man however, pushed off of him with ease.

Meila bolted towards the trapped door, but the strange man got in her way. He grabbed onto her wrist, and then he closed the door to the roof. Meila inched back; she tried to pull her wrist free, but his grip didn't falter. "Please, I just want to talk to you," the strange man said. He pulled off the cap he had been wearing. When he took off his dark cap, a disheveled tousle of blonde curls fell onto his forehead. The man stood a good six inches above her four feet eight inches. He was built, looking as if he often worked out. He was wearing dark colored clothes, or at least that is what she could make out in the dim light coming from the street lights below. Of the little she could see of his face, the piercing blue eyes seemed to captivate her. He moved his hand and Meila involuntarily flinched. She took a step back, remembering she was on an abandoned roof with this man.

"Will you please release me?" Meila inched back more.

The man raised his eyebrows. "That depends. Are you going to run from me?"

Meila said nothing to that. She pulled on her hand again, trying to wring free.

"I am not going to release you then. Unless you promise to give me a few minutes of your time."

The streetlamps didn't allow her to see much of his face, except for one of his eyes and some of his cheek and forehead. Some of his curly blond hair was visible too. She looked deep into his blue eye that she could see. She had learned to read people's eyes and their body language from a young age. He didn't look threatening. His eyes spoke of kindness and trust. She let her body relax. "Fine, what do you want to know."

The man's cheek moved up, indicating that he was smiling. "Well, first, let's start with names." He released his hold on her wrist. "I am Charlie."

Charlie. *Very nice.* If he hadn't been staring straight at her, Meila would have rolled her eyes. "Meila," she grunted.

He held out his hand. Meila just folded her arms. "What do you want."

"May I ask what you are doing on this roof with this man?" Charlie pointed to Mr. Narch, who was still on the ground.

"I was…*borrowing* it."

He frowned. "You were watching the lights. I saw you from my lookout post. What are you running from?"

Meila pushed her chin up higher. "That is no concern of yours, Mr. Charlie. My business is my business. You had your time. Now leave me be." She started to move past him.

"You are Old Man Manning's daughter, aren't you?"

She froze on the spot. *Play it safe.* "Who?"

Charlie's face went from kind to irritated. "Don't play dumb with me, Meila. Me and my crew have been watching your apartment since before you arrived here. When I saw you start to run, I left my post and followed you the best I could."

"That's why you were scaling the buildings?" Meila tensed. She pushed out a shallow breath. "And now you are going to take me to your boss, probably try to torture me, and then wait to see how much money my dad gives you to buy me back? Hmm? Just like everyone else?"

Charlie blinked. He shook his head. "We may ask you for some information regarding your father's business, but other than that, you can leave."

"You don't want me for the price that is hanging over my head? Maybe you want me for bait. I have been used as that many times." *By my father, mostly,* she thought.

Charlie smiled. "No." He pulled something from his pocket. "I apologize, but that is not how my agency does things." He pointed to Mr. Narch. "If you would like though, I could wake him up and give you to him instead."

Did this man not take anything seriously? "I am trying to get away from this life. From this world."

"I can help you. I know others that can help you too." He stepped toward her. "How about this? You come and answer some questions for me. You can leave the minute that you feel uncomfortable or feel that you have shared too much, then you can leave. If you continue to want our help, you will know where to find us and how to get in. If not, you won't see us again."

Meila looked at him confused. She wasn't entirely sure that this would go her way. Charlie must have sensed her hesitation because he spoke again. "If it makes you feel any better, I will be with you the whole time, and I won't let any harm come to you."

Meila felt a little bit better after he said that. She nodded her agreement.

"Good." Charlie reopened the trapdoor and motioned for her to proceed with him. He pulled out a flashlight and then followed her down.

CHAPTER 2

Meila checked the street again. She had been living on it for almost two weeks, and she was sick of it. She looked down at the card again. The man said to just walk in and ask for him, but Meila didn't feel right about that. It felt like a trap.

She tucked the card back into the pocket where she had found it. It hadn't been in there when she entered the Old Mill, but Mr. Charlie Schren must have slipped it into her pocket before she dashed away. She felt more comfortable with him then some of the men that had taken her, but she wasn't about to go on her own free will into this trap.

Meila pushed herself farther down the alleyway across the street from the building. She knew how to tell if a trap was set, so she would follow home this Charlie bloke, hoping he's ready to keep his part of the deal. She would wait for a couple more hours before taking refuge in the Old Mill. She just had to make sure that she was there before Mr. Narch locked up the building for the night. Meila watched the street, hoping that Mr. Schren would eventually make an appearance. It must be her lucky day.

Charlie Schren walked by in the next moment. He looked as if he just came from the gym. He carried a duffel bag on his shoulder, whistling an unfamiliar tune. Meila watched as he passed the alley she was in. She tucked her backpack further under the rectangular green dumpster and then looked back to Charlie. If he continued to whistle, he would be easier to follow. Meila climbed out of her hiding spot and spotted Charlie just as he was turning a corner. Meila was quick to follow him but tried to stay out of sight. He said that he could help her, and she sure was hoping that he could.

Meila trailed him for another few blocks before he walked into a building. Buildings, Meila had learned, were sometimes harder to track in. She had followed countless people on these roads, but she had never been inside this building.

Meila looked at the sun, her only testament of what time it was Mr. Narch locked the doors just after dark. She still had some time.

Meila sauntered over to the apartment building she had watched Charlie enter and pulled open the door. A man was at the front desk She considered asking him what room Charlie was in, but she didn't want to have anyone else know who she was. Instead, she smiled and moved toward the stairs, putting her hands in her jacket pocket, acting as if she were fishing out a key.

Once she knew that she was out of the man's sight, she stopped off on the second floor. She had no idea what floor Charlie lived on. She could knock on every door and ask for him, but alerting anyone of her whereabouts made her wary. Besides, there had to be more than one hundred doors in this building. That could take all night, time that she didn't have. She had made it this far though. She had to at least start somewhere.

She climbed a few flights of stairs, putting her in between the fourth and fifth floors. She heard a door open above and steps coming down rapidly. She couldn't see the people but gauged that they were coming from the seventh floor.

Meila turned around and ran back down a flight, opening the door claiming that it was the fourth floor. She closed it and waited for the voices to pass. The stairs were silent when she opened the door again, but she never made it one step onto that concrete. A hand clamped over her mouth, pulling her away from the stairs. She tried to scratch the arms and hands that kept her quiet, but another strong arm came around and grabbed her hands in one very large hand.

Her capturer dragged her down the hall and pushed open a door. She was shoved into a room and heard the lock click behind her. Meila knew that her father wouldn't be there to save her this time. As she turned around, she expected to see a gun or a knife, and someone demanding that she be silent. But as she looked, the man pulled off a hat and smiled. "Miss Manning! I wondered if you would follow me home today! What can I do for you?"

Meila just crossed her arms. "How did you know?"

Charlie threw his hat on the table. "How did I know that you needed help? Well, you have been living at the building that I found you in at night. But during the day, you mainly stay in alleyways or dark corners so that you're not recognized." Charlie pulled open the freezer and pulled out a pizza. "Do you prefer pepperoni and sausage or cheese?" He looked up at her, waiting for an answer.

"Is it poisoned?"

Charlie pulled out the pepperoni and sausage pizza and turned on the oven. "Miss Manning, I have absolutely no reason to kill you. As I told you before, I am here to help."

"Why did you try and kidnap me then?"

Charlie thought for a moment. "Oh, you mean when I covered your mouth to keep you from screaming for joy? And from our previous meeting, I have found that you have a tendency to try and run away. I admit that my execution of my plan didn't go as planned, but we are both here now."

"Strange way of making people not run away." Meila almost mentioned that he had almost done the exact same thing when they had first met. He held her hoʼ age on a rooftop. Well, kind of.

"Now"—Charlie sat down at the table; he motioned for her to join him—"what can I do for you?"

Meila hesitantly sat down. She was closer to the door, so if she needed to escape, she could. "You said that you could help me with anything. Are you willing to uphold your part of the deal?"

Charlie intertwined his fingers in front of himself. "Of course. What can I do for you?"

Meila took a deep breath. Her father taught her to trust no one but herself. So what was she doing? "I need a place to stay."

Charlie nodded and then stood. Meila stood as well. She moved closer to the door, ready to bolt. Charlie just smiled at her and pulled a key out of his pocket.

"I'm sorry, Miss Manning. I should have warned you that I was just pulling this key out of my pocket. I wasn't alerting anyone or pulling out a weapon, except I have learned that this can be used as a weapon—either this or a lock pick. People underestimate the power of these tools."

Charlie put the key on the table. "This is now your place. Here is the key. You should have everything that you will need. My team and I couldn't think of anything else that you may want, but if you think of something, you have my contact number."

Meila picked up the key. "How...why?"

Charlie smiled at her reaction. "I knew when I met you that first night, you wouldn't be going back to your father anytime soon, so I made sure an apartment was ready for you, although most of the decorations were left up to April. She grabbed a few items that she knew that you would need. But all of the food was done by me and Cody. Shanta came in and cleaned up after us. Marcus put up anything techy. I'm capable, but he doesn't even use instructions to put them up."

The oven beeped, interrupting Charlie. Meila silently thanked the oven. Charlie set the timer on the oven and then picked up a bag by the door. "You are free to stay here for as long as you like. Please make yourself at home." He opened the door and left her in peace.

Meila walked around the apartment. It contained a fully stocked kitchen, just like he promised. It had a small island in the middle next to a table. The floor was linoleum, but it moved to carpet just a few feet past the table. A small living room was connected to the kitchen. It had light blue walls and strange art. Two windows showed Meila the street below, along with a beautiful view of what she could see of the downtown part of the city.

She turned to one of the few doors in her apartment. Behind the first door, she found a closet. It had a washer, drier, along with some space that had been filled with sheets and towels and detergent. A few of the other shelves were empty, waiting for her to fill them.

She closed the closet and opened the door that led to the bathroom. She checked all the cabinets in this room too, also finding them full and ready for her to use. There was an extra door in the bathroom that led to a bedroom. This room had a window, a desk, and, of course, a bed. She moved to the bed. When she lived with her father, they were always moving. If she got to spend a month in the same area, she was lucky. She never had a place that she could call her own.

She hoped that this apartment could truly be hers. She moved to the window to find that it afforded her the same view that the two windows in the living room had. This one had an escape though. She unlocked the window and pushed it up. She climbed out onto the red fire escape and stood up. The sounds of the busy street sounded next to her. She could hear voices down from the street but could not make out what they were saying. The view was beautiful. She could see over the tops of a few different buildings around them. The fire escape showed her a view of the city. She turned slowly around on it, taking it all in. When she stayed with her father, they always stayed in run-down places, hiding from the police. This couldn't be more different. If she had some time and started to feel safe again, maybe she would come out and read in this small space.

She climbed back into her room and relocked the window. She could smell the pizza in the kitchen, and her stomach grumbled. She couldn't wait to eat! She opened her bedroom door, just as a knock came at the door. Meila walked to it but checked the peephole before opening. No one was out there. Her heartbeat increased. Meila unlocked the door and slowly pulled it open.

She looked up and down the hall but saw nothing. She looked down to find her bag she had left in the alleyway where she had been spying on Charlie, along with a bag of fresh fruits and vegetables and a note. She looked around before collecting the strange items and closing the door. She placed the bag of fruits and vegetables on the end table beside the door and took her backpack to her room.

She still held the note in her hand. She opened it cautiously, hoping it wasn't from her father or one of his men or enemies. She opened it and glanced at the signature—*Charlie Schren.*

Did he forget to tell her something? Curiously, she began to read the short letter.

Miss Manning,

I hope that the apartment is to your liking. I noticed that you had left this behind when you came after me. So, I had a friend bring it to me, and now I am returning it to you. I hope that was the correct thing to do. I had another friend of mine bring you some fresh food. I also ask that you stay inside for a time. I realize this is a lot to ask, but I believe some of your father's men or enemies could be out looking for you. Please contact me if you are in need of anything.

Thank you for being so understanding.

Charlie Schren

Meila read through the note a few more times. Of course, some of her father's men were still looking for her. She wasn't exactly wanted, but she disappeared with important information, information that her father needed. She just hoped that Mr. Schren was right about staying here. If she was found, she would be dead.

CHAPTER 3

A knock sounded early a couple weeks after Meila's uncomfortable run-in with Mr. Schren. She pulled her tired limbs from bed. She was going to hurt whoever was pounding on the other side of that door. She checked the peephole and found that it was Mr. Schren. She yanked open the door. "What are you doing here? And why so early?"

He just walked past her into the apartment and grabbed an apple from a bowl in the middle of the island. "Ah, Miss Manning! I am glad that you are up. I was wondering when you were going to uphold your end of the deal."

Meila shut the door. She was alert now. "Mr. Schren, I—"

He put up a hand. "Mr. Schren was my father. Please call me Charlie."

Meila put her hands on her hips, showing that she was serious. "Mr. Schren, I do not feel comfortable sharing personal information to someone that I do not know."

"I know that it is difficult, but you need to let those things go. You are trying to turn over a new leaf. Me and my team can help with that."

Meila shrugged her shoulders. "The only thing that I know about my father's business is he was into drugs and ammunition."

Charlie shook his head. "I think that you are still holding something back. You are not willing to let something from your past go.

Meila, you are going to have to move on. You cannot hide in fear all of your life."

"This, hiding? You, Mr. Schren, know nothing of hiding." She intended to walk back into her bedroom and slam the door, but his voice stopped her.

"You think that hiding has to do with fear. You think that hiding has to be done in dark, filthy places. Meila, it doesn't have to be.." He moved toward her, but she turned around and backed away.

"Hiding is not fear. Hiding can be more like watching from a safe distance, a safe distance where you can't get hurt," Meila said.

Charlie nodded, "I have been asked to bring you into the office just for a handful of questions. I told them that I would ask before I forced you to come with me."

Meila just stared at him. "You really need to work on your communicating skills."

Charlie looked shocked at her reply. "My communication skills?"

"Yes. First of all, you knock out a guy just to talk to me. Then you kidnap me and tell me that you want to help. I have never met a kidnapper that has wanted to help me. But you are just like all of the others. You just want me because I have the information you want." She backed up farther until she was in her room. "I am done being a pawn for my father." She slammed and locked the door.

A pounding came an instant later. "Meila, come on. Open the door. We can talk about this. I am not going to use you as a pawn."

Meila thought quickly. She made sure that both of the doors to her room were locked. She was on the run again just when she thought that she was safe. She never should have believed him. Never!

She threw on some jeans and a T-shirt. The pounding at her door hadn't stopped. He was persistent. She would give him that. She shoved some clothes into her bag. She wished that she could get some food from the kitchen, but that would mean facing Charlie. She wasn't about to do that.

The pounding stopped. She heard something click inside of her door. She had to get out now. She unlatched her window and climbed out onto the fire escape just as the door opened. She only saw Charlie's head pop through the door before she started at a run down the fire escape.

She saw a figure climb out above her and start after her—Charlie, most likely. She just needed to get to the Old Mill. It had been a safe spot for her before. It could provide some safety right now. Besides, she had been around it long enough to know how it was all laid out.

Once she hit the solid ground, she joined in with a group of people walking on the sidewalk. She knew that if she ran, she would become more of a target, easier to find. A handful of people split off before they hit the next corner. Meila knew that she could be found now, so she took off on a run. She turned her head to check behind her when she felt a hand come down on her arm.

The man pulled her back into an alley, but he wasn't prepared for what was coming. Meila smashed her elbow into his ribs, causing him to release her, but she didn't get far. Charlie's form came into view. He caught both of her arms. "Let me go!" Meila shouted.

Charlie's grip just tightened as she tried to escape. "Meila, I need you to listen to me, but we need to go somewhere more secure." He spun her around and pushed her forward. They walked a couple of blocks until Meila realized where they were, the building that she had staked out as Charlie's workplace.

She looked up behind her, Charlie had taken a hold of her elbow, escorting her toward the elevator. "Please, don't make me do this. My father will give you whatever you want. Please, don't hurt me."

Charlie's surprise showed. "Meila, I am not going to hurt you. Please, we will discuss this more fully once we are inside." Charlie pushed open the large front doors. He showed something to the security guard after the doors and continued to pull her forward. They climbed into an elevator, and Charlie pushed seven. Once the door closed, he released Meila.

"If you don't want my father's money, what do you want?"

Charlie looked down at her. "As I said earlier, you have some information that would be valuable to me and my team." He offered no further information when she tried to ask him more about it.

The elevator door opened, and they climbed off. He turned down the first hallway where they passed a desk and to a door. Charlie pulled out what looked like a credit card, swiping it before opening the door. He motioned her in first, closing the door firmly behind them. Meila took in the people that stood in the room. Charlie put a hand under her elbow and ushered her further into the room. "Meila Manning, may I introduce you to my team?" He pushed her into a seat and moved to the first person.

"This is Marcus. He is our specialist in gadgets."

Meila looked him up and down. He was about six feet tall. He was slender, but she could tell that he was strong. His hair hung down on his forehead, and he wasn't the most neatly dressed. His sleeves had been clumsy rolled up and only half of his shirt was tucked in. His fingers were greasy, but she guessed that it went along with the dirty rag that was hanging from his pocket.

Charlie moved on. "This is April. She is our multiworker. She does a lot of the paperwork for this place, but she is also a whiz with computers. She has great accuracy on the shooting range, and she is currently learning how to fly an airplane. She put most of the personal touches in your apartment."

Charlie pointed to the next woman in the room. "Shanta provides us with most of our meals."

Charlie was about to move on when Shanta spoke. "Charlie! That is not what I do and you know it!" She had a higher voice. It went along perfectly with her cat-eyed glasses. She looked in her late forties. She was more plump than the rest of the group, but she looked as if she belonged.

"Fine." Charlie crossed his arms over his chest. "Shanta used to take care of our undercover work, but has lately been staying off of the field and joining us more in the office. Her work has always been phenomenal, and now primarily buys us food."

Charlie was about to move on when the door behind them opened. Meila's head swung to the new arrival, recognizing him immediately. It was the man that she had elbowed. A younger woman with blonde hair helped him into the room, handing him the ice pack before disappearing back outside the room, closing the door behind her.

The man sent a withering glance at Meila and looked up at Charlie. Charlie introduced everyone else, but Meila didn't really hear it happening. The man that she had injured was sitting just a few seats away, glaring at her.

Finally, Charlie made it to the injured man. "This is Cody. He does all of our physical training. He works with most of us individually, but he's also got a pretty brilliant mind. He keeps up with a lot of the codes that get passed around down on the street."

Cody just stared at her, frowning. "This is her? She looks just as ugly as she fights."

"Cody!" That was Shanta's voice.

April spoke next. "Cody, she just got here, and she could help us. Can't you at least be kind to her?"

Cody just leaned back against the back of his chair. "She is the daughter of a crime boss. I don't think that she will give us anything. She probably has her father listening in on our conversation right now. She is just waiting for the right moment to run back to him."

Meila stood, ready to defend who she was. "That's enough!" Charlie's commanding voice stopped her. "Cody, you have been working the night shift. Get out of here and rest up."

The man stood and brushed past Meila and out the door.

"April, would you and Shanta set up voice recording in the conference room?"

Meila looked to April, the woman who nodded. She had short brown hair, and she looked to be in her early thirties. She collected a box from a closet and moved to another closed door.

Charlie pulled a file from his desk and moved toward Meila. "Now, everything that you will tell us will not leave this office. It is never discussed outside of the walls of this building either, so feel free to tell us whatever you feel is relevant to answer the question provided."

Meila nodded her agreement and moved toward the strange room.

"Also, if it becomes too much and you would like to continue later, we have a room prepared here for you, if you would like that."

"I can't return to my apartment?" Meila knew that she shouldn't have gotten her hopes up, but she thought that he was really trying to help her. This was twice today that she was wrong.

"You may return to your apartment when both of us have agreed about the information you'll be providing. Does that sound fair?"

Meila thought for a moment before nodding.

Charlie opened the door to the conference room. Meila hesitated only a moment before entering. This room was different than the last.

The last room had many desks and chairs. Boxes of unfinished cases lined the walls. Clutter was prominent throughout it. This room differed extremely from the last. It was clean. Not a single box could be found. As Meila stepped farther into the room, she noticed a large corkboard with pictures of people and places on it. She put her fingers on the board and walked farther, letting herself examine the rest of the room. A door was on the same side as she was walking, making two doors into this room.

Good, Meila thought, *another way that I could possibly escape*.

Meila let her eyes move on. A rolling whiteboard sat closely to the door. To the left of the board was a large screen. The rest of the walls sat empty. Meila turned her head to the noise of people entering. April had just finished setting up the voice-recording machine, and Shanta had brought in a stack of papers. Charlie had sat down in one of the seats by the machine. He indicated that she too should sit. She placed herself in the seat next to his, knowing that he would be the one to stop anything if she started to feel uncomfortable.

A box was placed in front of her. She didn't know what it was, but she was sure that it would serve a greater purpose. "What does that do?" Meila asked.

Charlie hit a button on it, causing it to click and then make a soft humming noise. "It will record what you say so that we can go back and monitor it later."

Meila nodded. Her father had something very similar; his was older, though.

"I ask that you please say all of your answers. This will only record your voice. It will not record if you nod your head yes or no."

Meila agreed to his terms and then looked back to the women who were seated across the table. Charlie opened the file that he had brought in with him. "April and Shanta are going to stay in here. Is that all right with you?"

Meila nodded, although feeling outnumbered and uncomfortable with the interrogation, she hoped to finished telling them the information they needed. The sooner this was finished, the sooner she could get away from this building and those she had met.

Charlie shuffled through some papers before settling on one. Meila could tell that it had a lot written on it. Charlie then slid a paper to each of the ladies before turning back to Meila.

"Just so that we have it on record, will you please state your name and who asked you to come in today?"

"My name is Meila Manning, and I was asked—well, more like forced to come here today because of Charlie Schren."

Charlie smiled at the answer and then consulted his list again. "Your father goes by 'Old Man Manning,' correct?"

"Yes."

"And you have lived with him for how long?"

Meila took a deep breath. "Thirteen terrible years."

Charlie nodded and made a note on his paper. Meila looked over at the woman. Shanta was writing almost frantically on her page, but April just smiled at Meila.

"You are his only living relative?" Charlie pulled her attention back to him.

"Yes."

"You don't know of anyone else?"

"He did say something about having a brother, but they were separated when they were young. I believe that my father has no one else. We searched for his brother for a couple of years. The only thing that we found was a headstone with his name on it."

Charlie nodded. "The information that I will be asking for next maybe very sensitive, and it is not to leave this office." He looked at the other two in the room; they both gave an agreeing nod. "Meila, let me know if we need to stop and continue this later."

Meila nodded and grabbed onto the armrests tightly.

"Meila Manning, are you aware of the business your father does?"

"Yes." Meila vainly hoped that he wouldn't ask more on that subject.

"Can you tell us what he did?"

Meila let out a sigh. "Very well. My father was into the drugs and ammunition selling process."

"What was your role in his company?"

"He would ask me to meet with new investors. Sometimes, he would allow me to oversee the shipments. He always asked that I would be in meetings with them. He learned in my early years that I could calculate things quickly."

"What kind of things did you calculate?"

Meila thought for a moment. "Anything. Not just the simple stuff. I mean, it started out that way. But once he learned how fast I could calculate numbers, he started asking for larger things. He would ask me to calculate how much manpower would be needed to make the shipping go smoothly. He asked me a handful of times to calculate how much ammunition or drugs we could fit in a certain amount of space, how long we should wait before the best offers come around. I would also look at those who wanted into my father's company. He knew that I could weed out those we could depend upon and those that we couldn't."

Charlie scribbled down a few more things before continuing. "Can you tell us more about life inside and outside your father's business?"

"Outside my father's business? There was no outside of my father's business. Those who usually wanted out would find themselves dead."

"Have you asked yourself why you are not dead yet?"

Meila blinked a few times. "No. Part of my role in my father's company was a pretty face. He would allow people to take me away.

I have been tortured and bruised and bullied more than I care to admit."

"Would your father let this happen on purpose?"

"Yes. It was part of the business agreements. My father would send me away, sometimes for months at a time, to go and look at other companies that we could de—" She swallowed. "My father loved to send me places that I could get in and find out their secrets. He told me countless times that 'me and my pretty face would get him through the door.' After I got him in, he would then destroy their company, making his own bigger."

Charlie nodded. "Just a few more questions before we let you go. Do you know anything about the drugs or ammunition that he is selling?"

Meila shrugged. "I was forced out of the meetings by the time that subject usually came out, but I can tell you most of the store houses that he has used. If you have a map, that would actually be easier. Some of them have strange names, but I can show you where they are."

Charlie nodded to Shanta, and she excused herself from the room.

"Do you know what came in your shipments or how much there usually was?"

"The amount changed often. It depends on what our supplier could get to us, but a normal load for this time of the year was about three or four truckloads."

"How often did these shipments arrive?"

Meila had to think. "A few times a week, but usually, we go to a different warehouse each time so that we didn't draw any extra attention."

"That makes sense. What about the supplier? Did you ever see him or meet him?"

"No. My father had another man that dealt with all that business. I was never allowed to be around when he came over. I still don't understand why."

Charlie glanced at April. She only nodded and wrote something down on the paper in front of her.

"Is there anything else that you can think of that would pertain to the shipments or how you were used in his operations that you think could be useful?"

"I heard my father speaking with one of his guards a few nights before I left. He was telling the guard how something big was going to happen. I am not sure if this was for a shipment, but they were putting together a meeting with a lot of people. I wasn't supposed to be listening in on that conversation." Meila blinked a few times, not wanting to look weak in front of Charlie. "I was punished for my actions."

Charlie grimaced before moving on to the next question. "Do you have any knowledge of those your father worked with?"

Meila had tucked those memories deep in her mind. "I know a few of the men that he worked with, but none of them had ever worked with anyone else, at least not that I know of. He did always have a group of strange men that attended the meetings. He made sure that I arrived in the room after they did and left before they returned."

"How did he make sure that you were in a secure place?"

"I was assigned a guard on those nights. The meetings could run late into the night. I was assigned a small room with no windows or ways out except for the door. It was a closet, but it was safe."

"Anything else about the drugs or shipments?"

Meila thought for a second. "Nothing comes to mind immediately, but I will think about it. I also know that each shipment comes with a list. A list of supplies that came in the truck, although it is all coded, in case it is intercepted into the wrong hands-"

"They wouldn't know it." Charlie wrote something else down. Shanta came back at that moment.

"Do you know the codes that are used?"

"On the papers or the streets?" Meila questioned.

"Are they different?"

"Oh, yes! They are very different. The terms used on the streets are different for each party, but they are discussed in meetings beforehand so that the correct ones can be used. Those that are on paper are just a different word for the actual item. Those were changed often as well."

Charlie nodded. "Can you break any of them?"

Meila shook her head. "Unfortunately, not. I was never taught any of that. If you think about it from a battle's view, I was the man up front, taking all of the shots and finding information. My father had men who would work on decoding for him."

Charlie nodded and then pointed to the maps that Shanta brought in. "Would you mind showing us where these storehouses are?"

"Why?"

Charlie smiled, probably for the first time since the long interrogation started. "We are trying to get some men off of the streets. We are also trying to put some of the bigger, um, dangerous companies out of business."

"So you are trying to make my father jobless and homeless. Which, in turn, makes me homeless and left on the street. Why did I agree to help you?"

Charlie set his paper down. "Do you remember when I found you that night on the roof?"

Meila glanced at the women listening to them. Shanta smiled, and April nodded, silently encouraging her to continue.

"Yes."

"I promised you that I wouldn't let any harm come to you." He looked at her for a minute. "And that is not going to change. You can have the apartment for as long as you want it, but we have to finish this case first."

Meila just stared into his blue eyes. She couldn't read anything but truth in them, so she nodded. "Fine. But I am going to go crazy if you try to lock me up in my apartment. There must be something else I can do to help."

Charlie smiled and pulled out the maps. "How about you just show us where these storehouses are, then we can talk about you possibly helping us some more."

Meila smiled, grateful that Charlie might be the right person to trust.

CHAPTER 4

Meila zipped up her jacket, wishing once again that she hadn't walked the longer route home. But she had her reasons. She had seen Charlie in her apartment building a few times, and it kind of creeped her out, so she had discreetly followed him home.

She was a block away from him, but she could tell that they were both approaching her apartment building quickly he turned and opened the door but just waited inside of the lobby. Meila thought about slipping around back and just going up the fire escape, but she had locked her window last night, so that was not a possibility. And she knew that the temperature would just keep dropping, so she crossed the street and made her way toward her apartment building.

She stepped into the lobby, grateful to be out of the cold. Charlie was sitting on the couch. He smiled when she made eye contact with him, but Meila just nodded and continued to the stairs.

It only took her half a flight to see that Charlie was following her up. She became even more concerned when Charlie stepped off on the fourth floor. She turned on him then. "Are you following me?" she accused.

He walked to her, a smile on his face. "Nope."

"Then are you trying to watch over me or something because I don't need anyone to look out for me."

He pulled out some keys. They looked much like the ones that she had in her backpack. "I just so happen to live at the end of the hall."

Meila didn't believe it. She crossed her arms over her chest. "I don't find that very likely. I think that you are lying to me." She held up her chin.

"Believe what you want, but the manager of the building gave me a pretty good deal—two rooms for a lowered price. It works out pretty great." He pushed past her and, true to his word, opened the last door, the only door that allowed a pretty good view of the entire hallway. "Now that you know where I live, don't be afraid to come by and visit." He closed his door, leaving Meila out in the middle of the hallway.

She moved to her apartment door, confused by what he had said. She knew that she would be able to process this better once she had food in her stomach.

* * * * *

Meila threw open the door to her apartment and pulled out some chicken tenders, throwing them in the oven to bake. She and Charlie shared an apartment building. He lived right down the hall from her, but he had never really come by her room. He came by that one morning to tell her she needed to come into the office. She had loved the job ever since. Charlie had told her how someone her age didn't typically have a job, especially a job as dangerous as this one. He let her know that he would make sure to give her plenty of time off so she could still enjoy her time as a child. But she enjoyed working. Besides the majority of the team was kind to her, and she appreciated not living in alleyways.

She had found food outside of her apartment a few times, with a note attached to it, telling her it was from Charlie or Shanta. Other than that, she didn't really talk to anyone. Charlie was the easiest to get along with at work. He seemed to actually care about what she found or her different outlook on life. Cody all but ignored her, but she found it was nothing new. He seemed to be shutting everyone out right now.

The oven beeped, telling her it was time to put in her dinner. Meila stood and pushed it in the oven, setting a timer and then moving out into the hallway. She paced up and back in front of Charlie's door before knocking cautiously on it. She stepped back, waiting for him to answer.

It only took a few seconds.

"Hey, Meila. Are you already here to take me up on my offer?"

Meila stared into Charlie's blue eyes. She didn't know how to respond. She had rarely been invited to anything, let alone someone else's apartment.

She shook her head, realizing what a bad idea this was.

"I'm sorry to have bothered you," she mumbled.

Charlie shrugged but didn't close the door.

"The invitation will always be open. My door will usually be unlocked if you ever do need anything."

Meila nodded and then turned on her heels, making her way back to her apartment and going inside. She pushed herself up against the door and let out a sigh, thinking over what she had just done.

CHAPTER 5

Meila knocked on Charlie's door before trying to push it open. It was locked! Wasn't it just last night when he told her his door was always open? Meila shook her head, doubting herself for the hundredth time since last night. She knocked again and then heard footsteps. She listened as the dead bolt was unlocked and watched as the swung open. Cody was standing in the doorway. "Cody? What are you doing here?"

He just grunted and moved past Meila down the hall toward the stairs. Meila walked into Charlie's apartment. She had never stepped foot into his apartment before, but it looked similar to hers. It was cleaner than hers, except for a few things that looked out of place. Had Cody moved them?

She heard noise in the bathroom but did not knock on that door. She instead moved around his apartment. It reminded her very much of her own that was down the hall, but this was a corner apartment instead.

She moved to the windows. They afforded two different views of the street. No wonder he always knew what she was doing. She turned around just as the bathroom door opened. Charlie walked out in his clothes that he would wear to work today. He opened his mouth to say something when he saw her. "Meila? What are you doing here?" Charlie's shock was apparent.

"You asked me to come over this morning. You said that you had something to discuss with me." Meila had worried about what that something might be. She had found a note on the floor by her front door. She had recognized Charlie's handwriting and read the few short lines on the slip of paper. It was a simple request, but she was still a bit worried about this meeting.

He motioned to the couch. "Yes. Every year at this time, I ask to meet with each employee, see how they are doing, maybe ask them what we can do to improve the team."

She nodded. "All right. What did you want to know?"

He sat down on the couch next to her. "How are you enjoying the job so far? I mean, you have had the job for a couple of weeks. Is it all right?"

Meila shrugged. She hadn't really been at the agency long enough to know how great of a job it was. But for the first time in years, she felt safe. She looked up at Charlie, who was waiting for an answer. Meila blinked a few times and then nodded. "I really like it. Thanks for getting it for me."

"No problem. You have been a good addition to the team. Just when we needed someone too."

They sat there for a moment in silence.

"So, is that it, or is there more?"

Charlie shook his head. "This is usually when I ask about home-life, but I have kept an eye on what you do around here. When you aren't at work, you watch TV or read a book."

Meila just shrugged. "It is just something to fill the time. I mean, it is the most peace and quiet that I have gotten in years, but I would at least like to talk to someone outside of work." She could see the wheels turning in Charlie's head. She didn't really care to hear what he had to say, so she tried to change the topic. "My TV would be better if it was bigger though. I have found that the TV you got me isn't as big as the one you have." She pointed to the one that was behind him.

He looked back and then smiled. "Being the leader or a coleader of the team has its perks. That is just one of them. Check this out." He grabbed the remote and turned it on; it had split screens. "This has come in handy more than once. Did you know that you can watch six different basketball or football games at the same time? It's incredible."

"And why can't I get one?"

"You have to become higher up in the ranking. Like I told you earlier, it goes to the leader or coleader or those that are the best on the team."

"And there is that cocky factor that I never miss. Well, I can tell you that Cody was probably looking to grab that from you then."

Charlie turned to her. "Why would Cody want this?"

Meila shrugged. "I'm not sure, but he answered the locked door. I thought that you said you never lock your door unless you're gone."

"I don't. I unlocked it before you came. I had thought that you had actually come and gone before I had gotten out of the bathroom."

"No. Cody answered the door. You didn't know that he was here?"

"Nope. Well, I am sure that he has a good explanation."

Meila rolled her eyes and stood up. Charlie was always fine that people did things as long as they had a good explanation. He was so strange. "Well, if we are done with this, I will go and eat breakfast then."

She walked to the door and was about to open it when Charlie spoke. "Mei."

That name stopped her. She had never had a personal nickname before, but she actually liked it. The only name that she had heard back with her father was mostly insulting. "Pretty face Meila, and that's all she is" or "Mastermind Meila." The last one wasn't bad, but she had only been ten when she had received it. She didn't like the idea of a whole operation resting on her shoulders.

"I just thought that I should open my doors to you," Charlie said.

She turned around. He had already given her so much. What more could he do for her? "You are welcome to come over anytime you want. I know that we work together, but it would be good to be friends."

She smiled. Friends. She nodded. "All right." Then she gestured to the TV. "Only as long as we are allowed to watch a movie on your 'much bigger screen than mine.'"

He laughed, and then she left him for just a moment to grab her breakfast. If he wanted to be friends, then she would take it seriously.

CHAPTER 6

Charlie held up the Manning file that the team had been working on. "We got him! He stepped into one of our traps last night."

The whole room cheered. Meila felt a little bit better, knowing now that she wouldn't have to worry about being so cautious when going around the town. Charlie instructed everyone to clean up any files from the Manning case and put them in a box. He asked them all to join him in the conference room afterward.

Meila only had a few files, mostly because she didn't have clearance for most of this case, so cleaning up for her was quite simple. She was in the conference room before almost everyone else. Marcus had already entered before her, but he was fiddling with something.

Charlie had yet to arrive, but he left the office just a few minutes after instructing everyone to join him there. Everyone else trickled in within the next half hour. Charlie was the last to join them, closing the door behind him. He put down a big stack of files that he had been carrying, passing them down each side. Meila went to open her folder, but Charlie put his hand on it, stopping her progress. She looked up at him. "What?"

"I'm sorry, Meila, but you still don't have the clearance to look at a lot of this information." Charlie slid her a different file, which was a lot thinner. "This is all that you are cleared to help with."

Meila opened the provided file and found many pages, but most of the information was scratched out. She flipped through them.

Several of them didn't even have full sentences that she could read. "Charlie, I can hardly work with this. This information can't be relevant, especially in the state that it is in." She held it up for him to see.

Charlie shook his head. "It is. Just keep looking at it."

Charlie turned to everyone and started the meeting. "We are helping another team with their case. They have been unable to make any headway in the last couple years, so I volunteered our team to try and help them. On the first page, you will see what we can discuss this time without the other team joining in."

Meila looked down at her first page. The first few lines had been drawn over. Charlie continued, but Meila didn't really listen. She flipped through the next few pages in her file; each one had different things marked off.

Another ten minutes passed before Charlie excused her, reminding her that she didn't have enough clearance to hear what they were going to say. She stepped out of the room, closing the door behind her. She dropped her useless file on her desk and grabbed her coat and bag. She hoped that something good was showing on television. She desperately needed a good diversion.

CHAPTER 7

Charlie hit the button to bring the elevator to their floor. "What is this all about?" Meila asked.

Charlie folded his arms over his chest. "We need some information that we think your father could provide, but he won't talk to any of the guys that we have sent in, so we decided to give you a try."

The elevator doors opened and they stepped in. Charlie hit G3. Meila had never been down that far before, but she knew that all the prisoners that they brought in were kept in levels G4 through G7. "G" standing for the underground levels. "Do you think that it is safe for me to be speaking to him? I mean, what am I supposed to say?"

Charlie shrugged but kept his eyes glued to the buttons in the elevator. "Just don't tell him that you work here. When he is released, he may come after you because of it. Maybe just tell him that you have been doing smaller jobs, living in a small house or apartment. I'm not sure, but you have an imagination, so use it." Charlie retorted.

Meila was slightly hurt. Charlie had never said anything so forceful to her. He had never even been rude.

They rode in silence the rest of the way down until the doors opened on G3, and they stepped off—the interrogation floor. Charlie showed his ID at the front desk, and then was handed a paper. Charlie took the pen he was offered from the woman behind the desk, quickly signing his name.

"What is that?" Meila asked, once the pair was seated and the woman behind the desk had disappeared.

"Since you don't have an ID yet, and I am the head agent over the Manning case, I have to sign for you to come in and speak with your father."

Meila nodded and turned back to see the woman had returned with a few guards. Meila stood, expecting Charlie to follow.

"Meila." his voice sounded from behind her. She turned, noticing that Charlie had stayed put.

She gave him a questioning look and she opened her mouth to reply to him.

"This next part you will have to do on your own. I wasn't given clearance to come back with you."

Meila felt a bud of anxiety start to grow in her.

"You're not coming with me?"

He shook his head.

"I can't."

She started moving back to him, but he put up a hand, stopping her.

"There will be a guard with you the entire time. I will be right out here, waiting for you when you are finished."

Meila nodded and turned back to the guard, following him through many doorways before stopping in a room with glass down the middle of it.

Meila followed the guard in and walked through many doorways before stopping in a room with glass down the middle of it. It had a seat for her to sit at and a telephone to be used for communication. The guard stood at the back of the room. He turned on a light, showing her father on the other side of the glass being seated. She watched as the cuffs came off, and he sat down. Surprise shown on his face. "Meila? What are you doing here?"

She smiled. "I was told that you were here. I thought that you would like to visit with someone that you actually know."

He just stared at her. "You shouldn't be here. It isn't safe. You should go back to the business and tell Hunter to come and get me out. The moment I get free, I will be coming back to get revenge on everyone that ever thought of putting me in this building. It's miserable."

"I'm sorry, Father."

He just grunted. "I don't want your pity, girl. Now, why are you really here? Did someone pay you off to get rid of me? Hmm?"

Meila was shocked. She wouldn't ever intentionally kill her own father. He was still a blood relative. "No one told me to come. I came on my own."

Her father slammed on the glass. His face was going more and more red. "Liar!" he shouted.

The guard struggled to restrain him and then cuffed him again. The guards voice came over the phone that had been dropped on her father's side. "Times up, Manning."

Meila hung her phone back on its receiver and stood. She watched as her father was escorted out. She then followed her guard through the hall of mazes to where Charlie was at. He stood when the door opened. "Well?"

She shook her head. Charlie thanked the guard and the person at the front desk. He put a hand on her back and escorted her out to the elevator. He waited until the doors closed until he asked what happened.

"He just asked who paid me off to kill him." She could feel Charlie's shock next to her. "But I think that I might have gotten through to him. Maybe if I went back to him, I could get something out of him."

When Charlie didn't say anything, Meila spoke again. "I would also need a better understanding of this case. Can I have better clearance?"

Charlie shook his head. "We have already been over this. You can't get any more clearance. We will just have to monitor what you say to him." He pulled a small book from his pocket and wrote something down. "I'll have Cody get on that."

The doors opened on the seventh floor. Charlie stepped out first, Meila followed more slowly. She was not in a hurry to get back to the only file that she could look at. She almost had it memorized by now. Charlie was wrong. There was nothing in that forgotten file.

CHAPTER 8

Meila moved down the hall behind the guard. She let out a deep breath, grateful her plan had worked. She had slipped a paper onto Charlie's desk early that morning. Seeing her father yesterday had unsettled her, and she knew she could be helpful if Charlie were to give her another chance. He hadn't even been paying attention when she pointed out he had missed his signature on one of the documents. She had brought that document down with her, showed it to the guard, and was now on her way to see her father again. Charlie hadn't known that she had come this time, and he was going to probably yell at her when he found out. She sat down on her side of the glass and waited until she saw her father's face on the other side to pick up the phone. "What are you doing here?" he sneered. "You come to try and get some information about me and the business?"

She just stared at him for a moment before speaking. "No, actually. I wanted to know why you came after me every time."

He looked surprised and sat back as far as the phone cord would allow him. "So, you want to know why I kept you?"

Meila nodded.

"Easy. You were a pretty face, just like your mother's. She got me to so many meetings. It was so simple. Once she ran, I knew that I had to keep you under lock and key. You know that you still have a spot in the business. Just get me out. Then we can continue what we do best."

"I already know what I do best. For you, that is to be a pretty face. I want to be more than that."

"Well, good luck with that. No one is going to want what you are. You can't legally change your name until your eighteen, so you are stuck being a Manning. That is a danger in some parts of the town, you know."

Meila leaned forward. "And what parts of town would that be?"

"Which one is it not in? In the north, you need to be concerned with Rodriguez and his men. My drug man from the west, and some dealers that live all around town." His face fell after he realized what information he just gave out.

Meila hung up the phone and mouthed a thank you. She rose and motioned for the guard to let her out. She looked back to see her father banging on the glass, yelling something that Meila was glad that she could not hear.

She thought about what her father had said on the quiet ride back up to the seventh floor. She climbed off the elevator with a blonde in glasses and a man with brown hair. They both took the second turn into where she guessed their offices were.

Meila continued on, thinking about how she still had a place in her father's home. Maybe she could use this to her advantage. She and Charlie got along well, but she couldn't always handle anyone else. She needed to keep her options open. Maybe if she did some training, her father would be proud of what she has done and maybe be more than just a pretty face. Yes, that is what she would do; she would become the best that she could be.

* * * * *

Meila watched from behind the two-sided mirror as Cody handed her father a piece of paper. Charlie found out that Meila had secretly seen her father and was putting a stop to it. He told her that it was too dangerous for her. She didn't really understand that. Her father was in jail. How could he be dangerous? But she knew that arguing with Charlie was useless, so she at least requested to be there when Old Man Manning learned the news.

She watched for a reaction and was not surprised when he jumped up. She moved closer to the mirror, smashing her face against it, allowing her to read a few of the words written on the page. A picture was next to it.

"What do you mean you're not sure?" her father's voice came barreling through.

"Sir," Cody calmly said, "we only got some information that she has been taken, and we believe that she is dead. We have not found a body or anything else saying that she is."

"Then why are you down here telling me instead of trying to find her? She has the most valuable information that could bring any agency like yours to their knees."

Meila rolled her eyes. Her father never gave her any important information. Unless he thinks that all of the warehouse addresses are important. Now the agency had all of those. He hadn't really told her those though. She had never learned anything from him.

"Besides, if you find her, I will buy her from you." her father's voice said, breaking through her thoughts.

Meila pushed off of the glass.

"That is all that your daughter is worth to you? Some price?" Cody sounded shocked. He shouldn't be. Meila wasn't even shocked. This happened more often than people would think.

Her father sat down and leaned back in his seat. "She's still alive, and you know where she is at."

Cody sat down too. The agent in the room moved so that he was leaning against the wall by the mirror. "We already told you. She's gone," the agent said.

Manning just nodded. "Tell me all you want, but I don't believe you. Just let her know that my offer still stands, she is welcomed back anytime." He stood. "I'm finished speaking with the two of you."

Cody just watched as Manning left the room. He waited a minute before standing and staring into the glass. "Manning doesn't believe that you are dead. Don't screw this up and be seen anywhere." Cody walked to the door and slammed it on his way out.

Meila sank down against the wall in the empty observation room. She had hoped that Charlie's strange plan would have worked, but now wished that her father's offer to work for him still stood.

CHAPTER 9

Meila cautiously approached Cody from behind. She knew that she needed to speak with him, but she needed to do so when Charlie was not in the room. Thankfully, Charlie got called into an unexpected meeting. Meila knew that she would have to do it soon, before Charlie reappeared.

Cody spoke before she took another step. "Are you just going to stand behind me and hope that I don't notice, or do you want something?"

Meila knew that this part would be much harder. She hated asking for help, but asking anything from Cody was difficult. She stepped up in front of his desk. "Cody," she lowered her voice, "I, um, need some help."

He only spared her a glance. He went back to the paper that he had been writing on. "Why don't you ask your best friend? You know—Charlie?"

"This is a favor that I would rather not ask him."

She had his attention now. He sat back in his seat. "You are doing something that he won't approve of?"

Meila nodded.

Cody put down the pen he had been taking notes with. "What do you want my help with?"

Meila took a deep breath and closed her eyes. "I need you to train me."

When he didn't answer for a moment, Meila opened her eyes. He leaned forward. "You what?"

"Charlie's expertise is needed on another case, and this other case has taken up a lot of his time." Meila took a deep breath and continued. "Charlie told me that you are in charge of most of the team's physical training anyway, so I was hoping you would help me."

Cody nodded. "Fine, but you have to do everything that I say. No questions asked."

"As long as they are physical and not being asked to quit my job," Meila negotiated.

"Fine." Cody put out his hand to confirm the idea. Meila placed hers in it, hoping that this training could be fast.

* * * * *

Charlie pulled a small leather-look-alike wallet. He flipped it open, holding it out to Meila. Meila put down her spoon into her soggy cereal, taking the leather wallet from him.

"What is this?" she asked, recognizing a picture of herself, along with her information.

"Your ID" Charlie simply answered, shoving another spoonful of cereal into his mouth.

Meila carefully pulled the card out from behind its protective plastic sheet. She could hardly believe what she was staring at. She turned to Charlie, clutching the car to her chest.

"Does this mean I can help with all of the cases? Full clearance?"

Charlie shook his head, still chewing his cereal.

Meila tried to not be too put off by not getting full clearance. She wasn't allowed to see everything her father's business did, but somehow, she was hoping this would be different.

"This does allow you to enter the building without me, go up to our offices on the seventh floor, it gives you access to the gym on the second floor, and it can get you into the courtroom."

Meila nodded, grateful to finally have her own ID. It would make her secret training with Cody a lot easier. Meila stood and put it in the pocket of her black jacket. She was excited to try to find something permanent.

Her father's offer still burned in her mind, but whenever she had stayed with her father, her place felt temporary. Maybe it was time that she considered staying with Charlie and his team.

* * * * *

Meila mentally kicked herself for thinking this. These were miserable Cody was going to kill her; she was sure of it. The gym on the second floor of the agency had always been a floor that Meila avoided. But when Cody dropped a note on her desk yesterday to meet him here before work, she didn't question. She knew that if she would ever be any help to the team or her father, she needed to be in shape.

Not that she hadn't been fit before, but not like this. She felt like her insides were about to come out. Maybe if she tried hard enough, they would let her go on a few missions.

Cody started her workout with a two-mile jog, another two on the bike, followed by multiple exercises that included weights. For his next trick, he had her run stairs. She felt awful.

He had told her that the cooldown would be easier, but she should have known that was a lie. He had made her jog three miles and walk another one. Cody then led her through multiple stretches. Meila had twisted and moved her body in ways that she didn't even know was possible. She barely made it back up the stairs to her apartment. Her body was screaming at her.

She had an hour before she had to go back to the office. She knew that she should shower and grab a bite to eat, but she just wanted to flop down on her bed and sleep. She ignored her aching body and grabbed her clothes, heading for a cold shower. She felt genuinely better after that. She grabbed a lunch that she could heat up at the office and then an apple and an orange from her bowl of fresh fruit.

She took the faster route to the office, walking quickly in the cooling air. She hoped that Cody wouldn't make her run outside.

The office was buzzing when she arrived there. She hung her jacket on its appropriate hook and then sat down. A file was placed in front of her and she opened it. She had never seen any of this information, but she was grateful to study something new. She turned her eyes downward and got to work, hoping that this information would help her keep her mind off her aching body.

* * * * *

It had been three weeks since Meila had asked Cody to train her. More than once, she had regretted asking him. She wanted to put men like her father behind bars, and keep them there, but there had to be a different way to train. She had fallen asleep during a group meeting due to exhaustion.

Cody usually worked the night shift; and requested that Meila meet him there toward the end of his shift to train. Most nights, she couldn't even fall asleep until midnight but had to be up at four so that she could meet him at the gym by five. She then worked out for roughly two hours and then returned home. Her shift began at eight, giving her an hour to shower, prepare a lunch, and return to the office. If this is how a working person's life was, she wasn't sure that she wanted it.

Someone tapped her on the shoulder. She looked up to find Charlie watching her. "Is everything all right, Meila? You've been off your game the last few days."

She nodded. She couldn't let him know. The few files that she had didn't really need her attention anyway. She had them mostly memorized. Nothing on them made sense. They were useless, making her role useless, something that they could do without. That is partially why she wanted to train, make herself worth something.

Meila realized that she had been woolgathering and that Charlie had asked her something else. "Sorry, can you ask that again?"

Charlie just shook his head. "Yep, something is definitely bothering you. I think that you are mad at me for not pushing hard enough to get clearance for this case, aren't you?"

Meila just stared at him. Either he was getting better at mind reading or her emotions were starting to show some more. She hoped it wasn't the second one.

"Come on, I'll show you what I do when I'm frustrated."

* * * * *

Charlie pulled Meila farther down the street. He and Meila had left the agency building just a few minutes ago. They had walked north of the agency building for a few blocks and had finally entered a concrete building. They walked through a pair of glass doors and entered into a small lobby. It contained a small desk with a door on one side. Five purple plastic chairs were leaning up against the wall.

A man was behind the counter, standing when they entered.

"Mr. Schren! It is good to see you again. Are you back for some more training? It has been quite some time since I have seen you around."

"It's good to be back." He put a hand on Meila's arm and pulled her forward.

"This is a good friend of mine, and I would like to teach her how to shoot. Can we go back?" Charlie asked, pointing to the door.

The man behind the desk nodded.

"Yeah. You know the way, right?"

Charlie nodded and pushed Meila on. They went through the door, walking through a skinny hallway until they reached another desk. The distinct sound of bullets flying through paper caught Meila's attention. She thought back on how her father trained his men. His voice was always sharp and biting when he was training new men. There was a small abandoned alleyway he usually used as his shooting range. This shooting range could not be more different. It was more controlled and her father wasn't there, hovering over her shoulder to tell her what she did wrong.

Charlie stopped at the next desk, he requested two guns and then turned to her. "This is a shooting range. I come here when I need to blow off some stream. Plus, it is part of training." He accepted the guns from the man behind the counter and then motioned to a door.

"But I understand that you may not need this training, as you have been doing lots of it lately."

Meila just walked a little bit faster. He couldn't know. Who could have told him? "How did you know?" she muttered.

"Well, it wasn't exactly the most secretive spot when you asked Cody. He hasn't told me himself, of course, but almost everyone else in the room did. I asked those on the night shift to keep an eye out for when Cody left for the gym. Then I just made sure that I didn't stop by your apartment until I knew that you had returned. But the real issue is, why didn't you just ask me? I mean, Cody is great and all, but Mei, from what I remember, you can't stand him."

Meila sighed as she put on the safety gear required to shoot. "I was desperate, and I knew that he wouldn't ask for a real reason. I knew that you would. He just cared about how hard he could push me until I quit anyway."

"And are you? Quitting?"

She shook her head. "Cody has been working me hard the last few weeks, but I could have handled it for a few more days."

Charlie stepped up to his mark. "Well, I told him that I would be taking over your training, but we will do it at a more decent time. And Mei"—he waited until she looked back at him—"I already know the reason you are doing this. Trust me when I say that no training can prepare you for what could happen in our line of work." He turned around and shot, hitting the bullseye every time.

CHAPTER 10

Charlie had knocked on her door this morning, announcing that she would start training with Marcus today. She had completed her training with Charlie just the week before, but he told her that he wasn't sure of what he needed her to learn next. I guess he'd made up his mind.

Marcus must have known too because he was anxiously waiting for Meila as she opened the office door. Meila left her things by the door and approached Marcus. She stood by his desk for a moment before he left to find a chair. He returned a moment later with a bar-stool from the kitchen. He placed at the side of his desk, motioning for her to sit before he did so himself. He seemed nervous.

He pulled out his kit that he always used when he tinkered. He held out a few pieces to her and then grabbed the tools needed. "Charlie asked me to teach you how to do what I do," Marcus said, a bit of sadness entering his tone.

"Yes. I tampered with some things when I lived with my father, which always got results. But usually, those results were insults or yelling from my father or one of his men to 'not play with anything,'" Meila said. She picked up the few things that Marcus put in front of her and started to tinker with them.

Marcus just nodded. He looked down at his work and started to work on another project. Meila knew that Marcus was quiet but never like this. He was being almost silent.

She looked back at Charlie, but he was too busy talking with Cody and April to notice. She glanced back at Marcus and then picked up the tools in front of her. After about twenty minutes, she couldn't take the silence. "Marcus, are you all right?"

He looked up. "Is it that obvious?"

Meila looked around the room; no one was paying attention to them. "I mean, you are just acting quieter than you normally do. Did someone say something rude or offended you?"

He shook his head. "It is nothing like that. I am just worried that...that my time here may come to an end."

Meila put down the tool she had been working with. "What do you mean?"

"Well, Charlie asked me to teach you everything that I can do. Is he trying to get rid of me?"

"No! No. He wants me to learn some new skills. He knew that I would enjoy this." She put a hand over one of his greasy ones. "You are still a part of this team. You are needed and important. No one, I repeat, no one could do your role as good as you."

Marcus smiled up at her and then continued on with his work. Meila picked hers back up to, wondering where those strange words had come from. A few minutes later, Marcus looked at what she was doing. "You are going to want to strip those wires before trying to use them. Otherwise, you won't get a strong enough current."

Meila nodded. She did as he instructed. They spent the next two hours working on the project that he had selected. Charlie had been correct. She enjoyed it, and Marcus had a lot to share when he opened up. She also really enjoyed the way that he taught, letting her try it on her own but correcting her if she asked. He would compliment her when something was done well or very close to being done right. He let her fail but wouldn't laugh when she did. He just offered a few directions and figuratively took a step back.

After lunch, she got back to her regular job. Looking through paperwork. Boring. But she had learned early on that the pay was good, and the people that she worked with were some of the best, so she put up with most of the things she was given.

She was concentrating hard on the case of a young girl when a hand came down on her shoulder. She put down the file and looked up. Charlie. "What's up?"

"Not much. I was heading down to the gym and wondered if you wanted to join me."

Meila put down the file, glad that she could get a break. They walked down the stairs instead of using the elevator. They had learned a few weeks ago that the stairs were actually a faster way to get to the gym. "How did your lessons go with Marcus this morning?"

"Great!" Meila said as she skipped down a few more stairs. "He taught me how to rewire a computer. It was interesting and fun. He is also a great mentor, which surprised me since he is so quiet."

She thought about the sad moment that they had earlier and opened her mouth to share it with Charlie. "Good, I'm glad that you like it."

"Yeah, me too. But today, he brought up a difficult topic."

They had arrived on the second floor, Charlie pulled open the door and let her enter. "A lot of topics are difficult for Marcus. Which one did he bring up today?"

Meila slowed her steps so that Charlie could catch up. "He spoke of being fired."

Charlie stopped walking. Realization struck in his eyes. "I was wondering why he kept looking longingly around the room yesterday." He shook his head, as if to clear it. "Do you mind if I go and clear that up right now? I promise that I will be quick."

Meila just smiled and told him that she could start without him. She watched him turn and practically sprint back to the seventh floor.

Meila had changed and started her first lap around the gym when Charlie joined her. "Crisis averted, although I should have been paying better attention. I should have seen that he was on edge."

Meila had been wondering why he had been so concerned about being fired, so she voiced the question. After being asked, Charlie moved his gaze straight in front of them. "I know more about Marcus's story than others do, but that still doesn't give me the right to share it."

"What if you just shared with me the basics, so that I don't touch on those subjects accidentally?"

Charlie considered it for a moment when he spoke again. "He was left behind when he was promised that he wouldn't be. I have tried to reinstate trust back into him."

Meila let that stew as they finished running their miles around the track.

"So I know that I told you that our training was complete, but I had forgotten that you had expressed an interest in another thing," Charlie said when they had stopped.

Meila was doubled over, trying to regain better control of her breathing. "What would that be?" Her breathing was getting better.

"Climbing."

A smile crossed her face. She had forgotten about that! She stood up. "Sure, where do you train for that? Outside?"

"Well, lucky for you, they actually have a wall inside that I started on. But our apartment is also a good place to train."

Meila looked at him.

"What? You think that I chose the apartment building because it was in a good location or anything like that? No way! The bricks, although very solid, have a lot of good places for gripping, making it easier for an escape. Plus, my buddy owns the building, so I got a good deal on the rooms."

"So if you care so much about the building, can I have your TV?"

Charlie laughed at the memory that they had shared there. He gestured for her to follow him. "Come on, I will show you this wall and how to climb it before you get any more crazy ideas going through your head."

Meila laughed along with him and then followed him, ready to learn how to scale a building.

CHAPTER 11

He watched from the rearview mirror as his daughter brought out Old Man Manning. He had been watching the streets over the last few months, observing what went on during the night shift at the agency building. His daughter had been working from the inside, going downstairs to visit Old Man Manning. She would check the guard routes and search for anything that might stand in the way of their plan. He had worked with Old Man Manning for years. He just hoped the man would cooperate and listen to what he had to say.

Two figures appeared out of the main glass door and made their way toward the black car he was driving.

He hit the Unlock button on the door right before his daughter reached for the handle and shoved Old Man Manning into the car.

"Any issues?" he asked when his daughter climbed in the front seat.

She shook her head and smiled.

"No one even questioned me on the way out." She dropped the fake ID badge of some random agent she had pickpocketed. She reached back to Old Man Manning and unlocked his handcuffs.

"Ready to be a free man?" he asked his old friend.

Old Man Manning smiled, a dark tint coming into his brown eyes. He nodded firmly once before they took off into the night.

* * * * *

Meila was deep into her work when a loud voice broke her concentration. "Emergency meeting!" Charlie yelled. He was staring at his computer screen. His face was a mixture of fear and anger.

Meila closed the files that she had been working on. Everyone else had stopped their work and moved toward the conference room. Meila joined them, sitting in her regular spot. Charlie waited for everyone to be seated before speaking. "We have a new situation that needs to be addressed. I know that we have closed this case, but it will need to be reopened—all of the files, anything that we had on it!" He slapped his hand on the table, causing everyone to jump a little.

They sat in silence. Meila looked around. Those that were there looked as confused as she felt. "Charlie, what case is it that we need to reopen?"

He rubbed his forehead. "The Manning Case."

Meila sat in shocked silence. A heavy weight started to grow on her shoulders. A moment ago, when she had glanced around the room, almost everyone had made eye contact with her. This time, everyone cleverly avoided her gaze.

"Why?" she asked.

"Meila, your father has miraculously escaped from the agency cells downstairs."

"Which means...?" she trailed off, worried what information she may learn.

April spoke from across the table. "Usually, suspects in cases like this are, um, urged to stay inside or to leave the country. This is primarily a safety precaution that we provide for them."

Meila looked back at Charlie. That did not clear up anything. "Meila, do you think that your father would come after you for any reason?"

She shook her head. "Doesn't he think that I am dead?"

Charlie nodded. "If he believes that a fall from the building you were clinging to could kill you, then he shouldn't be looking for you. But if he happened to see you or one of his men saw you in these past months, they may warn him."

Meila acknowledged what he was saying. "So, are you sending me away?" The weight grew some more.

"No. If they have already seen you, then sending you away wouldn't do anything, although it would be smart. You need to have an escort with you when you go out or allow others to get things for you."

Meila looked around the table again. "Am I going to have to move?"

Charlie smiled. "As I have told you before, I chose that building for many reasons. It has a good view and lookout points of the city. I can usually see things happening before they do."

Meila nodded.

"All right." Charlie turned back to the whole team. "Everyone else, I need you on file hunting. I am not quite sure where we placed those files. Also, fill in those on the team that work the night shift when they come around."

Everyone else left. Meila just sat there in silence, staring at her hands, trying to let the news that she was not safe anymore sink in.

"Mei, you okay?" Charlie had pulled out the chair by her and sat down.

She noticed that the door closest to them was closed, giving them relative privacy. "I just can't believe that he got out. I thought that I was finally safe and could maybe live a seminormal life." She heaved a sigh. "I guess that I am just disappointed."

"Disappointed in what?"

She looked up at Charlie. "When I was living with my father, he always told me not to get too comfortable. Things could change any day. I was just so happy to finally have something that was mine, I'm not ready to leave it behind."

"Mei, you aren't going anywhere. We are just going to escort you home. I live just down the hall from you, so keeping a watch out will be easy."

"What about when I am here? Are you going to restrict me to this office only?"

Charlie thought for a moment. "I know that if I said yes, you would do everything to break that rule, so I am going to say that you are free once you get in the building. But I would advise that one of us is with you when you are at the gym or shooting range. Just because they have windows that can be looked into."

She nodded. The weight felt like it had been lifted slightly from her shoulders, but she knew that it was still there. As long as she was in this building, she'd be grateful that she still has some freedom.

CHAPTER 12

Meila put the few files that she was allowed to see back down on her desk. She leaned back in her chair and groaned. Her father had been gone for almost a week, and no one had found any new information. Charlie had gone to a department meeting and was reporting anything that they had found. She hoped some other team had found some information they hadn't, but she knew that those chances were slim.

Meila stood, deciding she needed a bathroom and a little bit of exercise. She moved past the few desks and out of the door. Cassie wasn't at her desk, but she had taken a few days off, claiming she hadn't felt good. Cassie was the secretary to their team. She worked hard to keep all of their schedules straight, with all of the meetings and different cases they were working on. Cassie had curly blond hair that ended at her shoulders. She was friendly and easy to talk to. She showed up to work most days wearing jeans, a floral shirt, and sandals. A matching pair of earrings always dangled from her ears.

Meila walked to the bathroom but saw that a sign was on the door. She stepped up to it and tugged on the door. It was locked.

7th floor bathrooms are closed until further notice.

"What?" Meila's shoulders dropped. She would have to go down a flight of stairs before she could use a bathroom. *Fine!* she thought. *I guess that I don't need a bathroom.*

She started back to the main office. She hesitated before she opened the door. She heard her name. She looked behind her but didn't see anything. Her name was said again, and she realized that it came from inside the room. "She really isn't that good of an agent," a voice said.

Meila sat down so that they couldn't see her figure in the frosted window.

"Cody, she is still learning. We have to give her time!" That was April's shocked voice coming through the crack under the door.

"April, she is a screwup. I am just waiting for her big opportunity to come so that she can mess it up and leave."

"Cody, don't say that. You are tired because you worked all night and then came in again this morning. Meila is a nice girl and smart. She gave us details on the Manning case that no one could."

"Yeah, but she is only going to give us enough to lead us on a wild-goose chase. After that, she will take all of the information that she learned here and run back to her precious daddy." Cody said the last few words in a childish, whiny voice. "She probably aided in the escape. The security tape did show a girl."

"And it couldn't have been any girl?" April asked in mock astonishment.

"April, give me the benefit of the doubt. Come on. She has been trying to get out of here since the day she arrived."

"Cody—"

Meila didn't hear what April was about to say. Marcus had opened the door and spotted her. "Meila, what are you doing on the ground?"

She stood and pushed back against Marcus and glared at Cody as she entered the room. She sat down at her desk and thought of how much better her father would treat her, even if he did hold a price over her head.

It didn't take long for her to come up with a plan. She looked out the window and saw the dark clouds beginning to form. Good, no one would be able to follow her tracks. She shuffled through a few files before she knew that she wouldn't be able to concentrate any longer. She decided that she needed to leave. Being around Cody was only making her anger worse. She stood and walked out of the awkwardly silent room.

She moved out of the office door and turned the corner, proceeding quickly down the hallway. Charlie was just stepping from the elevator as she hit the button to go down. "Meila," he said.

"Charlie," she replied. She hoped that he would leave it at that, but she knew that he wouldn't.

"Where are you going?"

"Bathroom."

Charlie pointed behind her.

"The ones up here are closed until further notice."

He nodded, stepping off and holding the elevator doors so she could enter.

"Thanks," she said just as the doors closed. She had never been more grateful for a strange coincidence as bathrooms were closed. If Charlie knew where she was really going, he would have followed her. Or not let her leave. She knew that it was going to be dangerous, but she couldn't take Cody's sharp words anymore.

The elevator beeped, telling her she had made it to the lobby. She stepped off and made her way toward the glass doors. Now all she had to do was find her father. Now all she had to do was find her father.

CHAPTER 13

Meila glanced to the right of her. She recognized some of her father's guards in the building across the street from her. She had gotten their attention, but now they were shooting at her. She was hoping that she could just walk back to her father.

Meila threw herself onto the brick wall, needing to get some cover. The unforgiving rain made the bricks slick, but that did not slow Meila too much. She just needed to get around the corner of the building, and she could get out of the guards' firing range and to safety.

Meila ducked as the shot hit above her head. She was on the balcony a few floors up, being shot at by her father's men. They had spotted her but didn't truly know who she was. The rain was coming down viciously.

Another shot hit the brick wall next to her, causing the brick to slightly crack. Meila took a deep breath in as she swung herself off the balcony she had occupied and onto the slick wall. She moved slowly at first, testing the wall and seeing how wet it truly was. Another bullet whizzed past her and landed close to her head. She didn't have time to be cautious!

Meila moved faster to the corner of the building, hoping that it would provide more of a barrier between her and her father's men. She looked back to the lit windows across the street and saw the guards. Now each one had their guns pointed at her. How did she used to think of them as friends?

Meila felt her fingers start to throb. She took a deep breath and turned back to the more pressing matter. How to get down.

She pushed herself farther down the wall, remembering what Charlie had taught her. Meila looked to the building her father was in and sighed. She looked back to the task at hand and moved down the wall some more. The whirlwind of bullets hadn't really stopped, but they had slowed down some.

She started farther down the wall, but her left foot slipped. She looked down beneath her. She was still probably two floors up. It was way too far for her to jump without her injuring herself. She tried to secure her left foot, giving relief to her aching arm that was still recovering from her training and all the falls that had happened while learning to scale.

She made it farther down the building before she lost her grip completely. She fell to the ground hard. Thankfully, she had descended enough that she only fell about a little more than a floor. She tried to move her tired arms, but couldn't. She saw darkness come in from the sides of her eyes but saw nothing shortly after that.

* * * * *

Someone was shaking her. "Meila." The voice came from miles away.

She opened her eyes a sliver to see someone's muddy boots.

"Meila," the voice came more urgently and more distinctly. "Meila." Desperation hit as Meila recognized Charlie's voice. He was wearing his black slacks and a blue button-up shirt. The rain was dripping off of the hat that he was wearing. Meila blinked a few more times before his half-lit face came into focus. Concern and worry lined his face. Meila pushed herself up to a sitting position, letting the dizziness subside before she accepted the hand from Charlie to help her stand.

"Charlie? What are you doing here?"

"Attempting to save you." He turned to someone behind him and spoke. "Put Meila's dummy down here. Make sure to make her face nonvisible. She needs to have the blood coming from her head. Make it look like it is enough that she can't be saved." Charlie turned his attention back to Meila and slipped a jacket over her shoulders.

"I have a car parked halfway down the block. Are you fine to walk by yourself? Or do you need help?"

Meila thought for a moment before shaking her head and started toward the black four-door Camry ahead. "This is a new test that we are trying. I hope that it works because if so, you will be seen as dead."

Meila was quiet until Charlie put her in the back of his car. He pulled away from the curb and started back toward the middle of town. "Mei, what were you doing there tonight? Don't you know that you could have been killed?"

Meila nodded. She knew a lot about what her father did and how he treated people. He was a criminal. "Charlie, I know I shouldn't have tried to go back to him, but after listening to Cody, and others saying rude things about my father. I couldn't keep it in anymore, so I went back." Meila waited to see if Charlie would say anything, but when he didn't she continued. "I know about what my father does and the reputation he has, but he is all the family I have left."

Charlie was silent for a few blocks. He finally pulled into a lot next to their apartment building. He helped her out of the car and grabbed her bag. He grabbed her under the elbow and steered her into the building. They quickly took the stairs, and Charlie opened his apartment door for both of them. "Mei, you have got to stop doing this. It is getting ridiculous," Charlie said once he had shut the door. "When the team got the alert, you should have seen how frantic we all were. Mei, I know that you don't see us as family, but that is what we are, and we don't leave other family members behind."

Meila put her arms around herself and walked over to the couch, wishing that she could just sink into its cushions and disappear. "How did you know?"

Charlie smiled and plopped down in the chair across from her. "When you got onto that elevator, I could see the gears turning in your mind. I decided to call up a friend who owed me a favor. I asked him to follow you and try and keep you safe. I wish I could have come sooner, but I didn't know exactly where you were going until I got his call. I had hoped that you would have just come to your apartment." Charlie sighed and rubbed at his face. "He called and kept me updated once bullets had started to be shot off. I came as quickly as I could. Mei, a fall from the building where you were at in this condition could have killed you. You shouldn't have done it. So why did you?"

Meila dropped her hands into her lap, "You all hate me because of who I am, and why I am afraid to. I see it on everyone's faces when I am asked to do something. Don't you think I notice that you always have double-checked my work? It hurts to feel as though I am treated differently, so I made a choice. I was going to go back to my father. At least under his roof, people respected me. I wasn't made fun of. If I were, my father would quickly put an end to that."

"So you miss respect?"

"I...I don't know." Meila was so confused. She didn't really know what she wanted. She may have been respected in her father's house, but she wasn't liked. She knew a few people who actually liked her at the agency. Those in her father's house feared her. Her name was enough to bring fear into anyone's eyes; here, it didn't. But for the first time in a long time, Charlie and his team had given her something that her father never could—peace and safety.

"What did you find?"

Meila just shrugged. "I found that my father doesn't really want me back. The way that his men were shooting at me should have been a clear sign. I'm sorry, Charlie. I guess that I was just trying to prove myself, but I guess that I am just a screwup, just like Cody said."

"You listen to Cody way too much. Besides, he has been having some problems of his own right now, but he hasn't been able to sort them out. He just took his anger out on you." Charlie sat in silence for a moment. "He admires you, you know."

Meila looked at Charlie doubtfully. "Cody? The Cody I know?"

Charlie nodded, a smile starting to grow. "He said some good things on your behalf to keep you on this team."

Meila thought for a minute. She tried to picture Cody standing up on her behalf. She finally had to give up because she couldn't. Charlie held out his hand. "Please promise me that you are going to stop running from me and the team. We really are trying our best to help you. Besides, it is so much easier to talk things out, instead of having to chase after you."

Meila put her hand in his. She was becoming more confident around Charlie.

"Promise?"

Meila nodded. "I promise."

Charlie released her hand and stood up. He opened his arms and she ran into them. She squeezed him hard before he said good-night and let her leave.

CHAPTER 14

Meila stuck another bite of cereal into her mouth. Charlie walked into her apartment as she swallowed. "Morning, Charlie."

He didn't say anything but slapped the newspaper down in front of her. She picked it up and flipped through a few of the pages. "The hardware shop downtown is going out of business."

She dropped those pages onto the counter. "Charlie, I think that you are losing your touch. I mean, that hardware store is extremely vital to this case." She smiled at her own little joke and looked to Charlie. His smile, however, was not there.

He pulled the paper to where he was leaning against the counter and opened it to the next page—the obituaries. He pushed them toward her and then walked over to get himself something out of her fridge. She looked back at the page. There across the top was a picture of herself and a few paragraphs about her.

"What is this for?"

Charlie grabbed a bowl out of her cupboard. "You were the one that went on that crazy mission by yourself." He grabbed a spoon and then sat down next to her. "Next time, maybe alert someone before doing something stupid."

"Uh, ouch." She looked down at her cereal. She had barely opened herself up to Charlie, and he had to say something like that? "You know, I thought that Cody was the rude one."

"Mei, that's not what I meant." She heard his spoon drop in against his bowl, and she looked up. He was rubbing his face in frustration. "When you are on a team, especially like the one that we have, you always have a partner, someone to watch your back and someone you can confide in. You didn't tell your partner anything."

She shook her head. "I don't have a partner, so I don't need to report to anyone."

"You do have to report to someone." He pointed to himself.

"You aren't my partner." Meila let the disbelief be heard in her voice.

"I am," Charlie answered back.

Meila had to think for a minute. "But your partners with Cody."

He shrugged. "I can have more than one partner. Besides, I am one of the team leaders. I choose who I get to work with."

Meila let that sink in. Charlie wanted her there. That made the future seem a little brighter. Something still nagged at her, though. "But you don't treat me like a partner. You said that they share information. It seems that everyone has left me out of the loop."

Charlie nodded. "I know, but that is also changing." He put a bite into his mouth.

"Am I finally getting more clearance?"

Charlie's hand froze in midair. His spoon dripped with milk. "Not really."

"Not really?"

He put his spoon down and turned on his chair, facing her more fully. "I have asked those upstairs, and they are still hesitant. Now that they know what you did a few nights ago, clearance will be slower to come."

"Then how am I supposed to help? Maybe you can talk to those upstairs and see if they can give me a low-key case? They don't know how much I can do. If I was given a chance, I really think that I could impress them."

Charlie shook his head. "I have a few files that I can give you without getting into too much trouble. I will give them to you once we're at work." He turned back around and continued to eat his cereal.

"So, I can help with the case?" Meila asked hopefully.

Charlie just kept on eating his breakfast, ignoring her. Meila turned back to her breakfast but didn't really feel like eating it. She was excited to do something other than train.

CHAPTER 15

A week later

"What about the information specialist?" Charlie asked.

Cody looked to Meila and gestured for her to take the floor. All eyes turned to her. She stood and straightened her shoulders, stepping past Cody to where Charlie stood.

She turned to the group, looking in all their faces in turn. She took a deep breath and then began. "When I was let into the case"—she glared over at Cody—"I found things that others had chosen to overlook. For example, this page." She shuffled through Charlie's pages until she found the one that she needed; it was a picture of the apartment building that she had escaped from. "This building is not one of the more common buildings used. My father had a few places that he liked to stay, places that he felt safe. Those options are getting smaller and smaller, though."

"What makes this building or any building your father uses important?" Cody sneered from behind her.

"Well, my father always met with lots of people, whether it was new employees that I was over or if it was a shipment, or maybe he just needed to meet with some other bigwigs in the business. He would always make sure that each building had certain attributes."

Meila shuffled through a few more pages before discovering the correct information. She pulled them out and laid them on the table.

Fourteen different pictures lay before them. She turned most of them over, finding a simplified blueprint on the back. She pointed to the first few. "These are all on the south side of the city. He has used them more than once, which he didn't always do. He usually uses only a few at the same time.

"These next ones are on the west side. Those are in the east." She pointed to a few others. "North side." She held up the ones she had and said, "Center of town."

Someone let out a low whistle. Everyone was in shock. What they had thought of as useless information had been her treasure. A hand came down on her shoulder. "Well, it looks like Miss Manning should have been a part of this case the whole time," Charlie said pointedly at Cody.

Cody glared at the two of them for an awkward moment and then left, slamming the door behind him. Charlie's calm voice sounded behind her. "Keep going. I'll be back in a minute."

The hand left her shoulder, and Meila found herself at the head of the room, in charge. A smile lifted on her face. "My father used these buildings because of the good placement. All of them are in parts of the city that police can be found in, but not a numerous amount. He also made sure that it was a decent place for meeting. It had to have a large room, where he could meet with others, but it also needed a good escape."

"Escape from what?" said a voice.

"Anything. Anyone." Meila took another deep breath. "My father always made sure that I was out of the room before many of the dangerous investors came. Very few meetings went without hearing gunshots. I also would hear a lot of yelling and shouting. But I was locked away in some secret room that only my father and a few of his most loyal men would know about."

"So each building had some type of room you could stay in?" April asked.

Meila nodded. "Along with a secure room for him and his men. And also an escape from those as well. He always had a few men that would stay in the buildings next to ours." She gestured to the pictures. "As you can tell. Each of these buildings has those characteristics. Along with a backdoor entrance or a side entrance so that those coming and going wouldn't draw extra attention."

Everyone just stared for a moment, then all of a sudden the room was utter chaos. Pages went flying everywhere, and people hurried out of the room. Meila just stood in shocked silence trying to figure out what was going on.

After about thirty seconds of the noise, a strong voice broke through the noise. "Hold!"

Everyone went still and looked to the door. Charlie was standing there. "What is going on?" he demanded. He scanned everyone in the room, trying to get a handle on things. "I was outside in the hall when I heard noises in here that shouldn't happen during a meeting."

He looked at Meila. "Explain this."

Meila just shrugged, not understanding the confusion herself.

He turned to April. "Can you do better than Meila?"

She stepped up to Charlie and nodded. "Meila provided us with critical information, information that could possibly help us find her father. We were all just trying to get out of here and get to work."

Charlie nodded, then he turned to the rest of the room. "It is great that you all want to help, but we run things more smoothly than how you were previously carrying on, so I ask that you listen to the instructions given. I was unable to be here the entire time, so Meila will give out assignments."

Meila looked to the group, grateful that she could finally help. She thought of what needed to be done before she started to speak. "April, I need you and a few others to find out where my father has been. He doesn't usually stay in one place for too long, especially during this season. I need you to find out how long he was there and if he requested to use the conference rooms. Please choose a few to help you."

April nodded and then pointed at a few individuals, asking them to follow her out to the main office.

"Marcus, I need you to start looking at all the buildings that have these characteristics: conference room, spare room, side or back entrance, and enough buildings around it to be sufficiently guarded. Maybe see if you can track down his last address. He moves often and usually covers his footsteps pretty well, but it is something we can look into."

He finished writing down the requests. "Do I get a team too?"

Meila nodded and waited for him to quickly grab those he needed and leave the room.

"Shanta," she turned to the plump woman as she spoke, "I have a feeling that it is going to be a long night, so will you go pick up some food and beverages? You can join in on the search when you return."

She nodded and left.

"The rest of you, keep digging through files try to find anything that you think could be helpful. If you are wondering if it may be, come and ask me. I know my father's business pretty well."

Everyone else left, leaving just her and Charlie in the room. "What can I do to help?" he asked.

Meila shrugged. "I am not sure. I just hope that I am not sending everyone out there on a wild-goose chase."

"What is it you are trying to find?"

"My main goal is to find my father. He moved around a lot and was always trying to evade the law. I thought that he would have been caught long before now, so that is what I am going to have you do." She turned toward Charlie. "I need you to get in contact with all of the local police stations and agencies around here."

She moved to the map of Willowsville. "There has to be a reason as to why he hasn't been brought in yet, so I will need all of the charges surrounding him."

When Charlie didn't speak, she turned back around and looked at him. He was just staring at her. "Mei, are you sure you want to do this? That is why I didn't have you heavy involved in this operation. This is your father."

She nodded. "He may be my father, but he has done a lot of wrong, and if we leave him out on the streets, then he is just going to continue to hurt people. I want to prevent others from getting hurt, just li—"

She couldn't finish her thought. *Just like me.* Tears welled up in her eyes, and she turned away from Charlie. A hand came down on her shoulder. "I'll have Cody help me. He knows a lot of the men at many of the police stations. He might be able to weasel some information out of them that I wouldn't be able to get out." The hand left along with Charlie.

Tears leaked down her cheeks as she picked up all the pictures. She put them in the thick file that had been left on the table and then pulled it to her chest. She stood just inside the door, hiding behind the wall until her emotions were in check. She had to be strong for the team. They needed her, or she would make sure that they always needed her. What about after this case? Would they get rid of her? She shook her head, clearing that thought and then stepped out into the main office.

Shanta had returned with the food by the time that Meila had made it back to her desk. Shanta made a dramatic exit from the kitchen as she was being mobbed by everyone that was going to retrieve food. She smiled and moved toward Charlie's desk. "Okay, boss. I am done with my part so far. What else can I help with?"

Charlie pointed to Meila. "As much as I would love to claim the reward of all of the hard work being done, it is not me who should be getting it. Meila is in charge for right now, so report to her please."

Meila watched as Shanta put on her cat-eyed bright-blue glasses and trotted over to Meila's desk. "Okay, boss! I'm done. What can I do next?"

Meila smiled. "Well, I am glad that you asked. I just came up with a new possibility that could help us pinpoint where my father may be."

Charlie joined them at Meila's desk and sat down in one of the chairs across from the one Meila had placed herself in. "The drug my father sells and distributes has a growing season. If I remember correctly, that time is just about to end. His shipment usually comes from trucks in the north and boats from the west. He usually has his main meetings in the other three regions. What I need you to do, Shanta, is research this drug." She handed Shanta a file and then turned back to her project.

She turned on her computer and looked up, wanting to see if anyone had made progress. Instead she found Charlie's blue eyes staring back at her. She sat back farther in her seat. "Is there something that I can help you with?"

"I know that I am a little bit out of the loop with this operation, but would you mind explaining to me why you are having Shanta study this drug? It seems like you are sending her on a wild-goose chase."

Meila shook her head. "I have a reason." She opened the bulky file that she had brought from the conference room. She pulled out the blueprints of the buildings along with a few other items, intending to lay them all out on her desk but had a better idea. "Do you mind if we put this all up on the whiteboard?"

Charlie nodded and stood, motioning her to proceed with him. She picked up the file and stood. "Will you please grab the map that I first marked when I arrived here?"

Charlie stared at her as she walked; she stopped when she reached his side. "Yeah, but it may take me a few minutes to find it. I can't remember exactly where I have put it. Plus, I don't know if it has been moved."

She just nodded and continued. She closed the farther door in the conference room, hoping to stop people from overhearing. She had almost all the pictures up on the whiteboard when Charlie returned. "Here is what you needed, boss, but it still doesn't explain why you wanted Shanta to research the drug."

Meila opened the map, studying the various locations where her father's warehouses were. Only a few of them were next to buildings and hotels her father used. Others were next to abandoned homes, another place her father would hide.

"I had Shanta research the drug, my father called it fiedrum, because how it is transported." She made a few marks on the map and then pointed to them.

"My father owned a few different warehouses throughout town that stored both ammunition and fiedrum. When thinking back to the warehouses I have been in, I noticed how most of the warehouses, which had the fiedrum in it, were stored closer to the water. They were in tightly concealed boxes and would only be opened when a potential buyer was coming through. The ammunition could be stored anywhere, but I know my father kept most of it on the east side of town, farther away from the water."

Meila pulled out a green marker and a blue marker, drawing on the warehouses she knew had ammunition in them and which of them had fiedrum stored in them. A handful of warehouses in the center of town had both colors, indicating it had both fiedrum and ammunition inside.

"Could you tell what was coming to the warehouse by the truck they used?"

Meila shook her head and moved to the pictures she had placed on the whiteboard.

"My father would use different trucks every time. Most of the time, the truck size depended on what warehouse the shipment was being brought to and how much my father asked to be brought in."

"What about the warehouses where they were stored together?"

Meila thought for a moment, trying to remember those days she had fought so hard to get out of her mind. "The drugs and the ammunition were always brought in separately. Unless my father was moving them from one warehouse to another, then they were brought in together."

Charlie tapped his chin thinking. "Where did your father get the trucks?"

Meila shrugged. "I am not sure. He had another man that he worked with that always got that sort of supplies. I never met him though."

Charlie nodded. "So you are trying to figure out which warehouse has what in it and how it is transported."

Meila nodded. "It could actually help when we invade the building. If this drug is diluted or somehow stopped, that would be nice to know also. Really, if we could figure out where this drug was coming from, we could stop having issues with it. But if the building has weapons in it, then we know that we can't throw a bomb on it or something crazy like that."

Charlie looked up. "When have we ever thrown a bomb on something? Honestly, Meila, do you know anything about bombs? They create more damage than anything."

She waved him off. "I know. It was just the first thing that I thought of. Besides, bombs are not safe for those around the area." Meila nodded and pulled out a chair and sat down, staring at the layout in front of her.

Charlie took the map and hung it on the corkboard wall next to the whiteboard. He then sat down across from her and stared at it too. After about ten minutes of silence, Charlie spoke. "I think that you have something. Keep thinking about it. I have no doubt that you will figure it out." He stood, lightly punching her arm before exiting the conference room, closing the door behind him, letting her think on what she had learned.

CHAPTER 16

Meila was pondering something written in the margins of one of the pages, when a bright bit of clothing caught her eye. She looked up to see Shanta, her face full of concern. "Yes, Shanta?"

Shanta pulled out a notepad from the file she was holding and placed it on top of what Meila had been reading. "The information that you asked me to look up on fiedrum. It was difficult, but it is complete."

Meila held up the page and read through it quickly. It offered some new information, but she skipped over that. She traced a finger down the page until she found how it traveled. Fiedrum was transported on the sea. It usually came in a large plastic bag that had been placed in boxes and finally wrapped with another thin layer of plastic. Once it was on dry ground, it could be transported by truck. Fiedrum could be diluted by water, not stopped by it. She flipped over the page expecting to learn more, but nothing was on the back. Meila looked up at Shanta. "Is this all that you found?"

Shanta nodded. "It was a difficult topic to research. The Internet only had a few sources, all of which offered different suggestions. I went to a file that had most of the information that we already knew, but I did find that it has been given to people, diluted by water. But it didn't offer any information that I thought would be relevant to this case, so I moved on and looked at the maps that you had made in the conference room. That cleared some things up." Shanta motioned for Meila to follow her.

"What about the people that were given the fiedrum?" Meila asked as they walked.

Shanta shrugged in front of her. "The case didn't give me a whole lot on that. It said that some did die. Besides, this is an ongoing case. I spoke with the woman in charge, but their team is not making any progress, they can't find any new information."

"What did it do to the victims?"

Shanta turned on her, stopping her. She held out the file to her. "The fiedrum was given to the victim from they were killed. No one was ever alive to report the symptoms. Go on. Check it out if you doubt me. Shanta turned around but Meila called out for her before she got too far and continued into the conference room.

"Shanta, did you find anything about money that connected to fiedrum?"

Shanta turned back to Meila but shook her head.

"Not that I can recall. I will go and ask them." Shanta turned back around and made her way out of the office. Meila sat down and read over the rest of the information on the fiedrum. There wasn't much to learn from it. It consisted of only a few lines describing it, and no other cases had ever dealt with it.

The main office door opened, allowing Shanta to enter once more. She wiggled a finger at Meila as she walked to the conference room.

"The woman in charge told me they had looked into the financial records but did not find much. Anyways, let me show you what I did learn."

Once they were in the conference room, Shanta closed one of the doors. She moved to the map of Willowsville, where Meila had marked the warehouses, apartments and hotels. Shanta put one of her fake nails on the map pausing on the Old Mill, before dragging it out into the ocean to the west. "I learned from my search that fiedrum doesn't do well in wet places, but when I came in here, I noticed that a big chunk of your father's storehouses were in the west region. But I also noticed that it is one of his bigger regions."

Meila nodded.

"Then I noticed that you marked a hotel very close to this particular spot." She pointed to a hotel that was close to the water's edge.

Meila stood and walked up next to Shanta. "Did you, by chance look at how far apart the bay and this hotel are?"

Shanta nodded and smiled. "I put Marcus on it. He looked bored."

"Shanta!" A breathless voice came from behind them. "I am glad that I found you."

Meila turned to see Marcus rushing toward them. He held out a paper to Shanta when he came to a stop. "I found that information that you had been looking for."

Shanta took the paper. "Thanks, Marcus."

He turned and scurried out of the room.

Shanta held up the paper in between the two of them so that they could both read it.

> Bay Hotel is easily less than a mile's walk to the actual bay. There is an old port that is rarely used. Those that have seen it, reported also seeing trucks waiting to pick up the merchandise.

Meila looked up at the map and then to Shanta. "The trucks would make sense. That is how my father moved things. He rarely did it any other way. Do you think that we could perhaps get into that part of the city to see an exchange happen?"

Shanta shook her head. "That is not my area of expertise. You would have to ask Cody or Charlie. They would know better than I would."

With that, Shanta placed the new information on the conference table and started to walk towards the door.

"Shanta, what about having someone go undercover?"

Shanta stopped and turned around, looking back to Meila.

"I don't think we have had anyone go undercover. Charlie said it is too dangerous and your father could probably sniff out a mole in just a few minutes."

Meila nodded and Shanta turned, leaving Meila with a lot to process. Meila stared at the information for a bit longer. She knew one of her father's precious delivery's always were unloaded from boats, was nice to know it was fiedrum. Now the issue was how to stop it from coming in indefinitely.

Meila poked her head out of the door, but Charlie had left his desk. Cody and another agent were currently busy with the list that she asked him to create, but she still wished that she had someone to talk this through with.

CHAPTER 17

Meila hit the Pause button on the training video everyone had been required to watch. Charlie told her it was part of her training to understand all of the programs used, but Meila found the videos boring. Her mind was busy trying to figure out how her father easily walked out of the building. Or how he was flying so low under the radar that he couldn't be found. It had been a few weeks since the agency alerted them of his escape. Nothing had been said since. Her team had been working day and night, trying to find anything he might have left behind, but nothing could be found. He had covered his footsteps. He was out there somewhere, just waiting for the right moment to attack. She hoped they could be ready for what he may throw their way.

* * * * *

Charlie had asked them all to meet in the conference room at ten. It was getting closer and closer to ten thirty, and there was no Charlie. Cody wasn't there either, but he had the nightshift yesterday, so he wasn't expected to be here until this afternoon. The chattering in the room continually grew, but it immediately stopped when Meila stood. "I guess that we should get this meeting started. Um, April, let's start with you and your group. What did you find?"

When she didn't say anything, Meila just stared at her. "What, do I have something on my face?" Meila put a hand to her face but stopped when April motioned with her head to the door.

Meila turned around to look into Charlie's angry face. "What are you doing?"

"You weren't here, so I assumed, just like I did last week, that I could conduct the meeting."

Charlie folded his arms over his chest. "And what gave you that idea? You are not commander on this team. You do not have the right to be doing that."

"But after last week, I assumed "

Charlie cut her off. "Yes, Meila, that is what you do. You assume that you can have a leading role because that is what you had in your father's company. You do not have that here. I was just running late because I came from another meeting. Your role in this case has been revoked. You can go sit in the hall. Cassie isn't here today, so just stay put out there until someone comes and gets you."

Meila's jaw dropped. "'I have been temporarily removed from the case?' You have got as far as you have *because* of my contribution!" Meila shouted. "This isn't fair!" She slammed the conference room door before making her way out into the hallway.

She grabbed her jacket and backpack off the hook by the door, then she pushed open the main office door that led out to the hallway. Charlie had been correct. Cassie wasn't there. Meila wished that she was. Then she would at least have someone to talk to.

She sank down into Cassie's chair and crossed her arms, angry at Charlie. He was supposed to be the kind one! Cody was the one that she didn't get along with.

"Your pouting face is awful. But then again, you probably got it from your father, so that explains a lot."

Meila turned to find Cody walking down the hall. Meila looked at the clock on Cassie's desk. He was a couple hours early for his shift.

Cody stopped beside the desk. "Wait a second. Did they demote you? Did my complaint go through?" He raised a fist in the air excitedly. "Good! Now I don't have to see you anymore, and you won't be able to bother me. You do know that secretaries are supposed to do whatever their commanding officers ask them to do right? But you were supposed to already do that. You screwed up big this time, Manning."

He sneered and continued on. He scanned his ID and opened the office door. He leered at her as he began to close the door, but he thought better. Everyone had started to exit the conference room, and Cody hollered at everyone, leaving the door cracked open so Meila could hear.

"Hey, just thought I would let everyone know! We have a new secretary! She will be getting anything you need from her! And I am glad that she has been demoted!"

With that, Cody let the door close behind him. Meila didn't wait long enough to find out what happened next. She grabbed her backpack and headed for the elevator.

CHAPTER 18

Charlie had forced her to come into the office today, but she knew that it was pointless. Cody had her removed from the case, yet she made the most headway on it, so why was she being removed? It wasn't fair! It left Meila sitting in one of the chairs by Cassie's desk. She had her eyes closed and was sitting on the edge of the chair, her neck rested on the top of the chair.

Meila could hear muffled voices in the next room. She was mad that she couldn't be a part of it. She hoped that Shanta shared all the information with the team that she had shared with Meila. If not, that might put everyone a step behind. Meila sighed and let her mind wander back to a couple days ago.

Shanta had definitely done her part. Meila thought about how the drugs and the ammunition were transferred by trucks, no matter which storehouse they went to. Ammunition and the fiedrum could be stored at the same warehouses but a handful of warehouses were designated to just ammunition or fiedrum. She couldn't remember the reason why.

She tried to remember some of the deliveries that she helped with, the number of boxes that came through, the size of the room needed to hold them comfortably. The corners of her mouth slightly went up. She used to miss the days that went by in peace and quiet, but she had a job now, a purpose. Yet, delivery days had been her favorite when she lived with her father. They were filled with excitement for her father as they awaited a new arrival. She was excited to work alongside him and show him what she was capable of. Now, she approached the shipments the same way. She was excited for the day that she could help with another, but for a different reason. The sooner they could get her father off of the streets, the better.

She heard a shout from inside the room. Meila opened her eyes. The main room office door cracked open but then slammed shut. Meila went back to thinking about fiedrum.

Shanta told her that it doesn't do well with water, but it traveled on boats. That made no sense. Meila put her hands on her knees and sat up. She dropped her busy head into her hands and let it run wildly. She needed to see that map again. She remembered a few buildings that were by the water that had drugs in them, but they had been moved there after a certain amount of time. Perhaps the fiedrum just had to dry out. But why would you buy it if you had to let it dry out? That made no sense either. Shanta had brought her information about how tightly they had been packaged, but what if some water somehow got through? And what about after they were in the warehouses? The air was still humid.

She wondered if the team had thought about getting the drug wet. If the fiedrum could be diluted, then it would do less damage. Meila's brain spun faster and faster. *What is a good way to get everything wet?* Meila asked herself.

"Meila! What are you doing here? I thought that you were on the night shift?"

Meila opened her eyes and looked up to find Cassie walking toward her.

"Hi, Cassie. I am on the night shift for this evening, but Charlie had a stroke of brilliance and demanded that I come in. Besides, my father is still out there somewhere. Charlie is afraid to leave me alone for too long without protection."

"Ah." Cassie sat down at her desk, putting her bag and jacket underneath it. "What are you doing out here? Why aren't you in there trying to help the team put your father in jail?"

Meila sat back in her chair, her slumped position continued. "I was removed, as Cody likes to brag. I am surprised that you haven't heard anything about it? He has been telling everyone of his 'accomplishment.'"

Cassie just smiled sadly at Meila. "I'm sorry, but I hadn't heard that. I am not much in the loop of what goes on in the office. The most I see of anyone is when they walk in or out. They used to leave the door open until the last few years. It makes this hallway extremely quiet."

She let the silence drag on as she tried to figure out a way to stop her father. She closed her eyes and recalled some of the pages from one of her files flooded her thoughts. She rolled her head to one side of the chair, letting her cheek rest on the back of it. Fiedrum was so tightly packaged. If they could find a way to dilute it, maybe, just maybe it would stop them.

Meila opened her eyes and sat up taller.

"Cassie?" she asked.

Cassie finished up what she was typing before turning her attention on Meila. "Yes, Meila."

"If you wanted to get someone or something wet, how would you do it?"

Cassie shrugged. "I don't know. It depends on how wet you are asking?"

Meila sat up, pulling the chair closer to Cassie so that she could prop her elbows on the desk. "I am asking for a very tall person or thing, and they need to be fully submerged."

Cassie thought for a moment. "I guess that I would push them in a pool or the ocean."

That wouldn't work. Meila didn't want to take the time to try and figure out which warehouses she needed to empty into the ocean. Besides, she didn't know how fiedrum affected fish and ocean life. "What if you didn't have a pool?"

"A couple of buckets of water. Why?"

"No reason." Cassie looked at her unassured, letting the topic drop. She went back to typing while Meila was left to think. She grabbed a blank sticky note off Cassie's desk and a pencil. She started to draw out a design that she had seen in movies. It was a large bucket that helicopters used to dump water on forest fires. She wondered if she were to change it slightly they might be able to use something similar to it.

Meila drew it out, using arrows to indicate what bolts needed to go where or how much water it should be able to hold. She then put the end of the pencil in her mouth and chewed on the eraser.

"Meila! Don't do that!" Cassie scolded.

Meila pulled it out. "Sorry." She looked back down at the drawing. This much water should be able to diluted any fiedrum that her father had left in the storehouses. She stood. She moved past Cassie and scanned her ID.

She heard Cassie move behind her but knew that she was too slow. Meila had the door closed before Cassie could even grab the handle. She heard Cassie say her name and pull on the locked door. Everyone turned at the pounding.

"Mei, what are you doing in here? You have been asked to stay out of this case." Charlie pushed off the desk that he had been leaning against and moved toward her.

"Charlie, I know how to slow down and possibly stop the fiedrum. It is so simple that I didn't see it earlier."

Charlie turned her around, pushing her toward the door. "You don't have to worry about that anymore. You need to go back out in the hall and let the rest of us work."

She ducked under one of his arms. "But I have the solution!" She held up the sticky note that was full of words and drawings.

Charlie stopped. He held out his hand and took the sticky note. He examined it and then moved back toward his desk. He motioned for Meila to follow with a flick of his hand. She walked quickly with him as he examined her drawings.

When they made it to his desk, he stopped and asked a question. "Mei, this isn't new technology. Many people have used things like this before. Besides, what would it do?"

"We don't always need to use new technology to fix problems like these." She took the paper out of his hand.

"That's true, but what do you need that for?"

"It's how we can stop the fiedrum."

Charlie looked down at the file that he had been working on. "Mei, I know you are desperate and want to work on your father's case, but you can't anymore. Please, please go out and sit in the hall."

Meila clasped her hands in front of her, preparing herself to plead with Charlie. "Charlie! It will work! Just give me a few minutes of your time!"

Charlie sat down, unhappy. "Fine, two minutes. That's all that you get."

Meila nodded and then began, "Filmena told me that fiedrum travels somewhere to a port here that is less than a mile from one of my father's hotels and warehouses, but I remember that the drugs were often moved. My father never told me why." She put the sticky note down in front of him.

"I also heard that fiedrum can be diluted by water, but we don't know which storehouse it may be in, so we need to be careful there, but this can help." She pointed to the picture. "You do know how one of these work right?" Meila asked.

Charlie nodded.

"All we need to do is get inside of the buildings to know which ones have fiedrum in them." Meila plopped down on a chair in front of his desk, a victorious smile on her face.

Charlie leaned forward and picked up the paper. "Mei, even if we could get our hands on one of these contraptions, there would then be the issue of how to get it into the building and clean up after it. Can you imagine the damage it could create?"

Meila solemnly nodded, she had missed these flaws when the idea first came to her. She was tired of sitting out in the hallway and was trying to find a solution.

Charlie nodded. He held up the paper. "This is a good idea, but it won't work. We will just have to try another way. But I thank you for attempting to think of something. Now please go back out to the hall."

Meila stood and moved toward the door where the pounding had not stopped. Before she opened it, Charlie called her name. She turned around to find him running up to her. He held out his hand. "Your ID," he requested.

"What? Why?" Meila put a hand over it.

"Meila, I can't have you disrupting the team every time that you get an idea. It is great that you want to help. But you can't anymore."

She unclipped it from her shirt and begrudgingly handed it over.

"I will try and get it back to you as soon as I can," Charlie promised.

She just turned and opened the door. She pushed past Cassie and sat back down in her normal chair. She felt deflated and wished that she could go home, but she knew that it wouldn't be any better for her there, so she just pulled her legs up underneath her and hoped that the time would go by fast.

CHAPTER 19

A knock sounded at her door. "Go away, Charlie! I don't want to talk to anyone right now!" Meila yelled.

"Good thing that I'm not an anyone. Let me in, Meila. You know that I will come in anyway, even if you don't answer." Charlie's voice was outside her apartment door.

Meila knew deep down he was right, but Cody had pushed her past her limits. Over the last few weeks he had called her multiple rude names, pushed her out of the case and today he had humiliated her. She couldn't take it anymore. What was she supposed to do? Let him get away with it? No way, not on her watch.

She heard a scraping going on in the lock of her door, then a click. Charlie pushed her door closed behind him. "Meila we need to talk."

"I would rather not. Can we just let this be?" Besides, Charlie didn't try to stick up for her once over the last few weeks. Instead, he had kicked her out.

Charlie sat down across from her. "Let this be? That doesn't sound like you. You haven't sounded like yourself the past few days though. What's going on?"

"Nothing that I care to discuss with you." She reached for the remote to turn on the TV, but he was faster. He grabbed the remote out of her hand before the screen lit.

"Come on, Mei. You haven't been like this since you first arrived here. I am not going to let you slip back into being that person. Is this because you were pulled off of the case?"

She waved him off. "It's nothing like that. I just need some time alone to think this all over. I have a conflict, and this is how I've always dealt with it. My father never found it an issue."

"Your father never cared enough to make it his issue."

Meila's head snapped to him. Charlie put his hands out. "Mei, that's not what I meant."

She stood. "I don't care what you meant. Now get out."

He stood, a little more reluctantly though. "Fine. Can I at least make you promise that you're not going to run?"

Meila just pointed to the door. Charlie walked to it, pulling it open slowly. "If you do feel like talking, you know where to find me."

The door closed softly behind him. Meila knew that he would probably be watching out of his peephole to see if she left. Thankfully, she knew another way out.

Meila went into her bedroom, closing the door. If Charlie was going to come back, she would be ready. She put a chair under the doorknob, knowing that a pick wouldn't be able to get him in. Then she got to work. She pulled out her backpack, stuffing clothes into it. She also pulled out the last of what she had in cash from her job. She hoped that it would be enough to sustain her a couple of days. She wasn't quite sure where she was going, but she knew that she had to get away. Charlie would come back and check on her again, but she didn't want his help anymore. She had lived on her own before; she could do it again.

Meila scanned her room one more time before opening her window. She shoved her bag out and then followed. Charlie's fire escape was on the other side of the building. There was no way that he saw this coming. She took the stairs quickly, then jumped the last few feet from the ladder to the ground. She took off running. It felt so good to be out again, to be free—well, kind of free.

Meila turned to check behind her, turning back just in time to run into someone. Meila stumbled to the ground, scraping one of her hands and both knees as she went down. They didn't hurt too bad. Meila pushed herself up, intending to give this person a piece of her mind, but only one word came to mind when she saw the person's face. "April?"

April just smiled and grabbed Meila's uninjured hand. Meila tried to wrench it free, but she couldn't. "Please, April, I don't want to go back."

"You don't have to. I am just taking you back to Charlie."

"That's where I don't want to go. Can I please just escape him for a little while?"

April stopped, thinking for a moment. Finally, she nodded. "Fine. I have a place that we can go, but you have to promise not to run from me."

"Okay, I promise." *Just as long as you don't give me reason to run,* Meila thought.

April nodded. Keeping Meila's hand firmly in her own, April quickly walked the streets, making lots of random turns. When they finally went inside of a building, Meila had no idea which part of town they were in. April walked up to a man that was behind the desk. "Excuse me. I have a reservation. It's under Angie Harper Lee."

The man shuffled a few papers around, looking for the right name. He then grabbed a key from somewhere under the desk and handed it to April. He motioned to the elevator down the hall. "That elevator will be the quickest way there."

"Thank you!"

April pulled Meila along and hit the button for the elevator. Meila examined the elevator on the way up. No cameras. The elevator dinged as it passed another floor. Meila looked down to the elevator buttons. The lining was bent back in a few places. If she could—

"Don't even think about it," April cautioned.

The elevator dinged and the door slid open. April led the way down the hallway and put the key into the door. She motioned Meila in ahead of her. April checked the hallway before turning on the main light. Meila's mouth fell open. She was standing in a living room. She had never seen one in a hotel. Whenever she traveled with her father, he was lucky to get a few different rooms. Usually, they just stayed in motels where major repairs needed to take place. This was totally different. There was a kitchen and a massive TV. There were also a handful of doors that Meila assumed went to bedrooms.

Meila wandered into the kitchen as April began to pull food out of a fridge. Meila put her backpack down on a chair at the table. "Do you want to talk about it?"

Meila sighed. Was she ever going to escape this? "Not really, but you aren't going to stop bugging me about it until I tell you, huh?"

April just looked over at Meila and smiled. Meila watched as April pulled out fruit and vegetables. She cut many of them, placing the vegetables in a pan with oil. She picked back up a knife and started to cut the fruit. "Dinner will be ready in a little bit, but go and see if you can clean up the scrapes. There should be some supplies in the bathroom."

Meila just nodded, grateful that April didn't push the topic like Charlie had.

After cleaning herself up, Meila sat down at the now set table. April was pulling a pan off the stove, then joined Meila. "Are you hungry?"

Meila just nodded, hoping that April had just forgotten about Meila's earlier pleas. Meila ate hungrily, knowing that this might be her last meal for a while. She didn't want to run, but she didn't know what else to do. It had been a good solution so far in her life; why couldn't that continue?

April picked up her paper plate and dropped it into the garbage. "Go ahead and pick a movie while I clean up dinner. I will be in shortly to join you."

Meila gladly looked through her options, finally resting on a new one that she had never seen before. April walked in a few minutes later with a box of candy in her hand. "Were you planning on sharing that, or are you just bringing it in to force me to talk?"

April smiled as she sat down next to Meila on the couch. "I was hoping to do a little bit of both. Here." She handed Meila the box of candies. "So I understand that you are upset, but why?"

Meila looked back at the screen. She had been trying to sort through her feelings the last few minutes. She still didn't truly understand *why* she was angry, but she knew that she was. "Cody said some rude things."

"Do you care if I ask what he said?"

Meila popped a piece of candy into her mouth. "Okay, so maybe he hasn't really said rude things to my face. But he has practically ignored me. If he has to speak so, he makes me feel small and pathetic. The only thing that I have ever done to him is hit him in the ribs. I even asked for his help to train me, but I always felt like he was trying to push me too far."

April folded her hands in her lap. "So he makes you feel as if you are useless and a nobody?"

Meila nodded, letting a tear slip. She swiped away.

"All right, understood. I am going to let you in on a little secret."

Meila scooted a little bit closer, ready to learn.

"Cody is just jealous of all of the attention that you are getting."

Meila blinked. "So you are saying that he doesn't like me because I take the spotlight?"

April shrugged. "Cody and Charlie were inseparable before you came into the picture. They were like two brothers. They did everything together. I think that Cody is just taking his anger out on you."

Meila nodded. That made sense.

"Now the big question. What are you going to do to get back at him?"

"Charlie doesn't like it when I try to get revenge on anyone, including Cody."

"You are right, but I am not Charlie." She popped some candy into her mouth. "And I think that everyone in the office could use a laugh, so I think that we should do something to bring a little happiness back to the office.

"Besides, everyone has been a little bit on edge lately. Maybe we should do something that will bring a smile to a few faces."

"Are you sure?" Meila asked.

April shrugged. "You and Cody have been at each other for weeks. I am surprised that something hasn't exploded in either one of your faces yet."

Meila thought for a moment. A smile slowly spread across her face as she found an idea that would work. "You know that letter that Cody has been waiting for?"

Excitement lit April's eyes.

"I think I know a way to bring a smile to many faces. It includes a new gadget that I have been working on too!"

April grabbed her hands. "Let's do it then!"

CHAPTER 20

Meila had walked into work expecting to be sitting in the hall today, but Charlie pulled her into the main office. He had told her that Cody's demands had been looked over and reversed. She was not only allowed to help with the case again, but the board had given her clearance to see a few more files. The main office door opened and closed, April stepping in. She smiled at Meila and then sat down at her desk.

Meila looked down at her papers again. The notes that were from this meeting didn't make sense. New codes must have been written, and she had been off the streets for too long to know that. Cody burst through the office in the next moment, breaking her concentration. "It came, guys!" he hollered.

Meila and April looked at each other, excitement brimming in their eyes. Cody had waited for this letter for over a month now. A day didn't go by without him frantically checking if anything new had been brought to the office. Cody had turned in a request to be part of a new team that was being assembled here at the agency. Little did he know that the letter that he had been so eagerly waiting for arrived yesterday. The one he held was created by Meila and April.

Cody took a deep breath before opening it. A loud poof overtook the room. Meila had to cover her mouth to keep from laughing. Everyone else in the room looked shocked. Cody's face had gone black with soot. Charlie raised his eyebrows in mock. "This is the letter that you were so excited to receive?"

April handed him a towel to wipe off his face. She too was trying to hide a smile.

"Who did this?" Cody demanded. He scanned the room. "Meila Manning, so help me! I waited for this letter for over a month, and you tricked me. Let's see how good your training has really done ya!" He put up his fists. "Come on! Show me how tough you really are!" he yelled.

Meila stood, dropping all her files on the ground. "You want to talk about tough? Nobody gossips about me behind my back. If you have something that you want to say, just say it."

"I bet that is what your father did? I bet that he would tell you straight up how you were messed up, just someone to fool around with until he could dump you off for some amazing price—"

Charlie stepped in between the two of them. "That's enough!" He looked at both of them. "Cody, get back to work. The letter was sent to you yesterday, but you had the day off. I assumed that nothing would have happened to it during your day off." He motioned for Meila to grab it for him. "I hope its results are better than the previous one." He handed the letter to Cody and then rounded on Meila.

"After you clean up this mess, I will meet you by the elevator."

He stepped away from the desk when April chimed in. "Charlie, it wasn't her fault. I was the one who pushed her to do it. She doesn't deserve your wrath."

Charlie spoke without turning around. "That is very noble of you, April, but I need to speak with Miss Manning. I will speak with you after I have returned."

He left Meila to the mess that she had created. Cody had carefully pulled open the top of his new envelope and was almost done reading the letter when Meila had finished. The news must not have been what Cody wanted to hear. He didn't even comment when Meila was leaving. Meila closed the main office door behind her, only to have it be yanked open again. April stepped out, joining Meila in the hallway. Thankfully, Cassie had taken an early lunch, so she was not there.

"Meila, I hope that Charlie's punishment is not too bad, and I'm sorry for pushing you so far. I thought that it would have lightened the mood around the office."

Meila tried but couldn't muster a smile. "It's okay, April. I just hope that I am not done after today. You heard how angry he was. And he did say when *he* returns to the office, not when we."

April put a hand on Meila's shoulder. "Are you going to be okay?"

Meila just nodded.

"If you need a place to stay, go back to that hotel that we went to last night. When you get to the front desk, ask to speak to Gary and tell him that you are Angie Harper Lee. They will take care of you for as long as you need it."

Meila looked up at her. "Why are you doing all of this?"

She smiled. "You are one of the greatest friends that I have had in a long time, and once Charlie cools down, hopefully, you will feel comfortable going back to your apartment again."

Meila thanked her and continued to where Charlie was waiting around the corner and down the hall. Silence stretched on as they rode the elevator down to the main level. The silence continued as they walked the few blocks to the range. Charlie must be really mad if he wanted to shoot off rounds. She had heard from many others that he only did this when he was frustrated or extremely upset. She figured that it was partially both.

They were not any closer to catching her father. She felt as if he had betrayed her. She had wondered many times since their argument when he was going to push her out of his life. Everyone else had done so. Why would he be any different?

Charlie roughly pulled the door open to the gun range. They got their supplies and moved through the building and to the range, where they took their marks. Meila was preparing herself for an uncomfortable experience.

CHAPTER 21

After many rounds, Charlie let Meila go. Unlike last time, Charlie and Meila hardly spoke. She knew that Charlie was angry at her for what she had done to Cody's letter, but she was frustrated with him because of what he had said about her father. Charlie stepped up again shooting off another few rounds. She sat in a purple plastic chair, letting her thoughts continue to wander. Finally, Charlie put his gun away. "Meila, stop acting so childish. Honestly, it's just getting embarrassing."

Meila folded her arms and sunk farther into her chair. "I'm not. You have told me for months to start acting my age. Well, here you go. I am." She pulled her gaze to the floor.

He plopped down beside her. "Yeah, but I wanted you to have a few more years of childhood, you know, to have fun."

"To have fun. And you bring me to a shooting range?"

Charlie shrugged and bumped into her. "Yeah, this will be fun once you start to beat me again."

Meila smiled. "Well, my fun used to be a lot different, you know. Hiding for hours on end, hoping some of my father's enemies wouldn't find me—or sometimes my father. Then if I was caught, finding a way to escape and hoping that my father, or anyone, would be out there to help me."

Charlie chuckled. "Yes. As much fun as *that* sounds, let's concentrate on the present." He held out his gun and motioned to her shooting spot.

Meila grabbed the gun and walked to her spot, she pulled off the safety, and shot off a round.

After a few more rounds, she returned his gun to him and then sat down. "I'm sorry about what I did to Cody."

Charlie chuckled. "Honestly, after finding out how Cody has been treating you, I am surprised that you were able to keep your cool for as long as you did. I would have done the exact same thing that you did, but it would have happened weeks ago."

She punched him in the arm. "Then why are you so angry with me!?"

He shrugged. "I wouldn't really say that I was angry, but I think that you could have handled yourself better around Cody. But I also brought you down here to apologize."

She sat back, staring at the few other people that were there today. "I shouldn't have said what I did that night, and I'm sorry. I may not agree with what your father has done, but I need to remember that I am talking with his daughter. He is the only blood relative you have left. I hope that you are not planning on leaving the team anytime soon because of what I said."

Meila shook her head. "I was worried that you were going to kick me off the team. I have become rather attached to a few of them you know."

He smiled. "The feeling is mutual." He looked out at the shooters. "Can we try something new?" he said after a moment.

She gestured with her hands for him to continue.

"Instead of you running away, and me always trying to chase you down and find you, can you please just return to your apartment and pout? Or better yet, find a way to release that anger and make something good out of it!"

Meila groaned. "You sound like an ad. But for your sake and your health"—she sent a smile his way—"I will consider it."

"Thank you. Now, let's see how much I can beat you by today." He stood and shot off a round. Meila was starting to feel better already.

CHAPTER 22

Meila was furious. The team was no longer working on the fiedrum case. Or the case concerning her father. "What?" she yelled at Charlie.

Charlie stood up behind his desk.

"Out in the hall," he calmly said. He reached for her arm, but she skirted around his desk before he could touch her.

"About a month ago, I was being shot at, and you were overly concerned about my life. Now you don't even seem to care!"

The whole office was silent. Meila looked around at the shocked faces. She felt as if she might explode at any moment. She felt like a volcano that had stayed quiet for too long. She put her hands on her hips and looked at Charlie, anger apparent on her features. "This isn't fair! Get the case back. Go and fight for it!" She erupted.

Charlie looked around the room and dragged her out to the hall. He smiled at Cassie and asked that she go somewhere else. She stood and scurried away, sending one more glance there way before turning the corner.

"Where are we going? The shooting range?" Meila pouted.

Charlie turned on her, forcing her to stop moving. "And give you a weapon in the state you are in? No way." He indicated to the chairs that were against the wall, but Meila stayed standing. "Mei, cases come and go this quickly all the time. We have a bigger threat on our hands right now anyway."

"Oh, sorry. I guess that I was unaware that I am still in danger," Meila said sarcastically.

"Mei, you are still in danger, but this upcoming case is more important."

"Yeah, since *my life* doesn't seem to be important."

Charlie pushed her shoulder. "Stop it. Everyone in the office cares about what happens to you, but right now, we need you on this next case."

That caught Meila's attention. "Full clearance?" she asked

Charlie shook his head. "The board still doesn't approve of giving you full clearance to see what we are doing. You will have to wait a few more years to experience that."

Meila folded her arms. "Why did we have to move on?" She was hoping that her team could have closed this case before moving onto another one.

Charlie pointed to the chairs. "Sit down and I will explain."

Meila thought about resisting but knew that Charlie would probably sit her down if she didn't do it herself, so she sat down. Charlie pulled a chair out so that he was facing her. "The agency goes through many cases a day. Some of them can be solved within a few weeks, but most sent to our floor have already been tried by others. That is why our team has so many different strengths. We can see things that others don't. Some cases, like this Rodrigez guy, is very powerful in certain parts of the city. He has been spotted trading his goods. We have to move on from your father's case because he is not causing us problems right now."

"But we won't lose it entirely?"

Charlie speculated. "You still want us on the case, why?"

She shrugged, not really sure why she felt the need to be on her father's case. "Maybe it's because another team might see me as useless, where on this team, I know that I am not."

He nodded; understanding came across his face. "We will get back to your dad's case when we feel like we can, but these cases coming in are full of information. They shouldn't take long to complete."

"Why can't we just stop my father now? Go in with what we have?"

Charlie took a deep breath in before answering her question. "To be one hundred percent honest with you"—he turned his eyes upward, muttering—"I'm dead for telling her this." He returned his gaze back to her. "We don't have enough concrete evidence that he has gone back to his business. We think that he may be laying low so that we can't trace his footsteps."

Meila nodded.

"So, we're good?"

Meila let a smile climb onto her lips. "Yeah, we're good."

Charlie moved the chair back and then moved to the office door. "Come back in when you are ready."

Meila nodded, grateful that he understood that she might need some time to process this new information.

CHAPTER 23

Two years later. Willowsville, Washington

Charlie had been pulled into another department meeting. Meila was going insane. She sunk lower into her seat. Cody was standing in for Charlie, and he wasn't letting her do anything. When Charlie was in charge, he would allow her to look through files and something that no one else could. But Cody? He was a different story. She was given three case files. She had completed those yesterday when Charlie was, once again, gone.

She was going stir crazy now. She tapped her pencil on her desk; she had spun around in her chair and was considering even going down to the gym. Her energy was just building, but it couldn't go anywhere.

Meila finally excused herself and went to the bathroom. She walked up and down the hall by the bathrooms and by the elevator, hoping that Charlie would walk out of it soon. After thirty minutes of pacing, Meila resigned herself to go back and sit in the office. She knew that the longer she was out here. She would have to create a better excuse to tell Cody. One she knew he would never believe, even if it was the truth.

Cassie wasn't at her desk when Meila turned the corner that led to the main office. She must have been inside. Meila opened the door and found Cassie walking toward her. "Come on, back into the hallway. Nothing that these guys have said concerns you," she said.

Meila's shoulders dropped more. This was becoming extremely unfair. Anything that they found couldn't be shared with her because she didn't have clearance. She had more opportunities to do things while working under Charlie, but Cody was a stickler for rules. Charlie had always politely asked her to leave, but Meila knew that Cody would just yell at her if she stayed.

Meila slammed the door behind her and threw herself into a chair beside Cassie's desk. The main office door opened a moment later, and Cassie slid out. She looked over at Meila and smiled. "You remind me of a guy I used to date."

Meila sat up a little bit. "Excuse me?"

Cassie sat down behind her desk. "He would come and tell me about all of his problems. He would lounge around, just like you were doing. He would never listen to me when I said anything about my problems though." She took a sip of her drink. "So I broke up with him. Haven't dated much since."

Meila nodded. She looked at the door behind Cassie. "I just wish that they would treat me as an equal. In my father's house, I always had a job, although most of those jobs included running and hiding."

Meila covered her mouth. Charlie told her that she shouldn't talk about her father with anyone else but him. He said that they wouldn't understand like he would. She looked at Cassie but saw compassion on her face.

"I'm sorry, Meila. Do you want to talk about it?"

Meila thought for a moment before answering. "You don't mind?"

Cassie shook her head, sending her blonde curly hair bouncing. "It might surprise you, but I grew up in a difficult household. I bet I'll understand a lot of what you have gone through."

Meila smiled, grateful that she could have someone to talk to while Charlie was busy. "When I lived with my father, I had freedom as long as my father agreed with what I was about to do or go. He rarely lived in one place for more than a few months, so I rarely saw him. And when I did see him, it was always at meetings. I never really got to know him. He would go to meetings and then drink until he couldn't see straight anymore. I only ever knew him to be an alcoholic. I never found myself as a priority in his life, yet I wanted him to approve of me."

A tear slipped from Meila's eyes. She hadn't talked to anyone about her father like this. She tried not to think about what pain her father had caused her. Seeing how Charlie had been treating her, she knew her father had been wrong. Charlie only ever demanded details about how her father's business was run. He never dug into how she personally felt about her father or if she was doing okay. With Cassie, it was different, she seemed to be interesting and compassionate toward Meila. She really wanted to know how Meila was doing, but most of the information surrounding her father's case was classified. She swiped at the tear.

"You know everything that I just told you was classified. I don't even know if I was supposed to tell you."

Cassie turned back to her computer and started to type something. "Don't worry about me. I won't share it with anyone outside this office." She continued typing. "Meila?"

Meila slouched back in her chair again. "Yeah?"

Cassie stopped long enough to smile at Cassie. "Thanks for telling me."

Meila nodded and closed her eyes, hoping that the torment would end soon. She wanted to get back to the case the team was working on and stuff the memories of her father away.

* * * * *

Meila walked into the kitchen and grabbed a muffin Shanta had bought. She took a bite, wishing Charlie could hurry back from his department meeting. It must have been her lucky day.

Charlie walked into the kitchen, holding a file under one of his arms.

"Ah, here you are." He took a seat at the table in the kitchen and motioned for Meila to join him.

"I wanted your opinion on something."

Meila nodded and took another bite of the chocolate muffin.

Charlie placed the file in front of her and opened it. A pixelated picture sat on top. A few papers were underneath it. Most of them contained coded messages. Some which looked familiar; others seemed entirely foreign to her.

"Do you recognize the name Rodrigez?"

Meila thought for a moment.

"I have heard it multiple times. He and my father worked together every now and then. I know at one point they had a disagreement, but they have worked through it. Why?"

Charlie stood, grabbing a poppy seed muffin.

"Rodrigez is the next case we have been asked to focus on. I guess he is creating some issues in the northern part of town."

Meila nodded.

"My father is usually in the south part of town for a few weeks right now. Are you hoping Rodrigez might lead you to my father?"

Charlie shrugged.

"Rodrigez is the one I want to get, but if your father happens to be with him, great," Charlie responded, sitting back down next to her. "Do you know anything about Rodrigez which might help us find him or any useful information the agency may not know?"

Meila stared at the picture of Rodrigez.

"I don't know a lot about him. I was rarely in the same meetings as him and my father. My father always told me I wasn't needed during those parts of the meetings, so I was gone by the time Rodrigez came."

"Is his business similar to your father's?"

Meila shrugged.

"I noticed some of the codes they use are the same, but until I can look further into it, I won't know."

Charlie nodded and stood.

"That is all the information I can give you right now, but I am still working on getting you full clearance. Until then, work with what you can."

Meila nodded and turned back to the file, letting her head take over and process all of this.

CHAPTER 24

Meila closed the door to her apartment. She set down the bag that she had taken to the agency today and grabbed some food out of her pantry. She then opened her front door and locked it behind her. She walked across the hall and knocked on the door. She took a bite out of her apple while she waited. No answer. She knocked again. "Not now, Meila!" came a muffled voice from inside.

She pounded again. She waited for another minute before pulling out her pick. She leaned her ear against the door and started to move the tool inside. Something clicked, and the door opened. She pushed against it and let herself in. "If you really didn't want me inside, you would get a better lock system." Meila put down the handful of snacks on his table and then went and closed his door.

Charlie walked around the corner a minute later. His shoulder dropped in desperation. "I told you no. No, you can't come in."

He started to walk back toward his room. Meila followed him. "Charlie, this is twice now. You promised to let me in."

He pulled a suitcase from inside his closet onto his bed. "I know, but you can't be a part of this project. If your identity was discovered, it would ruin the whole mission."

She leaned against the doorframe. "So you are just going to leave me here? Hope that I don't get into trouble or am not recognized?"

Charlie shrugged. "I asked Cassie to keep an eye on you while I am gone. And since I am leaving, I asked the board if you could stay at the agency building. So, you are going to want to pack a bag too."

"Do I have to? Can't we just have a few people come here and watch over me?"

Charlie was already shaking his head. He put a few items into his suitcase. "Too dangerous, You will have to stay at the agency building."

Meila angrily sighed and rolled her eyes. She moved from his doorjamb to the couch. She listened as Charlie started to move around again. After about fifteen minutes, there was a sound of a zipper, then a big thud on the ground. "Mei, I know that you are not happy about this arrangement, but it is the only way that I know for sure that no one will get to you. I know that we haven't had much of an issue with your father for the last two years, but I don't want to leave anything up to chance. I even asked Cassie for her personal phone number, not her work number, so that I can call and check on you."

Meila turned her gaze to him. "You asked for a girl's number?" Meila let a smile grow on her face. "Charlie, are you okay? You told me that you don't go out with anyone? And Cassie…well, she is nice and all, but—"

Charlie put up a hand, stopping Meila's words. "That's not what I said, and you know it." Charlie's smile was slightly there.

"Charlie, really. You asked for Cassie's number?"

"For work reasons only."

Meila pretended to think about this. She looked around for his phone, seeing it on the table by the front door. "You asked for her personal phone number. It must mean you really want to get a hold of her. Have you talked to her?"

Charlie let out an exasperated sigh. "I told you why I got her number: to check on you. End of story."

"Mm-hmm." Meila got up and walked toward where she had put down the food. She looked back at Charlie. His back was to her on the couch. She grabbed a snack and then she grabbed his phone. "Well, it doesn't hurt to check!"

Charlie jumped up from the couch and reached for his phone. "No!" He reached around Meila and retrieved his phone before she had managed to do more than just unlock it.

"Why not?" Meila put her hands on her hips, keeping her eyes on the cell phone he held in his hand.

"Meila, the information for my mission is on here." He held up his phone. "It isn't safe to see where we are going."

Meila furrowed her eyebrows.

"Is that why I haven't been included in the meetings over the last few days? I am being pushed out of the loop because you are worried that I am going to ruin a mission?" Meila let that stew for a second before speaking again.

"I thought you trusted me."

He was leaving her behind, breaking his promise—just as everyone has done, just like her father. Charlie was the same as him. She ran toward the door, yanking it open and running down the hall to her apartment.

"Meila!"

She unlocked her apartment door but didn't close it in time. She hit Charlie's foot instead. He let himself in and closed the door after him. "Meila, I can't leave you like this because if I do, I will come home with a bigger mess on my hands then what I already have."

Meila moved to her favorite comfy chair and slouched into it. "Well, you should have just let me be a part of it."

Charlie ran a hand through his blonde hair. "I can't. All that I can do is promise that you will be safe."

Meila turned on him. "And what about you? Will you be safe?"

Charlie's face lifted. "I promise that I will be as safe as I can be."

"What about your promise to take care of me?"

"Hence, leaving you with Cassie."

"And you trust Cassie because—"

Charlie pulled his normal chair closer to hers. "We are not talking about that right now."

"If we talk about it, I'll feel safer staying behind."

Charlie closed his eyes. "Fine. Two minutes."

"Do you like her?"

He opened his eyes. "She's nice."

Meila rolled hers. "Anyone can be nice. I was expecting a 'she is very beautiful, and I think I would like to date her.'"

Charlie shook his head. "Mei, you are causing enough trouble in my life as it is. I don't need another woman to do that."

Meila let that sink in. "Fine, but you should know, she looks at you a lot."

Charlie scrunched his eyes. "So what?"

"Don't you know anything!" Meila got up and walked to her fridge.

"Hey, where are you going? The two minutes are not up yet!"

"Calm down, you big idiot." She held up the water bottle she had grabbed. "You know," Meila said as she walked back to her chair, "you could ask her out. See if she likes you."

Charlie's gaze had moved to the floor. "That would be breaking my promise to you, though."

Meila resisted rolling her eyes. "I let you out of the deal anytime you want to date someone. I can protect myself."

"No, that wouldn't work. That would leave you without someone to protect you for a couple hours."

"You have let me leave before."

Charlie shook his head.

"There may have been days we have worked different shifts or we weren't together, but I knew you were safe. We don't live too far from the agency building, and I know the agency building is well guarded. No one can get in undetected."

Meila thought for a moment, a smile grew. "You could leave me with some of the team at the agency."

"And have you do what?"

Meila shrugged. She thought of plenty that she could do. For starters, her lockpicking could use some work. She had a new gadget idea in her head that she would like to test, knowing that Marcus would help her with that. If she were left with Cody, they could work on her climbing and camouflage. He would most likely just ignore her. With April, she could learn to find her way into these secret files

107

without anyone else's knowledge. "Well, if any of the group is there, they'll watch over me."

"No." Charlie stood. "I have to get some rest before I leave in the morning. I will be over to say goodbye before I leave."

Meila didn't even bother to move. "When will you get back?"

Charlie opened the door. "I'm hoping no later than a week, just long enough to get some information and get back out. Keep the office in shape for me while I'm gone?"

Meila nodded, and Charlie left.

CHAPTER 25

Almost two weeks later

Meila pumped her fists in the air. She was getting the hang of this. She turned to April and Cody. "Can we test it?"

April looked up from what she was doing. Cody held up his finger, telling them to stay silent just a minute longer. Meila sat back down in her chair, anxious to get out of this white walled room.

Cody wrote furiously on the paper in front of him. He glanced up at the stack of papers next to him. He shuffled through them, pulling out one about halfway down. His eyes scanned the page. "April." He looked up, concern written over his face. He looked in between the two of them. With a flick of his wrist, he motioned Meila to leave.

Her shoulders dropped more, but instead of leaving, she walked toward Cody's desk. "What did you find?"

"Nothing that has to do with you." He covered up the papers he was working on. "Now, out."

"How come I can't know? Does it have to do with Charlie and the mission he is on?"

Both pairs of eyes jumped to her.

"I knew the night before he left. He straight up told me. I don't understand why you guys can't do the same."

April and Cody stared at her for a moment. Then they stared at each other for a moment. "Kid, this has nothing to do with you, nor does it have anything to do with Charlie. Go sit out in the hall with Cassie. She's supposed to be your babysitter anyway."

Meila's gaze went hard before she turned and stomped out of the office. She slammed the door, trying to release her frustration.

Cassie looked up at her, oblivious to what just happened. "You've decided to grace me with your presence today?"

Meila moved to a chair next to Cassie's desk and threw herself down in it. "It just isn't fair. I'm not allowed to do anything!"

Cassie moved from behind her desk to sit beside Meila. She held out a hand for what Meila was holding. Cassie took it from her, rubbing the small device between her fingers. "Is this what you were working on before you stomped out here?"

Meila slouched lower. "Yeah, but I didn't get to test it. Cody," she spat out his name, "kicked me out before I even got to explain what it was or how it worked."

Cassie sat farther back in her chair, examining the strangely shaped gadget. "How about you explain it to me?"

Meila closed her eyes. "You know that you aren't actually classified to know how this device works, right?"

Cassie sighed. "Yeah, but you would be surprised how many times the team has asked me to look over, you know, double-check?"

Meila put her hand out and felt the object be put in her hand. She held it up, seeing the design in her mind. "This device is used to help you hear certain things. It has two parts." Meila sat up, opening her eyes. "It has a second part that I am still working out the bugs."

An idea started to formulate in Meila's mind. "This one is strictly for listening. The other is for speaking. I have made it so you can hear conversation and information being passed by leaving one part in one room and carrying this one around with you."

Cassie smiled. "That is an interesting gadget, but I think it has already been invented. Sorry." She stood and moved around her desk.

Meila waited for Cassie to start back up on work before she put the device in her ear. She held the button on the top of it until she heard voices coming clearly into it.

"Transported tonight. How are we going to get this information to Charlie? He hasn't been at any of our meeting spots." That was Cody.

"He is a good agent. Just because he has missed a couple of check-ins doesn't mean that he has jumped back into that business."

Meila could see Cody shaking his head in her mind. "Someone is going to have to go in after him. I think we need to pull in Agent Thompson."

April shrieked. "Shanta! No! No way." Something scraped in the background. "I vote that I just shoot Rodrigez. If you could get me up to the neighboring roof, I could get a clear shot and this whole situation would be solved."

"If only you had enough bullets or if I thought the area wasn't going to be well manned."

"So you can take everyone out on the way up, and I'll just follow you at a safe distance. Besides, there aren't that many buildings around the Old Mill anymore. There wouldn't be too many good look out spots."

Meila pulled her gadget out of her ear and turned to Cassie. "I'm going to run to the bathroom real quick."

Cassie nodded, not even looking away from her computer. Meila walked calmly down the hall and turned the corner, but instead of entering the bathroom, she took off at a run toward the stairs. She knew what she had to do.

CHAPTER 26

Meila had second-guessed herself ever since arriving here. If Charlie found out, Meila knew he would be furious with her. The man she had taken out was tied up and gagged in an alleyway a few streets down. She had taken his jacket and hat, trying to replicate his look. She had also drawn a symbol on her arm, noticing that he had one. She walked up to the Old Mill wondering if those transporting the merchandise would see their stark difference. She was skinny, short, and young. Most of these men had large arms, but not always the brightest brains.

A truck's horn honked loudly, pulling Meila back to the present. She turned her gaze down, hoping she could pull this off. A man approached her. "Hey! How are the bites around this part of town?"

Meila hid her smile. This was an old trick her father used to use. She hoped that her part hadn't changed. "A little slow for my liking."

The man stepped closer to her. "Where's Lito?"

Ah. Lito must have been the man she had taken out. "Got called back urgently. Boss had something for him to do."

The man nodded. "Fine." He motioned toward the Old Mill. "You know how to get in?"

She smiled and nodded. He walked toward the truck, and Meila turned toward the building. She walked around the corner and then made sure that she was out of sight. She pushed on the side door, the door she had always come through when she came here, hoping that it was unlocked. Fortunately for her, it was.

She ran through the mill, thankful no one was in it. When she reached the side with large doors, she yanked them open, letting the truck in. She watched as men unloaded the truck, mentally counting the crates and barrels. She had seen many boxes close to this size, but they seemed to be heavy. The ones her father always ordered had been lighter. She moved to one of the crates, slightly lifting the lid. She looked around to see many men watching her, so she dropped the lid, hoping she would get a chance to look at them later. Maybe Charlie already knew what they were anyway.

Once the truck was almost empty, a man walked up to her. "Rodrigez said that he had a message for me. What is it?" a man with a stack of papers said.

Meila looked down, trying to formulate something in her mind. The man grabbed her wrist. He pulled back the sleeve of the borrowed jacket and looked down at her. "You are not one of Rodrigez's." He pulled a gun from his back. "You must be a snitch." He held the gun to her throat. "Now, tell me who you work for and what they want, or you'll never see tomorrow."

Meila watched the rage grow in this man's eyes. *This unplanned mission had been going so well! Why did it have to change now!*

The man crumpled to the floor. Meila looked at him a little startled. She looked around her. Many of the men's gazes were on her. She took only a moment before doing what she did best. She ran.

CHAPTER 27

Meila panted as she turned the corner. She dodged a few pedestrians and then checked behind her to make sure that she wasn't being followed. She had lost a few of the men that were following her a few streets back, but she knew that they would still keep an eye out for her. She glanced over her shoulder before ducking into an alleyway. She moved farther behind the building and shrunk herself against a large rectangle dumpster.

She took in a few deep breaths, trying to slow down her ragged breathing. She had been running for a good half hour, and unlike the men that were chasing her, she couldn't exchange places and take a break.

Footsteps entered the alleyway, and Meila closed her eyes, pushing herself closer to the dumpster. The feet came a few steps closer, pausing and then shuffling again.

"Diego!" a voice came from behind him. "We had a sighting of the girl down another block."

The feet ran from the alleyway, but Meila waited for a few more seconds before allowing herself to relax. They had almost found her. She was losing her touch.

When she lived with her father, he had sent her to do things just like this. She would help with shipments, and then she would run. Exhaustion was starting to set in, but she knew that she had to keep going.

She cautiously made her way out of the alley, swiftly across the streets. She needed to get back to the agency building but had to make one more stop before returning.

* * * * *

Meila made her way up the stairs at the agency building. She walked down the hallway, turned the corner, and walked toward the main office. She figured that her team should get caught up on the details. After that, she figured they would kick her out. She had gotten into a situation that did not even concern her. She hadn't thought about how dangerous it was until she had hid in an alleyway.

Cassie wasn't there. She shouldn't be. The sun had set just about fifteen minutes ago. The day shift should have gone home almost an hour ago, meaning Meila would only run into the very small skeleton staff the night shift allowed. At least that was a relief. The door to the main office was closed, but Meila saw that the lights were on. The night shift must be already hard at work. Meila scanned her ID and watched as the light went from red to green. She quickly knocked, announcing her entrance before pulling the door open.

All eyes turned to her. She had been wrong about a few people working the night shift. Everyone was there, including Charlie. "Meila?" Most of them sounded surprised. Most of them looked as if she came back from the dead.

She shrugged off the unusual jacket and hung it on a peg by the door. "I guess I should start off by apologizing." She lifted her head and tried to give a smile to the team.

"Where have you been for the last few hours?" Charlie gave her a pointed look, one she knew all too well. Charlie picked up the receiver of his phone and punched some numbers in. "Call off the search. Agent Manning has returned." He slammed the phone back down and then looked up at her, expectantly.

"I overheard a conversation about Rodrigez's men. I thought that I could help, so I went in after the few hints I had."

Cody shook his head. "That was classified information. You don't have access to those files. How did you find out?"

She held up the device. "It works, quite well actually. And I am grateful that I left this"—she walked toward her desk where the other half was—"In here, or else I wouldn't have known where to find Rodrigez and his men." Meila looked back to the jacket she had borrowed, remembering the paper she had found. She started to move toward it but paused when Charlie spoke again.

"And it's a good thing Cassie had called me when she did. I just happened to be able to spare your life. I arrived just in time to see a man hold a gun to your throat. Thankfully, I had my gun on me and shot him through the window. I called the office from the rooftop across from the warehouse and asked the team to keep an eye on for you until I got back. I was worried that you had tried to return to your father again."

Meila hung her head, disappointed in her actions, but she had nothing else that she truly wanted to say.

Charlie scowled. He turned to everyone else. "Thanks for coming in or staying late. You are free to go now. Meila and I will take the night shift."

Meila's shoulders dropped. She had acted like someone else today, ran for forever, and had worked the day shift. She was exhausted.

As everyone left, some putting their arms around her shoulders, saying they were grateful that she was still alive. Most, like Cody, just glared at her as they passed. She smiled the best that she could as they passed her. She sat down at her desk and started to fiddle with her gadget again. If she was going to stay here for the night shift, she would at least try and accomplish something.

Charlie sat on the edge of her desk. "Are you going to tell me the real story now?"

"You think I lied about something?" she sneered.

Charlie crossed his arms over his chest. "Hmm, well, with that tone, you definitely did."

Meila put her gadget down and stood so that she was eye level with Charlie. "Ask away! I'm not scared to answer."

"Why were you in that part of the city? I've warned you about going there. People are still looking for you, hoping to get revenge on an old enemy."

"Well that *enemy* is somewhere else in the town. They should be searching for him, not me."

"You said that you had more information about this stuff. Explain."

Meila lifted her hand. "I used this to get past most of their men. I noticed that the man that I had knocked out had a tattoo on his left hand that stretched from his wrist to the first knuckle of his thumb. It was small, but I figured that it might be significant, so I found a pen and quickly sketched it in the same spot. It got me past most of the men there. Their pass codes and wording were some of my father's old sayings. That part was easy. The truck itself was like any other that you would see in that part of town.

"As for the supplies? Big crates. They had to be pulled off the truck with care. They were also very heavy. It took a few men to try and move them."

"Did you see what was in them?"

Meila shook her head. "Nah. I was about to, but it was drawing too much attention. Besides, this was just a holding place for the items. They won't be unpacked at the Old Mill. They will wait for a buyer to come in, or they will move them."

"Which do you think will happen?"

"Probably the first one. The man who almost sho—" She couldn't quite get that word out. It stuck in her throat. The reality that she could have died today had already sunk in during her afternoon detour. Charlie put a hand on her arm.

Meila shook her head, attempting to clear it. She then continued. "The man who figured out I was the fake asked for the message from Rodrigez. Since I didn't know it, I found myself in some hot water."

Charlie gave her a crooked grin. "Thank goodness I was there to save you."

Meila tried to smile back but found it difficult.

117

"I will continue working tonight, but you need to lie down. I knew you wouldn't freely give all of that information to everyone else as you would if it were just me and you." He pushed her toward the door. "Just promise me that you won't run out on me."

She could tell that he was joking with her. She nodded in agreement anyway and moved out into the hall, ready to get some much-needed sleep.

She was about to close the main office door when she remembered something else. She had gone back to the Old Mill, after everyone had cleared out and found a paper lying out. She didn't know what any of the words and letters meant, but maybe it would help. She walked back in and grabbed the strange jacket. She searched all of the pockets before she found what she needed. She went over to Charlie's desk and set it down on top of a stack of pages.

He looked up after she laid it down, confused.

Meila just shrugged. "I found it lying on the ground when I went back to the Old Mill. I hope that something useful can be pulled from it."

Charlie just nodded then went back to his work. Meila walked to the elevator, where she went down to the fourth floor or the comfort floor, which she needed badly right now.

* * * * *

Meila felt a hand on her arm. Muffled voices were starting to make more sense. "He won't answer what we have asked. Perhaps if we pushed harder, or if we—"

The hand on her arm moved. Then Charlie's voice sounded. "We can't tell him that she lived. If he knew, countless ideas would come to his mind. Keep trying. You'll get it."

Meila opened her eyes. The bright light made her regret it though. She put a hand up, shielding her eyes. Blinking her eyes, she let everything come into focus before attempting to sit.

"Meila, lie back down. You don't have to be up yet. I just came down to check on you." Charlie put his hand on her shoulder and gently pushed her down.

Meila tried to shrug it off. "I'm fine." She pushed his arm away with one of her own. "Fill me in on what has happened since I've been"—she gestured toward the bed she had been lying on.

Charlie retrieved a glass of water for her and then motioned to the other man. "This is Agent Walker. He has been assigned to the Rodrigez case."

Meila nodded then looked back at Charlie. "I asked for an explanation, not an introduction." Meila took the water offered to her and took a sip.

Charlie sighed and pulled up a chair. "I was assigned to you and your father's case. I found that they had a connection with Rodrigez's case. I didn't know for sure though until you brought in this paper. Progress on both of our cases have been slow. The paper you brought in last night helped us link these two men together and perhaps find a way to stop them both."

Agent Walker spoke next. "The document that you brought us was invaluable and enough to put his men away for some time."

Meila looked in between the two men. "But—"

Charlie rubbed his hair in frustration. "He was gone before the police showed up. His men gave us a name that we haven't heard in some time." Charlie's arms went tighter. "Meila, he gave us your father's name."

Agent Walker exploded. "This little brat is what?"

"Oh." Meila closed her eyes and took another sip of water. That was a name she hadn't heard for a while. Her team had moved on to different cases. They had kept that one open, just in case Old Man Manning was spotted or did something drastic, but he had stayed pretty quiet over the last few years.

"You mean to tell me that...that this girl, this thing"—spit flew from Agent Walker's mouth—"is why he has been hunting my agents?"

Charlie put a hand up when Agent Walker came closer. "Yes, she is the daughter of Manning, but she isn't like him. My team and I have helped her change."

Agent Walker just watched her. "I want out." His gaze turned to Charlie. "I want nothing more of this. Get me out."

Charlie gestured to the door. "I can't help you with that. If you want out of this case, you will have to go to the board. They are the ones that assign the cases. Go complain about your assignment to them." He shook his head, clearly disgusted.

Agent Walker glared at Meila and then turned and stomped out. Charlie turned his gaze to Meila. "How do you feel."

Meila shrugged, and moved to swing her legs off of the bed. She wished she hadn't, both of her legs were sore. She had run for a long time yesterday, and she hadn't experienced that type of fear for the last few years. She had been anxiously waiting for the men to arrive at the warehouse and then she was nervous after she had escaped. "I've been worse."

"Well, try and get some rest. I really hadn't meant to wake you up when I came in earlier. I had come to check and see if you needed anything. You had a pretty rough day yesterday. The team will probably work through most of the day. I'll come and get you before we have our main meeting tonight."

Meila nodded and laid back down. She let herself drift back into a dreamless sleep.

CHAPTER 28

Meila was being shaken. "Mei, time to get up." Charlie's voice sounded miles away, but Meila opened her eyes. She put a hand to her head. She was not ready to get up yet, but she knew that the team needed the information that only she could provide.

She sat up. "Okay, let's go." She swung her legs down over the bed and walked with Charlie out of the room. They climbed into the elevator, and Charlie hit the seven. Back to her old sweet office. They walked in silence until they made it to the conference room. Everyone was in their usual spot, leaving Meila's seat towards the head of the table open for her.

She smiled at everyone around the room, grateful to see familiar faces smiling back at her. Charlie captured everyone's attention by clearing his throat. "All right, so we have been over the few files that were extracted from the Old Mill. What have we found?"

The team looked down at the papers in front of them. No one spoke. Meila slid over so that she could look at Cody's copy. He didn't even look up. Meila quickly read the information and then spoke. "This was one of their bigger shipments, at least according to these lists. The numbers at the bottom, I believe, are dates of past shipments and the sizes. Those at the top of the page would have been yesterday's deliveries."

Charlie nodded. "Meila, when you first started to work here, you told us that guys like this have many warehouses. Could these shipments just be to this one warehouse on these dates?"

Meila took Cody's page, holding in front of her. "I'm not sure. If we knew what was in those crates, it might be easier to narrow down."

Charlie nodded and then looked at April. "I sent the white powder samples we retrieved from the warehouse down to the lab. I looked on them while you went to get Meila, but they are pretty busy, so they had just barely started to test them."

"What about the men that were apprehended?" Meila asked.

Charlie looked to Cody. "We have another agent who will be bringing in some pictures along with a list of items we found at the Old Mill. Most of the pictures are of the men that we apprehended."

"What about fingerprints?"

Cody just stared at her. "Why would that matter?"

Meila looked around the faces of the room. They all were just staring blankly at her. "None of the men were wearing gloves. If you went directly to the warehouse after I returned, they wouldn't have had time to clean all of their fingerprints."

"So what?" Shanta posed.

A voice came from behind her. "It means that you could still see who is out on the streets, those that still need to be apprehended. Fingerprints are good to have on file anyway."

Meila turned around to find Agent Walker with a big pile of papers in his arms.

"Cody, go see if you can get some men to do those fingerprints. Also, check on those results from the lab. Don't come back until you have gotten answers from both," Charlie demanded.

Cody stood and left, scooting past Agent Walker on the way out. Meila stood and grabbed some of the papers in Agent Walker's arms. She sent a small smile his way and then helped him pass out the pages that he had brought in.

"I had Agent Walker collect everything that his team already had from the case. He will be joining us in this case, I will now turn over some time to him."

The agent walked up in front of everyone, worry apparent on his face. He pushed his square glasses back up to his nose and then began. "My team and I have been trying to get this guy behind bars for the last few years. He calls himself Rodrigez. We are not sure if that is his real name, but everyone on the street knows him by that name. He has a big gang, but only a few of them have caused us problems. We know that he sells ammunition and weapons in large amounts. What we don't know is the amount. The information that Me"—he cleared his throat. "The information that Miss Manning provided us has been helpful, but this is just one warehouse."

"Do you have any evidence that he has more than one warehouse or somewhere he stores them?" Meila questioned.

Agent Walker blinked a few times and then looked back at the pages that he had handed out. "My team and I are not certain. We had a man on the inside of Rodrigez's business, but he was badly injured yesterday, apparently right after you left the building. He, unfortunately, has not been released from surgery, so questioning him at this time would be impossible."

Cody walked in at that time. He held up papers in his hand. "I have pictures and results from the lab." He passed them down both sides of the table.

Charlie stood back up and took control. "Meila, do you recognize any of these guys?"

Meila looked through all of the pictures that Cody had brought up. She pointed to a handful of the men. "These men were definitely there. They helped unload the truck. This man"—she pointed—"drove the truck." She moved to the next one. "He was also there, but he didn't help unload or anything. He just stood there and watched."

"Was he holding anything, a paper perhaps?"

Meila closed her eyes, letting yesterday's surprising outing come back to mind. "No. He wasn't holding anything. I don't think he was a lookout either. He was too far into the building."

Agent Walker made a quick note on his paper. "If we were to go back to the storehouse, would you know which crates were brought in yesterday?"

Meila shook her head. "I was scared when I went back, but I had wondered if they might have left something behind. I grabbed the slip of paper, then I heard a noise, so I got out as quick as I could. I figured that it was too dangerous for me to try and get anything else." Meila held up the copy of the page she had found. "This is a list of shipments. It tells us how big the shipments were and the date they were dropped off at a specific location." A plan started to formulate in her mind. If only she could get back into the building.

The meeting around her continued, but she zoned them out. The gears were going, and there was no use in trying to stop them. She needed to get back into the Old Mill, but she knew that it would be too dangerous. Rodrigez's men were no doubt watching now, especially now that this information got out. The cops were also probably roaming around the Old Mill. It wouldn't look good if she tried to break in. Her chances of being caught were high.

She checked the page again. The next delivery wasn't listed, but she assumed that much. Delivery dates, especially future ones, were not left out for anyone to see. She examined the past dates, trying to find a pattern. The dates were so strange, though. She sat for a moment more before she realized the odd silence in the room. She Looked up to find everyone staring at her expectantly. "Um, sorry. Did I miss something?"

Charlie placed a paper over the one that she had been examining. "I just asked you if you knew of any special circumstance for a drug called 'fiedrum.'"

Meila thought for a moment. She shook her head. "I'm sorry. It sounds familiar, but I don't remember the exact details surrounding it. Is it a white powder that came in the boxes?"

Charlie nodded. "The analysis report says that they have been passed as bath salts, but there has to be more to them. Especially if your father is storing and selling them."

"The woman in the lab told me she had never seen anything like it before. She said that she would continue to run tests to see how it would react. She said that she would send an update once she had one," Cody commented.

"All right. Please get those results to me and Agent Walker as soon as possible. Other than that, I think this meeting can be adjourned. Those of you who worked the day shift, go home. Those who work the night shift, let's get going." Charlie stood and left the room. Everyone else seemed to drift out, except for Meila.

She looked back down at the pages that they were handed out during the meeting. She stood and moved to the whiteboard. She was supposed to work the day shift but had slept during most of it. She figured that no one really cared if she stayed. She made sure that she was out of the line of sight from the door then got to work.

She hung the pictures on the whiteboard. Something about the paper that she had found wasn't correct. It had been way too easy to access. Most papers, especially like this one, were kept under lock and key or only given to extremely important people. It wasn't something that was just left on the ground in plain sight.

She turned over the page. She must have had a copy. There may not have been anything on the back, but she wanted to double-check. She placed it on the table next to her. She put a hand up to her face, placing her chin in her upturned fingers. All of this information had to link together somehow. But where?

A knock came from behind her. She turned around to find Charlie watching her. "Mei, I was headed home. You want to come?"

Meila thought for a moment. Maybe talking it through with Charlie might help. "Can you stay for a little bit?"

He walked farther into the room and acted as if he was thinking. "Hmm...stay here and possibly see if anything new can be developed about this never-ending case or go home and sit in silence by myself? I think I have a few minutes." He answered, dramatically plopping into a chair next to her.

Meila rolled her eyes. "Do you know how to get your hands on the original paper that I brought you?"

Charlie folded his arms. "We sent the original to be scanned in the lab. We are hoping that it can tell us about where it may have come from, maybe some fingerprints. The lab told me that we were the sixth piece of evidence that was brought in this morning. I asked to have the results as soon as possible, but we haven't received them yet."

Meila offered a small smile, then pushed on. "I think that I need to get back in the building."

Charlie was shaking his head before she even finished. "I knew that your mind was going during the meeting, but, Meila, these men are dangerous. I don't think that you fully understand that."

It was Meila's turn to shake her head. "My father would put me in those situations so he could prove that he was more powerful. He would do it to prove that nothing stood in his way."

"Well we are not run by your father. We don't do the same things that he does. What I say goes, Meila. I don't want you anywhere near that building. Rodrigez or one of his men could easily recognize you. Besides, you are supposed to be dead."

"Charlie"—Meila sat down across from him, looking intently into his blue eyes—"I got in and out yesterday without anyone else's help. I can get in and out again, without being noticed."

"You only got out of there yesterday because I was there." He hooked a thumb back to himself.

"No, I went back again. That is when I found this page."

"And you didn't see anyone or anything."

"No one was watching, at least not that I could see. I only found this page, though. I am sure that if you let me go back there, I can get more, especially if Rodrigez or some of his men were there! Charlie! That would even be better!"

"No, Meila, it's too risky."

Meila's shoulders dropped. "Charlie, please, I need maybe twenty minutes. I could get more information than anyone."

Charlie just stood. "I think that you have had too much excitement for a couple of days, Meila. I will let you examine that page tomorrow. Come on. Let's go home."

* * * * *

Meila looked at the page again. Just as she had suspected, nothing was on the back of it. She placed it back down and ran her fingers through her hair. Her head dropped and she propped her elbows on her knees, before resting her head in her palms.

"Anything?" Charlie asked.

Keeping her head buried, she shook her head. She felt and heard a chair being placed beside hers.

"It's okay if you don't find anything. Maybe it was just an old paper that wasn't needed anymore," Charlie said.

She looked up at him. "You really think so?" Meila asked, doubting that he actually believed that.

He shrugged. "Mei, I don't know. What if they were watching you and knew that you were going back. Maybe it was a trap, but you were lucky and got out before something bad happened."

"Charlie, I don't think that it was. Maybe they thought that I was going to run to the police? That always scared my father. He would up and move all of his supplies and wipe the whole place clean before the police even got there." She pointed to the page on her desk. "Everything in that warehouse could be gone before we can pull a search team together." She paused, waiting for this information to process in Charlie's head. "But, if you let me go back—"

"Which you won't be," Charlie stated.

"Charlie, I know what I am looking for. I can get the information that we need."

"Out of the question, Meila. Please, just this once, listen to me and stay put. This situation is sticky, and it will only get worse if you were to jump in."

She leaned back and folded her arms. "You don't trust me?"

He sighed. "Of course, I trust you. I just need you to stay put. You can't go anywhere, especially now that Rodrigez might be looking for you."

Meila tried to think about what he was going through. She finally nodded, admitting defeat.

"Thank you. Now, please keep looking through the files that you can. I think that you will find something soon." Charlie stood and moved his chair back over to his desk, letting her do her work in silence.

Meila wasn't super proud of her choice, but she didn't care to face the consequences of the mistake of going against Charlie again.

CHAPTER 23

Meila slipped on her backpack. She checked the streets; they were busy. Good! That would give her some cover. She checked the peephole before opening her door. She looked toward Charlie's door but quickly diverted her gaze, knowing he wasn't there. She moved down the hallway and pulled open the door to the stairs.

She looked over her shoulder and then moved down the first flight. She heard voices down below and stopped. She listened for a moment when she realized that neither one of the voices belonged to Charlie. If he ever found out about this, she was dead.

Meila started down the stairs again. She passed the people but kept her head lowered so that she didn't make eye contact with them. She pushed the door open to the lobby. Empty. The man at the front desk had just walked into the back room. The time was now.

Meila stepped out of the stairs and pushed herself toward the front door. She glanced back, but the room was still empty. She made it outside and started to walk. She knew that running would make her more of a target, so she tried to keep her pace steady.

Charlie was still at the agency building. He had another meeting that he had been pulled into. Meila looked down at her watch. She should be able to make it to the Old Mill before dark and possibly make it back to her apartment, all before Charlie returned. She planned to slip away once it was dark.

She turned the corner slowly, knowing she had run into April the last time she had come this far. But no one was there. Not a single soul. *That's strange*, Meila thought. She took a couple of steps into the unusually empty street. She felt the hairs on the back of her neck start to raise.

Someone tapped her on the shoulder. She spun around. "Charlie? I thought that you were in a meeting?"

"I was. It ended early when I got a phone call from the apartment manager." He folded his arms over his chest. "The question is, what are you doing out? I told you how dangerous it is for you to be on the streets. Did you think that I was joking or something?"

Meila shook her head. An idea popped into her head. "I was going to pick up some groceries," Meila lied. She hoped that Charlie wouldn't see through it.

He sighed and then grabbed her arm and dragged her back toward their apartment building.

"Wait," Meila tried to fight back but knew that it was useless.

"Shanta can pick up anything that you need. You can use that excuse until we reach my apartment. Then the real story is going to have to come out."

Meila let herself be pulled back to the apartment building, wondering how she was going to explain this one. Charlie nodded to the man at the desk, and then they walked up the stairs together. He opened Meila's apartment door and ushered her in. Meila dropped her bag on his kitchen table and pulled out a chair. "How did you know that I was going to leave?"

Charlie opened the fridge and pulled out a water bottle for both of them. He set one in front of her and then sat down across from her. "I didn't, but I knew that you might one day try to do something like that, so I talked to Rick, the apartment manager, and asked him to call me if you ever tried to leave."

Meila sunk down farther into her chair. "You are acting like my father. He always had me followed. Made sure that I felt free, but I never really was."

Charlie shook his head. "It's not like that, Meila. The chance that you have a large price over your head, one that is continually growing, is big. We can't have you wandering around the town. Besides, you are supposed to be dead, remember the fall you took on that rainy night? We are trying to keep you safe."

Meila put her head against the back of her chair, letting her eyes stare into the ceiling. "So it's going to be how it was when I first started to live here? Everyone cautious, no one really talking to me unless they are forced. Things like that?" Meila asked, dreading the answer that she knew would come.

Charlie thought for a moment. "No. Everyone talks to you now without force, but you will just need to be more careful. Besides, you promised." Disappointment colored the last few words.

Meila closed her eyes.

"I know, and I'm sorry, but I knew that I could get in and back out safely." Meila opened her eyes and sat farther up. "Charlie, we need those papers out of that building."

He shook his head. "Mei, that is what my department meeting was on. The lab found some traces of fiedrum on that page. The page that you found was enough. Agent Walker and his team are going to take over this case. Agent Walker knows a lot more about Rodrigez and his business. We have been released."

Meila stared back at him, shocked. "But there is more that I can find! I know that if I were given a few more days, perhaps a week or two—"

Her words died when Charlie put his hand up. "I'm sorry, but it is out of my hands. Meila, you have to understand that this is how our unit works. We help other teams get over a bump in the road, then they keep pushing through the case. If we are lucky, we get to hear the results."

Meila's back slumped. "Can you at least let them know that there are more papers out there, that could be of more use? And maybe suggest having someone go undercover?"

Charlie nodded. "I'll make sure to mention it." Charlie started toward the door but stopped when he touched the doorknob. "I actually came to give you good news."

Meila turned her head so that she was looking at him.

"I asked the board for permission to give you full clearance. They agreed."

Meila stood, excitement taking over the resentment she was just feeling. "Really?"

Charlie nodded. "When we start our next case, you will be allowed to see everything that everyone else does."

He turned toward the door again and opened it. "Goodnight, Meila. I will see you tomorrow." He closed the door.

Meila jumped up for joy, squealing as she did. She was allowed to truly help with cases now!

* * * * *

Meila stayed seated after Charlie had finished the meeting. They had received a case that they would have for about a week. Her father was still out there somewhere, covering every step he took. Every effort they put into finding him had backfired. There still had to be more. Somewhere, there was a piece missing from this whole puzzle. She just wished she knew where to begin to look for it.

A knock came from behind her, and she turned to find Charlie standing in the doorway.

"You okay, Mei? The meeting ended five minutes ago, and everyone is already working except you. Did everything make sense during the meeting? Are you struggling with this huge amount of work?" Charlie smiled as he sat down next to her.

Meila shook her head. "It's nothing like that."

"Something is bothering you, though."

Meila nodded. "How could my father be lying so low under the radar that we can't even find a trace of him? It has been two years since he escaped. How is he surviving?"

"Meila, there are many ways he could be doing it. He could live under a different name, buy everything with cash… You didn't want me to answer that question, did you?"

Meila shrugged and Charlie stood.

"Why don't you come help us with this case? You need to get your mind off of your father. I promise I am keeping your father's case in my mind, but we need to move on to more pressing cases."

"I know, Charlie."

"All right," Charlie stood. "Let's get going then."

Meila gathered her things and took them to her desk. She pulled out certain parts of the file, searching through different parts to find where this business went wrong. When Meila felt as if she had found something, she looked up, letting her eyes scan the room. Everyone seemed busy, but she had a question.

Charlie was on the phone, talking to someone in hushed tones, and April and Cody were discussing something with Marcus. Shanta had been moved to the night shift, so who else could she ask?

Her eyes settled on the door out of the main office. Cassie should be out there, and hadn't she told Meila she has helped the team in the past before?

Meila stood and made her way over to the door. She held the file in her hand and was about to step out of the office when she heard Charlie's voice behind her.

"Meila, where are you going?" He came up behind her, pulling her hand off of the door.

"You were all busy, so I was going to go and ask Cassie a quick question. She told me a while ago about how she sometimes helps with the cases."

Charlie looked at her, confused.

"Cassie has never helped with the cases. She doesn't have clearance to do so."

Meila furrowed her eyebrows.

"But isn't she your secretary?"

Cody sniffed in indignation. He walked toward the pair standing by the door. "Cassie helping with cases?" He forced out a few laughs before Charlie spoke, abruptly stopping him.

"Cassie is more of a glorified receptionist. If we have a meeting coming up, she lets us know. She takes any calls we don't answer or runs simple errands when Shanta isn't here. Other than that, her job is pretty boring. She doesn't have clearance to look at anything from our cases. She doesn't even have clearance to enter this room without knocking."

Meila nodded. "So, in other words, she can't help me?"

Both Cody and Charlie shook their heads.

Meila nodded and sat back down at her desk, pulling out the file and searching for the missing piece.

* * * * *

Meila picked up a book from her room and stepped out onto the fire escape. The weather had turned warmer, and there was a slight breeze, making it a perfect day to sit outside and read. She sat down on the rough steel gratings, which were somewhat uncomfortable, but Meila didn't mind. It was a nice day, and she intended to enjoy it.

Meila had only read a few pages when she heard voices down below. Meila closed the book and put it down beside her. She scanned the streets before she recognized a familiar face. She stared for a moment before darting back toward her window and throwing herself through it.

Her breathing came rapidly as she remembered the terrifying face of one of her father's men. It was Hunter. He had found her.

Meila's breathing had still not calmed down when she heard her apartment door open. Meila grabbed the nearest object she could find and stood behind her closed bedroom door. Hunter had found her and was coming to take her back to her father.

Not now! she thought. *I love where I am at. I finally feel as if I belong and have meaning in this world!*

Her door pushed open slightly, and Meila lifted the object in her hands above her head, realizing now it was the book she had been reading. She was about to bring it down on the intruder's head when a hand reached up and snatched the book from her hands.

Meila instinctively went to run, but a hand grabbed her arm. She wacked at it wildly, hoping Hunter would let her go.

"Meila!" a familiar voice said. Her guard immediately fell, and the hand let go of her.

"Mei, are you all right? You seemed like you were going to kill me with the book you were holding." A smile played on Charlie's lips, a teasing glint apparent in his eyes. Meila tried to match his smile but could not muster one to appear.

"Charlie, I saw one of my father's men down on the streets. His name is Hunter. He is one of the best men my father has ever had. He has found me, Charlie." Meila let out a deep breath before continuing, whispering this last part. "My father has found me."

Charlie moved to the window and crawled out onto her fire escape. He stood out there for a few minutes, scanning the streets. Meila had moved to her bed, sitting, waiting for Charlie to come in and inform her of the bad news.

"Mei, even if it was Hunter down there, I don't think he saw you."

Meila turned around and glared at Charlie. She looked at him long enough to watch him come back into the room before she turned her back on him and spoke. "How would you know? You weren't here, and who knows how long Hunter has been down on the street looking for me?"

Charlie sat down on the bed beside her. "Mei, I know your father's men are on the streets, but I don't believe they are looking for you. Your father believes you are gone. I know it can be difficult, but Hunter may not have been out on the streets looking for you. These groups are always after someone. You will probably see your father's men from time to time, but you make sure to see them as if they are any other pedestrian walking past you."

Charlie placed a hand on her shoulder. "If Hunter was trying to track you down, he would be searching in alleys and places they believed you could afford. This end of town is kind of pricey for someone your age living on their own."

Meila nodded, understanding what Charlie was saying. She was paranoid. She had been free for almost two years. She had a job that paid well for her age.

"I am safe, right?" Meila asked, not an ounce of confidence splattered in the question.

Charlie patted her on the shoulder and lifted his hand.

"If it was too dangerous for you to live here, I would get you out."

Meila looked over to him and lifted the corners of her mouth.

Charlie stood and moved to her doorway and into the kitchen. "Dinner will be ready soon."

Meila thanked him but stayed put. She turned her head toward the window and then stood. She maneuvered herself cautiously over to the window before slowly closing it and latching it. Her safety needed to come first. If Hunter was really after her, she wasn't going to make the chase an easy one.

CHAPTER 30

Four years later. Willowsville, Washington

Charlie handed the folders to Meila, asking her to pass them out. She did so quickly as she listened to the new case that they had been given. "All right, so if you look at the information in front of you, it will look familiar to a big chunk of us."

Meila looked down at the file once she sat back down in her spot. It had a few pictures that she didn't recognize. She pushed those aside and pulled out a few more pages. None of them looked familiar until the last page. It was the page that she had found a few years ago. She looked up at Charlie. "I thought that this case would have been solved by now."

He shrugged. "Me too." He turned to the whole group. "So as many of you probably know, this is the Rodrigez case. I need everyone to look over the notes and the new information the other teams have found. We will reconvene after that."

Everyone started to leave, but Meila stood and stopped Charlie's progress. "My suggestion, about someone going undercover. Was it made?"

Charlie looked at her confused. It took him a minute for understanding to cross his face, but it did. "I did ask the group to look into that, but they must not have seen it important." He pushed past her.

"It didn't seem important? Who thought that?"

Charlie walked to his desk, with Meila following close behind him, eagerly waiting for an answer. "The man that was in charge of that team."

Meila could tell that Charlie was holding something back. "And who was that?"

He took a breath and then answered. "Agent Walker."

"What?" Meila moved around him so that she was looking into his face. "He still doesn't trust me? We helped him with his case!"

Charlie looked up. "I'm not sure what he thinks."

A possibility jumped up to the front of her mind. "Are we going to have to work with him?" she asked hesitantly.

Charlie lifted one shoulder and let his gaze go back to what he was working on. "A little bit. I was told that we would be working on his case for a few weeks, but I will try and have him come in when you aren't around. I know he hasn't always been the kindest to you. He now knows who you are, but I am not sure how he is going to act around you. Until I know how he is going to be like to work with, I will make sure the two of you don't work together much."

Meila nodded and thanked Charlie. She moved to her desk and started to work on the case, hoping that it would distract her from the thoughts of Agent Walker.

* * * * *

Meila had picked up a box from the outside the elevator. Charlie had requested that they get everything that they could for the Rodrigez case. It had been four years since they had even touched this case, but no team could make any kind of headway on it. Charlie didn't want to leave out anything in this next search. All of the files that even mentioned Rodrigez's name, or someone in his gang, had been brought to this floor. Meila hoped that Charlie now regretted that decision.

When they had climbed out of the elevator this morning, the hall had been lined with boxes stacked five or six boxes high. It was almost eleven o'clock, and Meila was gathering up the last few boxes. Charlie had sent everyone else to work and then was off to a meeting.

Meila was the only one given the task of sorting through the rest of the papers and boxes left in the hall.

Meila turned the corner and ran into someone. The box was dropped in the contact and tipped over, forcing off the lid and spilling its contents everywhere. Meila sighed as the woman bent down and started to pick up the files.

"Meila! I am so sorry. I should have been paying better attention to where I was going!"

Meila bent down and helped Cassie pick up the files. "It's okay. After doing this for a couple of hours, I must have zoned out and wasn't watching where I was going." Meila said, placing the files that she had picked up back in the box.

"What are you doing with all of this information anyway?" Cassie asked.

Meila shrugged. "I'm not sure. Charlie just asked that all of it was given to us, so here it is," Meila said as she took the few files out of Cassie's arms and placed them in the box.

Cassie nodded and then continued on her way. Meila moved on past Cassie's desk and then on into the main office. She placed this box on her desk and then started to go through it, knowing that she would have a long day of sorting ahead of her.

* * * * *

"You made sure that no one will find even a trace of me in those files, right?" a voice said over the phone.

"Of course they won't, Dad. I've wiped your name totally out of the system. Don't worry about what I have done here. Once we are back to our business, there is nothing that you have to worry about. Besides, you have your own issues to work out. You have to get in and talk to Old Man Manning. That is going to be tough enough on its own."

"Don't worry about that, I have a way in. You just make sure that you gain that girls trust. Get her on our side. We will need that extra leverage."

"And what if that doesn't work?" the second voice asked.

"Oh, it will. My plans always work."

* * * * *

Meila pulled open Charlie's door, knowing he was home from work. She placed her keys on his end table and moved to his living room to sit in her favorite chair. She picked up the TV remote and turned on the TV, flipping through the channels until she finally settled on some black-and-white Western. A commercial came on, and Charlie stepped out of his room.

"Find something good?" he asked, pointing to the TV.

Meila shrugged.

"I am going to go and grab some food from a nearby takeout. Is there anything I could get you?" Charlie asked, pulling his keys out of his pockets.

"A hamburger sounds good," Meila responded.

Charlie nodded and left his apartment. Meila muted the TV and walked over to the fridge and pulled out a water bottle. She took a drink when she heard a scratching on the door. Meila tensed up, feeling the hairs on the back of her neck start to stand up. A pit dropped to the bottom of her stomach. Something was up, and Meila was worried about what it may be.

The scratching on the door continued. The doorknob started to turn, and Meila dropped down behind the island in the middle of Charlie's kitchen. Her breathing quickened as she listened to the heavy footsteps walk across Charlie's tiled kitchen floor. The person must have stepped onto the carpet because the footsteps had softened. Meila dared a look around the counter. The man's back was to her. He had opened up the small entertainment stand under the TV and was rummaging through it.

Her breathing became normal as she recognized the sandy-blond straight-styled hair.

"Cody?" Meila stood, and so did Cody, surprise apparent on his face.

"Meila? What are you doing here?"

Meila furrowed her eyebrows. "Charlie and I eat dinner together every evening. He went to go and get some food."

Cody nodded, looking uncomfortably at the open door. He made his way toward it, moving quickly before Meila could attempt to stop him.

"Wait, Cody! What are you doing here? You are supposed to be at the office, aren't you?"

"None of your business, Manning," he called as he made his way to the concrete stalls. Meila quickly followed him, pulling the door closed behind her. She ran down the stairs after Cody.

"You have done this before, Cody. You were in his apartment a few years ago. Why?"

Meila jumped the last few stairs out of breath and watched as Cody ran out the glass doors of their apartment building. He had disappeared into the busy street before Melia had made it outside. Frustrated and disappointed, she made her way back upstairs and twisted the knob to Charlie's apartment but found it locked. She put a hand on her back pocket but remembered her lock pick was inside of her room. She leaned her head on Charlie's door and closed her eyes. She was in such a rush to find out what Cody was up to she didn't think about how she was going to get back in.

Ten minutes had passed before Meila saw Charlie enter the hallway with two brown bags in his hands. His eyebrows furrowed when he saw her.

"Mei? What are you doing out here?" He handed the bag of food to Meila and pulled out his key ring, sorting through it until he found the correct one to open his door. He opened the door and motioned for her to enter. Meila stepped back into his apartment, placing the food on the counter.

"Cody stopped by."

"Oh, did he need something?" Charlie asked, closing the door and making his way over the food he had just purchased.

"Well, he broke into your apartment and then got some stuff out of the cabinet under the TV."

Charlie looked to Meila. "He broke into my apartment? Hmm." Charlie lifted a hand to his cheek, rubbing it slowly, thinking.

Meila made her way over to where she had found Cody. She lifted up the few pieces of paper Cody had left out. None of them seemed to be important. They were the instructions to the TV, the remote, and a warranty on the microwave.

"Do you bring any of the files from the office here?" Meila asked, replacing the pages in the cabinet.

Charlie shook his head. "I like to keep all of my work at the office. The minute I get home, I try to forget about work and relax. Why?"

Meila let the gears spin in her head. "Why else would Cody break into your apartment? If he wanted to talk to you, he would have knocked or called on the phone. Cody was searching for something, but he didn't want you to know about it. He was surprised when he saw me and ran out of here before I could get two sentences from him."

Charlie shook his head. "Don't worry about it, Mei. We can go in a little bit early tomorrow and ask Cody why he came over last night."

"Yeah. That sounds great," Meila answered sarcastically. "Let's ask Cody why he was acting strangely. Confront him about why he broke into your apartment, yeah." Meila rolled her eyes. "Charlie, be serious. You can't just ask Cody what he was doing last night. If he broke into your apartment, he probably didn't want to be found."

Charlie nodded. "I know, Mei. I will talk to him tomorrow, though. Just promise me you are going to drop it. I will discuss the matter with Cody, and if it is an issue, then I will let you know. But please keep your mind focused on the current case."

Meila shrugged but did not say anything.

"Meila," Charlie pressed.

She sighed. "Fine. I promise not to poke into it anymore."

Charlie smiled at her and handed her a burger.

CHAPTER 31

Charlie dropped a stack of files on Meila's desk. "I need you to look over these," he requested.

Meila picked up the first file. "What am I looking for? A murderer? Or perhaps where they are now?" Meila's mind started to run faster and faster with each new possibility that she may be looking for, at least until she opened the first file. "William Walker. Male, five feet seven inches." Meila moved her finger down his briefing page until she found the cases that he had worked on. She looked up at Charlie. "What is this for?"

He placed himself in the chair across from her desk. "Since Marcus's expertise is needed on a different case, I have decided to pull someone in who is already familiar with this case and the information we have been going through. Unfortunately, he was removed from the case last year because the board believed that he was stalling. But I believe that he was sincere in his search. This case has been ongoing for almost six years. We need to solve it. I need the best people that I can get on the job. Agent Walker is one of the best agents this place has. We need all of the best people that we can get."

Meila moved Agent Walker's file to the side and flipped open the next one. It only contained some empty pages. She moved on to the next one to find the exact same thing.

"He is the only one here. The rest of these are empty." Meila knew the moment that she said it, Charlie was trying to tell her something. She looked up at him expectantly.

"What are you trying to say?"

"Mei, he is our best chance. I need an experienced man for this case."

Meila shook her head. "Charlie, you must be crazy. This man wanted out of this case because of who I am."

Charlie just shrugged. "He wanted out because he thought that you were dangerous. He has found that you aren't the person your father is. He is going to be our best chance in this case."

"If you think that he is the best fit, why did you care to inform me? You do all of the hiring and firing." Meila rose, hoping that Charlie would get the message that she didn't want to speak about this anymore. But as usual, Charlie didn't pick up on the hints.

"Mei, I just wanted to warn you. I didn't want to surprise you, and I respect your opinion. I try to make these kinds of decisions as a team decision. I think that everyone should get a say of who they are working with." Charlie replied, following her to the closest stack of boxes.

Meila pulled a box down from the stack and opened it. "Well, you can't always make everyone happy. You have to do what is best for the team." She saw Charlie tense.

"Fine. If you will excuse me, I have to go speak with some people upstairs." Charlie stomped away, leaving Meila to do her work.

Meila placed the box on her desk and pulled out the first few files. April was at her desk the next moment. "Are you all right, Meila?"

"I'm fine. I just have a lot of paperwork that I need to get through before my shift ends." *In eight hours*, Meila grumbled.

"Okay," April answered hesitantly. "Shanta left breakfast for anyone who wanted it. I believe that she put it in the kitchen."

Meila looked up at April. "Thanks, but I would just like to get back to work."

April looked a little hurt but turned and walked back to her desk.

Meila watched as the door opened almost an hour later. Charlie walked in and asked everyone to gather around. "I know that most of you already have met this guy, but I'll introduce him anyway. This is Agent William Walker. He has done a lot of the field work on this case, so he will be joining us. He will be temporarily filling Marcus's shoes, but his role will be different. He knows almost nothing about gadgets or how to work them. He has been working on this case for some time, so he is going to be the expert that we can go to. He will be working at Marcus's desk."

Charlie looked up, expecting people to object. When none came, he waved everyone to get back to work. Agent Walker put his hat and jacket on the rack by the door. Meila lowered her eyes when he walked toward Marcus's desk. The desk was kiddy corner to hers.

Meila looked over at Charlie, but he was busy talking to a few other agents. April had gone into the kitchen to grab some food. She wouldn't meet Meila's gaze when she walked back out. Did anyone *not* know that she didn't want this man here? He accused her of being a criminal!

She saw a gray suit move in front of her desk. Speaking of the man, he stood right in front of her. "Can I help you?" Meila tried to embody the best Cody look that he always gave her.

"I was wondering if you had eaten yet. I haven't got the chance to do so yet but would love something before I start."

Meila shook her head. "Why, so you can yell at me some more? Didn't get your share a few years ago?"

Agent Walker looked embarrassed. He pushed his glasses up his nose higher, then wrung his hands. "I actually wanted to apologize for my actions. If you would be so kind as to grab something with me, I would explain it better, especially with less ears listening."

Meila looked around. Many of her coworkers had their heads deep in work, but she knew the sense in what he was saying. "Fine, but only a couple of minutes. I have a lot of work to get to."

Relief was evident on Agent Walker's face. They filled their plates and sat down at the empty table. He ate a few bites before beginning. "I really am sorry that I yelled at you. I was having a bad day, which

I know does not justify my actions. Do you mind if I explain a little more about myself so that you can see why I exploded?"

Meila had shoved food in her mouth to keep from saying something that she would regret, so she just nodded.

"Very good. Fifteen years ago, I married the love of my life. After a few years, we had twins. I set my younger son down on his stomach to sleep one night. He passed away that night. I knew I needed something to distract from all of my heartache and pain, so I threw myself into trying to find a job. I started work here shortly after and was asked to be a part of a team that worked out in the field. They learned quickly that I did better the behind the scenes than when I was out in the field. Miss Manning, I had only worked in the office for a year, almost two, but I moved up quickly."

"Does this have anything to do with me? Because the only thing that I have heard from your mouth is all about you."

He put up his hands. "I was getting there." He intertwined his fingers in front of him. "I was proud of my station and started to boast. Unfortunately, my boasting was passed along to some very powerful men here in the city. A month later, my wife and four-year-old son were kidnapped. I blew up at you that day because"—he took in a breath—"because it was your father that did it."

Meila nodded. She understood that. Her father would threaten family or loved ones to get his way. It was awful.

"They were dead by the next week." Agent Walker pulled a handkerchief from his pocket and stopped a tear from rolling down his face. "So I apologize for speaking so harshly to you. I thought that you would be very much like him. Maybe that you came to finish the job."

Meila put her hand on the one that wasn't mopping up his wet eyes. "I'm sorry. I always heard that my father did those sorts of things, but I have never met a person that suffered the consequences for it." Meila released his hand. "So what are you doing here?"

"I decided that I was going to make a change in my life. I used the anger and the hate stuck inside of me to help put the bad guys in jail."

Meila smiled. "I understand that completely." She held her hand out. "How about we start over?"

Agent Walker stuffed his wet handkerchief back into his pocket and then took her hand. "I would like that very much."

A few minutes later, the two of them walked out of the kitchen, discussing the case. When they reached her desk, Agent Walker nodded and went to his borrowed desk. Meila smiled. He had been one of the first people that she connected with. Yes, he had yelled at her, but that was ages ago. It was the fastest that she had even bonded with anyone since leaving her father's house. She was grateful that she had made a friend, a true friend that hadn't been made because of Charlie. Well, mostly not because of Charlie.

* * * * *

Meila had gone out for just a few minutes to go on a walk around town. She knew Charlie probably wouldn't enjoy her doing so, but she was tired of being holed up in her apartment and the office. She needed an out for a few minutes.

Meila had only made it a few blocks, making her way toward the agency building, before she recognized a voice. She turned around, searching for the owner of this certain voice. She paused for a moment, listening to Cody's voice. Where was it coming from?

She was walking around a corner when a hand tugged on her arm.

"What are you doing in this part of town?" The nails dug into the flesh of her arm.

"Cody? What are you doing in this part of town?" Meila echoed.

"I had a meeting on this side of town," he answered begrudgingly.

Meila blinked a few times, trying to process what he had said. "A meeting with whom?"

A familiar face stepped out from behind Cody, and Meila felt a scream come in her throat. He had long brown hair, a mustache, and goatee. He was wearing his normal attire of a baggy olive-green shirt with his brown pants. He was holding a gun, pointing it straight at Meila.

"Mastermind Meila. Won't your father be proud to see you." Hunter, one of her father's goons, stepped closer to her.

Hunter grabbed Meila's other arm. Meila struggled against his grasp. She turned to Cody.

"You turned me in? How could you?"

Cody shrugged. "How couldn't I? You were getting in the way of my success."

"Meila!" a voice said from far away. She punched at the hand that was holding her.

"Meila!" the voice said again, but this time, it was drawing nearer. She was being shaken. Meila opened her eyes to find herself in her own room. She rubbed her face and found Charlie staring at her.

"What is going on?"

"I came to get you for work, but you weren't up. Are you all right?"

Meila nodded. "I'm sorry. I thought I saw Hunter again."

"Aw. That makes sense. You were throwing punches at me the moment I grabbed you." Charlie sighed. "Where was he this time?"

"Just a few blocks away from the agency. He started to drag me back to my father."

"I thought you had worked past all of those things."

Meila shrugged. "I did too, but I guess not."

"Did you get away from him?"

Meila shook her head. "Charlie, Cody was with him. He was the one who turned me in. He wants me gone, off of the team permanently. Cody told me I was in his way of succeeding."

"Hey, don't start to think like that. You have value on the team, and don't mind what Cody said in your dream. He does not see you like that in real life."

Meila took a deep breath. "Are you sure?" she asked.

Charlie nodded. "I wouldn't have told you if I didn't think it was true. Now, go and get ready for work. I think you need to focus on the Rodrigez case and get all of this fabrication out of your head about Cody."

She got out of bed, and Charlie excused himself to get her some breakfast. Meila quickly changed and threw her hair up into a tight ponytail. She then made her way into the kitchen, quickly eating breakfast before stepping out onto the street with Charlie.

Meila cautiously watched every person who passed her. She knew her father and his goons were out there somewhere, but they hadn't had much of a sign from them in the last couple of years. Her father was laying low, even though he had escaped years ago. Something big was going to happen, Meila just hoped they were ready for it.

CHAPTER 32

Meila looked at the file again. She ran a frustrated hand through her hair. She had been over the file that Charlie had given her so many times. None of it fit. Cody walked past her. He looked at the file she was working on. He laughed. "Good luck getting anything out of that one. I looked at it for days on end but didn't get anything from it. Trust me. If I couldn't get anything out of it, you most definitely won't." He moved past her and sat down at his desk.

Meila looked back at the documents and zoned everyone out. Rodrigez had been spotted in many different parts of town. Each one was completely unique. Each shipment he helped with was approached in a different manner. There were no visible patterns he had left behind. He must have known that he was being watched.

A file was dropped in front of her. Meila mumbled a thanks to whoever it was and opened the file. The first few pages listed the crimes that he had committed. The next few pages were about the ammunition that he brought. The next page was a map. It had marks on it, showing buildings agents had already checked. The back side of the page had the dates that each one of those buildings had been checked. Notes were written under each date, most saying, "Empty, wiped clean." A few others read, "Agents attacked on first attempt, could not proceed, upon returning it was found empty, wiped clean."

Meila dropped that page. The last few pages consisted of pictures of Rodrigez or his men at the storehouses listed on the map.

Someone hit her desk. "Meila. Meila. Come on, can you hear me yet?"

She looked up to find Charlie standing there. "Sorry. I was thinking."

Charlie nodded. "I know. I have been trying to get something out of you for the last few minutes. Instead, you just took my file and looked through the whole thing."

Meila closed the file and handed it back to him "Sorry. What can I help with?"

Charlie sat down at one of the chairs in front of Meila's desk. "I was wondering if you could look further into where Rodrigez's main warehouse is."

Meila wrote down his request. "Why?"

Charlie put his left ankle on to his right knee. "We had a few men slip into a truck of Rodrigez's, but they were stopped before they made it to the final destination. One of them died and the other is in critical condition."

"Oh, so we are trying to find the main warehouse because...?"

"It is similar to killing the roots of a tree. It is a waste of time to try and dig up each root individually. Instead, cut the tree at the trunk and put poison on it to kill the rest."

Meila smiled. Sometimes, Charlie said the weirdest things, but they always made sense in the end. "Has anyone tried to just follow the trucks?"

"Well that's the thing. Just like your father, they used borrowed trucks, so the truck is returned to the respectable company, and we haven't been able to track where they picked up the delivery. Some agents have gone to ask questions, but I doubt the company will know the answer. That is why we need to find the main building. We are hoping there is some kind of evidence to where all this ammunition is coming from."

Meila nodded. She thought back to the first file that she had received on this case. She opened the bottom drawer of her desk and shuffled through all of the files before finding the correct one. She opened it. She read a few of the words that hadn't been scratched out. None of them made sense, together or each by itself.

Punished. Ate. Balloon. More and more just random words or phrases popped out at her. She vaguely was aware of Charlie standing and moving to his desk.

She held up the next page next to it. She placed the edges right next to each other. The scratched-out lines connected. She looked to where the empty spaces were at, finding that they also connected. Meila pulled out the next few pages, arranging them until large letters started to form. Meila smiled. It wasn't the words written on the page that mattered. It mattered what word the pages created! Meila looked at the remainder of the pages. She needed a bigger space to work in.

Meila collected the loose papers into her arms and put the papers back into the file. She closed it and then went over to the copier. She quickly copied each page. She grabbed a black marker off of Marcus's desk, which was the closest desk to the copier. Then she moved into the conference room, needing a bigger work space.

Meila placed all of the copies down on the table. She placed the file of the originals down on one of the chairs. She then grabbed the Sharpie she had retrieved from Marcus's desk and pulled the first copied sheet over to her. The lines where words had been crossed out were still faintly visible. She took the marker and drew over them, connecting the few lines that had all been crossed off until there was a clear empty space. She laid her completed page down and moved on to the next one. Once she was done, she moved all of the extra chairs out of the way, spread out all of the pages, and let her brain take charge. She shuffled the pages around until she found the letter *J*. Next was a *G*. Meila continued to move the pages until the word *building* formed. She stepped back a few minutes later. It still didn't make sense. She stepped back up and moved around more until she felt more certain this time.

When she did, she heard someone step in behind her. She found Charlie and April watching her. "The pages that you gave me weren't useless. I just didn't see the information that was there."

She looked back to the copies and the word that was hidden within the pages. It spelt out *Justice Building*. Charlie spoke from behind her. "April, go grab Cody. He needs to see this."

Cody came in after a minute, followed by April and a few more of their coworkers. Cody stepped up next to Charlie and Meila. "That file wasn't as useless as I thought. Why did you have me brought in here?"

"You had the file with the map of all the other buildings that have been tried. Where do those buildings stand compared to where this one is?" Charlie inquired.

Meila held up a finger and ran through the group of people that had started to gather and stare at her work. She grabbed the file off her desk. She held it up as she went back in. She already had it opened and to the right page by the time that she had reached Charlie's side. "The map doesn't even come close to where the Justice Building is. All of these buildings are closer to the water on the west side of town, but the Justice Building is closer to the northeast side of the city."

Silence came from behind her. She turned around to see astonishment from everyone's face, except Cody's. "She's right. Maybe Rodrigez has more places where he is storing his weapons. That would describe why he has been in weird places at weird times."

A few in the group nodded. Charlie turned to April. "We need to find out what we can about the Justice Building." He raised his voice. "Everyone else, back to what you were doing."

Meila started to leave, but decided she could be involved in what they were learning. She had, after all, been the one to find out about the Justice Building.

April sat down at her computer and started to type rapidly. A few seconds later, the result came up. She clicked on the first one and started to read aloud to those who had followed her to her desk. "The Justice Building was previously used to bring justice to those who needed it. It was opened in the early spring of 1996 but only stayed open for a few years. The building was built into the side of a small hill. By the time you make it to the back of the building, you will be staring at a green grassy hill and cement stairs."

April paused for a moment on a picture of the Justice Building. Meila thought she recognized it. The gears in her head spun faster and faster as she tried to recall how she knew this building. Charlie's voice broke through her thoughts.

"Jump down and see if it says anything about where it is at today or what happened to it," Charlie demanded.

April was quiet for a moment while she searched. "The building was closed for its regular maintenance work when a bomb went off inside. Thankfully, no one was killed in the explosion, but many were injured. The bomb caused half of the structure to crumble. The building is not in working condition today but has a beautiful view of the city.

"Many tourists have taken pictures there, some highlighting the view of the city, other images show off the building and main road that was forced to be closed. It is on the city's list to get it fixed but will have to wait to get clearance to reenter the building, as it is unstable."

Meila looked at Charlie. Cody spoke from behind them. "There would have to be another way to get to the building. The main road in front of it is closed, but it says that tourists have taken pictures of the beautiful view that it provides. April, look up a map of the area around the Justice Building. There has to be another way to get to it."

April nodded and did as Cody asked. A moment later, she had found a back road that led to the backside of the building. Cody clapped his hands. "Bingo!" he shouted and then moved back to his desk.

Charlie put a hand on April's shoulder and thanked her. Meila stopped Charlie when he tried to get past her. "Why is it such good news that we can get up to the Justice Building?"

Charlie pointed back at the map that April had left up on her screen. "If we can get up there, then so can Rodrigez. The building has been out of operation for almost a decade, so that makes one of the best places to hide something. No one wants to get near the building because of the state that it is in. Rodrigez and his men will be the only ones who are trying to get into the Justice Building. If the tourists know about the bombing, they won't be eager to enter it anytime soon. You heard what April read. *Tourists* love that place. Besides, the roads to get there are out of the way. You can hide the fact that many trucks are going up that way. It is mostly in a high-rise building part of town. Trucks are always going through that part of town. No one would suspect them."

"They were hiding in plain sight?"

Charlie nodded and then smiled. "But not for much longer."

CHAPTER 33

Charlie pulled on Meila's arm.

"Can you at least tell me where we might be going?"

He hadn't said anything but had dragged her out of the main office, onto the elevator, up to the tenth floor, where Charlie had pulled her through countless doorways, and was now taking her down a strange yet familiar-looking hallway.

Charlie looked around before speaking, as if that was necessary. Meila was pretty sure the last person they had seen was the blonde on the elevator. "The board has seen our group's work and has put us back on your father's case, full time."

Meila could hear the excitement in Charlie's voice. They just had a major breakthrough on the Rodrigez case. So why switch now?

Meila stopped in the hallway, waiting for Charlie to halt and turn back to her.

"Nothing has changed in my father's case for the last two years. Why is there a sudden interest in it now?"

Charlie stopped walking and turned toward her. "The board looked deeper between the connections we made in the two cases. The board has found I found some evidence possibly connecting the two cases. We won't be dropping the Rodrigez case, but we will work on them simultaneously. I made the inquiry to the board, and they sent a few people to dig into this new idea. You are a link that knows both parties."

Meila shook her head. "Agent Walker knows Rodrigez better than any other agent around here."

Charlie shrugged, the smile never leaving his face.

"That's why you brought in Agent Walker. You wanted more experience and someone who was familiar with the details of Rodrigez's case."

Charlie nodded enthusiastically. He was almost skipping; he was so happy. "The board asked to speak with you specifically. You said that your father used to deal with this man. Did you know him?"

Meila shrugged and stepped up her pace to keep up with extremely happy Charlie. "He worked with my father for a couple of years. I must have met with him because that was my job, but I haven't seen him for years."

Charlie nodded and looked forward. He stopped at a door in the middle of the hall and knocked. A soft "come in" sounded from inside. Charlie opened the door, and Meila stepped inside after taking a deep breath. She looked at all the faces of those around the room. Many nameless faces stared back, except for Cody. She saw him trying to look all superior here. It wasn't working.

A hand came down on her back. It pushed her farther down the table, placing her in between Charlie and some unknown woman. The woman smiled over her shoulder. Meila just nodded and watched as someone stood at the front of the room. "Thank you for all joining us this afternoon. We have a few things to discuss, and then we will dismiss those that can't hear the rest of what we have to say." The gentlemen looked straight at Meila. She wasn't affected by that too much.

"The Rodrigez/Manning case has been handed over to Agent Schren and Agent Lopez. They said that they would gladly take over the case, and now, Agent Walker has been moved to their team. This may be a permanent move, but we are not sure. Agents"—the man turned his attention strictly to the few of them—"what can you tell us about the case?"

Charlie stood. "Unfortunately, at this time, not much. We were given this case a day ago, and all of the data and information needed to even begin to dig into this case is still being transferred to our unit.

But we did bring someone who was an acquaintance with Rodrigez." Charlie pulled Meila up and pushed her forward.

She stood there, uncertain of what Charlie wanted her to say. She turned back to him and lifted her hands, showing that she didn't know what to do. He just smiled and motioned toward all the people that were waiting.

"What do you know about Rodrigez?" The man's voice pulled Meila's attention back up front.

Meila took in a breath before stepping forward. "He worked with my father, but I was never in the room when they discussed his business with my father."

"Yes, we are aware of your father's business. What was his connection with Rodrigez?"

"I am not entirely sure. My father and Rodrigez did not get along when I lived with him. I cannot say what has changed their relationship."

The man at the front of the room turned his eyes to Charlie, who was standing behind Meila.

"I thought you said she would bring us new information?"

Meila turned to see Charlie shrug his shoulders.

"No, sir. I was asked to bring Agent Manning up because she might have a connection to Rodrigez. I was going to question her on my own, but you advised me against it."

The man at the front of the room raised one of his eyebrows. "So this is my fault?"

"No, sir. I believe that we can take the information that Agent Manning has provided and still use it for our benefit. Two crime bosses are joining forces. If we can find where they are, we can potentially take down two major criminals at once."

The agent at the front of the room sighed. "Very well. What do you know of Rodrigez's business?" the agent pressed on.

Meila took a few steps toward the agent at the front of the room while she continued. "I have looked into a few things with his case before now, enough to understand that he is dangerous. Right before I ran away from home, my father met with Rodrigez. They had met a few times before this meeting, but those meetings were used for the selling and buying of merchandise. My father mentioned something about how this meeting would be different." Meila closed her eyes for a second, trying to recall what her father had said.

"When I was younger and living with my father, I overheard a conversation about this. He told one of his guards that Rodrigez was in trouble and needed some help. My father said it wasn't time for him to overtake Rodrigez, but this was a few years ago. I am not sure if this information could be useful." Meila looked at Charlie. He nodded, silently urging her to continue.

"Was that everything said between your father and his guard?" the agent at the front of the room asked.

Meila nodded.

"My father noticed that I was listening in on their conversation. He didn't know that I was there, but once he found out, he made sure that it never happened again."

The man at the front of the room sat down on his barstool. "Miss, do you know what Rodrigez does for a living?"

Meila shook her head.

"I have heard of a few crimes that he has committed, but I have never known specifically what Rodrigez does. I have also studied the files we have been given on him, but it does not state specifically what he does. To my understanding, he sells ammunition, which my father buys and then sells at a better price. I have been told that he is dangerous and not to mess with him."

"Miss, let me tell you that this case was handed to you because of the success your team seems to have. We have sent many agents after this man, and many have lost their lives over this."

"You haven't been able to get close to him?"

"He owns a very profitable ammunition and weapon company. Do you see why no one else has been able to get close to him?"

Meila let that sink in before nodding.

"Is there any other details you can provide us with at this time that another team might find worth knowing?"

Meila was taken back a bit by the frankness of his words but shook her head.

"Very well." The man looked at a woman in the first few rows. She hadn't stopped writing since Meila had started to speak. "Thank you for your input. You are excused."

Meila blinked a few times. She had been dragged up here by Charlie to attend this meeting. It had been a long, confusing trek through the halls and then she had spent two minutes explaining herself. Maybe they were looking for more information on both her father and Rodrigez's businesses.

"What about my father's business? Does anyone need help with it?"

"No, Agent Manning. You have been asked to leave. We thank you for your contribution, but please allow the rest of us to get on with this meeting."

Meila opened her mouth to suggest something else, but a hand on her back stopped her. Charlie pushed her toward the door they had entered and pulled it open. He nudged her forward until they were both out in the hallway. He led her away from the conference room, through the maze of hallways, and almost made it to the elevators before speaking.

"Why did I feel like I was no help to anyone in that room?"

Charlie shrugged.

"Sometimes, I feel that way in those meetings too, but the information you just shared could be valuable to our case. I wish you did not have to come up here to tell everyone, but maybe it will end up helping some other agents' case."

Charlie pressed the button to call the elevator to the tenth floor. They waited in silence until the doors opened and Meila stepped on. Charlie stayed in the hall.

"You're not coming down?"

He smiled. "Not yet. I still have the rest of a board meeting that I have to be in." He turned his back and started to walk away as the doors closed.

* * * * *

Meila walked over to Charlie and handed him the file she had finished. He had the phone to his ear, speaking quietly.

"Find anything new?" he asked, covering the receiver.

Meila shook her head.

"Did you find anything new?" she repeated, subtly looking in Cody's direction.

Charlie followed her suit and frowned.

"Meila, he is clean. Don't worry about Cody. I have worked with him for years, and he does good work."

"I know, but—"

The look Charlie gave her cut her off. She knew Cody was a hard worker, but she still wondered if he might have alternative motives. She knew she could trust Charlie, but Cody? No way.

CHAPTER 34

A week later

Meila looked at the white board again. She couldn't believe that Rodrigez was running his business out of this shabby place. Half of it was falling apart, the other half was still together, but there was only one way to get there. How had no one noticed his large delivery trucks going up there?

The Justice Building sat on the most northeast side of town. It was built close to the side of a hill, making one of the best lookout points on the top of that hill. The hill was just tall enough to afford anyone a beautiful view of the city and the glistening ocean farther out still. There was a small wooden fence stopping tourists from accidentally falling down the south side of the hill and onto the main road, which led to the front of the Justice Building. A steep set of cement stairs made their way down the west side of the hill and met a single door to the Justice Building.

Meila looked back to her notes. She and Charlie were going to go in and see if any shipments were there or find any information that could be useful. Charlie was in another board meeting. She knew that those in charge were not happy with this decision. There were only a few ways in and a few ways out. Both of the south entrances had been cut off when the building had a bomb explode, leaving three entrances. One to the east, and two toward the north. The west side only had windows.

Charlie had suggested using the north entrance. It seemed most likely the one that tourists would accidentally stumble on, but they would have to wait until they go into the building. They hoped to find another way to get in. Or another way to get out.

He had also proposed that only he and Meila should go. They needed to be as discreet as possible. If too many people were seen approaching the building, that could trigger Rodrigez, and he would run.

April walked into the conference room and placed a paper on the table in front of Meila.

"Charlie just called from the tenth floor. He said that he would be working late tonight. The mission is to be run tomorrow morning, regardless of what Charlie learns tonight. He is worried that Rodrigez is going to move."

Meila nodded. It would be better to sneak up on this guy, he had slipped through their fingertips so many times. She hoped that tomorrow they could truly get him.

Meila pulled on her borrowed jacket, too anxious to work and waited for Charlie. The team had found out that Rodrigez, and some of his men were spotted at the Justice Building downtown. She and Charlie had been asked to go in looking like tourists and check it out. She hoped that this plan worked.

Sometime later, Charlie opened the main office door and stepped in. He scanned the room until he saw her and waved her toward him. "Time to go. They just sent the car."

Meila nodded and tried not to pretend to be nervous. She had only been on a few missions, most that she had created, and most of them had been semisuccessful. This one was different. Everyone knew about it and was counting on her.

She and Charlie stepped onto the elevator and sat in silence as it made its way down to the main floor. They stepped out of the elevator and they moved out of the front doors. The cold air enveloped them as they walked across the street to the parking lot. "What do you think is going to happen?" Meila asked.

"Not now," Charlie said. He kept his eyes glued on the parking lot ahead and he moved up and down the aisle of cars. He finally pulled open a car door and motioned for Meila to climb in. He got in behind the wheel and started the car. He pulled out of the lot and turned the car northward.

"Do we usually talk about the mission on the way there, or do we sit in silence?"

Charlie looked over at her. "We can talk about it. Just know that you can't say anything about it in public. We have to pretend that we are tourists."

"Okay, but how are we going to get inside the Justice Building? I mean, when I was reviewing this spot yesterday, it seems like it was a popular tourist area."

"So we shouldn't have a hard time blending in. We will just watch those around us and see what they do. If they are moving toward the building, it will be easier to sneak in. If not, then we are just going to have to be clever."

Meila nodded.

The rest of the ride was done in silence, but Meila's mind was running in circles, so it wasn't a boring ride to the Justice Building. Charlie pulled into a grassy area and parked.

"What are you doing? I thought that we were supposed to drive up *behind* the Justice Building?" Meila looked around and was confused to see the city to the left of her and luscious mountains to the right.

"They sent in a team ahead of us, and they are going to give us an all clear signal. But we still have to be tourists, so I brought us to the lookout spot for the city. It is just a few minutes' walk to the building." Charlie opened his door and jumped out.

Meila recognized a few familiar faces around the grassy hilltop, all dressed as tourists. Some would keep an eye on Charlie and her. Others were only there if something went wrong. Only she and Charlie would enter the building. Meila followed Charlie to where a big group of people were standing. She looked out at the view and sighed. Her nerves were going crazy, and Charlie wasn't willing just to jump in with both feet. She looked over her shoulder but didn't see anything out of the ordinary. She looked forward again, scanning the town for trouble. Nothing. Man, such a boring day. She checked behind her again.

"Stop doing that," Charlie whispered in her ear. "People will start to look and wonder. We don't need any extra attention."

Meila glanced at the groups of people there. You had your few families that were trying to control their kids. You had the older couples, who were brought here on a field trip by the assisted living home. Next was a few couples along the fence line. They were too happy to even realize that anyone else is here. Meila watched as a few of the visitors took pictures together and laughed and talked.

She pulled out her phone and turned to Charlie. She didn't say anything, just walked up to him and put her face by his. She turned on her camera and let a few clicks go by before stepping away.

"What was that for?" Charlie angrily asked. "You were mad just a minute ago that we weren't diving into this case headfirst, and now you want to play tourist?"

"If you want this to go down correctly, then yes. You said that we need to blend in. I think that we can take a few pictures and then move around. Trust me." She had a plan in her head but wasn't sure that he would really follow her.

He just nodded and reached for her phone and took a few pictures of the city below them. This ruse lasted for the next ten minutes as they stared out at the city. Finally, a man walked over and leaned up against the fence. He just nodded at the city once and then walked back toward the cars.

Charlie grabbed Meila's hand, tugging her back toward the cars. They paused for a moment by them, taking a few pictures of the building and then turning around, snapping a few selfies of the two of them with the building. Meila scanned those standing on the green grass in front of her before she felt Charlie pulling her to the Justice Building. They only had to go down half of the cement stairs before they were out of view of everyone else. They entered the building through a gaping hole, most likely made from the bombing that took place.

Charlie released her hand, and she blinked her eyes, trying to let them adjust to the light before continuing on. The broken skylight allowed light to seep into the middle of the room, but left the outer edges and corners dark. She heard a click of something and then a light was shining on her.

"You ready?" Charlie's voice came from behind the light.

She put a hand up to her eyes and moved toward him. "Yeah." She followed him through the building. They checked a few more rooms but found them empty.

Meila's breath quickened as they entered the next room. It too was empty, but there was a hum of something on the other side. Charlie motioned that she should stay back as he approached. Meila watched in terror as her best friend walked up cautiously to the door and pulled it open.

Meila only remembered hitting the wall before she opened her eyes and was staring at the hazy outline of the grass. She tried to sit up, but found it too difficult. Pain shot through her right shoulder and down through her arm. "Great," she grimaced. She looked down and saw a sling over her body and she had a blanket wrapped around her shoulders.

"Oh, good. You're awake. How do you feel?" a voice said from behind her.

Meila looked to the face but didn't recognize it.

Another joined the first in the bright sun, and Meila smiled. "Oh, dear! Are you all right! You should have seen the commotion that happened at the office when we heard that a bomb went off in the Justice Building! We were all going crazy, wondering what happened to you and Charlie."

Meila couldn't help but smile at Shanta's theatrics. Meila had been told that Shanta was dramatic, but she knew she saw it firsthand like this. "How's Charlie?"

Shanta bit on her lower lip, looking uneasy. "Well, he was closer to the bomb, so he has a few more injuries." Shanta pointed across Meila. Meila whipped her head around to see an ambulance and a stretcher across the lawn with a man on it.

Meila pushed herself up and escaped Shanta's arm that had been put around her. She ran to Charlie's side. It was a crooked run, but she was still a little bit in shock from her injured shoulder. She sat down by him and reached for the hand closest to her. She looked down to find it in a white bandage. She noticed some deep red burn under the white bandage. She watched as the bandage slowly took on a wet look. She didn't dare put him in any more pain than he was already in. She looked up his arm and found that the fire had only caught him up to his elbow. His leg was also bent the wrong way.

She turned her eyes to his face. He was trying to smile. "It's better than it looks," he tried to joke.

"How—"

He shrugged his shoulders. "I'm not sure. I think that someone must have been watching nearby before the bomb went off. Maybe it had a timer on it. I don't know. But the impact was strong. You weren't a ton of help either." He smiled.

Meila struggled to put a smile on her own face as the events of the day and what could have happened came rolling in like a tsunami on the beach. A hand came on top of hers. "Hey, I'll be all right. Just give me a few days, and I will be back to my old self."

Meila nodded.

The paramedics came up from behind Charlie and started to unwrap the oozing burn, making it visible. Meila watched as Charlie's face went from teasing to agony. She squirmed as she was forced to back up. An arm came around her, and Shanta's face appeared by her. "How about you go home and get some rest, huh? I will go with Charlie."

Meila nodded and followed the nameless agent to a car.

CHAPTER 35

Meila mindlessly followed the agent through the halls of the agency building until they reached the elevator. The agent hit the nine. The elevator had others in it, so no one spoke. Meila wished that someone would. Maybe it would help her fill her mind with something other than what had happened today.

Most of those in the elevator got off on the second and fifth floor. The agent that had gone with Meila ended up leaving her and getting off on the eight floor. She did, however, give her instructions that she should check on the man that was wounded and then report back to her office. Meila nodded and tried to remember the instructions.

The elevator dinged, telling Meila that she had arrived at the ninth floor. She clambered off and moved to the desk. "Hello, dear. How can I help you?" the nurse said.

Meila rubbed at her face. "I am here to see Charlie Schren. He was just brought here."

The nurse nodded and then picked up the receiver and spoke into it. After a few minutes, she placed it back down and turned her eyes to Meila. "He just barely came in, and they are getting him stable. If you still wish to see him, you are going to have to wait awhile."

Meila nodded and moved to the chairs beside the desk. She closed her eyes and let sleep overcome her as she waited to see Charlie.

* * * * *

"Excuse me, miss?" Someone tapped on her shoulder. "Excuse me."

Meila cracked her eyes open and remembered the previous events that had happened. She sat up, rolled her tired neck. She then looked at the nurse.

"Mr. Schren has been moved to a room. Unfortunately, the doctor said that you could only go in there for a few minutes. Would you still like to see him?"

Meila nodded. The nurse motioned for her to follow and swiped her badge at the door. She led Meila down a long hallway, finally turning at the last door.

Charlie lay there, bandages covering most of his burns. Meila moved around the nurse and stepped into the room. She moved to his side and was reaching for his hand when the nurses voice stopped her. "I am sorry, miss, but he is not supposed to be touched. We found burns on both of his hands, and the doctor has taken care of those already. We are just waiting on another doctor to arrive before they start to do more of the serious burns."

Meila nodded and she stared at the half-covered face. "Is he going to be all right?" Meila asked.

The nurse nodded and then gestured that Meila's time was up. "He has fought for his life this far. I daresay that he won't let anything take him now." The nurse smiled as Meila stepped past her.

They walked down the hall together, and Meila left the nurse at her desk, knowing that Cody would probably need to hear about the details of the day.

* * * * *

Meila made her way slowly back to her office. She wished she could have spent more time with Charlie, but the other doctor had come to take a look at his burns. Meila knew she couldn't sit out in the foyer of their makeshift hospital forever.

Meila pulled her ID out and swiped it, waiting for the door to unlock. She pulled it open when she heard the familiar sound. Everyone was inside the main office, except Cassie. She was not required to stay past five o'clock. It was closer to six now. She approached her desk and moved around a few files until she could easily see her brown desk. A hand came down on her shoulder, and she turned to see April smiling behind her.

"Are you all right? I heard Charlie took the bulk of the bomb."

Meila nodded. "I was just checking up on him. The doctors and nurses think he will survive."

"How are you holding up?"

Meila shrugged. "I keep going over the scenario, but I know I couldn't have changed what happened. I don't know where to start to look for information."

April nodded.

"Oh, so you finally decided to grace us with your presence," an angry voice said from behind her. Meila turned to see Cody's face, disapproval and frustration clearly being shown.

"I was told by an agent over two hours ago that she had sent you back to the agency building. Where have you been?"

"I was visiting Charlie," Meila mumbled, dropping her head and staring at Cody's brown shoes.

"Well, congrats. While you've been wasting your time, the rest of us have been working hard to try and find out who could have done this."

Meila stood, finding a sudden burst of energy. She didn't deserve this type of treatment from Cody any longer. He had pushed her and made her feel as if she was nothing. Her emotions welled up inside of her and came tumbling out.

"*I* was the one on the mission with him. *I* was there when the bomb went off. And where were you at, Cody? I was told you were his best friend, but you don't even care about him! You would rather stay down here than face Charlie!"

Cody snapped at her. "That's enough! We have heard enough from you, Miss Manning!" he spat out her name. "You have tried and tried to prove that you are worthy of being on this team, but I am second in command. Charlie isn't here right now, so you have no one to protect you. I don't want to hear another word come from your mouth." He grabbed at his hair, pulling at it. "I am *sick and tired* of hearing about you and your difficulties. I demand that you just grow up, or you can get out!"

The whole room sat silent. Cody pulled a chair to the wall. "You can sit where I can't see you. Maybe then I might be able to get some work done."

Meila sat and went to open her mouth, but Cody put a hand up stopping her. "I don't want to hear a word from you either. You almost got one of our teammates killed. You have lost my respect because of it." He turned and walked away from her.

"The rest of you. Get ready. I want to know why that bombing happened and where it came from. Marcus said that it was a short-wired bomb, meaning that it could have been set off from a close location. If the person trying to set it off gets too far away, they will be out of range and it won't go off. I need a few of you to go out and search the building nearby and see if you can find any clues. The rest of you can stay behind and keep going on this case. Plus, you can watch this trash and make sure she doesn't go anywhere." He pointed to Meila. "If she does, make sure that she clocks out. We don't need her wasting anything else."

Cody grabbed his jacket from off his hook and walked past Meila.

CHAPTER 36

Meila drew on the whiteboard.

"Hey, um, Mei. This meeting is going great, but you want to tell us what you're doing?"

Meila had completely forgotten that she had asked them all to meet; she had been so focused on what she was doing. "Yeah, sorry." Meila pointed to the first picture at the top. "That is the Justice Building. Charlie and I were asked to explore it to see if we could find any evidence that Rodrigez was using it." She turned back to the group. We were hoping to find someone or something that could help bring us closer to Rodrigez. Everything that we saw did not look out of place until we hit our third or fourth room. We heard a buzzing going on inside, and Charlie told me to wait for him. I can't remember if he got to the door and opened it or if he just made it to the door." Meila blinked a few times before continuing on. "Charlie was closer to the bomb when it went off. He has spent a few days in rehab but is doing better now. I was left with a few small bruises and cuts."

"Here"—she pointed to another building—"is where we think Rodrigez might be sending supplies to my father. We are not certain on what is going to be there, but we do know when and where this building will be used. These are the people you will need to be looking for." She held up a folder filled with pictures. "In order for this entire plan to work, they cannot get in the way.

"Questions before we break?" Meila looked around; nothing from the team. "Good. April, will you take a few of the new members and run them through codes. See if we can get the names of what is going in and out of the building."

April nodded and then called out a few names and left.

"Cody, I would feel better to have a team on the ground and in the air. You and Agent Walker should be able to come up with a list of supplies and trustworthy people to do that. Once it is completed, I will double-check it."

Cody snorted but did not move. "Can I ask who put you in charge?"

Meila folded her arms. "Please deal with the assignment you have been given. If you have a hard time with who is running this operation, you can take your leave, and I'll ask Shanta to come in."

Cody stood. "The list will be on your desk by the end of the day."

Agent Walker just smiled and walked out after the storming Cody. Meila finished assigning everyone to their roles, then she left to find Cassie. She smiled when Meila interrupted her. "Meila! What can I help you with?" she said cheerfully.

"Cassie, how did you know that I wasn't coming for a friendly visit?"

"You? A friendly visit?"

Meila put a hand dramatically to her heart. "You wound me." She smiled at the friendly secretary. "I'm in need of some security footage that would have been used a couple of weeks ago." Meila handed Cassie a sheet of paper, listing the dates she needed.

Cassie nodded after glancing at it. "Okay. Is there a specific time that you need or a certain area that you need to see?"

"Nope. Just all the footage you can find for those dates."

"And I assume that I will be giving them to you?"

"That would be best. If you can't find me, just leave them on my desk."

Meila thanked Cassie and then went up two floors to the hospital part of the building. A nurse greeted Meila at the desk when she arrived.

"Hi. I'm looking for a patient that came in just a few days ago. They said that he would be moved today."

The nurse moved to some charts. "What's his name?"

"Charlie Schren"

The nurse flipped through some charts. She finally stopped on one and then looked up at her in confusion. "Well, you were correct about him moving, but he didn't move rooms. He's left the hospital."

Meila blinked a few times, processing this information. "Did he say where he was planning to go?"

The nurse smiled. "Even if he did, I am not allowed to release that information."

Meila nodded and then thanked the nurse. She let her feet take her mechanically back to her desk. She collected a few things to take home with her and then asked April to take over part of her night shift. She felt daggers at her back coming from Cody. She didn't care. She couldn't deal with Cody and his biting remarks now. She briskly walked home, hoping Charlie had perhaps returned there.

She didn't even bother to stop in her apartment; she just went straight to Charlie's. She knew that he probably would answer if she knocked, so she pulled a pin from her braid and started to fidget with the lock. She knew that her pick would have been faster, but she didn't want to be in her apartment currently.

Finally, she heard a click and the door swung open. Meila stood when she saw a lump of pillows and blankets on the couch. "You could have just knocked, you know."

Meila walked over to him. "Would you have answered?"

He tried to shrug but ended up just wincing at the pain instead. "Eventually."

Meila rolled her eyes and plopped down on the floor. "How's your pain?"

"I've felt worse."

"When is the last time you took pain meds?" Meila stood and went and looked around his kitchen. She found a list that had been written out with strange names on it. The other side had times, one which had come almost two hours ago. She held up the list. "Where's your medicine?"

"Meila, I am fine. Please, leave me be."

Meila spotted them the next minute. Picking up the first one on the list, she shook out two and filled up a glass of water. She took it to him and then went to his fridge. She pulled out some leftovers and put them in the microwave.

"Meila, I don't need a nurse. That's why I came home," Charlie complained.

"Yeah, I know that you don't need a nurse, but how about a friend. You bothered me all the time when I first got here. I have all the right to do the same to you now."

Charlie just sighed but accepted the food. Meila turned on the TV and watched until he fell asleep. She checked her watch, seeing that she was due at the agency soon. She left a note for Charlie along with some more food and medicine that he could take while she was working her shift. She then grabbed her black jacker and left him to sleep.

* * * * *

Meila picked up the rock from the ground and threw it in frustration. It hit the green grass and rolled a bit before stopping. She had requested a search of the building, but nothing was there. She begged Cody to allow an extra two teams to join theirs in the search, which had been granted, but the search had brought up no new information. There was no trace of Rodrigez or any indication that this building had been used by him the last couple of months. She could have sworn she recognized this building.

An agent made their way past Meila and over to Cody.

"The building finished collapsing after the bomb went off. We have some men working on the parts of the building which are safe to be in, but this place has been wiped clean. The only fingerprints we have found and matched to anyone is Agent Schren, who touched a few doors."

Cody nodded. "Manning," he called.

Meila turned around and made her way toward Cody.

"Go back to the agency building. I can handle everything from here."

Meila planted her fists on her side. "Cody, why can't I stay? I helped put this whole plan together."

"And I am in charge. When Charlie isn't here, it is up to me." He put a finger up, stopping the protest she had ready on her tongue. "And me alone to guide this team. Right now, your services would best be used at the agency building."

Meila knew it was useless to fight. Cody may not be right, but she wasn't doing any good here, and she didn't want to create a scene.

She folded her arms over her chest. "Fine," she dolefully answered.

Cody waved to someone who was standing just a little ways off. It ended up being April. He left her with some instructions before turning and making his way to the Justice Building, where the investigation continued without her.

CHAPTER 37

Cody looked like he was going to blow. It had been about three weeks since the bomb went off at the Justice Building. Charlie had finally started to come back to work, making life easier on Meila. Cody had been looking daggers at her ever since she had returned. She had taken over the team just because she knew the most about this assignment. She just barely learned that she had become second in command, pushing Cody out.

Meila smiled and accepted the compliments from her coworkers. She shot Cody a glance, gloating that she was better than him.

Charlie placed a hand on her shoulder and moved her toward the conference room. "That's enough gloating, Meila. You'll soon find out how valuable he can be. He's one of the best on the team."

Meila looked up at him in disbelief. "Cody?" Meila laughed as Charlie closed the door to the conference room. "I'm pretty sure that he hates me."

Charlie pulled out a chair and motioned for her to sit. He leaned against the table as he reminded Meila, "I haven't met very many people that actually get along with Cody. Besides, he is just angry that you are moving up faster than he is."

Meila smiled at that. She really couldn't believe that she got a promotion.

"Now, bring me up to date on where you are with this case."

Meila slumped. "I hope that you are not looking for good news because you won't get any."

Charlie shook his head. "If I want good news, I will ask for it. Right now, I am asking for an update."

Meila stood and went to the board. "The Justice Building was empty when we arrived. I have been thinking about that for the past few days." Meila held up a finger and ran back out to her desk, returning shortly after finding the information she needed. She put it down on the table in front of Charlie. "This building has been heavily guarded for years. I remember my father taking me there when I was young. Security was everywhere."

"That's why you asked for a few extra teams. For backup." Charlie stated.

Meila nodded. "That place had been deserted for some time before we even arrived." Meila sifted through a few more pages. "But the document clearly states that a new shipment was to come in that day. These days were not very flexible. You couldn't easily hide all the supplies these guys were getting. I mean, truckloads."

Charlie nodded, showing that he understood. "You think that they have a new holding place then? Maybe a new way of disguising them?"

"I think that they may not need to have them shipped anymore. I think that they are building a new stash. Here. In the United States."

Charlie sat down, processing all this information. "Any ideas why?"

Meila shrugged. "Easy. Their cutting out the middleman and their supplier. The less people that know how to do their job, the more that they are needed and the more they are paid."

"Do you think that someone here would know how to get in, maybe find out how this is happening and how we can better control it?"

Meila moved to the foggy window on the door that led out to the main office. She thought of each person and their skill set. None of them quite fit. April, although a genius, has always had a hard time blending in. Cody would probably mess up the mission on purpose, all while trying to make it her fault. She didn't know enough about Agent Walker to send him. Charlie was too big to go unnoticed. She had made the Old Mill project possible but only because she had been new to the agency. She still had most of the knowledge that her father gave her, but the codes changed often.

A name popped into her mind as she turned back to Charlie. He put a hand up, not even letting her speak her idea. "I know that look. Whatever it is, the answer is no."

Meila crossed her arms over her chest. "You haven't even heard what I was going to say, so you can't shoot it down before you've heard it." Meila walked over to him and he sped against the table. "It might also be our only chance of getting in."

Charlie dropped his head into his hands, frustrated. "Fine. Let's hear it."

Meila took a deep breath. "Old Man Manning."

Meila watched as Charlie rubbed at his forehead, knowing that if he didn't care for her plan so far, he wasn't going to be ecstatic about this next part.

"All we would have to do is get me inside."

Charlie jumped from his seat. "No." He started pacing. "There has to be another person who could tell us where this warehouse is or where we can get better information from."

Meila watched him pace. "You can say all you want, but you know that I am right. We have been trying to get Rodrigez for a while now and if we can get to him through my father, then we should at least attempt it. He still has guys working for him and Rodrigez. Plus, I think I know where I can find him."

"Meila, it's not safe. Remember the last time you did something impulsive like this? You almost got yourself killed."

Meila nodded. "Yes, but you were there for me. You promised that you always would be. Has our agreement changed?"

"Meila, you ran from home, and we have almost successfully put your father in jail permanently. Do you really want to risk him escaping or killing you?"

"He won't kill me. If he wanted to do something like that, he would have when I was younger."

Charlie grabbed her arms. "Meila, I know that you don't fully understand this, but he is a madman. Another death, even his own daughter's death, won't hurt his conscience."

She leaned forward. "We have to get this information. Without it, all our work will be for nothing. Please, at least let me try." She pulled her arms from his grasp and walked from the room.

* * * * *

Meila hadn't seen much of Charlie over the last few days. She knew that he was still trying to process the information she had left him with. They both knew that she was the best person to get back into her father's business. She knew that trying to convince Charlie about this plan was going to take some time. She hoped that enough time had passed. She had been tracking her father over the last few days, but if they waited too long to initiate this plan, he could move.

Meila approached Charlie. She had kept glancing back at his desk all morning. He had been staring at the same file for the last thirty minutes. The look in his eyes told her that he was not focused on it. His thoughts were elsewhere.

"Charlie, do you have a few minutes to talk?'"

Meila watched Charlie's eyes come back into focus and his shoulders drop. He knew what she had come to discuss with him, but she knew he wasn't too happy with her choice.

"Mei, I really don't want you to go. I'm sure that someone else can start at the bottom of the business and work their way up."

"And risk someone else's life? I don't think so. Charlie, I will be careful. Besides, I have finally found where my father might be in a few weeks."

Charlie looked up at her.

"Where is he going to be?"

"I am pretty sure he is going to be at the Old Mill." Meila said, briefly dropping her chin so she could look at her feet.

Meila heard Charlie sigh, dropping his head into his upturned palms too happy with this plan. "My father used to have supplies sent there. I think that I can get in unnoticed. I have been out of the system long enough that no one would recognize it."

Meila waited for an answer, but Charlie stayed silent, his head resting on his hands. "What do you think?" she tentatively asked.

He lifted his head and stood. "Is there anything I can say that will convince you not to go through with this crazy plan?"

She shrugged, knowing that he already knew the answer to that. He sighed again, letting out some of his frustration.

"Charlie. I know that I could do this. Besides, I was the one that suggested that we get more information from the Old Mill. I still think that I could get in there. Please, you have to give me a chance."

"Fine, but you are going to have to go under some training before we send you out. I am not comfortable with you doing this, but I know you'll do it one way or another. I would rather prepare you for what may happen." Charlie scratched his head, his forehead was wrinkled in deep thought. "Do you even know what information we need?"

Meila just stared at Charlie. She had never seen him like this. "Trust me. I know what these pages look like. It is not like I am moving back in with my father. This is going to be a simple mission. All we have to do is get me in and then back out."

Charlie shook his head. "Fine. Let's start looking for something that you might need once you get in."

Meila nodded and opened the conference door, excited to see what this training process looked like.

CHAPTER 38

Meila took another step toward the Old Mill. She still had another few blocks before she was there, but she knew that someone was following her. She looked into the reflective store window next to her. Charlie's blonde curly hair caught her eye. She shook her head but knew that she wouldn't be able to get rid of him until she spoke to him. She turned her mind back to her mission and thought back over all she had learned.

After three weeks of extensive training, Meila finally felt ready. She knew that most people received a lot more training going into these types of things, but she lived with her father who expected her to face these situations weekly. A hand came down on her forearm, forcing her to stop.

Meila turned to see Charlie watching her. She knew that he was worried. He had told her many times since she had brought up the idea and all the way through the very thorough training. She knew that he would back her up with her decision, though.

"Are you sure you want to do this?" Charlie asked under his breath, interrupting her thoughts.

"This is the only way that I can for sure get the information needed." Meila pulled her borrowed cap lower. "Besides, last time, I didn't have backup. This time will be different."

"Mei, I'm not saying that this isn't a bad idea, but you were nearly killed last time you tried to do something like this. Why do you think it will be so different this time?"

"Charlie, the team is never going to take me seriously if you are always babysitting me. That may have worked for the first few years, but now? I took care of myself for the first thirteen of my life. I need to learn how to do that again."

"Getting yourself killed is not going to get you any closer to the information needed. Besides, the team knows that you do your part."

Meila shook her head. "This information is crucial. I have a plan, and I have leverage."

Charlie stepped closer to her. "What is this *leverage* you speak of?"

Meila kept her gaze lowered, not wanting Charlie to see the anxiety building in her eyes. "My name. I learned from a young age that 'Meila Manning' got me through any door."

Charlie put hands on both sides of her face. His eyes serious, fear creeping in through the sides. "Meila, the men that you are dealing with today, these mobsters, they are dangerous. I don't believe you know what you are doing."

She pushed his hands away from her face. "I lived with a mobster for thirteen years. Don't you dare try and lecture me on not knowing that they are dangerous." She took a deep breath then continued. "My father used to send me into meetings exactly like these. *He* hadn't trained me. Trust me. I feel a lot safer now than I ever did then."

Charlie's face didn't soften like Meila expected it to. A truck rumbled by in the distance. "Fine. Nothing I say won't change your mind?"

Meila shook her head.

"I didn't think so. Be careful, and don't be late to the spot." He left her standing on the sidewalk by herself.

Meila watched as Charlie walked away from her. As the sun started to sink behind her, she made her way to the Old Mill, her thoughts clouded by the fear she had just seen in Charlie's eyes.

CHAPTER 39

Meila jumped behind the closest brick column. She tried to steady her breathing, but it didn't work. Her nerves were flying off the roof. Meila hadn't been this nervous since she had lived with her father.

She closed her eyes, thinking back to the conversation she had with Charlie just before starting this crazy mission. She should have listened to him. Instead, she assumed that the building would be empty and that she would be able to get in and out quickly without even being noticed. But right as she had entered the building, she had heard voices.

She had tried to speak with them, but they immediately pulled their guns on her, and she ran to safety. Now she was stuck, hiding, in fear that she may not make it out.

A shot sounded, hitting the wall behind her. She forced herself to open her eyes and push forward. *I need an escape.* Meila ducked as another bullet went wild. Meila looked around. On the other side of the room, a window, about halfway up a brick wall, caught her attention. Where was her cover or her backup? *Where is Charlie?*

She closed her eyes as another bullet hit above where she was at. Her gut tightened, telling her that the men were getting closer. If she didn't move soon, she would be left in the hands of men like her father. She had to move. They were tracking her. She needed to get out of this building. Once she was out in the dark, she could easily blend in with the crowd. She moved behind another brick column. *Breathe*, she reminded herself.

Meila looked up. An idea came to mind. She knew that if she could get to the roof, she could get out. This building was made of brick, making her escape simple and stable. She knew there was a hanging rope ladder in the office. She just needed to find a way to get up there. She had learned how to scale a wall from Charlie, but she had to get there first. She slid down the brick column, sitting on the ground, hoping that it hid her enough from the men that were hunting her. She pulled a few bullets from her back pocket. Then she double checked that the documents she had taken were still in the inside of her jacket. Footsteps sounded on the wood planks next to her.

It's now or never, Meila. She pushed her gun up to the ceiling and shot, hoping that it would bring her some cover. She knew that darkness would help keep her alive just a little bit longer. She pushed against the pillar that she had hidden behind and moved toward a set of stairs. She knew that it led to a small office on the second level that contained an old rope ladder. She hoped that it might be her escape. Meila tucked herself closer to the pillar before quickly peeking around it, making sure it was clear before she ran for the stairs. The way was clear, and Meila ran to the wooden stairs, ascending them with as little noise as possible. Meila aimed her gun across the large mill. She shot out a window. Then she moved for the lights around it.

"Boss, she's up on the deck!"

More shots fired near her. One of them shot through her left shoulder.

Umph. Meila bit her lip, trying to keep from screaming. Her left shoulder went numb. She couldn't even move that arm. She grimaced as she lifted her right hand to it. She touched it—wet.

Meila moved to the ladder but knew that it was hopeless after being shot. In order to get up, she would have to drop her gun. With Rodrigez's guys so close on her tail, she knew that it would not be possible. The light in the office started to flicker. Meila's brain was running a hundred miles per hour, trying to think of another solution.

The window! She looked across the mill, and her escape plan started to make sense.

She moved quickly to one of the sets of stairs. She stopped, footsteps coming up them. *How many guys does Rodrigez have?*

Footsteps sounded closer on the stairs, and Meila turned to the small room. She threw herself in the corner near the door and threw a blanket on herself. She held her breath, partially because she did not wish to be found and because the blanket stank.

Two men burst in the room just a moment later. The first crossed the room, and the second stood near the door. Meila lifted her gun and shot the closer man in the leg, causing him to drop his gun. She kicked it away and then threw the blanket off of herself and rushed toward the other man who had taken his aim. In the closed space, Meila knew that he most likely wouldn't miss. Before she even really thought, she rushed toward him and tackled him. She heard a crack as she pushed him down, and when the man hit the ground, she could tell that he was unconscious. A dot of blood was on the desk behind him.

Meila covered her mouth but did not linger for long. She knew that she had to get out. Meila picked up the gun from the man that she had shot in the leg, who was screaming in agony, and then ran down the stairs. She slid behind a brick pillar as footsteps ran past her and up the stairs. Commands shouted in Spanish sounded throughout the building—someone to find how to get most of the lights back on. Others guard all the doors.

Then she ran. Meila kept close to the many different boxes filled with the various illegal items her father and Rodrigez sold. She avoided all of the doors, knowing men would be waiting for her there. She instead went to the window she had previously broken. She moved up the wall quickly as she could without causing too much blood to smear on the wall.

The window had shattered at her bullet impact. She carefully pulled herself through, then started to climb down the other side of the wall. She paused, waiting to see if any commands were being made inside the building. Silence. She jumped to the ground and took off as fast as her legs would take her.

After running a few blocks, a car came into view. She ran a little bit farther until she could see her reflection in a store window. She had to keep an eye out behind her; she didn't want anyone to sneak up on her.

The car came to a screeching halt at her side. She tensed up. She couldn't see who was inside or what they had. "Meila? What are you doing so far away from the meeting place."

She let out a sigh. "I should be asking you. You promised that you would take care of me. Well, guess what, I was in trouble. I needed your help, but you weren't there."

Charlie had gotten out of the dark-tinted windowed car. "Yeah, I am here to help you." He pulled her toward him, embracing her. "But you have to tell me where you are going to run off to *before* you leave. And maybe next time, don't shoot out the lights. My 'older-brother' skills aren't that great yet." He smiled when he pulled away.

Meila smiled back, but it faltered. She started to see black spots in her vision.

"Charlie, the Old Mill, where you found me…"

More black spots. She felt herself falling but couldn't recall hitting the ground.

CHAPTER 40

Meila rolled over in bed. She winced as she remembered that her shoulder had been shot. She sat up in bed and rubbed at her face with the hand that wanted to move. The other one felt as if it was tied down to the bed with a weight.

Meila threw the covers off, and she changed into sweats and a baggy T-shirt. She heard shuffling in the kitchen, and she moved cautiously to her doorway. Charlie had been over last night to remind her that she wasn't needed at work today. He never said anything about anyone coming over, though.

She cracked the door open slowly and listened as the loud shoes moved around her kitchen floor. Familiarity struck when a voice came too. Shanta was singing, rather obnoxiously, in Meila's kitchen. Meila propelled the door the rest of the way open. Shanta stopped her tune when Meila stepped into the kitchen. "Meila! Honey, how are you doing? The office has not been the same without you."

Shanta pulled on Meila's good arm until she was sitting at one of the kitchen stools. She then placed a bowl of sliced apples down in front of her. "Eat up. I was told that I needed to call the office once you were up. The last few days have been boring for me. So that's why they let me come and stay with you. We both know that I am much better with dealing with people than doing anything behind a desk." Shanta smiled behind her blue sparkly cat-eyed glasses.

"Well. If you are up—" Shanta stopped and started to look around the apartment. Meila tried to follow her gaze but couldn't due to some pain that came when she turned her head too quickly.

Shanta moved across the room and picked up something black off of the floor. She brought it to Meila and put it over her head. She then tugged on her bad arm. "Ow! Shanta! What are you doing?" Meila insisted, pulling away from her. She looked down to see the sling that she had discarded last night. Charlie had told her that it helped, but she insisted that she was fine. She really did not need to be fussed over.

Shanta put her hands on her hips. "What do you think I am doing? Helping you heal!" Shanta moved back toward Meila and put her arm in the sling.

"Just in case you forgot, you were shot a few days ago. It got the top of your shoulder, but you lost a lot of blood because of it. You also moved around quite a bit and pushed yourself. I mean, why did you tackle that man, with your bad shoulder, and then decide to climb out of the building? You are crazy." Shanta shook her head and then continued on. "Anyway, the doctor said that you would be woozy for a few days but to keep you out of the office and always have someone with you."

Meila closed her eyes and picked up a slice of the apple. She thought back to the past few days. They were all a blur in her mind. She vaguely remembers a doctor speaking and being brought back to her apartment. She remembered how Charlie stayed with her last night, but her mind only really thought of sleeping right now. "May I go back to bed?" she asked Shanta. She kept her eyes closed and reached for another slice of apple.

When Shanta didn't answer immediately, Meila opened her eyes and looked around until she saw her. Shanta's expression showed worry, but Meila should expect that. Besides, this entire plan had been her idea, and she was the one who got hurt.

Shanta finally spoke. "Very well, but finish the apple first and then take some more pain medication."

Meila nodded and did as she was told.

After a few minutes, Meila was back in her room and ready to sleep. Shanta put a glass down by her bed, telling her that she will need to drink it if she wakes up. Then she told Meila that she would be back in a few hours to give her more pain medicine. Meila tiredly nodded, pretending she heard that and then climbed under her covers.

* * * * *

Meila felt someone tapping her shoulder. "Mei, you up? It's time for dinner. The team came by earlier, but you were still asleep. Are you good to get up now?" Charlie asked.

Meila shrugged and rolled over so that she was facing Charlie. "I guess," Meila said. She pushed herself into a sitting position. She looked to the empty glass that was on her nightstand, vaguely remembering Shanta coming in and giving her medicine.

Charlie put a hand out and gently pulled her from bed. "The team brought over dinner, but I didn't know what you felt like eating, so I put most of it in the fridge." He helped her to the kitchen table. "How do you feel?"

Meila shrugged. "I have felt better."

Charlie looked at her, knowing that she was holding something back. "Really?"

"I'm just tired, mostly."

Charlie moved to the fridge. "Well, you had one crazy day. Plus, the doctor put you on some pretty heavy meds. Are you ready for some more?"

Meila nodded. Her shoulder was sore again. "What about the team? How are they all doing?"

Charlie put a container of something in the microwave. "I will catch you up on that in a minute. First, you need to eat and get your strength back. Doctor said that you need to be out a week before you come back into the office. After he makes sure everything is healing correctly, you can start physical therapy. Once you are done with physical therapy and the doctor clears you, you'll be cleared to come back and work full time."

"And the case?" Meila asked, hoping that she hadn't been shot for nothing.

Charlie shook his head. The microwave buzzed, telling him that time was up. He pulled out the food and laid it on the table. He pushed it over until it was in front of Meila and then spoke. "Eat first, then I will tell you about what we found."

Meila obediently ate the alfredo he had put in front of her. They didn't talk while she ate. She just ate and Charlie turned on the television.

Once she was done, she pushed the container away from her and moved over to her favorite chair. Charlie turned off the TV. "Are you ready to learn what we did?" he asked, a spark of excitement lighting his eyes.

She nodded.

"All right, well. Thanks to your instructions before you gracefully blacked out, we apprehended most of the goons at the mill. We have caught more trying to come and get their leader. Now, we are trying to get him to fess up on some stuff and get evidence for what he has told us."

"Have they offered you any new information that could be useful?" Meila asked.

Charlie shrugged. "Not really. I mean they gave us some stuff but came to find out that the previous team on the case already knew all of that, so it wasn't as helpful as I thought."

"But Rodrigez is in jail?"

Charlie shook his head no. "We thought it was him, but it is just one of his right-hand men."

Meila thought for a moment about what he said. "Then why are they trying to get him out?"

"What?"

Meila moved so that she was sitting across from Charlie. "Think about it. If this man has some valuable information, that would be a reason to get him out. Or perhaps he is vital to one of their plans. Think about it Charlie."

Meila watched as expressions crossed Charlie's face. He smiled after a few minutes. "I think that you are on to something, Mei. I'll make the suggestion to the team. We'll see if we can get him to crack."

Meila smiled back at Charlie, grateful that she could still be of help.

CHAPTER 41

Meila trudged into the office. She had been at home for almost two weeks. She was sick of lying around and doing nothing! She turned the corner to the main office. Cassie wasn't at her desk, but that was all right. She probably would have told Meila that she wasn't supposed to be there. Meila already knew that.

She swiped her badge at the door and then pulled it open. No one was at their desk, and the conference doors were closed. Meila put her black jacket on her peg and then walked over to her desk. She turned on her computer and put in her password one handed.

She opened up the shared document that the whole team uses. It showed all of the cases that they could currently or were currently working on. She checked for Rodrigez's name but couldn't find it. Meila read through the list again, hoping that she had just missed something. She searched for her father's name as well, but also found it was no longer on the list.

The door to the conference room opened and then closed. April had stepped out. "Meila!" she said. She quickly made her way across the room and gave Meila a hug. "It's good to have you back. Does Charlie know that you are here?"

Meila shook her head. "He told me this morning that I needed to stay in bed and rest. He makes it sound like I lost a limb and need to stay home until it grows back."

April moved to her desk. "He is just concerned. He probably doesn't want you to overdo it."

Meila sighed. "I know, but I am going crazy sitting at home, wondering what to do with my life."

April looked up from what she was doing to glance at Meila. "Wasn't there a time when that is what you preferred to do?"

Meila shrugged. She tried not to think about the time that she had just sat in apartments with her father. She did not care to go back to that life. "Yes, but that was before I knew that I could fight against my father and men like him. If I can help make this city a better place for someone else, then I am fine with that."

April made a face and then pulled something from her desk. She put it in her arms and then scurried back to the conference room.

Meila went back to searching the list, trying to find the information that she needed. Both doors to the conference room opened. A lot of people came spilling out of the room, most of which Meila didn't recognize. Those that she did know, started to come out, and they pulled a few files from their desks. They then gave them to the unknown faces and those people left. Meila just stared around the room at the faces and actions of her teammates. What were they doing?

Charlie walked out of the conference room. He made eye contact with Meila and motioned for her to come with him. She walked over by him, and he pulled her into the empty kitchen. When he didn't say anything, Meila spoke. "Aren't you going to ask me what I am doing here?"

Charlie shook his head. "April already told me, so I guess that I should catch you up on everything." Charlie opened a box that was on the counter. He pulled out a donut and then pushed the box to Meila. She pushed it back toward him and gave him a look, telling him that she was ready to get to work.

He swallowed his bite and then began. "The people you just saw, was the team that was taking over the Rodrigez case. I spoke with the board this morning. They told me they had set up a team that they believe could handle this case, so our team debriefed them this morning and then handed the case over to them."

"So I can't help with it? What about my suggestion of having someone go undercover?"

"I told the new team about your idea and they said that they would look into it. No promises, though, Meila."

Meila sat down at a barstool in her kitchen. "Already doubting this new team?"

Charlie shrugged and took another bite. "I thought that we had a good handle on the case and this team just decides that they actually want to do it. It just sounds kind of strange to me."

Meila nodded, understanding his feelings. After a moment of silence, except for Charlie's chewing, she spoke. "Well, should we get started on the next case then?"

Charlie smiled in between bites and motioned for her to go ahead. Meila adjusted her sling before reentering the office with a grin beginning to grow on her face.

CHAPTER 42

Four years later, 2011. Willowsville, Washington

Meila sat down on the edge of Charlie's desk. "Why can't I do it?" Meila held up three fingers. "This is the third time that the Rodrigez case has come to us. Each time, my father's name is brought up. Why can't I go to him and see if I can find something? Or I could go undercover!" Meila's head churned with ideas and possibilities of what she could do.

"Mei, we have been over this, time and time again. It is way too dangerous for you to try and do this. You are too connected with this case that you probably shouldn't have gotten involved."

"Go ahead and try to pry me from the team. It's not going to work. Charlie, I know more about this case than anyone else. I don't see why you can't see me as qualified."

Charlie stood.

"Mei, I don't want you falling back into your old ways."

Meila rose her eyebrows. "You are worried that I might go back to my old ways? Charlie, that was almost ten years ago! I am a completely different person now!"

"I know, but who knows how long it will take for you to find the information we need? Besides, what if it ends up taking longer than you thought? There are so many things that could go wrong.

Your father is one of the main issues. He isn't going to open his arms for you to fall into. That is not how men like him work, Meila."

"Thank you, Charlie," Meila retorted sarcastically. "I am aware, you are not the only one who has been working on putting these men behind bars for the last few years."

"Not to mention I would have to find someone who would fit into this team, someone who is thorough and hardworking, someone who has been trained to see the world differently," Charlie continued, as if not hearing what Meila had said.

Meila didn't bother trying to say anything. She knew that Charlie was frustrated with her, but why had to do this.

* * * * *

He stared at Old Man Manning.

"You mean to tell me my daughter has been alive this entire time but no one dared tell me?" he accused.

The other man nodded his head.

"She is planning to come back to you. Make sure you have a room ready for her when she does arrive." The man stood.

"How do you know? She has known I have been gone for years. Why would she try to return to me now?" Old Man Manning questioned.

"You have been flying under the radar. She is lucky she found you and not one of your rivals."

Old Man Manning nodded and stood.

"And she is finally coming home to help me run the business," he muttered, a spine-chilling smile creeping onto his face.

The man nodded once at Old Man Manning and stepped from the room. A smile slid over the man's face as he took a step toward the shadow and made eye contact with another familiar face.

"Rodrigez."

The man nodded.

"Do you really not recognize me?"

Rodrigez shook his head, taking a step closer to the man, examining him. The man steepled his fingers and put on a smile.

Recognition finally hit Rodrigez's face, and he took a step back, fear evident.

The man chuckled and then turned and left.

* * * * *

Meila glanced at the note she left Charlie, double-checking if she had left the keys to her apartment by it along with some money. She knew he had taken care of paying for her apartment for years; and now she would be gone for a couple of days, weeks at most, along with a meeting spot on the other side of town, a safe spot she could run to once she had the information the team needed. She made sure to leave out where her father currently was, not wanting to bring Charlie into this whole mess. She just hoped he would have enough sense to stay out of it.

Meila pulled the door to her apartment door closed, listening as it automatically locked, and then made her way toward the cement stairs. She made her way down them quickly and mentally went through the list she had created. It was her cover story. It still had some holes, but it would work for what she needed to accomplish this evening. She had been writing it up for days, knowing she would have to live it once she arrived at her father's. She had to stick to it no matter what. She couldn't tell him she was working for the very people he was trying to destroy. If so, she would be dead within minutes. She repeated the list in her head, knowing she couldn't let anything about her real life slip out.

She had gone over the maps with Cassie. She then made Cassie promise that she wouldn't mention any of this to Charlie, at least not until he found the note in her room, explaining that she had gone to get the information needed.

She had known that her father had just been staying in some abandoned homes down in the south and central part of town, but he would be moving closer to those in the east. His drug shipments would be slowing down right now, so being in the west side of the city would not be wise for him.

Meila pulled her jacket closer to her body. She hoped that she was getting closer. The sun was setting over the water, but the buildings had long ago covered her from the warmth of it.

She heard a popping noise behind her. She looked down at her feet and smiled into her jacket. Her father hadn't stopped using his old tricks. That noise to anyone one else was just that, a noise. But to Meila or anyone who had worked with her father, that was a common noise. Her father was around here somewhere. Now, it was a matter of finding him.

Meila glanced around at the surrounding buildings—a few old apartment buildings and a shop that was up for lease. The popping noise was made from behind her, meaning her father's men were watching her, but they were behind her. Meila paused for a moment, taking in the vicinity. The apartment to her left connected to an alleyway. Meila took in what she could see of the other streets. Her father needed that extra way to escape. This had to be the building he was hiding out in.

She looked up around her. This was not a building that he had previously used, but she would try it. She moved around the side of it, looking for a door or some sort of way in. She found a door just along the back side. And to her luck, it was cracked open.

She checked behind her, feeling the hairs on her neck stand. She pulled it open and stepped inside. The hallway was dark. Meila blinked her eyes, trying to let them adjust. She heard voices farther down the hall and moved toward them but not before a blanket came over her head.

She reached out trying to find who had put it on her. Two hands came down on her arms and pulled her forward. She tried to struggle but found that it did no good. The voices were getting closer, and she heard a door's squeaky hinges. The voices became more distinct, then they stopped. Her arms were pulled behind her and tied down with a rope. She was pushed farther into the room and then placed on her knees.

She heard an eerie voice from behind her. "Who is this?" it said.

The second voice grunted. "Don't know. The guards alerted us of her presence, but she walked straight into the back of this building like she was looking for something."

Someone kicked her leg. "Speak! Who are you?" That was the first voice.

"My name is Meila Manning."

The room went silent. Meila waited, hoping that they would pull off the blanket on her head. But they didn't.

"Can't be. She died. I saw it happen. She is lying!" A few other voices joined in, agreeing.

Meila tried to jump up, but a hand was placed on her shoulder, keeping her down. "No! You were misinformed. I have been living in the alleys for many years. I have worked a few jobs where I knew I would not be recognized. I have since then been living in small places that I could secure. I have been looking for my father and his business for some time, but I haven't been able to find you until today. Please, take off the blanket or get my fingerprints! I can prove that I am who I say I am."

A few voices sounded from behind her. They debated for some time before a voice came in front of her. "Describe your business that you did previously for your father," the familiar voice demanded.

"I was his way in, a pretty face. I also spoke with new employees and helped with a few shipments."

The room silenced again. "What about the night that you left? Hmm?"

"I was captured. It wasn't by anyone that you know. They called themselves 'the agency.' They asked me for information, but I wouldn't give it to them. I was kept in a cell for a couple months, but I escaped."

"Why didn't you try to come back then?"

"I already told you. I was trying to find you but was barely surviving. That is when I started to do small jobs. I even got in on one of the shipments, but they wouldn't disclose where my father was at."

She waited for a moment and then heard a chair scrape behind her. The blanket came off her head, and someone pulled her up. "We are grateful to have you back." Her father stood in front of her.

She smiled, not sure what to hope for. Meila watched as relief crossed his features, and then a mixture of disappointment and anger. She wanted to lean in for a hug, but she also knew that her father wouldn't accept it, so she pasted on a smile and asked for the rope to come off. The rope was removed, and Meila turned around and saw many faces.

"I'm sorry for barging in during an important meeting. I have been searching for my father for years and have finally found him," Meila blurted to the group, recalling the story she had created earlier.

"Good, I was in need of a pretty face. That is what this opera tion needed."

Meila turned to her father. "Where can I help? If you are meeting, something big must be about to happen. What were you discussing before I came in?" She searched around the room, waiting for someone to answer.

"We are not at liberty to talk about that with you in the room." her father replied after a few seconds of silence.

Meila looked back at her father, shocked. She didn't really know what to expect when she came back from the dead, but it wasn't this. She expected to possibly be tested, but she figured that she would be let back in pretty easily.

"I'm sorry, Meila, but you have been out on the streets for too long. You do not have the right amount of my trust to be in the rest of this meeting." He moved away from her and to his seat at the head of the table. "My men will be watching you, and Hunter will stand guard at the room I have assigned for you. We will be at this location for some time, so feel free to unpack what you have brought. You will be starting training in the morning. Goodbye, Meila."

She was pulled from the room. She hated this waiting period. She thought that she would have full respect once she rejoined her father's business but she should have known better. Meila was pulled up the stairs and shoved into a room, much like the one that she had escaped from. It had a twin-size bed against the far wall, a window showing you the street a few floors below. Her door closed behind her, and she saw a shadow of two feet standing in front of it.

She pulled the curtains closed over her window and turned on the light. She had an adjoining bathroom and a closet. No sight of food, but she assumed that most of her father's men ate in the main conference room downstairs. During meetings like this one, food was served in one place instead of to each and every individual room. Her stomach growled in protest, but Meila knew she couldn't do anything about that right now. She had bigger problems.

She sat down on the plump bed. Charlie was right. She had no idea what she was getting herself into.

* * * * *

Cody brushed his hair aside in frustration. Information was being leaked. This was the third time the Rodrigez case had come to their team. No new information had been found. How could no new information be found over the last few years? Someone had to be taking information or not sharing this new information.

He had looked into every agent on his team, searching through every inch of their apartments. Every member on their team was clean. April, Shanta, Charlie, Marcus—even Meila was clean. None of them took files home. They didn't speak of their cases outside of work. None of them went anywhere suspicious. They didn't meet with anyone who had a bad streak.

Cody looked around the room. Marcus was the only one still working. Shanta was in the kitchen. He could hear her sandals flopping around on the tile. Cody glanced at the files once more, looking at the picture of Meila, her dark-brown eyes staring back at him. He closed the files before hiding them under a fake panel in the bottom drawer of his desk. He would continue to keep an eye on his coworkers. He knew one of them was spilling the beans. He just wished he knew who it was and stop them.

A knock sounded at the door, and Marcus got up to open it. Cassie poked her head in.

"Hey, Cody. I just wanted to let you know the files from the Rodrigez case have started to arrive. Do you want me to start bringing them in?"

Cody shook his head and stood. "The morning shift will be coming in soon. They should be able to handle it."

Cassie nodded and smiled. She closed the door, and Cody sat back down.

Maybe he hadn't looked at everyone, but Cassie was just a glorified receptionist. There was no way. The door to their office was always closed, and she didn't have access to anything on their computers. She was just a secretary.

CHAPTER 43

A hand was over her mouth. Meila's breathing increased as an arm moved over her arms and pulled her out of the window. Meila tried to function, but her limbs felt numb. She tried to kick or scream for help, but her body felt immovable.

After a block of being dragged around, she finally felt some feeling come back to her limbs and mouth. She tried to scream, but it was muffled. The person who held her captive had her in an alley; who knows where they were going or what he would do to her.

Meila had been through enough of these. She pushed her elbow into the man's gut, feeling him fall slightly away from her. She bit his finger, forcing him to release her.

She turned toward him, ready to attack again, but the kidnapper spoke before she could. "Gosh, Meila! If I knew that you were going to act like this, I never would have come!"

Meila let down her defenses. "Charlie?"

He held his finger she had bitten, looking at her, smiling. "Who else do you think would attempt a crazy mission like this? Cody?"

"What are you doing here? I purposely gave you a meeting place on the other side of town. Why couldn't you have just followed those instructions?"

Charlie shrugged. "You were the one who set up a meeting place. I just didn't follow your directions. I knew that you would probably lead me away from this place from the very beginning. So, yes. I disregarded your meeting place and started to search for you. Besides, you know I don't always follow the instructions given." Charlie let out a deep breath. "I really came because I needed to make sure that you weren't going to get killed, so I have finally tracked you down and have been watching you the last few nights. Anything new?"

"Yeah. I'm surprised that you got me out so easily tonight. My father's men have been watching me like a hawk. He didn't truly believe the story that I pieced together. I thought that it was pretty decent, so I'm currently in a probation period, so I won't be able to get any new information until I'm more trusted."

Charlie nodded, "Just make sure that you don't get too deep undercover." He turned and started to disappear into the dark alleyway.

"Wait, Charlie. Are you still angry with me?" Meila asked hesitantly.

Meila watched as Charlie stepped closer shaking his head.

"I can't be angry with you anymore. You are in the middle of a mission and now it is my responsibility, along with the rest of the teams, to make sure you get home safely. You make sure to get what you need and then get out."

"Don't worry about me. I know how to take care of myself." Meila started to walk away. "I have to get back. They're going to notice I got out, then we won't be getting any information."

"Fine. Let's try and meet up here again in a few nights. Crack your window on the night you can do it. I will see it and be waiting here."

Meila nodded once more and started back toward her apartment.

* * * * *

Meila pushed the letter toward Hunter, one of her father's favorite goons. "Looks like you've done it again, Mastermind Meila."

She smiled at the nickname. All of her father's men knew her as that—Mastermind Meila. "Thanks, Hunter. Anything else that I could do today, or am I excused?"

Hunter stood and walked across the room, pulling in a guard before closing the door. "Just one more thing, then I will release you."

Meila sat up a little bit taller. "Do you know that agency building that your father was being held at?"

Meila nodded. She knew about that building long before she had started to work there. "Of course. I was permitted to go and visit him weekly."

"Miss Manning, how come you were allowed to go and see him, hmm? Weren't they suspicious that you would help him break out or maybe kill him?"

"Kill him? He's my father. He may not be the best thing in the world that happened to me, but he is all the family that I have left. Killing him was never an option."

"Interesting." Hunter drummed his fingers along the table. "How did you see him every week?"

Meila knew that they were trying to get her to spill something, and it wasn't going to work. She had kept secrets worse than this from her father's men; she could do it again. She closed her eyes, remembering the list she wrote out and had left at her apartment. Her cover story was outlined on it. She had to stick to it the best she could. "I was scanned on my way into that dark building. I always had guards around me, no matter what. I was put in cuffs on my arrival, and they didn't come off until after I left."

No one spoke in the room for a moment, and Meila opened her eyes, glancing between the two men in the room with her.

Hunter looked at the other man in the room. "What do you think?"

Meila heard the voice get closer behind her. "That's how it was whenever I went in. She's telling the truth."

Meila sighed in relief, she was glad these guys were believing her cover story.

Hunter looked back at her, almost embarrassed. "Sorry to doubt you, Meila, but we had to be for sure."

"It's fine. I hope that this does not happen again, though. You know that my father will not tolerate his daughter being questioned."

Hunter nodded. "He asked to see you if this turned out the right way."

"Very well. I haven't seen him much since I have returned."

The guard opened the door for her, and Hunter led her to her father's conference room. They knocked preceding their entrance.

Meila looked at all the men's faces as she entered. A few of them she recognized, others she had only seen on pictures. Then she saw her father. He had not been the most caring while growing up, but she stood true to what she knew. He was all that she had left of her blood family.

He nodded to her, and she nodded back. He then turned and continued on. "Rodrigez said that he has had some trouble with the agency. He has currently stopped his supply coming over. That is why he has come to us for help. But I need a few more of his men out of this arrangement." A few men in the room laughed at this.

"I need someone that they won't recognize, though, someone who is fresh. Since I cannot go myself, I have decided to put someone else who I wholly trust in this situation." He gestured toward her.

"This is my daughter Meila. She is smart, and I have watched her grow under my intense care the last few weeks. I have no doubt that she will do great things." He looked at her, a smile almost lighting her face.

"Everyone is excused. The plans are all set. All we need to do is put the bait in. That will be done as soon as she is ready."

Meila moved to where her father stood as everyone else filed out of the room. "Catch me up on what we're doing here."

He shook his head. "This is a need-to-know plan only. The only thing that you need to know is that this is your final test. Your job here—your only job here—will be the same as it always was. You get me in the door, you and your pretty face." He reached out and touched her cheek. "The same thing that I only ever used your mother for."

She jerked away from him, angrier than ever. "Fine, I'll be your pretty face, but I want more information, or I'm out."

He moved to his spot at the table. "If you leave, then I will kill you." He glanced up at her, probably trying to see if it scared her. "If you stay, though, I will tell you a few more details of the plan."

Meila thought this through. She needed this information for Charlie. If her father was planning something good, he needed to know. If they could stop her father before something happened, she needed all the details they can get. She also knew that her father never went back on his deals. He had broken more promises to her then he had kept, but it was the only way. She nodded.

"Very good. Once you are in, I will have Hunter and a few of my men follow and finish off the job." He stared at Meila for a moment, as if waiting for her to object. When she didn't go asking questions, he nodded and started to stand.

"Wait, may I ask a few questions?" Meila asked, hoping he would stay so she could understand more of what she would or could do.

Her father looked down at his watch. "One question." He answered wearily.

Meila took a deep breath. One question. She let the gears start to turn in her head as a plan started to form.

"Why can't I take out a few of the men on my own?"

"Meila, I have never taught you anything like that, so no. You can't take some of the men out on your own."

"Let me prove it."

He shook his head. "That plan is already in motion. I am not going to delay it so that my daughter can play some fantasy game."

"Father." Meila sat down across from him, hoping that he would actually listen to her. "You won't have to delay anything. Let me get caught sooner than planned. If I can take out a huge amount of them before you have to get there, then your men will have to do less work."

She could tell that his gears were going. He was thinking about it. "Fine, but if you do not have it completed, then my men will interfere."

She held out a hand. He hesitantly put his in it, and they shook. "It's a deal." She released his hand and then stood. "Now, if you will excuse me. I have to go and make myself presentable."

She turned and walked out of the room without even looking back. *How am I going to get this information to Charlie?* She only hoped that she could figure that out before they left.

CHAPTER 44

She looked out the window again. She saw no signs of movement, but she had put out her sign. She just hoped that Charlie was serious when he said that he would be there.

Meila cracked her door open. No one was out in the hall. Her father was in a meeting, so she would be left alone for a good amount of time. She just hoped that it would be enough time. She shut her door silently then slid out of the window. No one was on the street, so navigating to the meeting spot would go by quickly.

She walked quickly, wishing that she would have brought a jacket to ward off the early chill that was coming in this year. She just rubbed her arms as she walked. She looked around, trying to see if she was being followed but saw no one. She slipped into the strange alleyway and looked around. The lights that were coming from the street were not enough to provide the light needed to actually see anything.

She moved farther into it, hoping that her eyes would adjust, when she stepped onto something soft. "Ow!" came from right behind her.

"Charlie! I'm sorry. I was hoping that you got my message, but I wasn't sure. Is your foot all right?" She looked down but could not see anything but darkness.

He grabbed her by her arms. "I am fine, really. What is it you wanted to tell me?"

"My father told me of some of his plans. He is even letting me take part in the execution. I leave in the morning, a new part of town, a part I don't think you know well enough to call for backup. I will have to take care of myself on my own."

"What will you be doing?"

"The only details that my father gave me were need to know. I will be his way to get through the door, as usual, but I asked if I could be the one to take out the man."

Charlie's eyes widened at her last statement. "Meila, you have never killed anyone in your life. Trust me, you don't want to start now."

"Hold on a minute. I never said anything about killing. I will go in, assess this man, and then I'll decide what needs to be done. If I have to, I will kill him, but that will be my last resort."

"What does your father think?"

Meila put her head down. "I don't need his approval anymore."

Charlie nodded. "And what if you find that your target's life should not end tomorrow?"

Meila shrugged her shoulders. "I saw some fake blood that my father's kept to fake the death of some of his men."

"Why would he do that?"

"So that he could continue to use them, but they aren't wanted anymore. He did it to a few of his men when I was young. I just plan to knock out this man and then put some of the blood on him. Do you still have one of your cards?"

"Yeah, sure." Charlie dug around in one of his pockets until he pulled out one of his cards, placing it in Meila's hand.

"I will send him to our team."

"What!" Charlie stepped back. "What are we supposed to do with him? What if he gets out and starts sprouting sonnets of what you did for him?"

"Just make sure that he flies under the radar for a while, maybe get him out of the country. I don't know. Think of something."

Charlie rubbed his head in frustration. "Fine. If you can get him to us, we will try to help him. What about after?"

"I'm not sure yet. My father said that this was my last test. If I can make it through this, I will be able to get us more information than ever."

Charlie sat silent for a moment. "Are you sure you want to do this? I can get us out safely right now."

Meila thought for a moment, but she already knew the answer. "I'm sorry, Charlie, but you know that this information is critical to this case. I can't let the team down now."

She glanced out at the street. "I need to get back. I still have some things that I need to get done tonight. I just hope that I haven't been gone for too long."

"All right, but, Mei"—Charlie waited until she turned back around to face him—"be careful."

She offered him a small smile. "I always am." She turned back to the road and walked briskly back to her apartment, hoping that she was really ready for what tomorrow would bring.

CHAPTER 45

Meila checked the street again. She had two men that had tailed her for the last two blocks. One man walked ahead of her not too far, but he was watching her every move. She kept her head up, not acknowledging any of them. Her father had taught her to treat them as if they were invisible, it would give her the upper hand. Most of the time, a trap was set up for them anyway. This time was different though. Usually her father's men would dominate these traps. She was the only one going into this arrangement. She just hoped that her plan really would work. If she was going to be a valuable part to the team, she would have to prove it to either the agency or her father. But she dearly hoped that it was the first option. If not, she was condemning herself to a life of misery.

She felt another man come by her. "Manning?"

"You asked to see me." Meila glanced at him.

"Good. You are to follow me to a car." He gestured to turn around and walk the other way. She followed, knowing that her cooperation would get her far. It always had.

The strange man grabbed her elbow, pushing her to step up her pace. Meila resisted the urge to yank her arm away from him. Play the part of an idiot. That's what her father always told her on these missions. If she actually ever listened to him, she would have died a long time ago.

They approached a black Sedan with darkly tinted windows. The license plate had been torn off the front and most likely the back too. There was a long scratch along the side of the vehicle but not quite long enough to make it unique.

The back door opened, and the man practically shoved her into the car. "I apologize, but I need to make sure that we are not being followed. Also, I will need to check you for wires or a tracking device," He said, climbing in the car behind her.

Meila nodded and sat as still as she could while he ran through the humiliating search. She had slipped a handkerchief and a small vial of chloroform into her pocket before leaving. Thankfully, the man went through the search quickly, completely missing that her right jacket pocket was a little bit larger than the left. Once she was pronounced clean, the car pulled away from the curb and down many unfamiliar streets. Meila had been placed in the middle seat, making it harder to follow where they were at. The clock in the sedan was also broken, so no watching the time.

After a while, the black car drove up through a more deserted part of town. Night hadn't started to fall yet, but Meila knew that it would be here soon, making everything more complicated.

The black car drove through a strange gate and toward a building. Meila glanced through the windows, not a whole lot of guards around. Hopefully, if her father kept his promise, they would have someone to watch out for her.

Once the car came to a stop, Meila was let out and became surrounded by four men. Meila looked up at the building, a classic two-, maybe three-story home. It belonged to someone with finer tastes but no cameras. That would make her escape easier.

Meila was escorted by the group of guards into the house. The entryway was vast, a chandelier hung over their heads as they moved down the hall before entering a much smaller room. Three of the guards spread out amongst the edge of the room. The last one escorted her to a seat across from a desk. Meila had expected something shabby, maybe a warehouse or an alley. She was on the wrong side of this one. These guys probably got a whole suite to themselves. Her father shoved her in a small apartment downtown.

Footsteps sounded behind her. She turned to see an older gentleman walk in. "Thank you, Sergeant, for bringing her in. Did you have any trouble?"

"None," the man who stood beside her answered.

"Very good. Very good." The older man turned toward Meila. "Miss Manning, I presume?"

"Yes, sir. Thank you for meeting with me on such short notice. My father would have come, but he is still a wanted man."

The older man moved toward her and held out his hand, smiling. "Mr. Miller," he introduced himself.

Meila took the man's hand and firmly shook it once before dropping it and taking a seat.

The man walked around his desk and sat down. "Yes, but I would do anything for an old friend. Now, what do you need to discuss with me this evening?" Meila opened her mouth to reply to Mr. Miller, but he cut her off.

"Did you know that he was one of the first men that I helped? I am so grateful that he has guided so many others in my way so that I can help them too. Starting a business can be hard, especially when you are hurting for money. Giving him another small cut wouldn't hurt me at all." The older man pulled out his ledger and laid it on the table. He then picked up some glasses and placed them on the bridge of his nose. "Did your father specify how much I should be giving back to him? He has done so well to keep on paying me."

"He is paying you?" Meila questioned. She did not know that her father paid anyone, let alone someone who didn't know the true nature of his business.

"Oh, yes. He has been paying me for years. It helps keep the feds off of his back."

Meila shook her head, trying to comprehend everything that he was saying. "Do you mind if I ask how?"

Mr. Miller shrugged. "I know quite a few feds around this part of the town. When Manning asks me to, I let them know of a different location of where his competitors may be. I pay the feds more than what they are getting paid, and I stay out of trouble. It also keeps my family out of it too. My son-in-law has decided to go down a much different dangerous path. He pulled his daughter away from me also." A sadness entered the man's tone. "I do not miss them very much anymore."

Meila nodded, pushing down her feelings. She came to show her father that she was loyal to him. She hoped that he found out soon because she was missing her apartment and all the time she spent at the agency.

"Sorry, I am blabbering on." He leaned forward and looked in his book. "How much did you say that he wanted?" Mr. Miller asked, looking up at her over his glasses.

"My father told me that he wanted his out. He said that you would know how to access this."

He nodded. "Yes, I do. That is quite a sum, though. Plus, I have an employee that manages all those accounts. I can give your father a portion right now, but not the whole sum." Mr. Miller pulled out a blank check, quickly writing out a good chunk of money before looking back up at Meila. "I will speak with my employee about the remainder of the money your father has in his account and get back to you." He made a note on the paper in front of him.

Commotion started up in the hall. Meila turned at the unexpected noise. A voice came from behind her. "Sergeant, take your men and please investigate."

The door closed behind the sergeant, leaving Meila alone with Mr. Miller. Meila knew that now was her chance. "My father said that he wanted me to ask you one more thing."

"Please, my dear, ask away." The man smiled.

"This is not really a favor. It's more of a request." Meila stood, pulling a napkin and a small bottle of chloroform from her pocket. "You are in his way. He needs you gone."

The man's eyes widened with shock. "You are going to kill me?"

Meila just walked around the desk, dousing the napkin before she put it up to his nose, knowing that he would be out before he could even struggle. She then pulled out a small bottle of blood and dumped some on him, making him look dead. She then shuffled around a few things in his office, making it seem as if he had struggled a bit before she ended him. She put some blood on his fingers.

Meila then moved to one of his bookcases, carefully pulling out a larger book that could have done damage. She placed that next to Mr. Miller on the desk before taking her chloroformed rag to wipe off any fingerprints she might have left. Meila could never actually kill anyone, but if she wanted to get on her father's good side, she had to make it look like she could. Thankfully, his men were not as sharp as those working at the agency. Her father rarely checked his men's work. She hoped that it would be the same for her. It hadn't started out that way, but she had worked for him when she was young, and her father had always trusted her to do everything right. He just trusted her. Even if she did not really have his love, she hoped that she had gained his trust. Her plan would go a lot smoother if he did. Meila picked up the check from the desk, depositing it in her jacket pocket before looking around the room, double checking that she had done everything. Her finger grazed the card Charlie had given her. She pulled it out and slipped it into the man's sleeve, taping it down. He would be dead long enough for authorities to call him dead, long enough for him to call Charlie and get all of the information to him.

She closed the door, thanking him for his time, and left the building. A car waited for her out the front door, Hunter in the driver's seat. Meila pulled open the door and climbed in. She barely had time to shut the door before Hunter zoomed down the driveway. "How'd it go?"

"Good." Meila held up the check for Hunter to see. "Father got a portion of his money, and the money man is out of the mix. How is the other side doing?"

"They have eliminated most of those that needed to go tonight. Your father has a more imaginable way of getting rid of the others." Hunter smiled.

Meila shuddered at the thought. Her father had tortured people when she was young. She used to have nightmares of the screaming that she heard. He, thankfully, thought that she was too young for that experience. She hoped that he still thought that.

Meila watched the clock and the street signs as they passed through the rest of town. "Who created the distraction to pull the guards away from me?"

"Me and a handful of the guys. You sure that man is dead?"

Meila nodded and looked out the window. "He shouldn't be a problem anymore." Especially if he could get in contact with Charlie. She knew that he wouldn't let her down. "Can I ask you another question?"

Hunter shrugged.

Meila took that as a good sign and asked her question. "How come we are getting rid of so many people?"

Hunter thought for a moment before speaking. "Your father doesn't want to be double-crossed in any of the deals that are made, so he double-crosses them first."

"Doesn't that defeat the whole point of making an alliance?"

Hunter stopped at a stop sign, turning left down the next road. "Your father gets what he needs out of people and then eliminates them. Mr. Miller and his men were just one example. He has been doing this for years. He has grown more powerful lately. He doesn't want his reign to end abruptly, if you know what I mean."

Meila nodded and let the conversation drop. They sat in silence the rest of the way back to the meeting place. The silence allowed her to process what her father might have planned, but then, she had never been able to really predict what he would do.

Once they returned to the apartment, there was a quick meeting. Meila updated everyone on her part, and she heard the rest of what went down. If she calculated correctly, there were seventy-nine in this business. Thirty-seven had already fallen and another twenty-three tonight, leaving the business in the hands of roughly nineteen people left, give or take a few just because Meila couldn't kill.

The meeting was dismissed soon after, and Meila went to her room. She immediately moved to her window, staring out at the empty street before cracking it open. She hoped that Charlie was really watching her. She really needed to speak to him.

CHAPTER 46

She peered out of the door. Meila was glad that she wasn't caught earlier tonight, but she had to see Charlie. She had cracked her window as soon as they had arrived home, but a guard had been at her door the entire night. She was hoping that once it got darker, he would be released or moved.

Finally, she heard the heavy footsteps move away from her door. She checked for a shadow but didn't see one. Meila glanced around her room once more, before deciding that a jacket wasn't going to be needed. The nights had started to cool off, but she was only going to be gone for a short amount of time. She looked back to her door and saw that no shadow had returned. Grateful, she tiptoed to her window, opened and eased it closed again. She went down the fire escape noiselessly and felt like running to her and Charlie's meeting place.

She checked behind herself before going into the dark alley. The street was blessedly empty, which was not strange for this time of night. She moved far back into the alleyway before daring to speak. "Charlie?" she whispered.

Arms came around her. "Mei, I was worried. You cracked your window almost two hours ago. What kept you?"

"There was a man guarding my door. I knew that I couldn't leave until after he left." Meila released Charlie and looked him straight in his eyes or where she thought his eyes were. This alleyway really was too dark to see anything. "Have you heard from Mr. Miller yet?"

Charlie's dark head went up and down. "Cody has got him packing up, discreetly, of course. He was quite easily persuaded to leave the country and will be doing so before the end of the week. I don't think that he will be coming back anytime soon."

Meila sighed a breath of relief. "Oh, good. I am happy for him."

"As am I," a voice came from behind them. Meila turned around, only to have a bright light shine on her face. "Mastermind Meila, back in trouble again, are we?"

Meila knew that she recognized that voice. "Rodrigez?"

"Ah, I am glad that you know my voice. Now, how about we turn you back over to your father because I have told him the truth. Imagine his astonishment when I told him that his little girl, who supposedly came back from the dead, really works for a company that he has tried to destroy for the past three decades."

Meila moved farther back until she was against Charlie.

"Oh, don't think about running. I have pulled Hunter along with me. We both know why he really got his name."

Meila swallowed. She had heard tales about what Hunter had done to his enemies. She did not wish to endure any of that. "Fine. You've got me." She put her hands out in front of her.

Rodrigez pulled out another flashlight, shining it on the others that were there with him. He had most of his crew, along with a few of her father's men. "You're not the only one that he wants. He wants the man behind you too. I need proof that I am not crazy. I was lucky when I accidentally found myself this far down town and saw you. I followed you to this spot and heard you talking to someone, so I called a couple of my men to follow you around. Good thing too. I knew that I would repay you for what you've done to me," he sneered.

Meila and Charlie were forced to the ground. Their arms were tied behind their backs. They were ushered back to the hotel, where her father was waiting for them in the conference room. Meila opened her mouth as if to say something, but a hand came down across her cheek, stopping her. "How dare you! I let you back into my home, my life, and you betrayed me!" her father yelled.

"I know, and I'm sorry, but—"

Another slap stopped her again. "No daughter of mine would ever do that."

"Please, Father, who are you going to believe, what I say or what criminals say off the street?"

Her father's red face just went a shade darker. That's not what she expected. "I have no family left. They are all dead to me."

"Please."

"Silence!" her father shouted. "You will be put in jail where I will all of those who have betrayed me. I hope that I never see you again. I should have listened to my mom when you first arrived. You are a stranger to me, and you have tried to destroy me." He looked to the men behind them. "Take them away. I wish to have no more garbage in my life."

"Please, Father! I can explain!" she cried.

Her words were not even heard. A black bag was placed over her head, and Meila felt herself being pulled. They were dragged from the room and put in the back of a car. The guards that had pulled them from the building pulled off the sacks and then climbed up front. The car pulled away from the curb and left her father and the building behind. Meila leaned against Charlie's shoulder and cried. Even though she had never really been close to her father, hearing him say those awful words had hurt her. She was now really alone in the world, no blood relatives to turn to anymore.

Charlie just sat there and let her cry. Finally, when her breathing became normal he spoke. "Where do you think they are taking us?"

"Who knows? I have heard stories about a place that he sends people to. I have never heard of anyone coming out alive."

Charlie just nodded. "My promise still stands. I will protect you, whatever the costs."

She took her head off his shoulder so that she could look him squarely in the face. "Thank you, Charlie. Knowing that you would be there for me has really helped me get through some hard times."

"That's what brothers do." Charlie smiled.

Meila shook her head. "I do not have family anymore, Charlie. You heard what my father said."

"I know, but family doesn't always mean blood. I count everyone on the team as a family member. Whether you like it or not, you are part of the team and family now too."

"That means a lot right now."

Charlie nodded and then stared out the dark tinted windows, watching the streets go by. "You say that no one has ever escaped this place?"

"Yep," Meila sighed.

Charlie turned back to her. "You want to make history?"

"What?"

Charlie's smile grew. "Let's be the first to escape this horrid place."

* * * * *

Cody heard footsteps out on the pavement before he turned to the window. A black Sedan had been parked in front of the dilapidated meeting place, but Cody had inspected the vehicle earlier. There was nothing about it that made it special, and it did not look like a car that had been stolen. He had stepped away from his post for just a moment before hearing the car start and zoom away. Cody's attention had been pulled back to the front of the building, though. He knew that Old Man Manning was inside. He couldn't wait to see the old man's face when he found out it was Meila, his own daughter, who had turned him in.

Cody checked the window, thinking about the busy day that he had. Mr. Miller was safely on his way to Europe where the man would disappear for many years. Cody moved the drapes a little bit further back, revealing more of the street. Darkness had come, and the streetlights lit the road and sidewalk pretty well. He hoped that it would be enough.

Cody watched from his position in the apartment as Old Man Manning stepped from the building across the street. He had very few guards flanking him, but Cody knew that he would most likely have more hidden around him.

Cody smiled as he recognized the second person stepping from the building. This night could not go any better. The two men that the agency had been trying to capture for the last ten years were at the same place. This made his job so much easier.

He pulled out his radio and gave the command, "Target in sight. Move in."

Cody quickly moved down the stairs of the building, knowing that others were keeping an eye on Rodrigez and Old Man Manning. He pulled on his protective helmet before stepping outside. He had required that all who were helping with this mission wear a Kevlar vest, bulletproof helmet, and bulletproof pants. He felt that everyone should be prepared for anything going in to take these two down.

He stepped outside and lifted his gun. He knew that the building he was in and the buildings on each side of it had been cleared. About a half hour ago, there had been some commotion in an alleyway a few streets down, but Cody knew that Charlie could handle that.

"Put your hands up!" Cody yelled, catching the two crime bosses' attention. They both reached for their weapons that Cody knew they carried. More shouts came from around him as a big chunk of his team filed out of the other buildings, creating a barrier. A few men came around the corner north and south of him. Other agents came from behind Old Man Manning and Rodrigez, bringing a handful of Old Man Manning's guards.

Rodrigez and Manning watched as more of their guards were brought down, weaponless and defenseless. Their backs were to each other, watching the fleet move closer to them.

Cody moved closer but noticed that neither one of them were going to give up without a fight.

Manning cocked his gun and shot at the agent closest to him. It hit the man's bulletproof vest, and he still staggered back a few paces. Cody moved closer, and Manning turned his gun on him, but before he could get a shot off, a bullet hit Manning's right shoulder, causing him to drop his gun. Rodrigez turned to see what happened, and an agent rushed him from behind and ripped him free of his gun. Rodrigez turned and tried to lay a punch on the man but was too sloppy. The agent kicked the back of his knees and pushed him to the ground. Another agent jumped on top of him and tackled him to the ground. He was quickly in handcuffs, just leaving Old Man Manning.

The man turned toward him and threw a punch with his left arm but missed Cody. Cody turned and smiled smugly. He was just about to tell him that his fighting skills were worse than his daughter's, but Old Man Manning's fist connected with Cody's face, sending him backward. He did not fall over, but he stumbled. Another shot came from somewhere, barely grazing Old Man Manning's torso. Blood seeped through his shirt, and he looked up to Cody before lifting his fist and trying to hit him again.

Cody anticipated this swing and ducked, grabbing Old Man Manning's arm as his momentum pushed him past Cody.

Cody stood, still holding Manning's only good arm.

The man screamed out in pain, but Cody didn't put much thought into it as his hands were handcuffed, and Cody pushed him to the ground.

Finally, Old Man Manning would go behind bars and stay there. Rodrigez wouldn't be causing the agency any grief, and the team could be complete once more.

Cody handed Manning off to another agent, and he made his way into the apartment building. Cody glanced in the first few rooms but only found agents in them. The agents were taking pictures and collecting the arrested men's belongings. Cody quickly looked through them, trying to see his best friend.

Cody stopped in the next room. This one had belonged to Meila. He recognized her black jacket that she must have left behind. He picked it up and made a mental note to give it to her.

Cody stepped back out into the hallway to see Agent Walker running toward him.

"They are not here," he said, breathless.

Cody scrunched his forehead. "What do you mean they are not here? This is the only building that we couldn't check while Manning was in his meeting. They have to be in here."

Agent Walker vehemently shook his head, sending his few last strands of hair flying on his head. "We have searched everywhere. Even tried to call out their names, but no response."

Cody shook his head. "They have to be here." Charlie had just told him yesterday that this is where he would be. This is where Old Man Manning had to be taken down. What had gone so wrong in the plan that he wasn't here anymore?

Cody took off the protective helmet, the same that all of the agents had been wearing, and let it drop to the floor. His best friend had left him behind.

Soft footfalls approached him he turned to find April making her way toward them. She smiled and held up a sniper rifle.

"Sorry I missed him so bad on the second shot. He wasn't supposed to move the way he did."

Cody nodded and held Meila's jacket out to her. He knew that Meila wouldn't accept it from him. He did not even really care for the girl.

"Why do you have this? Charlie told us that he would be waiting for us here. Meila should be around here too."

Agent Walker spoke before Cody even opened his mouth, "We searched the entire building. Neither one of them have been found."

April shook her head. "Are you sure you checked everywhere?"

Agent Walker nodded his head, glasses bouncing up and down.

Cody moved past April and toward a set of stairs that would take him downstairs and outside.

"Cody? Where are you going?" April asked as she followed.

"If Charlie and Meila aren't here, then I do not know where to search. We never arranged another meeting place. But I have an idea that there is one person that knows her whereabouts. If I have to finish beating it out of him, I will."

Cody threw the door of the building open to find two undercover police cars sitting in front of the building. He moved to the first and pulled open the door. Rodrigez poked his head out. Cody had no patience for talking to the man, so he pushed his head back into the car and slammed the door closed. He bolted his way over to the other car and opened the door. April and Agent Walker stood behind him.

"Where is Charlie?" he demanded.

Old Man Manning smiled. "I have no idea who you are talking about," he answered smugly.

"All right, I have a simpler question." Cody leaned in closer. "Where is your daughter?"

Old Man Manning snorted. "I don't have a daughter, only a memory of one who would do my every bidding."

Cody grabbed the man's shirt, wadding it up and pulling him down to meet Cody's eye level. "Where did you send them?"

Manning leaned closer. "To a place you and your friends will never be able to find. I sent her to a place where she will be forgotten."

Cody shoved the man back into the car and closed the door. He turned to April and Agent Walker. "There was a black car out front of the building before Manning came out. Did you see a license plate or anything that would make it easy to find?"

The pair thought a moment before they shook their heads.

Cody rubbed his face and started to walk away from the car. "We need to find them. April, I want you to get onto the security cameras around town and see if you can find anything. Agent Walker, round up the rest of the group. We are not going to stop until we find out what happened to them."

CHAPTER 47

Meila had fallen asleep. She knew that this compound was a long drive away. Charlie was lightly bumping into her to get her to wake up. "Hey, wake up. We are almost there, but I think we need to discuss something before we arrive."

Meila blinked, trying to waken herself the best that she could. She tried to stretch but was stopped by the cuffs that were around her wrists. Charlie waited until she looked back up at him before starting. "Please remember that I am doing this for your best interest, but I think that we need to go under assumed names. If we are seen as smart, then we can get in big trouble. Trying to escape will be a lot harder, so I need you to think of me as dumb."

Meila blinked. "Charlie, I can't think of you like that. I could never think of you like that."

"I know. It will be difficult, but it *will* make everything easier in the end. Also, you are to refer to me only as your brother. I will think of you strictly as my sister, nothing else."

Meila nodded. "Anything else that I need to know before going undercover?"

"Don't tell anyone anything that could give away your true backstory. It is easier to fight against lies than fighting the truth."

"Okay."

The brightly colored leaves disappeared as they drove through a gate, toward the compound. It was a big gray building, fenced in with concrete walls. Meila would examine the wall later, hoping that it may be a way to escape.

The building reached many levels into the sky. It was surrounded by green grass, except for the blacktop they drove on. Inmates were outside in their orange jumpsuits, a few with a white T-shirt on underneath. She noticed many of those that did not have the white sleeves on had marks on their arms.

She turned her attention back to the overpowering building. Each window looked as if it had been carved out. The whole building, she assumed, must be square. The corner they were driving to angled steeply into the building, creating some shade.

The car stopped, and she and Charlie were dragged away from the car. Her father's men turned around and were gone before Meila had gotten her feet under her. A gate closed behind them, probably one that could be easily shorted if she were given the correct tools and time to do so.

The guard behind her pushed her forward and into the building. There they changed into matching jumpsuits, mug shots were taken, and they had a number tattooed on their wrists. A red band was also burned into her arm, just above the elbow. Her entire arm throbbed from the pain of the branding. Meila had seen animals being branded and had never really thought about what pain they went through. Meila looked down at the red blistering band around her right arm. A small triangle sat on top of it. When she asked the guard what it meant, they just ignored her.

She was placed in a cell by herself, after learning that the driver of the car told them that she had some mental issues. She was fine with that. It allowed her time to think. It allowed her time to try and find a way out of this crazy place. She touched her arm where they had branded her. It was still tender, but she figured that it could have been worse.

Shouts came from outside, pulling her attention away from herself. She stood and moved to the window. It looked as if someone had tried to get over the wall but must have failed. She saw an orange blob out in the distance that was on the ground. Guards ran toward them. *What was on that fence that kept them from going over?* she wondered. She sat back down on her cot. Maybe Charlie could find out. She wasn't going to be much help if she were stuck inside her cell with no one to talk to.

* * * * *

Meila sat down next to Charlie. "Find anything?"

He took a bite of the sandwich, which they had been served. After chewing, he answered. "You heard the shouts yesterday?"

Meila nodded. She pushed her tray farther onto the table, resting her elbows where the tray had been. "I saw two orange blobs out my window, but that's it. Do you know what happened?"

Charlie shrugged. "I didn't hear anyone important talking about it, but I just assumed that someone was trying to escape."

Meila looked at her food. "Which means that escape is going to be even more complicated than I was planning." Meila scooted closer to him. "Any plan, yet?"

He looked over at her in astonishment. "We arrived here yesterday, and you are already ready to leave? Mei, a breakout plan takes time. I need to see the layout of the building, how many guards, weapons, what we have outside the fence. There is a lot that has to be done before we even think about escaping." Charlie took another bite from his sandwich.

Meila thought for a few minutes. If he needed that information, she could get some of it for him. She started to make a list of things that she needed to do. She needed to watch how many guards were on her floor and how often they changed. She had to figure out how far away she was from Charlie's cell and how to get there.

She lifted her head to the railed section of floor above them. A few guards paced on them. One door led out and in. Each guard had a gun. If she could get closer to them, she could probably get Charlie the amount of bullets each one had.

"Are you going to eat, or can I eat it for you?"

Meila pulled herself out of her thoughts and looked at her food. She picked up the apple and bit into it. "What about your act?" Meila asked, leaning closer.

"I will only do it when we are around others."

Meila gestured to the almost full cafeteria. Charlie just ignored her and picked up her sandwich and took a bite.

CHAPTER 48

Meila walked next to the wall, dragging her fingers along it. It was smooth, just as Meila had found from the very beginning. No grooves or juts that she could stick her fingers in and throw herself over. Meila sighed, frustrated. A whistle suddenly blew.

Meila moved toward the sound. She saw many of the other inmates running and then stopping behind one another, starting to form a line. Fast footsteps sounded from behind Meila and someone bumped into her. "Hey! Watch out!"

The man turned back to her. "Don't you know what is going on?"

Meila shook her head. He grabbed her arm and pulled her toward the line. Meila tried to pry her arm free, but the man's grip just intensified. "When your cell block is allowed to go outside, the guards whistle you in. That means your time outside is done. If you don't get in line, they put extra guards on you and move you floors. Trust me. They would move you to one of the top floors. I haven't heard anything good about the people that go that high up into the building."

The man put Meila in front of him in line. "They do this every time that your floor goes outside?"

The man nodded and then put a finger to his lips, telling her to be quiet. They were escorted inside and up to their cells. The man behind her smiled when she was pulled from the line and her cell was unlocked. She went into her cell and heard the lock click behind her. She sat down and stared at the white brick wall across from her.

CHAPTER 49

A few months later

Meila saw Charlie the minute that she walked into the lunchroom. Unlike the last few days, though, he didn't smile at her. Meila watched him as she waited in line to get her food. The man next to him looked familiar, but she couldn't place where she knew his face. She stepped up in line and retrieved her food and then moved to her normal table. "Charlie."

He looked up at her as she sat down. "Meila." He turned toward the man with the familiar face.

"This is my sister Meila." He turned back toward Meila. "This is JP Simmon. He was moved to my cell yesterday."

Meila nodded to the man. He pointed at her. "You were the new one that I pulled into line! I knew that I recognized you somewhere!"

Meila nodded and smiled. "Thank you for doing that."

JP shrugged. "It's no problem. I don't mind helping out the newbies that come in. I don't know why some people think that they will figure it out, but they never do."

Meila nodded.

"JP said that he has been here for a couple of months. He said that he knows the layout of the building. He was just about to explain it before you came in and so rudely interrupted."

Meila was shocked by what Charlie was saying to her, but what was even more surprising was his degrading tone that he did it in. JP's voice broke into her thoughts. "The first floor has security on it—guards rooms, main security office, really anything that the guards need to survive. The first floor also consists of medical rooms. Nurses and a doctor live on that floor. Everyone that comes in goes through the guards. If you are a new inmate, then you see the medical staff.

"The second floor is just a bunch of empty rooms. The floor wasn't being used when I arrived here. I heard they don't put anyone on that floor because it would be too easy to escape from. Third floor has the cafeteria and a few cells. The fourth floor still has the cafeteria, but only the guards."

"The guards eat in here?"

JP shook his head. "Naw, they eat on the first floor, but they patrol the cafeteria from behind a thick layer of floor to ceiling glass on the fourth floor."

Meila nodded. She looked up to find a few guards surveying the room. The glass was there, almost floor to ceiling. The only thing that wasn't glass, was the balcony they were walking on, and about a foot of white bricks that lined the bottom of the glass wall.

"The rest of the fourth floor is just cells. The fifth, sixth, and seven are also just cells. Floors eight and nine are interrogation floors. I haven't been up there, but I have heard that they question you harshly. Most inmates come back broken from it."

"Broken? What do you mean by broken?" Charlie asked.

JP shrugged. "I have never personally seen anyone come back from those floors, but I have heard stories that they all just come back quiet. They don't speak to hardly anyone, and they don't want to leave. After a few weeks, they usually disappear.

"Anyway, the rest of the building is a mystery to me. No one has ever been that high, except for a few of the guards, but they don't speak to any of us about what is there."

Meila nodded and turned back to her food, nibbling as she thought. She looked around the room. About forty people were in the room. That was two floors put together for lunch.

Meila's eyes moved up to where the guards watched over them. Only four guards, one guard for ten people. *The odds seem to be on my side*, Meila thought. *How come no one has had a successful escape?*

Meila ate the rest of her lunch in silence, listening to what the boys were saying but not participating unless they asked her specifically. She needed time to process this new information.

CHAPTER 50

Meila put a bite in her mouth. "What have you done since yesterday?" JP asked.

She swallowed and then spoke. "It was my cell blocks turn to go outside, but it was raining, so I just stood out in the rain and froze. Spring is here in full force, but the temperature still isn't rising"

Charlie pipped in. "At least you got to go outside. Our outside day got canceled due to some lunatic." Charlie hooked a thumb toward JP "He got into an argument with one of the guards, so the guard took away our blocks outside time as a punishment. Could be worse."

Meila smiled. Commotion started on the other side of the cafeteria. "What's happening now?"

Charlie stood, "I will go check it out." He moved toward the commotion and pushed through it.

"Does he ever stop?" JP questioned.

"Stop what?"

JP took a bite. "Being annoying, showing off, talking. Take your pick. The list is a lot longer than that."

Meila smiled. "He didn't used to be like that."

"What, annoying?"

Meila rolled her eyes. "No, that hasn't changed. He used to be kinder, act more his age."

JP took a drink of his juice. "What about you? What did you do before you were sentenced here?"

Meila thought for a moment. Charlie warned her that she needed to stick to the backstory they had created, but she figured that she could branch out a little bit. "I worked in the tax business. In my spare time, I learned how to build new things."

JP looked at her. "Then how did you get stuck in here? Did you not pay your taxes or something?" He laughed.

Meila offered a small smile. "I found myself in trouble, so I went to someone that I heard could help. Instead, this person sent me here. He wasn't as much help as many claimed that he would be."

"I'm sorry." Silence was there for a moment. "What new things did you build?"

Meila smiled, grateful that she could actually tell the truth on this one. "I have only ever successfully built one thing."

JP leaned in closer.

"It was a two-piece machine. The first one was a listening device. It looks very much like a smaller headphone. It could fit in your ear, but no one would be able to tell that you are wearing it unless they see you from the side. The other piece is just a little bit bigger. It looks like a small box with a speaker on it. The only way that it is turned on is through the headphone. The second piece picks up any-one's voice in the room. It becomes quite convenient, especially when you need to learn new information."

JP raised his eyebrows. "What information would you need to learn, hmm? Maybe a new tax form that is coming out?" JP laughed again.

Meila opened her mouth again, but thankfully, Charlie came in to rescue her. "Supposedly, an inmate punched another inmate. It is all sorted out now." He slid in beside JP. "Oh, by the way, Meila, JP said that he has a friend working on the outside trying to get him out. He offered to let us tag along. How does that sound?"

Meila's mouth dropped open. She had been trying to think of a way to get out of this place, but she given up hoping that it would happen so soon. She assumed that it would take months for her and

Charlie to escape. Besides, she did not anticipate anyone ever joining them.

"Do you have any details of a plan?"

He just waved his hand. "Not much of one, but once I do have one, you guys will be the first ones to know."

Meila smiled as the bell rang, signifying that lunch was over. She waved to the boys and took her leave, grateful that she had hope again.

CHAPTER 51

Somewhere north of Willowsville, Washington; early spring of 2011

Meila set her tray down by Charlie's. "We had this last week," she said.

"Well, unfortunately, we don't get much of a choice of what we eat," JP said from across the table.

Meila shot him a look. "So when are we getting out of here?"

JP lowered his voice. "I've got a guy working on it from the outside. We should be out of here in a couple of weeks."

"Good," Charlie grumbled. "I am ready to have my own room back. Sharing with you sucks."

"Well, sharing with you ain't that great either." JP glared at Charlie.

"Calm down. You two look like children fighting over a toy." Meila looked to Charlie. "If JP has a man working on it on the outside, then we will be out of here in no time. Until then, we need to figure out how to get the plans."

Charlie sighed, folding his arms. "Fine, you're right anyway, Meila. Will work on getting the plans. Any ideas how?"

JP looked up at the security camera that kept watch over the cafeteria. "I have one, but are you sure that it is safe to talk in here? I mean, this isn't the first jail that I have been to. This one is more secure than I regularly work with."

"Are you saying that you are scared? Dude, this is nothing compared to our last mission." Charlie went off into a long one-sided conversation about their last handful of missions.

JP leaned closer to Meila and whispered, "Is he always like this? Why can't we just leave him behind again?"

Meila shook her head. If they were going to get out of here, she knew that she would need her brother's help, regardless of how dumb he acted. He was the brawn in the group. "What is the actual plan," Meila questioned.

"I have most of it made up in my mind, but until my outside man can get back to me, I can't give you final details." JP grimaced.

"Fine. What do you have planned?" Meila was getting impatient. JP had been telling her and Charlie for the last few months that he was going to get them out of here. This is all they ever heard from him.

Charlie had finally noticed their whisperings and leaned in. "What are you saying that is so secretive, or is this something that a brother shouldn't hear?"

Meila rolled her eyes. She looked away from her brother and JP. She examined the room, calculating the amount of guards, their ammunition, and what inmates were there. JP recaptured her attention again. "Here's what is going to happen: when I get word from my outside man, that's when everything goes down."

JP turned to Charlie. "You'll need to take down as many guards as possible, then I'll need you to get me downstairs."

"Downstairs?" the other two said in unison.

"We're going to have to take the director's car out of here. He is the only one that gets in and out of this building without any extra security. We will meet up on the second floor to draw less attention to ourselves. Very few prisoners are held on that floor anyway. I am not quite sure what to do once we get there, but it is a start."

"What about the director's car? Won't it be searched before leaving?"

JP shook his head. "Guards just follow him until his car is at the end of the encampment, but they stop at the gate. After that, we are free to go."

"This sounds way too simple. Besides, what will I be doing?" Meila posed.

JP turned fully toward her. "Your part, my dear, is very important. I need to start shorting out all of the cameras."

Meila raised her brow in confusion. "I ask for my part, and you go back to talking about you."

JP held up a hand "You seem more familiar with these types of circuits and wires. I will need you to tell me how to change them *before* the fighting happens. If the guards in the main room get a hold of what we are doing before we even start, the whole place will go on lockdown."

"Why can't I just do all of the wiring? I have already tampered with it to make the guards believe I am not who I say I am," Meila challenged.

JP didn't look too happy at her suggestion. "You asked for my help to get you out of this old tin bucket. You don't double-cross me. You are going to have to do it my way, or I'll just leave you here to rust."

Meila looked at her brother; he just shrugged. "We won't double-cross you, but you better not leave us behind either."

JP looked at her longingly. "That's not part of the plan, and my plans"—he hooked a thumb toward himself—"*always* work."

* * * * *

Meila was escorted back to her lonely cell. She would rather have it that way. It allowed her to think of this plan. The female guard locked the door behind her. *That was new.* Meila looked at it in surprise. Was something going down that she didn't know about?

She walked back to the door, looking through the small window it had. She turned her head, looking both ways out of the door. No one. Meila took her chances; she pushed on the door. Unfortunately, it was locked. She walked to her barred window and looked down on the grounds. Nothing out of the ordinary was happening.

Meila turned around and slid down against the wall. Closing her eyes, she let out a frustrated sigh. JP's plan has to work. If not, she was going to kill him.

* * * * *

A week later

Meila was pushed out of her room. "Room inspection," the angry officer said.

"No. This is unfair." Meila shook her head in disbelief. "This is the third room inspection that I have had in two days. A male and female yesterday," *a female who looked very familiar,* "and then you today." Meila followed the guard back into her cell. "You watch me day and night. I should have my privacy at this time of the day. It is my right—"

Her complaint was cut short by a slap across the face. "Your rights were stripped from you the moment you stepped onto this mountain. Your name no longer exists outside of this murky hole. Do you understand?" The police officer moved his hand to where his Taser sat.

Meila grudgingly nodded.

"Good, get out of my way and let me do my job." He slapped handcuffs on in front of her and then pushed her toward the other officers.

Meila moved out into the hallway and sat with the other police officers. After about twenty minutes of inspection, the police officer finally came out.

"What is it you do in that cell?" the officer demanded.

"Even if my rights have been pulled away from me, I can still keep my thoughts to myself."

The officer moved forward and grabbed the front of her jumpsuit, pulling her right up to his nose. "I found that the camera had been blanking out but only in your cell, yet the wires haven't been tampered with. Then there is this." He held something up to the side of them.

Meila had to crank her neck to the side to see what he was holding. It looked like the lockpick Meila had once owned before she was in jail, except her kit didn't have blood on it.

"We need to move this one to a more secure vault. She harmed the prisoner in section 201."

The officers on either side went to grab her. Meila knew that she needed to act fast if she was going to ever see that escape plan come into play. With her cuffed hands, she got a hold of the angry officer's pistol. She pulled it loose and shot both of the officers to the side of her. She went to shoot at the angry one, but he was quicker. He had pulled his laser from his belt and had her on the ground before she could fully turn toward him. She felt pain and fell to the ground, blacking out on the way down.

* * * * *

Meila woke up in a strange room, in a strange bed. She lifted her head, trying to get a better look around the room. Pain split through her head when she tried to lift it. She laid it back down. She tried to move her hand to her head, but found it restricted. She turned her head to look down, lifting her hand enough to see it. It was handcuffed to the table. She turned to her other side, finding the same result there.

Ugh. Meila turned her attention back to the room itself. It was small, with no window, except for the one on the door, but she was too far away to see anything useful. As far as she could tell, there weren't any other instruments in the room, only the bed.

She turned her gaze to the ceiling. Only a dome video camera. Harder to disable than most of the others used here in the jail, but if she could get the right things, it would easily be doable.

The door opened to her new cell. Meila saw two figures walk in and up to her table. "Good," the first man said. "Inspector, she's awake."

Another sound of footsteps sounded from out in the hallway. "Good. Very good," a new voice came into the room. The voice came from beyond her head. It was heavily accented, though Meila couldn't say from where, nor could she crank her head far enough to see who it was.

The first two men scooted back, letting the new one farther into the small cell. "Inmate 6657, do you know who I am?" the strange voice said.

Meila shook her head slightly but then stopped. The pain was coming back.

"Still in pain, are you?"

"Yes." Meila briefly closed her eyes. When she opened them again, one of the men had left. "May I ask what you better yet, what am I doing in this cell?"

The man who first came into the room spoke. "The officer who Tasered you let his Taser run too long. Due to his stupidity, you have been knocked out for six hours."

Meila processed this new information in her head. She had never been up against a Taser before. Yet, she had never heard of anyone being knocked out because of one.

"There is something here that you are not telling me. Tasers don't knock people out for that long."

The inspector sighed and looked back to the other officer. "You are right, 6657. But we cannot discuss this in front of you. What we need from you is some information."

Meila looked in between the two. "What about a trade. I give you information. You unlock me and get me out of this cell."

The inspector looked at her for a moment. Meila could tell that he was calculating something. "Fine, but information first," The inspector agreed.

"I'll give you what I can but no promises."

"Then no promises on our end either."

Meila gave the inspector a cold look.

"I want to know why you did what you did."

Meila closed her eyes. She had done a lot in her lifetime. Was he asking about what she did to get into this jail, or was he asking about the move and Tasering that just happened? Meila opened her eyes and saw both of the men just staring at her. "I don't know exactly what you want to know. You are going to have to be more specific."

"I am asking about the incident that just happened today."

"It was just an inspection that happened today, except this is the third one I have had in two days. My block only gets one inspection a week, due to the lack of staff. It was a male who checked it first, and then a female came. Both of them came yesterday, though. Then today, I had another inspection done by a male."

The officer pulled out a notepad and started taking notes. The scratching of the pencil helped Meila think this through.

"It was not a regular time for the inspection to come, but whatever. I know what happens if I don't obey, so I sat in the hall and waited for him to finish." Meila paused, not sure how to get through this next part.

The inspector nodded, trying to get her to continue.

"He accused me of having something in my cell, but I had never seen that exact tool before. It was covered in blood." The image came to her mind. She pushed it back. When these two left, she would stew over it some more. "I then pulled his gun out and shot at both of the other officers. I remember falling to the ground, but it's pretty foggy after that."

"Do you recognize this?" The man held up a small object.

Meila craned her neck so that she could see it better. "That is the object that the guard accused me of having. I have not seen it before he'd shown it to me."

The investigator nodded his head. He held up a picture. "Do you recognize this man?"

Meila looked at the picture and examined the man. He had blonde hair, similar to Charlie's, but it was not the exact same. His face was turned to the side, a purple lump forming on the side of his head.

Meila shook her head.

After a few more seconds of scratching, the officer put the notebook away. "Thank you for your time. I will have someone come in and release you. You will be taken back to the cell block that you originally came from."

Meila nodded, and both men left the cell. True to their word, a few officers came in and returned her to the sixth floor, where she belonged.

It was night before she had been returned. The lights had been out in her cell for over an hour. She could hear the security camera move as she paced. *I know that I didn't have that tool yesterday in my room.* She knew she would have to wait until it was daytime before she could check some other places.

She pulled the sleeve up on her jumpsuit and could faintly see what was there. Not like she really needed to look anyway. Each jail had their own way of marking a prisoner or number. That's how they could tell the difference between worker and inmate. She sighed. She had the mark of a prisoner. Escape seemed harder and harder each day.

* * * * *

Meila was allowed to go early to lunch. She sat at the normal table and waited eagerly as Charlie and his inmate walked in together. Surprise registered on both of their faces. JP quickly walked over to her after getting his food. "Where have you been? My man got word to me about two days ago."

That was news to Meila. They told her that she would have only been out for about six hours. She had seen both of the boys at breakfast the day before.

Her brother joined them then. "Long time no see, sis," he commented as he moved in to sit next to her.

"Yeah, you too, Charlie." She shook her head, then turned back to JP. "What did your man say?"

"Not much. But not much needed to be said." JP took a sip of water then continued. "He can get us out tomorrow, but we have to have everything ready on our part."

"What else do we need to do?" Charlie asked. "I didn't think much needed to be done until we could actually leave."

"I have been working on the security cameras. I can't get them to come down. I tried but heard that it resulted in a prisoner almost dying."

Meila perked up. "That was you?"

JP looked at her warily. "What do you mean 'that was me'?"

Meila leaned closer, pulling Charlie closer too. "An officer came to my room yesterday for a surprise inspection. He said that my room had been going black on their screens upstairs. Were you hacking into the system yesterday?"

JP quickly shook his head. "It couldn't have been me. After breakfast, we were outside for the rest of the day, except for meals. Speaking of, where have you been for meals?"

"I told you, surprise inspection, then I was on lockdown. They think that I killed a man."

Charlie touched her shoulder with one of his massive hands. "Did you?"

Meila was startled by this accusation. "Kill a man? No way!"

"That explains the extra guards," JP reinserted himself back into the conversation.

Meila looked around, noticing for the first time that there were, in fact, two extra guards in the cafeteria. "What else happened," Charlie nudged her.

Meila looked down at her partially eaten meal. "I blacked out. I woke up later to find myself in a windowless room. Some men came in later to talk to me. After that was finished, I was moved back to my cell. The only light of day that I saw was this morning."

JP grimaced. He opened his mouth, but Charlie spoke first. "So you don't really have any idea how long you were gone?"

Meila shook her head. "The men that came in and spoke with me told me roughly six hours. Why? How long have I been gone?"

The two boys made eye contact, shock apparent on both faces. Meila looked in between the two of them. JP finally answered, "Three days."

Three days. "What happened while I was gone?" Meila asked.

"I saw my man, like I said earlier. He can get us out tomorrow. Just make sure that you don't do something stupid in between this time." He glared at Meila.

"Most of that wasn't my doing. Lay off me," Meila said sharply.

Charlie joined in. For the first time, he actually sounded like himself. "JP, what time are we meeting up with your outside man, and what do we need to do before we secure our freedom?"

JP's expression changed and moved to Charlie. "I've most of the cameras running at my will. They will change what needs to be done at my command. The director will drive in at roughly two thirteen tomorrow afternoon."

Meila changed her gaze to the clock on the wall. *I have roughly twenty-six hours left in this hole*, she thought.

"What about once we get out of here. Do we have an escape car, helicopter maybe?" That was Charlie's voice.

"My man said that he could get a car down to the main gate. We just have to get down there." JP paused for a moment, counting something on his fingers. Then he turned to Meila. "What are we looking at weaponry wise?"

Meila took a quick scan of the room, then looked up at the ceiling and walls of windows before them. She then closed her eyes, visualizing what she knew about the rest of the building. "If we can get our hands on a couple of guns, that would definitely be better. I say that we will run into thirty to forty guards, not to mention the reinforcements that will come when the alarm goes off."

JP swallowed a bite. "No alarms should go off. I've got enough rigged that I could control both the cameras and alarms. It's just the guards that will be our concern."

"No concern for me." Charlie popped his knuckles, making his jumpsuit once again look too small on his muscular frame.

Meila looked in between the two of them. "Good, then we will be ready for tomorrow."

* * * * *

Meila heard her door click. *Time to go.* A smile appeared on her face. She climbed out of her bed and walked to her cell door. She sat there and listened for footsteps. Nothing. Good. She pushed against her door. It moved! She was really getting out of here! A pit fell in her stomach. Her gut told her something was not right, but Meila pushed it out of her thoughts, telling herself she was nervous.

She looked out again but saw no one. The regular lights that had been on all of the security cameras now were firm, not blinking. She walked swiftly down the hall toward the main hallway. She knew where to go from here. The cafeteria was down three flights of stairs and around the corner.

She quietly slid up against the wall, then peeked around it. No guard. She walked as silently as she could towards the cafeteria, stopping again and checking before entering. She heard the noises of the cooks shuffling around in the kitchen, getting prepared for dinner.

Silence, just like it needed to be. Then all of a sudden, she heard a banging. It was coming from in front of her, across the cafeteria. She quickly moved back through the door she had just come through, pulling it closed behind her, just enough to cover herself. She then moved so she could see through the crack in the door.

Meila held her breath. Had the boys gotten into trouble? They hadn't made a sign or a signal to tell the other if there was an issue *this* early. All of the signs and signals came in after they met up.

She shook her head. No trouble should have come to them yet. JP said that he had watched the guards' routine enough to know what to expect.

It was his frame that filled the doorway, leading into the cafeteria from the other side of the jail. Meila quickly slid from her hiding place and checked that no one had seen her before reentering the cafeteria. Charlie walked in a step behind JP. She heard the complaint as they got closer. "We were *supposed* to be escaping quietly," JP muttered, then turned to Meila as she arrived at her brother's side. "Your brother is an idiot. He practically just announced to all of the guards that we would be escaping today."

Meila gave her brother a look of pity. She felt bad that he had to room with this. JP had rarely said anything nice to her brother.

Hopefully, after today, they wouldn't be seeing much of JP anymore. Once they escaped, he could go his way, and they could go theirs. *When did Charlie ever not fight back?*

Meila cleared her head. They had to escape first, and that escape was happening now. "Lead the way, JP." Meila could feel excitement growing in her. She had been looking forward to this day since she arrived here, but something else was growing in there too. *Regret? Disappointment? Anxiety?*

She paused her thoughts long enough to realize that JP looked embarrassed for the first time. Her apprehension came instantly alive. "What happened?"

JP sighed. "Change of plans. I watched all morning for the director's car to come in, but it didn't. Thankfully, a delivery truck has backed up next to our exit. Unfortunately, I have no idea when it will be leaving. But it is our only hope of getting out of here, so I say we give it a shot."

Charlie nodded his agreement. "I can't be cooped up here much longer."

Meila agreed with him on that.

"Okay. Follow me then."

JP led them through many doors and down a few flights of stairs, all of which Meila had never seen. Once Meila felt as if she was certainly lost, JP stopped them at a door and pulled out a pick. He leaned against the door and pushed the pick into the lock. He made quick work of it. They were barreled in a room less than thirty seconds later.

JP quietly shut the door behind them. Meila surveyed the room—a cell, much like hers, except this one had four beds instead of one. It too had a camera, but its light had gone out. Charlie moved to the window at the edge of the room. He looked back over his shoulder. "You sure this will work?"

Will what work? Meila shot JP a look; his gaze was strictly on Charlie.

"Yes, but we will wait until we are one hundred percent ready. If not, it will alert the guards too early."

JP moved Meila to one side, instructing her to pull all of the sheets off of the beds. JP then collected them and tied them all together. "I will lower both of you down and then I'll climb down." he explained to them as he finished up the last couple of knots. He then smiled and looked at Meila. "Ready?"

She tried to form a smile but couldn't. JP turned to see Charlie nod his head. Charlie started to press against the bars, slowly bending the metal that she thought was impossible to move. She noticed that it painstakingly started to wilt to one side but only after a few minutes of pushing.

Meila felt a hand on her arm and jumped. JP took a step back. "Sorry. I didn't mean to startle you. You just seem upset. Is something wrong?"

Meila shook her head. She didn't want to share all of her secrets with JP. He didn't need to hear what she was thinking. "Okay, fine. Don't tell me. Here. Put it around your waist and tie a knot so you can be lowered down."

Meila took the tied sheets and added another knot. JP checked it and then nodded satisfied. He pushed her toward the window and then put a hand on Charlie's shoulder. "That will be big enough. Now get ready to move fast. Once the alarm sounds, we might have three minutes."

Charlie took the end of the bedsheets and tied one end to the metal bars. *When had he learned to tie that knot?* Meila asked herself perplexed.

He then covered his fist and checked with both of them before putting a big hole through the window. Meila stepped up, knowing her part. She slid out of the window. The maneuver down was faster than she thought it would be. She hit the ground and pulled the makeshift rope off of her. It was quickly pulled back up.

Meila moved to the truck, checking her surroundings as she did so. *No guards.* The handful of cameras that she could see had no light, saying they weren't going. Meila had reached the truck and peeked over the open driver's side window. Empty.

She pulled open the door and checked the back. Also empty. A beeping came from the dash. The keys had been left in the engine. This might be easier than she thought.

Bang, bang!

Nope! She went to open the truck door but instead looked in the side mirror. The rope was still in the air but nothing else. She checked the other mirror, seeing JP run up along that side of the truck. "Go, go, go!" he demanded as he hopped in.

"Where's Charlie!"

"He got hit by the fire. Couldn't save him. He wants you to get out of here and be safe. He put your protection in my hands. Now drive."

Meila shook her head. "Not without him. You promised."

JP muttered something under his breath and then reached for the keys. He turned them and climbed over by her. Meila quickly got out and ran to the back of the truck. Charlie was lying there, blood pooled around him, ghostly white. She knelt down, not caring about the stain that was surely going to be left there. She wrapped her arms around his cold, damp body.

She heard the engine get revved up and then move farther away. Guards came out of every visible exit with their weapons raised. She raised her eyes to the sky, seeing the sun shining brightly behind the building.

A fall from the second floor, along with the gunshots, must have killed Charlie. Meila should have followed her gut. She shouldn't have worked with JP. He was dangerous; he had gotten Charlie killed.

CHAPTER 52

Nine months later

Life was hard without Charlie. Nine months. Nine miserable, hard months. Some part of her still carried hope that Charlie had escaped earlier and was out there trying to find a way to free her. The hope was quickly squashed when Meila realized the situation she was in. No one knew where she was, and no one really cared.

Everyone must have moved on with their lives, Meila thought to herself. *Me?*

Meila figured she would just end up staying in the compound until the guards got tired of her. She did not know very many people who left this place alive. There was no hope of ever leaving this place. It was empty, full of white walls and smashed hopes and dreams. Just like her.

* * * * *

Meila walked into the cafeteria. It was already buzzing with many people. A few inmates walked in behind her and started speaking in lower tones. "Escape isn't impossible. A man has already done it."

"But, Joey, that was months ago! They have tightened security. I have already tried the wall, but instead of making it over, I ended

251

up on lockdown. I don't think that getting out of here is possible. We have thought of everything that we can."

Meila turned around to see the three people with their heads tucked down. "Not to mention that the guards have doubled along with the weapons that they carry," Meila said.

The three of them looked up at her. The tall man in the middle spoke. "How did you know?"

She gestured to those around the room. "It was quite easy. Also, another good thing to point out. Don't make it look like you are trying to escape. They put extra guards on those that do."

She turned back around and picked up a tray. She got her food and then sat down in her regular spot. A few minutes later, the three inmates standing behind her spread out their trays, joining her. "Can I help you with something, or did you not hear that I eat alone?" She preferred to eat alone ever since Charlie had left her. She had, in fact, gotten into many fights over this particular table and had won.

A woman sat across from her. "We want your help. We want out of this place, and we heard that you almost accomplished this. How did you do it?"

Meila put a bite into her mouth, not wishing to speak of this right now. She had been having such a good day! Why ruin it? "My escape resulted in the death of someone that I care about very much. I have never found that killing people is a way out."

The two guys that sat on both sides of the table, shared a look. "We know JP. He was my cellmate before he was transferred to a different one. Most of his parts are still in my cell. He hid them pretty well in the ceiling. Unfortunately, we can't get to them. The guards are always coming in and checking it out, and don't forget about the security camera too."

Meila nodded. She could easily short out the camera if she could get there. "What floor are you guys on?"

The tall man spoke again. "I'm on the fourth."

Meila had been on that floor before. She started to calculate how many guards and cameras were on that floor.

The other man spoke. "I was on the second, but they just moved me to the fourth also."

Meila looked at the girl.

"I am on the sixth floor, just a couple of doors down from you, actually."

Meila nodded. She knew that this woman looked familiar. "And what have you done to get yourself stuck in this place?" Meila asked.

She took another few bites before the tall man across the table spoke. "I stole a car and drove it up here. I was told to meet a few people by the gate, but only a delivery truck came out."

Meila looked up at him. *A delivery truck?* Meila thought for a moment. *Was this JP's outside man?*

The man next to her spoke. "I have been put in many jails, but I escaped most of them. As for the one that I didn't have a set escape plan, well, let's just say that I was lucky that I got out alive." The man creepily smiled. Meila would have to keep any eye on him before she agreed to do anything with this team.

"I was incorrectly told I committed a crime I didn't commit. I was being transported to the courtroom when someone took a wrong turn, and I found myself being shoved into a cell here," the woman next to her explained. "How about you? What are you doing here?"

Meila swallowed and then spoke. "My father was angry with me. This is where he sent me," she answered. That wasn't too far from the truth, right?

The woman smiled at her. "We have another two in the group, but we only see them at lunch."

Meila nodded her understanding. "You were speaking of escaping before I interrupted you." *Plus, you were speaking of JP*, Meila thought.

The tall man nodded. "Yes. We have bits and pieces planned out, but we cannot form a whole plan. We heard there is someone that almost made it out of here and to ask her. After some asking around, we found that person was you."

Meila acknowledged that and asked how they were going to escape. The woman spoke. "Well, we have tried to go over the wall when we are allowed to go outside, but the guards catch up too quickly."

"What is on the top of that wall?" She had meant to ask JP, but she had been too busy trying to figure out how his plan could go wrong that she forgot.

"Nothing of importance. A couple of dead birds, bugs. But once you are outside the wall, they have sensors all through the forest. That is where you really need to be careful," the tall man answered.

"What kind of sensors?"

The man next to her took over filling her in. "All kinds. They have heat, infrared, motion. They have a few more classified ones that I didn't get to read about. But these sensors will set off knock-out gas. Most which will kill anyone but the guards."

Meila was shocked at this man's knowledge. She assumed that she would have to completely make up this plan, but they had it mostly laid out in front of her. It was as though someone dumped out a puzzle in front of her and asked her to put the pieces together. This was going to be easy. "Why wouldn't it affect the guards?"

The man next to her pointed at the branding done to him. It was the same as hers. They are the same as anyone's in this compound. "They have a different marking than us. The chemicals that they burn onto our arms are easier to detect, especially between all of those sensors they have."

Meila nodded. "So how do we bypass that?" she asked.

The tall man jumped back in. "We aren't sure. That is why we started to ask around, see if anyone has escaped or tried to."

"So you are asking for me to help you escape?" She looked in between the three of them. All of them nodded. "And you're not asking for anything in return?" Meila asked.

"If anything, you would be saving our lives. There are no laws this high up. We all came here without even being put on trial. We know that after a while, they just get rid of us. If you could help us escape, we can all get back to our normal lives. Most of us would still be indebted to you once we got out."

Meila sucked in a breath. She had never done a plan without Charlie, at least not a successful one. She finally nodded. If she was going to really do this and help everyone escape, then she needed to clear her head and let it get to work.

* * * * *

Meila was walking back from the strange conversation between herself and the two new recruits that they had found, Daren and Kyle.

She had met the rest of the group yesterday at lunch, although it had been a few weeks since she had first seen the group work together.

She had found that the man who had sat next to her the first day was Bart. He was great with anything that had to do with electricity.

Joey was extremely tall. He was darker skinned and was very strong. She would guess that he and Cody were very much alike, except that she actually liked being around Joey. He was much kinder than Cody had ever been to her.

Bianca was next. She was shorter than Meila's own five-eight, but she too was strong, although she wasn't really strong in the physical sense. Meila had seen more of Bianca because they were on the same floor. She too was kind.

She had met Daren just yesterday but was glad that she did. He was covered in tattoos, but she found very quickly not to fear him. He was always making a joke about something or somebody. She didn't really know what he offered the group, but she would help him escape just the same.

Kyle was just here too. He couldn't have been there for more than a month. He watched everyone carefully, fear dominating his face. He was still jumpy and was eager to escape.

Daren had made jokes all through lunch about the guards, keeping everyone laughing and happy. Even in the circumstances the group had found themselves in. She shook her head at Daren's strange attitude toward everyday life. She sometimes envied an easier life.

Voices pulled Meila from her thoughts. Two guards down the hall were speaking but had not realized that she was there yet. She ducked into the nearest open door and listened as they moved closer.

"That's what happened? A man really got away?"

The second voice scoffed. "Barely. That's why security has been tightened."

"How long ago did this happen?" the first voice asked as they passed.

"Probably about a year ago. Security has really relaxed since that escape, but give it another month and we will be back to running our normal staff."

The feet stopped moving.

"Wait, you guys didn't catch him on the mountain? What good is the use of the mountain and the sensors we have laid out in the forest if we can't use them?"

The other guard stayed quiet for a moment.

"An inmate would be crazy to try and escape from here. We have the most advanced technology that is used in any compound or prison. Not to mention that the closest town to this place is a good few hours' drive or a few days of running. We have plenty of time to catch people on the way down."

"Then why didn't you catch the one that escaped?" the curious voice asked.

Meila poked her head out of the door to see the two men face away from her, but one of them obviously seemed upset.

"We couldn't trace him because he stuck to the roads. The roads do not have any sensors on them. In fact, they don't have anything close to it right now, but that will change before summer rolls around here in a few more months. Once security has lifted here, then we are having more sensors placed near the road to keep the inmates from getting any ideas."

The second guard nodded, and they continued their way down the hallway. Meila listened until she couldn't even hear their footsteps before leaving the small closet that she had concealed herself in. She moved toward her awaiting empty cell. She had much to tell the others.

* * * * *

Meila looked around the group, receiving many different looks from the faces of her new friends, anything from surprised and astounded to nervousness.

"That is really what they said?" Joey asked, surprised.

Meila nodded. "Word for word. I know we wanted to escape in a few months, but if we could ready in the next few weeks, I believe we could have better success. If we wait too long, the number of guards is going to go increase. And we need to get out before the new sensors are put throughout the forest."

Daren nodded his head, agreeing with her.

"So what else do we need to figure out before we escape?" Meila questioned, looking at the faces waiting for a response.

Bart broke the silence and put his hands in his lap. "I was able to get up and see the things that JP left. I am not entirely sure what you may need, but I brought you a few maps that I believe could be helpful. I couldn't bring them to lunch with me, but we had time outside yesterday. I have placed them under one of the tables outside. The table points toward the main powerline into this place."

"I'll try and get them this afternoon when we go out," Meila answered.

Bart nodded and then continued, "I haven't had a chance to play with any of the wires quite yet, so I haven't been able to tamper with any of the cameras in any of our rooms and hallways, but I think that given another week, I should be able to get up there."

The guards on the balcony above shifted abnormally, and one moved toward the door out to the hallway.

"I've got a place that we should be able to hide, but I need to make sure that someone gets a guard's key."

A guard entered the cafeteria. Meila looked to Joey who turned toward Daren and Kyle.

"Can you find out what is going on without causing too much of a scene?"

The two nodded and stood, moving toward the guard.

Meila turned back to Joey. "What about the wall?"

Bianca caught her attention and spoke. "The wall on our side is flat, but due to so many recent modifications, the other side of the wall creates a slope. There is a little bit of a gap to get to the slope of the wall. It might be a few feet that we have to drop. I did notice a long cord that is connected down to the outside of the wall. I believe it is the main power source. If we can get to it, it could make our escape smoother."

Meila nodded.

"To get over the wall shouldn't be too difficult. I can lift anyone over." Joey declared.

Meila agreed. "Is that everything?"

"Besides the maps that I left you outside, I do not think that we can plan anything else right now." Bart summed up.

The guards blew their whistles, signaling that lunch had ended early. Meila stood and made her way toward her cell.

* * * * *

Meila looked at the maps again. She looked at the road leading out of here. She put her head back against the white brick wall. She had been studying these maps for almost three weeks. She knew that the best way out of here was to follow the road, but it was such a long and drawn-out way. It was safe, though. If she was going to get everyone out safely, she would have to do so the smartest way.

She closed her eyes and hit her head against the brick wall, bringing pain to the back of her head. A beeping sound came from above her. Bart had told her that he could easily take over the guards' cameras for about an hour a day without them getting overly suspicious. He allowed her the same hour every day to study the maps. When he was about to switch the camera, he would send a small warning before doing so.

She slid the papers into the sheets of her bed, knowing that it was one of the safest places in her room.

She laid down on her bed, knowing that it was the position that Bart had asked her to do so that it seemed that she hadn't moved in some time. She watched as the camera's light went from blinking to solid.

She sighed, ready to get out of this way of life.

* * * * *

She heard her door click and watched it swing open. She looked up, but no one was there. She stood and cautiously walked to the door. She then heard a voice call that lunch was ready. Meila walked down to Bianca's cell door and waited for hers to be unlocked too. She heard a click and then Bianca's voice. "Are you ready to do this, Meila?"

She smiled at her new friend. "I'm not sure what we are doing yet but sure!"

She and Bianca walked down the three flights of stairs and down to the cafeteria. The boys were already eating their food at Meila's normal table. Once they had grabbed their lunches, they joined them and joined in on the conversation. "Have you learned anything new that could help us escape?" Joey was asking the girls.

Both of them just shook their heads, but Meila was the first to speak. "I need the gear that JP had."

Bart nodded. "We got up there yesterday after hours, but we couldn't tell what to look for. It would help to know what you need."

Meila thought for a moment and then informed him that she needed a handful of the tools that he had along with a few other odds and ends. "I have some friends that would probably help us if they knew how to, but I am not sure how to get word to them."

Meila thought back to JP and his having a few people that were on the outside. She assumed that none of these guys had that same luxury. Most of them were put here by mistake.

Joey took back over the discussion. "We have everything planned on how to get out, thanks to Meila. Now it can hopefully happen."

"Yes, I have thought over what you told me about the plan, and it will work great, but what about the sensors? Have we found a way that may prevent them from stopping us?"

Bart jumped back in. "Not yet, but we aren't about to give up."

Meila nodded. She looked across all the faces at the table. All were in very deep thought, except for one. Daren had put a straw in his milk and was blowing into it. It was creating bubbles that were soon going over the side of the plastic carton.

Meila stared at it for a little bit longer before a thought came to her. Her eyes widened as she went through the possibility that it may work. A slow smile spread across her face before she announced that she may have found their way back home

CHAPTER 53

"Mail!" the officer yelled down the hall. Meila heard her door unlock and be pulled open. She had been surprised that they even received mail at this place, but she found that it was mostly mail that others didn't want.

The mail was never addressed to anyone at the compound, but she wondered if the team knew where she was at, that she would receive mail. She had four envelopes. The first two had been credit card ads; the third consisted of coupons to a store that was going out of business. The fourth one was unlike the others she had retrieved; it was not addressed to a place that she recognized.

Ever since they had started giving out the mail, just after JP left, she had laid out a map in her mind. She had known where each one of her letters had come from and where it had gone. This one was entirely different. It was addressed to someone named Angie Harper Lee. She couldn't place where it was going, and there was no return address.

She flipped it over and put her finger under the seal. She checked the window to her door before she continued. She broke open the top and then started to pull out the letter, when something heavy dropped inside.

The letter had not been bulky when she first got it, but now, she could tell that there was something in it. The letter was handwritten in cursive. She hoped that it brought her some type of information.

To whom it may concern,

A young woman was wrongfully accused of what someone else did and is now facing the consequences. Angie Harper Lee and her team have asked permission to take over the information on the case and hopefully be successful.

We will not give up on her. Please see that she receives the few wires that have been placed in here.

Meila put her hand in the envelope and pulled out a few familiar wires. She felt them in between her fingers for a little bit before she recognized them. They were parts to her ear piece that she had used to overhear conversations going on in the office. These wires would help her make the side of her gadget that you spoke into. If she made it correctly, she would be able to say something to her team. They wouldn't be able to say anything back to her, but this was a start.

She turned the envelope over, shaking it delicately, but nothing else was in there. Meila leaned back against the wall. She rubbed the wires between her fingers, knowing she would easily be able to find the rest of the needed parts around the compound.

She looked back at the short note. Angie Harper Lee! Of course! That was April's alias! Meila picked up the note, grateful that the team still believed in her. She had thought about giving up, but now she knew that she couldn't. Her family would never forget about her.

CHAPTER 54

Meila stared outside her cell window on the sixth floor. A few weeks earlier, she had retrieved all the supplies needed to finish recreating her talking device. She only hoped that it was working and her team was listening on the other side. She tucked it into the white sleeve under her jumpsuit and walked back to her cell door.

Time seemed to pass faster, especially now that her mind could be filled with a plan and she felt a shimmer of hope. Meila had given up trying to figure out which day of the week it was. Everyday felt the same here in the compound. She was excited to see what had changed outside of the concrete walls, but tried not put all of her hope into this idea. She had just met the whole group a little bit over a month ago, and no solid plan was in place quite yet. But she was getting closer.

About a week and a half ago, they had decided on a signal that the guards wouldn't be suspicious about. Kyle had suggested that it be outside so that it would be easy to see. Meila had agreed with him and decided that it would be on her favorite table that Bart had put the maps under. It was easy to see from her window and from Bart and Joey's too. Kyle and Daren were the only two that would have to search to see the sign. Thankfully, Bart suggested that they help contribute to the signal so they knew when the escape would happen.

Daren and Kyle's unit had gone outside this morning during their allotted time. Daren and Kyle had placed all of the remaining snow on the table that they could find. The weather had been colder up here in the mountain, snow still covering some of the yellow grass. When Joey and Bart had gone out this afternoon, they had spread it out, showing Meila that everything was ready. Tonight was the night.

Unlike the last failed escape, Meila didn't feel nervous or anxious about getting out. She was more worried that something might happen like it did last time. She knew this time, though, that she would just carry on. This team had made her vow to do so.

They had seen each other at lunch just the day before, and all swore that they would continue on if something were to happen to one of them, especially Meila. They knew that the guards wouldn't let her live through another failed escape. She had been under higher security since she, JP, and Charlie had attempted to leave. If this plan did not work, she would be a goner for good.

Just like last time, the door to her jail cell clicked and swung open. The lights on the security cameras had gone from blinking to solid. Meila checked the hall before entering and then moved to Bianca's cell. Her door was already open, but she was looking out the window. "We aren't going to get too far if Kyle doesn't light up the distraction. You said that it was a vital part of the plan." Bianca said, keeping her gaze on the darkening sky.

"I know, but we need to get moving so that when our cell doors go on lockdown with the alarms, we can get out."

She nodded and moved with Meila. They checked the corner and the stairs before quickly and quietly making their way down to the meeting spot. They had decided the stairs on the fourth floor was a good meeting spot. Guards only came on the stairs when they were changing floors. That only happened every hour on the hour. Meila knew that the guard change had just barely happened. Plus, security cameras were very scarce on the guard stairwell. No inmates were allowed on them, so why would there be a need for security cameras on it?

The boys were waiting for them, and they progressed onto the next part of the plan. Kyle left to go and fulfill his part, and the rest of them continued to the cafeteria. Meila had been reminded about this from Kyle. He had noticed that all the guards, during meals, stood on a balcony. This balcony went around the entire room. It allowed the guards to watch everyone at once.

When a lockdown happened—they were expecting one to happen anytime tonight—the team knew they had to be ready. Guard entrances automatically unlocked when anyplace the prisoners would have access to were locked. Bart went on to explain that it is easier, especially with this type of setup because then guards wouldn't have to swipe their card when in a hurry. Daren had slipped a key card off a guard when he had inspections today. They wanted to be ready for anything that could possibly go wrong tonight.

Joey pulled the door open to the balcony above the cafeteria, and they all snuck inside. Joey had suggested this room because he knew the guards wouldn't suspect anyone to be in here. He told her that all of the guards would be busy with the alarms and the fire. If they were to hide anywhere else, the guards would most certainly find them. There was a short wall about a foot high that should hopefully protect them from any guards glancing up as they passed.

"Lie down on the ground and up against the edge. The short wall should protect us from being seen," Joey advised as she passed through the door.

Meila lay down and waited for Kyle to come through the door. She knew that once he came, they could leave. She could hear Bart breathing next to her and Bianca down the line was muttering to herself. Had none of these guys ever done an escape mission?

A loud blaring beeping came from everywhere in the building, and footsteps started to come from every direction. Meila closed her eyes, hoping that they wouldn't be discovered. A few minutes ticked on as loud feet ran through the cafeteria below them. Meila heard distant voices ring throughout the building, and then silence. The lights went off, and the alarm stopped. The fire must have worked. The power was gone. The door opened, sending just a little bit of light toward the group. Kyle's head popped through in the next moment. "All set! Let's get out of here!"

They all stood and moved toward the door. Joey led them through the dark building quickly and outside. They all paused, looking to the team's fine work. Daren's voice came up next to her. "Good idea on the fire. It gives the guards a great distraction."

She smiled back at him and then pushed on with the rest of the group. They ran in the opposite direction of the fire and toward the wall, about thirty feet away. A smile grew on her face as she thought about the fire. She couldn't believe her luck in thinking of ideas, but she wasn't about to admit that Daren had really been the genius of that plan. When she saw his milk overflowing his glass, she knew that the same could happen to any type of electricity. She made this so that it would overload the system. Not only that but the fire should be enough to damage the power supply above the wall. She asked that the fire be started by those lines so that when they were running down the mountain, they couldn't be tracked.

They had barely made it to the concrete wall before Joey had hoisted Meila up on his shoulders so that she could reach the top of the wall. Meila placed her hands on top of the wall, quickly lifting herself the rest of the way. She heard a crunch as she sat down. She wished that she could have just slid down to safety after seeing the sight up on this wall. It was covered with dead eroding bugs. Meila managed not to gag before focusing on the task at hand. She reached down to help lift Daren and then Kyle. She looked back to the guards just in time to see some pointing at them and pulling out their guns.

"Time's up!" Meila hollered down.

Bart and Bianca came over quickly, and Joey yelled for them to keep going.

The guards had pulled out their guns and had started firing. Meila's breath quickened as she threw herself down the outer angled wall. Joey arrived shortly after.

"Run!" he yelled. No one needed to be told twice. They all started off at a dead sprint down the large mountain.

Meila heard voices behind them but didn't dare stop to find out what they were saying. More shots fired around them, and the group scattered into the trees.

Meila's breath came fast, but she kept it quiet, knowing that if she ever went back to the compound, she would never get out. She ducked under a large tree root and some green brush that was coming up. Meila listened to the crunching of dead leaves as the guards looked around.

The footsteps came closer, and Meila held her breath. Meila sunk down a little bit lower, hiding underneath some green brush. She kept repeating in her mind, *I can't go back.*

The black boot stopped in front of the brush and moved it slightly before moving on. Meila kept her breath in, knowing that the guard was still around somewhere.

She waited for what felt like forever before the brush was moved again. Meila ducked, trying to hide further under the brush, but a hand took a hold of her wrist, stopping her.

"He's gone," Joey said.

Meila sighed and lifted herself from the brush around the trees. "Where is everyone else?"

Joey pointed to his right, and Meila saw the group starting to form.

"We all split when we heard the footsteps," he started to explain. "There were three of them that came down. One started back up the hill, telling the others that he would go and get a car, and the others stayed down here to take care of us. The only thing is they don't know that we are not captured."

"What if they have the sensors back up?"

Bart shook his head, moving closer to Meila.

"That isn't possible. The fire was big enough. We broke the connection between the backup generators and the rest of the building. A building that size will have lost power about"—Bart looked down at his watch—"six minutes ago."

"Good. Then why are we still standing around here? All I have heard come from your mouths is that we are still stuck in the forest with men after us. And we are just sitting around," Kyle butted in.

"I agree with Kyle," Bianca added her voice. "We need to move. Give it an hour, maybe a little bit more, and this whole place will be swarmed with guards."

"Okay, but the original plan was to stay close to the roads. That was our path. Now what?" Bart questioned.

Meila took a deep breath and willed the gears in her brain to start to turn. She saw the map she had created laid out in her head. Following the road was the logical idea when she had first thought of the plan. That was out of the question now. She closed her eyes, examining the map much closer. She saw the regular route, the planned one. She saw a new route starting to come about. After another minute, she found the new route.

"Okay, new plan," Meila said, opening her eyes. "The old route isn't going to work. Guards are going to be down here soon, and they are going to stay close to the roads. They know that it is the easiest way out of here. There is a much straighter route, but I am not sure what the terrain looks like. And I am not sure how long it might take, but I think that it is worth a shot."

Meila looked around the group, waiting for someone to object. When no one did, Joey waved, motioning that Meila take the lead. She nodded and began the long trek down the mountain.

Meila led the group at a quick pace to try and keep distance between themselves and the guards. They had crossed a handful of roads, crossing back and forth, and Meila was hoping that she was leading the group in the right direction.

The sun had come up, and the night chill was finally gone. The group was tired and agitated, but Meila knew that they needed to keep moving.

Daren stopped, putting his hands on his knees. "Can't we just stop for a few minutes? My feet are killing me," he complained.

"Well, you should have worn better shoes. That is all that there is to it," Bart replied.

"Well, you should have worn better shoes," Daren mimicked. "I'm sorry. I guess that I should have asked the guards before I left. I can see that conversation going over great. 'Excuse me. A group of us are planning to escape tonight, and I would like to be able to run away from you for a long time. Would you mind if you could get me some nice sneakers?'" Daren scoffed. "I guess it just slipped my mind before leaving."

Meila rolled her eyes at his exaggerated and tired state.

"You could have at least tried it," Kyle whispered.

Kyle didn't whisper it too softly, though. Daren heard him and turned to him, laying a punch to the middle of his face.

Kyle swung back, but Daren was ready for him. He dodged his fist and planted a foot in Kyle's gut. Kyle fell back in pain but quickly got up. He didn't get too far, though. Bianca had jumped between them.

"That is enough, you two! We are all tired and all ready to go home. But we need to get each other home."

Meila stepped up next to Bianca, "She's right. We need to keep moving. I understand that you are tired, but staying here and bickering gets us nowhere." Meila stepped closer to Kyle. "Put your fist down."

Kyle lunged forward and tried to get past Meila. A large hand jerked him back before he could get much farther.

"That's it!" Joey pushed Kyle to the ground and stood above him. "If you want to stay and fight each other, then be my guest! But the rest of us are going to move on and get out of here!"

Kyle thought for a moment before turning to Daren.

"Get the hint?" Joey asked, waiting for Daren to back down.

Daren put his hands down to his sides and then nodded.

"Good. I agree with the women. There is not enough distance between us and the compound. With the way you two were attempting to fight, I wouldn't be surprised if they are moving closer to us every second." Joey looked over to Meila. "Keep going."

Meila looked around before remembering which direction they had previously come from. She started their pace again, pushing them a little faster than they had previously gone. They were all tired, and Meila couldn't wait to climb into a real bed tonight.

After a while, the group came up on a road, and Meila slowed the pace. They were almost at a complete stop when they had come to the edge of the road. The group backed up a way and listened. The rumbling of a car could be heard in the distance, but Meila figured that it was far enough away that it wasn't an issue.

The group crossed the road quickly as the rumbling got closer. She looked to Joey, hoping that he would have an idea.

"Let's hang low for a moment and let everyone catch their breaths," Joey suggested.

Meila nodded, and the rest of the group hid behind trees and large roots, waiting for the car to drive by.

A black four-door came around the bend at a slow pace. Its headlights were on, meaning that darkness would descend upon them soon.

The car came to a complete stop just a few yards down the road. A head popped out from the car before cautiously whispering. Meila couldn't see the face of the man, but she knew that he looked familiar. Joey tugged on her shoulder, telling her to get back a little bit further. The voice came closer, and the group seemed to hold their breath.

The man came closer. The three that were closer to him all looked in Meila's direction, surprised. She just stared back at them, confused.

The man came a few steps closer before whispering, "Meila?" The man took a few more steps down the road and whispered her name again.

She peered around the tree and looked to see the face of who was calling her name. She jumped out of the trees and ran toward him. She threw her arms around him and sighed. "JP!"

She had never been so happy to see him in her life! She pulled back from him and then waved to the group in the trees. "It's okay. We have been saved!"

She watched JP as the group came out of the forest. His expression softened when he saw five others, and she could tell that he was counting in his head. "Everyone climb in. I hope that I have enough room."

Meila and Bianca climbed up front, and the four guys squished in back. JP turned on the car and flipped a U and started back down the mountain. He turned to Meila. "Where to?"

She looked at everyone in the car. Each one took a turn, telling where they could be dropped off. Meila waited until they had silenced before speaking. "How did you know where I was at?"

"You told me about your device. You told me that one day when we were outside. You said that you could speak into it, and I could hear it, so I made one once I escaped but remembered that you did not have all the supplies needed. I just made sure that the right parts got to you."

She smiled. She was grateful for this man! Why did she ever doubt him?

* * * * *

Sleep had come quickly after they had made it around the first mountain. Meila figured that they would be driving for a good two hours before they even saw the outline of Willowsville. She sunk down in her seat and let her aching limbs rest.

Meila blinked awake as JP pulled the car to their first stop. As each member was dropped off at their intended destination, they patted her arm or thanked her for helping them escape. She smiled and thanked them right back. Once it was her turn to leave, she climbed out and thanked JP. She did not know if she should really trust him, so she had him drop her off a few blocks north of her apartment and the agency building.

Before she could close the door, JP spoke. "Meila, if you need help with anything, please let me know."

She smiled and said that she might take him up on that. She closed the door and watched the black car drive into the night, grateful that JP had been there to pick them up.

She hesitantly made her way to the hotel where she had been dropped off and pulled the door open. She stepped inside and moved to the desk. Meila looked at the attendant's name tag but found that it didn't say Gary. She instead asked to use the phone and had to think hard before remembering how to get to her old office number and trying to figure out how to get past security.

After speaking to a few different people, she was finally directed to the correct place. She heard it only ring once before a strong voice came over the line. "You have reached the agency building. Would you please mind stating your business?"

The voice was demanding, and Meila took a stab at who she was talking to. "Cody?" Silence filled the other line.

"May I ask who this is?"

"Cody, it's Meila."

"Meila!" She heard relief and excitement fill his voice. "Meila, where are you at. I will send you a car and bring you to the agency building."

She looked around the hotel hoping to find a sign or possibly what street it was on. "Cody, I can't tell, but I know that I am only a few blocks from the agency building. I'll just walk."

"No! You could be farther away from the agency building than you think you are. Besides, we have a lot we need to discuss, so having someone come to get you would be better. Can you possibly describe the building or what is by it?"

Meila moved as far as the cord would allow it to, but it didn't allow her to see more than she already could. "I'm sorry, I don't know, but I do remember coming here before. I was with April. She asked for Gary at the desk and used the name A—"

"Angie Harper Lee. I know where you are at. Look for a gray four-door out the window." He hung up after saying that.

Meila put down the phone and thanked the attendant. She moved to the window and waited to go outside until a gray four-door car showed up. She hesitantly approached it until Agent Walker's head came out of it. She moved to the car and climbed in, grateful that Cody didn't come himself.

Agent Walker only seldom spoke, telling her that everything would be explained to her after she arrived and got some much needed sleep. She allowed herself to be shown to a room and lay down on a cot. She fell asleep before her head even hit the pillow.

* * * * *

A noise came outside of her door. Meila half expected a guard to come in and yell at her, but one never came. She cracked her eyes open and looked around the room. Her limbs loudly protested when she tried to move them. The memories of the last few days came back in full—the fire that her makeshift team had set, running for miles, seeing JP again.

She pushed herself to a sitting position and looked around the room. Some food and a water bottle had been placed on a small table next to her bed. Some clothes had been placed on a chair next to her temporary bed. She slipped out of bed and changed into the clean clothes, glad that they were her own and that they still fit.

She picked up a jacket that had been placed on the back of the chair. It was her black jacket, the one that she had worn since before meeting Charlie. She pulled it close to her, breathing in the smell, realizing it smelt like home. Tears sprung in her eyes, and she was grateful to be there again. Her ID was there too. She sat down on her bed and let the tears flow.

One other item of importance had been placed next to the bed. She picked up the box that she had made while at the compound. This small box had saved her life. If it wasn't for this small object, she would still be stuck in that miserable place. She placed the box in the pocket of her black jacket.

After a few minutes, she clipped on her ID and ate the food that was provided. She moved to the door and took a deep breath. She hoped that this wasn't some kind of dream, and she would wake up to find that she was really back at the compound.

She pushed open the door and looked both ways down the hall before walking toward the elevator. She only took a few wrong turns before arriving at the metal doors. Meila pushed the button indicating that she wanted to go up and stepped onto the empty elevator. She pressed the seven button and waited as the elevator ascended.

She stepped off the elevator and only got lost once before she saw Cassie sitting at her desk. Meila could tell that she had recently dyed her hair. It was bright and happy to go along with the smile that appeared when Cassie recognized Meila.

"Meila!" Cassie stood and moved around her desk, embracing Meila. Meila stepped back from Cassie and smiled. "I am so glad that you are back and safe. It will be good to have you back. The office just hasn't been the same without you."

"Thanks, Cassie. It's good to be back and not stuck on some forgotten mountain." She looked to the door behind Cassie. "Are they waiting for me?"

"Yep! But I think that they too will be glad to have you back."

Meila moved behind Cassie, scanned her ID, and went through the door. All activity stopped when she came through the door. The whole team was there. April ran to her and threw her arms around Meila. "I am so happy that you are back!" she exclaimed.

Shanta hugged her next, then Marcus and Agent Walker. Cody just put a hand on her shoulder. "Good! Now that you're back, maybe work can get going around here again.

Meila just frowned. Shanta took her arm and started to pull her toward the kitchen. "Where are you taking her? I said that we would have a meeting the minute that she arrived," Cody complained.

Shanta waved him off. "She has just been at the compound for nineteen months. She deserves a few minutes before she is forced back into work."

Meila was grateful that she couldn't see Cody at that moment. She was sure that he had probably rolled his eyes. She did, however, hear him mutter something about how Meila may have had too long of a break.

Shanta took her into the kitchen and pulled out another water bottle and some food. Meila graciously accepted the offering and hungrily ate. Even though she had some food downstairs, she hadn't eaten a whole lot the last few days. Her nerves would not have allowed it anyway.

After a good twenty minutes, Meila let Shanta pull her into the conference room, where everyone else had congregated. She sat in her regular spot, and Cody stood at the head of the table, starting the conference. "Thanks for everyone's help these last many months. They have been long and tedious, but we did get one member of the team back." Everyone clapped before Cody moved on. "But work here at the agency building never ends, so I'm turning the floor over to Meila. She is going to tell us how she got away."

Meila wasn't expecting this, but she stood anyway. She looked at the sea of faces; many of them were not familiar, but she began anyway. "I have been at the compound for the last nineteen months. Charlie Schren passed away when I was almost there for seven months. I lost hope for a couple of months, knowing that I was in a position where I could easily be forgotten. When I felt like I had a purpose, I felt that hope start to build again. I started to work with a new team eight months ago and together these last four months, we had developed a plan on how to get out.

"It started when I found out there wasn't anything on top of the concrete wall that surrounded the compound, then finding that all of the wires that control the cameras were above one of the walls of the compound. I met most of the group then. I was still struggling with the fact that Charlie had died, but I knew that this would distract me. I told myself that I could grieve later."

I guess that time has come, Meila thought. She cleared her throat and then pressed on. "We prepared for weeks, using supplies left behind by JP, a man that almost got me and Charlie out the first time. We used many of his tools. One of the inmates made a light beam strong enough to start a fire. Another one knew how to short out the cameras long enough to allow us to escape to a prearranged area. Other's knew what to listen for when guards came through.

"We started a fire that burned the main wire, stopping all security cameras from recording. Of course, my team had already been at a safe spot so that our cells would not lock down on us.

"My makeshift team had almost made it completely over the wall before we were recognized. Some guards tried to come after us, but we lost them on the mountain. We kept away from the roads, knowing more guards could be coming after us. After a while of running, JP, the man who tried to help me escape the first time, came and got us." Meila pulled the box out of her pocket. "I had parts sent to me slowly, and I created this. I did not know if anyone was even on the other side of it, but JP found me, so I assumed that he was there for me. He drove us down the rest of the mountain and dropped us off where we asked him to. That's when I called you guys."

Meila waited for a moment before asking if there were any questions. Silence echoed throughout the room. Cody stood and thanked her. He said a few more things and then dismissed everyone to get back to work.

Meila let a tear slip. She hadn't really believed that Charlie was gone. Even though she knew that he had practically died in her arms, but she had been hoping, by some miracle, that Charlie would be here waiting for her. But now that she was here, she knew that he wouldn't be coming back.

April sat down next to her and put an arm around her shoulders. "Cody asked me to fill you in on the last case. He noticed that you didn't really listen too well during the second half of the meeting."

Meila mumbled and looked up at April. April smiled tentatively at her.

"Cody is working on getting you clearance again. Since you were held in a jail, the state took away most of your rights. Cody is fighting to get as many as he can. It could still be a while, though. Usually, you have to go to court for something like this," April explained.

"I know," Meila replied. Someone had died while up at the compound. She would not be surprised if she was summoned to be seen in court for that. But that was not the problem right now. Her team needed her help on the next case.

Meila nodded, allowing for her to proceed. "I know that this might be hard to hear and believe, but we got your father." April removed her arm and pulled a file up from the other side of her chair, sliding it in front of Meila. "The details are in there if you want to read them."

Meila just looked at the file. This was the last case that she had been on with Charlie. She wasn't ready to go over it yet. She slid it back over to April. "Why don't you just sum it up instead?"

April nodded. "We got him the night that you and Charlie disappeared. Rodrigez was with him. We got them both, and they have both been to court and found guilty. They are being held in the state prison, where they are under constant supervision. We still worry that some of his men are on the streets. We have found a big chunk of them, though. Both of their businesses have been shut down. All of their merchandise has been taken into our custody. Thanks to you, the world has become a safer place."

Meila nodded. She dropped her head into her hands. She was glad that he was finally behind bars, but Meila was starting to feel the weight of Charlie's absence. Something was placed in her lap. She lifted her head enough to find keys—her keys.

"We kept both yours and Charlie's apartments. We figured that you might want some stuff out of his or out of yours. We have pre-paid for both of them for a couple more months, but that charge will be difficult for you to handle on your own. I don't think that you will be able to afford to keep both apartments. The agency has only kept them so you can decide which one you want."

Meila spoke from her slumped position, "Why did you keep them both? I assumed that I wouldn't be coming back here." When Charlie had died, she did not have much of a desire to escape.

"Did you really think that we would have given up on you that easily? Meila, you are a part of this team, and we do not leave others behind. When we heard that Charlie had died, we were all devastated, but most of us were more worried about you. We knew that you were the closest to him. We hoped that we wouldn't be hearing that you had left us too."

A hand came over one of her own. "Please let me know if there is anything that I can do to help." With that, Meila heard April stand and leave Meila alone to think.

CHAPTER 55

Cody lay a hand on Meila's shoulder. "Do you want to talk about it?"

Meila shook her head. She was sick of being asked that question. She had received sorrowful looks from everyone in the office. Almost everyone has tried to talk to her about it, but it wouldn't change anything. Charlie was gone. This time, he wasn't coming back. Her best friend, her partner in crime, her brother had left her behind.

Meila blinked back tears, determined not to let anyone else see them. She was furious with herself. She let her guard down. If she wouldn't have done that, Charlie would still be here.

Cody turned her chair so that it was facing him. "Meila, you're going to have to open up about this. Grief is a hard thing, especially when you feel like you have to bear it alone, but you don't. You have all of us. We all are sad that he's gone, but we have to move on."

Meila stood. "You know nothing of my pain! You sit behind a desk, or you're in the gym. Charlie was *my* brother. He is the only true family that I have had! So don't you dare talk to me about grief. Trust me. I have lost more than anyone."

Everyone had stopped working at that point. Cody folded his arms. "You don't think that any of us have had grief? Agent Walker lost his wife and two sons because of your father. Shanta lost her parents because of a bomb. April lost a boyfriend to the business that your father runs. My younger sister was murdered because of men like your father. None of us here are without scrapes."

Meila shook her head. "Yes, but you all had someone to turn to. Charlie was that someone for me. He knew me even before I truly knew myself. None of you can say that for me."

Cody nodded. "You're correct. We can't change that, but Charlie told us when you started here that we needed to let you in. He didn't tell us anything besides that you were going through a rough patch. Now, as you are going through another rough time, we ask that you take his advice once again: you let us in." Cody turned back to his desk.

Agent Walker awkwardly patted her arm on the way back to his desk. Everyone went back to work. Meila excused herself to use the bathroom. The tears were flowing long before she got there though. She made sure that no one else was in there before she sank down the wall and allowed herself to truly cry.

Charlie had been gone for almost a year, but she had been trying to escape during those last few months. The first few months he was gone, it was hard, but some part of her was holding on to some sort of hope that Charlie had faked his death and escaped. But that couldn't have happened. He was cold in her arms. She saw the blood. She saw his injuries. No one could have survived what he did. Ever since late January, she had been busy trying to piece together the escape plan. She told herself that she would grieve once she was free. But now that she was free, she wished that she had something that would distract her.

The door opened with a swish, Cassie's familiar form filled the doorway. "You all right?"

Meila nodded.

Cassie sat down on the ground next to her. "Cody asked me to keep any eye on you. But last time I remember you heard some bad news, you practically ran from the building. I'm glad that you didn't try to run this time."

Meila just stared at Cassie.

"Anyway, Cody said to tell you that the teams got a case that should help you push through this time."

Meila shook her head no. "I didn't think I would have clearance for this case."

Cassie shrugged. "Has that ever stopped you before? Didn't Charlie let you work on most of the cases without clearance?" Cassie winced, realizing what she had just said. Charlie's name wasn't said much around the office.

Meila looked back forward. She wasn't interested in doing a case right now. She didn't care about what it was about or who was in danger. Someone was always going to be in danger, and someone would always get hurt. Cassie laid a hand on Meila's arm "I know that I am only a glorified secretary, but I heard that it has something to do with the man that tried to escape with you the first time."

"JP."

Cassie nodded. "Or something like that. But Cody started without you. He didn't know how long you would be in here."

"What else did you hear about the case?"

"Something about putting this man away. Besides, don't you think it would be good to get working again? Fill your mind with something else?"

Meila nodded. Why were they trying to put up a case against JP? He was trying to help Meila and Charlie escape. In the end, he had been there to get Meila and a few of her inmates when they escaped. He hadn't done anything wrong. If anything, Meila should be put on trial. Meila stood and thanked Cassie, then left the bathroom. She had to go in and prove that JP was innocent.

Meila pushed open the office door. No one really acknowledged her entrance, so Meila stomped over to Cody. "This case around JP won't stand. He was innocent, and I can prove it."

Cody didn't even look up from his work. "He is a criminal that was in jail. He escaped many more jails and compounds before that one. You don't really know this man, he hasn't done one right thing a day in his life."

Meila slapped her hands down on her desk, wanting him to listen to her. "He is the one that almost got me and Charlie out the first time. He even came after me the second time. He is changing."

Cody leaned back in his chair. "Already replacing Charlie so quickly? Just a half hour ago you wouldn't speak to any of us. Now you are full of words." Cody threw out a fake laugh. "Besides, we have evidence that will put him away for life. The lawyer that Mr. Simmon has hired does not get along with the judge that was assigned to this case. He'll lose."

Meila was stunned. This man had helped her escape. She was only recaptured because of her own doing. This man was a friend to Charlie. Okay, maybe not quite friends, more like forced friends.

"Fine. If you think that he is going to go away for life, I will defend him."

Cody blinked. "Meila, I think you are taking your anger out in the wrong place. This man has killed thousands. He needs to be brought down."

Meila pushed away from his desk. "Not the man that I knew." She grabbed the file that had been placed on her desk and a box full of odds and ends for the case and headed for the conference room. She closed and locked the door after her.

* * * * *

She smiled to herself. She was getting through to this girl. She could tell. Her father would be proud. She walked back to her desk, picking up the receiver and dialed the number to one of her father's friends. She wasn't finished doing damage yet.

CHAPTER 56

Two papers had been sitting on Meila's desk when she arrived this morning. The first was a note from Cody telling her that the rest of the team had taken the morning off, giving her some space. He also was letting her know about the temporary offices on the floor below them. The next one was a note from Agency Boardman Six. It informed her that she was allowed to see any case files that she needed along with some other privileges. A sticky note had also been placed on her desk. Meila recognized Cody's bold handwriting. This note was to inform her about JP's court day. It was almost two weeks from today. They would be issuing their opening statements on May 17.

Meila put down the papers. She had met with JP's lawyer this morning. He was good at what he did, but once he found out who the judge was going to be, he flipped. Meila just left him to have his temper tantrum. She had been waiting for him for about ten minutes now.

Meila had gone over the case again, and she had finally found something, something that might keep him out of jail. Mr. Tate, the lawyer, walked in the next moment. Meila stood and held out the documents to him. "I think I found a loophole."

Mr. Tate looked at the documents. He looked up, waiting for her to begin her explanation. "JP has done some pretty awful things, but he has already done time for them. We are up against some people that I know well. They are going to try and see the worst in him, find the things that he hasn't served time for. We can't let them win."

Mr. Tate nodded. "What is the loophole you found?"

Meila's shoulders dropped. *Did he not hear a single word that I just said?* "JP has already served time for these previous crimes. He just has to finish the time that he was supposed to serve at the compound."

Mr. Tate just stared at her, a blank stare. "So we want to keep him out of jail, and you know how to do it."

Meila was getting frustrated. They were never going to win the case with this man. "Do you have anyone else, an employee perhaps, that could help with this case?" Meila asked, hopeful that the answer would be positive.

He shook his head. "What about you?" His gaze all of a sudden intense.

"What about me?" Meila said, leaning back in her chair.

"You work here."

Meila nodded, indicating that bit of information was obvious. Mr. Tate leaned forward in his chair. "You run the case."

"I already am. You have done zero work since I met you a few days ago."

He waved a hand and put his briefcase on the table. He opened it, covering his face. Meila rolled her eyes as she listened to the shuffling of papers happening. Finally, the briefcase closed, and the man handed a paper to her.

"Power of Attorney." Meila looked up to Mr. Tate. "What is this?"

Mr. Tate took the paper back.

"It tells me that if someone is unable to be at court, I can sign for someone else to be there in my place." Meila was catching on now. "You want me to defend JP," she stated.

Mr. Tate nodded. "You know him and this case better than anyone. If anyone could save this man's life, I believe that you can fill that role perfectly."

Meila smiled at Mr. Tate. She was beginning to like this man. If he hadn't thrown a tantrum ten minutes ago, she might even consider him a friend.

Meila took the paper back from him. "So how do we do this so that you can relinquish this case to me?"

Mr. Tate pulled out a pen and began checking certain boxes and signing his name. He then pointed to a few places where she needed to sign. Mr. Tate then pulled out one more sheet of paper "Here's a note confirming that I can't be there. If the judge questions my whereabouts, this should stop all of his arguments."

Meila mumbled and accepted the page. She set it in her stack of things that needed to stay at the office.

Mr. Tate shut his briefcase and nodded toward her. "Thank you. You have no idea how much I do not want to attend court next week."

"And deal with the judge?" Meila joked.

Relief crossed Mr. Tate's features. "Yes, that will be a benefit all on its own." He stood and collected the few papers, placing them in his briefcase. He closed it and reached his hand out. Meila put hers in it, and they shook. "It was a pleasure doing business with you, Ms. Manning. Please, don't ever contact me again."

Meila blinked at his strange way of ending their deal, but she shook it off. He was a strange little man anyway.

Meila picked up the backpack that she brought and put the few files left on the table in there. She followed in Mr. Tate's footsteps and left the agency building. She walked the streets and listened to the busyness of the city. She opened the door and waved to the man at the desk in the lobby. He smiled at her, and she moved on past him to the stairs. He had been a friend of Charlie's too. Did he know that he was gone?

She unlocked her apartment door and pushed it open. She closed it and fastened the three new locks she had installed. She wasn't going to have anyone ever just walk into her apartment, like Charlie used to do.

She felt tears start to form in her eyes. She blinked rapidly, hoping that they would disappear. To distract her, she opened her backpack and pulled out the files. Before opening them, she went to her fridge and found some leftovers. She warmed them up and put them down next to the files. She prepared herself for a long night of working.

* * * * *

Meila's eyelids fluttered open. She pushed her head off the table where she must have slept. She put a hand to her tired neck. She rubbed it and looked around for the source that had awakened her. Her phone was going off. She moved her backpack closer to her and pulled out her phone. She shut off the alarm, not grateful that it was already six thirty.

Meila stood and moved to the bathroom. Her appearance was not great. There were marks on her face where she had slept on the table. She tried smoothing the marks, but nothing happened to them. She stopped and moved into her bedroom. She changed clothes and fixed her hair and makeup and then went back to the table.

Most of the notes she had made last night probably wouldn't be helpful, but she had to review each of her sources and make sure JP stayed out of jail. Meila packed up all of her files she had brought home, grabbed some food for lunch, and then went to the agency building.

She showed her ID at the door and walked to the woman at the front desk. "Hi, I am looking for a temporary office?" Meila thought about this last night. She didn't think that she could face Cody every day until the trial was over.

"May I ask you what you are working on?"

"A court case."

The woman looked down at the computer in front of her and was silent for a minute. Meila started to drum her fingers on the counter, unable to stay still. Finally, the woman looked up. "There is one on the sixth floor. And"—the woman bends down and pulls something out from under her desk; she handed Meila a key—"here is the key to get in. Also, since you are on a court case, know that you are allowed to use the interrogation rooms on G3. And the court-room, when the right date comes, is on floor 3." The woman smiled.

Meila smiled back and thanked the woman. She moved to the elevator and hit the button for the sixth floor. She stepped off in the strange hallway and looked for the number on the door that matched her key. A few minutes later, she pushed open a door to a small office. It was nothing like the main office on the next floor, but Meila knew that it would do.

She put her jacket on the peg by the door and closed the door. There was a whiteboard along one wall, a corkboard on the one behind the chair. A window showed her the west side of town. A table was fashioned in the middle of the room, a single chair behind it. She peeked out of the door again and saw that the bathrooms were down the hallway. She closed the door again and started her work, grateful that she wouldn't have any distractions.

CHAPTER 57

Meila rolled her tired shoulders. This case was not as simple as she had originally thought it was going to be. She looked up to the corkboard. She had placed everything that she had found useful on it. It wasn't even half full.

The box that she had taken from the main office had been useful, but it had security tapes that she didn't have the right technology to look at. The files had been just about as useful as the tapes, nothing to possibly keep him out. JP had given a statement when he first arrived here, but everything in it would go against him. Not to mention, that she had found out that he had recently also stolen a car. How was she supposed to keep this guy out of jail if he kept putting himself in bad situations?

She rubbed a hand over her face in frustration. She had no idea what to do. Cody had been correct. JP would end up serving some time in prison, regardless of what she tried to do.

Meila thought of her file and shuffled through her backpack. It wasn't in there. She must have left it up in the old office. She pulled her ID off her jacket and made sure that she had the key to her temporary office. She walked out of the door and locked the door, not wanting anything else to vanish.

Meila walked to the elevator and pushed the button to go up. She had accidentally hit the seven this morning when coming up, but thankfully, she got off before that.

The elevator came up, and it had a few other people in it. She stepped in and hit the seven. Conversation wasn't really possible as she was only going up one floor, so Meila didn't say or make eye contact with anyone in the elevator.

She stepped out and walked slowly toward her old office. She stopped right before the turn and listened. It was quiet. She poked her head around the corner, but Cassie wasn't there. That would make this a little bit simpler. Meila moved to the door and stopped, hoping not to hear any voices. The room seemed silent.

She put her ID up to the sensor and was glad that the light turned green. She pulled the door open and walked in. April was on the phone, Marcus was doing something with gears and wires. Shanta wasn't there, but Meila wondered if she was moved to the night shift.

Cody was at his desk, leaning back in his chair and chewing on a toothpick. "Have you come to admit that I was correct?"

Meila walked toward her old desk, missing this office already. "Nope. I have just come for a few files that belong to me."

Cody stood and moved so that he was in front of her desk. "You will have to eventually accept that I am correct because no matter how hard you fight, I will always win."

Meila looked up at him. "And why would that be, Mr. Lopez?" Meila snapped.

He gestured to the room around him. "Because I have people around me, people that know me, people that have let me in." He smirked.

Meila looked back down and pulled the files that she needed out of her desk. "Well. I wasn't given the comforts of a team, but I don't need them." Meila stepped out from behind her desk and sauntered toward the main office door. She turned back to Cody at the last minute, allowing herself to say one last rude thing to him. "But at least I am not stuck with you. You see, when I worked here, the others liked me. They're just stuck with you." She leered. Meila turned and slammed the door behind her, letting a satisfactory smile stay on her lips as she went back to her new office.

* * * * *

Meila put the files down on the desk, mad that she was struggling to make any progress on this case. She hoped that Cody was having less luck than she was, but she knew that was probably impossible. He was correct on what he said. He had a whole team behind him, a whole team to support him. And whom did she have? No one.

Meila touched her arm, letting memories from the compound come flying back in. While in jail, each inmate had been given a specific number—you practically had it burned into your skin, just on the underside of your wrist—and a colored band around your arm.

Charlie had promised Meila that they would get it removed or find a way to cover it. Now, Charlie was gone, but the number still remained—6657. In jail, that's all you were, a number.

A memory flashed through her mind, something about Charlie and his death. A man… It was gone. She tried to recall it but couldn't.

She craned her neck. The amount of work she had put into the case did not reflect at all in the progress she had made. The court date was coming up for JP, yet she felt as if she had very little information on how to help him. She was stiff, but she had just worked a night shift. She couldn't wait to go home and climb into her bed.

Meila listened as the clock in her small office ticked. She tried to concentrate on the files before her, knowing JP's court date was quickly coming up. Frustrated, she closed the file and glanced up at the clock, realizing she could go home. She pushed open the door and rode the elevator to the main floor. She greeted a few people on the way in and said good morning to the guards at the door.

The cold morning air was still upon Willowsville, but Meila hardly felt it. She crossed the street and turned toward her apartment. She was deep in thought when she bumped into a man. "Hey, watch where you're going!" Meila reprimanded.

He just nodded to her and then turned back and kept walking away. Meila stood and watched his back for a moment, thinking that he looked familiar. She shook it off and blamed it on her lack of sleep. She moved back into the busy part of the sidewalk and continued on her way home.

CHAPTER 58

Meila sat down behind the glass, slightly terrified. The last time that she had been in a room like this, she had been yelled at by her father for lying to her. But this time, a friendly face came in front of the dimly lit glass. They both picked up the phones, and Meila spoke. "Hello, JP. How are you doing?"

He shrugged, but the smile never melted away. "I've been in worse places than this, so I'm doing okay."

Meila nodded. "Do you mind if I ask you a few questions?"

He shook his head and waved his hand, showing that he was ready. She looked down at the list that she had created the night before. "How long were you in the compound?"

"Six months. Six miserable, agonizing months."

Meila made a note of this in her notepad and then looked for the next question. "How did you know where to get supplies for the cameras?"

Meila looked up at JP, but he just smiled and answered. "Someone before me had almost completed it before I went in, so all I had to do was finish the job and connect it to the right system."

"What about me? How did you know where to find me that night on the mountain?"

He moved his face closer to the glass. "I had been searching for you for many days, knowing that you had received the wires that I had sent you. I made sure that they seemed harmless enough when I put it in the junk mail pile that went up there, then I drove that road every night."

"How did you know that it would be night time when I escaped?"

He shrugged. "I wasn't sure, but I knew that you would lay low in the forest by the compound during the day. Moving at that time would be too difficult. The sensors would have picked you up immediately, so I figured you would lay low during the day. That made it so you would most likely be moving during the night. Besides, if someone would have come after you from the compound, moving during the night would have been easier. If you were moving the group during the night, it meant my chances of finding you would have been easier during that time."

Meila jotted down a few things to help her remember this conversation and then moved on. "What about the time that you have served for the car theft?"

JP put his elbows down on the small table in front of him, frowning. "You mean the car that I borrowed from a friend in order to get you out?" Meila hadn't known that. "That car was mine at the time that the cops took it away from me. And getting you out seemed crucial."

Meila nodded, agreeing with that statement. She asked him a few more questions and then left him to the mercy of the guards. She wandered back up to her temporary office and looked over the information that he had given her. Nothing extremely useful but still some details that could help her squeak out this case, she hoped.

CHAPTER 59

Meila handed the judge her "Power of Attorney" documents. He quickly looked through them and nodded to her.

"Everything seems to be in order here. You may take your seat next to the defendant."

Meila thanked the judge and then turned to the table to her right and took a seat. She smiled at JP and placed her briefcase on the table, pulling out the notes she had taken from her hours of research.

The judge cleared his throat, and Meila lifted her head, wondering if she had missed something, but the judge was looking at Cody.

"Where is Mr. Johnson?"

Cody stood, a familiar paper in his hand. "May I approach the bench, Your Honor?"

The judge sighed and nodded.

Cody handed the papers to him, and the judge replaced the glasses on his nose to read them. He flipped through them, just as quickly as he had hers. Finally, he nodded to Cody and spoke, "Very well. Let's see what the two of you came up with to battle for this man's life." He gestured to JP, who had just been brought into the room and sat down behind Meila's table. JP smiled up at her, and Meila smiled back.

Her eyes scanned the room, stopping on a few of the officers. Some were placed by the judge on the wall by Cody's table. The officer that brought JP in, moved and took his place against the wall, far enough away not to be included in the case but close enough to stop anyone from getting too violent.

She looked back to the judge, who gave them a few instructions on how today's court would be run since neither one of them had their assigned lawyers to represent them. The judge dismissed them from the bench, and he asked that the small audience be quiet through the proceedings.

She sat down next to JP and leaned closer to him. "How are they treating you down there?"

He grimaced. "It could be better, but I have gotten to eat a few more meals a day than I usually do. And you come and visit, so that is enough for me." He smiled.

She nodded and turned her attention back to Cody as he called his first witness. A man stepped out of the group of spectators. Meila recognized him but couldn't place his face until he sat down under oath. Cody stepped up to the man and asked his first question. "Sir, will you please state what your occupation is?"

"I am a security guard."

Meila knew that she had recognized him from somewhere!

"And where do you work?"

The man looked at Cody confused. "I am currently waiting to start my next job."

"All right. Let me rephrase the question." Cody steepled his fingers before speaking. "Where was your last place of employment?"

The man thought for a moment. "You mean you are asking where I previously worked, sir?"

Cody smiled slightly, nodding, encouraging him to continue. "The latest that you had."

The man pushed himself farther back into the chair before answering. "I worked up at a jail in the mountains."

Meila's heartbeat sped up.

"Which building?" Cody pressed.

"Many call it just the jail in the hills, but I have heard it referred to as the compound here."

Meila sucked in a breath. This guard had been there while she had been there! That is where she knew him from!

"And how long were you there?" Cody asked.

He shrugged. "I had been there for a couple of years, but I was let go."

Cody pretended to ponder this. "Did they tell you any reasons why you were let go?"

"I was actually quite grateful that I got to stay there as long as I did. We had an escape about a year into my time there. There were three of them that had attempted the escape. Only one escaped."

The courtroom sat in an awkward silence while Cody jotted something down at his desk. He looked up after a few moments and stared at the witness.

"The other two?"

The guard cleared his throat before continuing, "One of them we captured and kept on strict lockdown for about six months. The other, unfortunately, passed away."

Cody nodded. He turned and walked around his desk, keeping his gaze from meeting Meila's. "What did you do to try and find the man that escaped?"

The man leaned forward in the witness seat. "In the main guardroom at the compound, the guards all knew about a radio. If someone was ever to escape, we were to tell the person on the other side."

"Did you ever hear back from the mysterious voice?"

The man shook his head. "No one at the compound even knew who was on the other side of it. We often thought that it was the police and we assumed they would have spoken back to us, but the radio always sat silent."

"What else can you tell us about the escape?" Cody asked.

"The prisoners escaped from the second floor. Due to having a small staff, we were unable to keep very many guards on that floor. Very few prisoners were kept on that floor because of that problem. Besides, we did not see this as a problem because the bottom floor contained the remainder of the guards and all of the controls for the compound. We did not think that anyone could escape from the jail without trying to get through us first."

"Did you ever meet the owner of the compound?" Cody asked.

The guard thought for a moment. "No. There was a female who would come up every now and then and bring us supplies, and she told us she was the owner's daughter. But that is the only time we ever heard of the owner. He never came personally to see us."

Cody nodded and then turned to Meila.

"Your witness."

Meila nodded and tried to think of what to ask him. She stood and started to pace in front of the witness stand. "Sir, did you know any of the specifics of the prisoners held in the compound?"

The man looked up, giving her a surprised look. "That was not our area of expertise. We were employed to keep the prisoners within their bounds."

Meila stopped and tried to level him with a stare. "So you don't know a single person that was in the compound."

He shook his head. "We weren't allowed to interact with those living there."

Meila nodded and then continued to pace. "Sir, may I ask what your duties or the duties of others were inside of the compound?" Meila glanced over at Cody, expecting him to object, but he just nodded to her, giving her a knowing smile.

"The duties varied between each officer. We had some that were strictly in the halls or watching the cameras. We had some that only worked on the floor."

Meila's head snapped back to the witness.

"And of course, thos—"

"Explain to everyone else what 'working on the floor' is."

The man rolled his shoulders back before answering. "It means those that worked outside or on the main floor. They never saw any inmates unless they were outside."

Meila nodded. "What other jobs were there?"

"Mail officers, wellness officers, and"—he ticked them off on his fingers—"the searching officers."

"Please explain for those who do not understand who those might be." Meila continued to pace, always keeping her gaze on what was in front of her.

"Mail officers searched all the junk mail that people didn't want and found it safe to bring it to the compound. Wellness officers were pretty much like nurses and doctors that worked there. They met new arrivals and marked them. Search officers are exactly what their name is. They search each cell for dangerous materials, but there are only a handful of them, so they only can search a floor a day."

Something flashed in Meila's mind, another memory, but she pushed it down. "What about cars coming in and out of the gate?"

The witness thought for a moment before answering. "Cars were not searched, but they were scheduled and had to answer someone before the gate could be opened."

"What did these cars bring in?"

The man shrugged; he opened his mouth to reply but was cut off. "Counselor, where is this questioning going?"

"Judge, I am trying to place and figure out how Mr. Simmon could have left the compound. If the cars were not searched on the way out, then a number of prisoners could have escaped."

The judge considered her answer and then nodded, indicating that she should continue. She thanked the judge and then turned back to the witness. "Why weren't the cars searched on the way out of the compound?"

The guard shrugged. "It never really occurred to us that someone would try and escape that way. Most of the prisoners in the compound didn't really seem to mind. This had been one of the cleaner jails that they had been in. There wasn't a whole ton to do up there, but most seemed okay with that. Plus, we have very good security once outside of the wires. We had sensors outside of the compound, which would tell us if some unknown object was moving. We also had some infrared cameras and heat cameras throughout the first few hundred feet of the forest surrounding the compound."

Meila began pacing again. "What about the gate that leads into the compound?"

The guard sat up taller and watched her pace. "We opened it from inside of the guardroom. If the place were to ever go into lockdown, the gate automatically locked, not allowing anyone to enter nor exit."

Meila nodded and sped up her pacing. "You mentioned earlier that you had infrared. How far down the mountain did that go?"

Silence echoed on for a minute before the man answered. "Just a few miles down the mountain. They stopped when we hit public property."

Meila kept her head down, watching her feet walk. "But the road did not have infrared sensors on it?"

The guard shook his head. "That would have been too difficult. Trucks that brought up supplies once a week set off the alarms. Plus, whenever the asphalt was hot, our system would send us a message telling us that someone was out there."

"That's not how those sensors work."

He sighed. "I know, but these were unlike many other infrared cameras. When prisoners arrived, they were marked with a special chemical. This camera had a way of telling us when a prisoner had escaped because of their marking. We did have some other infrared cameras, but they started to go crazy, so we switched over to this new gear. The first few times that it happened, we sent guards out to make sure that no one had escaped. After a while, we just got tired of the alarm going off. That's when the new gear came in. It really helped."

Meila looked to Cody to see him intently staring at his notebook. She looked back to the witness. "Now that you have had some time to think about this, sir, do you mind if I repeat one of Mr. Lopez's questions?"

The guard shook his head.

"Please do not answer swiftly. If a name comes to mind, any of us would be willing to know who."

The man nodded and leaned back in his chair, obviously ready to answer.

"Do you know who owned the building?" Meila asked, hoping that she would at least get that answer.

But the man shook his head. Meila stopped her pacing, waiting to see if any other questions came to her mind. When nothing came, she nodded and then sat down.

Cody stood, releasing the security guard off the witness stand and calling his next witness. The rest of the day went like this, but

Meila did not really pay attention. He brought up no new information that was needed to help her win the case.

Finally, court was adjourned for the day, and Meila watched as the guard took JP from the room. Meila looked back to her things and then started to clean up. Cody stopped by her desk on the way out. "I'm surprised that you didn't question the third witness that I had on the stand. She could have offered you some valuable information." He smirked.

Meila just shrugged. "Everything that she presented, I already knew, so why question something that I have previously researched," Meila closed her briefcase. She reached down and picked up her jacket before leaving Cody with some parting words. "Honestly, Agent Lopez, you are going to have to do better than that to beat me." Meila leered and then turned and left the room.

CHAPTER 60

Cody called his next witness to the stand. Meila wanted to hit her head against the desk. It had almost been a week since they had started debating in the courtroom. This case was even getting old to her. She wondered how long the judge would allow this to continue.

"Mr. Perez, can you tell us how you are involved in this case against this man?"

Mr. Perez just shrugged. "I knew of him. My old boss used to have me watch him."

"And your old boss was…" Cody left the sentence hanging.

"He called himself Schren." Mr. Perez said, then he nodded, as if confirming the information that he had just laid out.

Meila looked at the man, letting her mind recall where she might have seen him, but her memory came up blank. Cody asked him how he had found Mr. Schren. "We used to be on the same team. I mean, we still are, but he worked with my unit very often before he moved up the chain. He used me and a few other team members often, but we never did anything, except to watch people.

"First, it was a young girl a few years back, then he didn't need us for a few years. About two years ago, he called me and asked me to watch the guy over there"—Mr. Perez pointed at JP—"and report if I saw him make contact with the woman sitting next to him."

Meila looked at the man. She was feeling more confused by the minute. She felt like this man spoke in riddles. He used to watch JP? Why? And why did Charlie have her watched?

"I ran into the young lady on the street just the other day. That is what reminded me that I hadn't reported to anyone about what I had seen." Mr. Perez stopped his testimony. He glanced around the room, as if looking for someone to tell him that what he was about to say was against the rules.

Cody motioned for him to continue.

The man spoke hesitantly at first, but his confidence quickly fell into place. "It was really quite boring at first. The man would just go and get coffee in the morning then proceed to work. He would work until five and then go home. He didn't have a wife or anyone that lived with him, so the TV was on very often.

"Mr. Schren asked that we look deeper into what this man did, so we followed him more closely. We found that he didn't actually work at the building that he went to five days a week. We got his name from Mr. Schren and went to the apartment housing where he lived. No one by the name of Mr. Simmon lived there.

"He disappeared from town. We searched for almost a whole year. One of my men a few months ago called, saying that he had seen a man with a similar shape and look as the man that we had been searching for. We have been watching him ever since."

"You lost contact with Mr. Schren at the same time, did you not?" Cody questioned.

Meila stood. "Objection! Your Honor. This case is not about Mr. Schren. It is about Mr. Simmon."

The judge nodded. "Objection sustained. Counselor, you are to ask questions that pertain to this case and this case only. Do you understand?"

Cody nodded and then moved to his table.

He picked up a file and read something before returning his attention to the witness. "You said that this man disappeared and then reappeared nearly a year later. Can you recall the actual date?"

The man held up a finger and then pulled a small book from his pocket. "I started writing things down when I watched people. I would record the exact time that I was called and what was discussed during that phone call. My memory cannot always be trusted."

Cody nodded and pointed to the book. "What do your notes say?" he prompted the man.

"My man called me at six-thirteen. He reported seeing Mr. Simmon driving out of the mountains and then stopping at a gas station just a few blocks away. My man was supposed to be watching for another person, but when he recognized Mr. Simmon, he thought it might be smart to follow him."

"Did your man have any contact with Mr. Simmon?"

The man shook his head and flipped a few more pages in his book. "I told him to wait while I collected a few things. I knew he was a wanted man for a few different crimes. After I called the agency to get approval for a warrant, I went and spoke with Mr. Simmon."

Cody nodded. "How did Mr. Simmon accept the news?"

The man flipped a few more pages in his small booklet and moved his finger quickly down the page, searching for some information. "He did not really care. He did, however, make eye contact with a woman who looked to be in her thirties and shook his head. He then sat in the car quietly. We have tried to find the woman, but no luck."

Cody nodded and turned to Meila. He paused for a moment, staring at her, and then moved to the table where the evidence had been laid out. "Mr. Perez, you were the one that brought me some of these items, were you not?"

The man on the stand nodded. He pulled out his booklet again and opened it, quickly finding the page he needed. "I brought them to you on April twelfth. I was bringing Mr. Simmon to the agency building for questioning. I did not undertake those, but I instead met you on the seventh floor and relinquished the following items to you. Items included a lock pick and truck keys." The man looked up at Cody after finishing reading the note he had made in his book.

"Did you search the truck?" Cody asked.

Mr. Perez nodded, flipping a few more pages before reading. "It was a white blank truck. It was found empty."

Cody nodded and moved away from the stand and to his table.

"Your witness."

Meila moved out from behind her table. "Mr. Perez, do you recall anything dangerous that Mr. Simmon was doing while you were watching him?"

The man on the witness stand sat silently for a full minute before finally being able to answer. "No, the man who put us on his case did say that he wasn't doing anything wrong. Well, at least at that time. Mr. Schren had noted that Mr. Simmon had committed quite a few crimes before suddenly disappearing."

"So why did you watch him? Other than Mr. Schren telling you to do so?"

Mr. Perez shrugged.

Meila was astounded. She usually went into a job that she knew why she was doing it.

"I have always been told not to question those in charge. I am getting paid and have a roof over my head. Be grateful for what you have."

Meila nodded. "Mr. Perez, I ask you to think about when your man called you, saying that he had found Mr. Simmon. Were you officially put back on the case?" Meila turned around and faced Cody. She walked toward his table, watching his expression crumble.

Mr. Perez's voice forced her to turn around. "No," he answered unassured. "All of the crimes that he had committed, his sentences had been completed."

Meila moved to her table and picked up a file. "Your Honor, I found that no case was ever created against Mr. Simmon. And those that have been, he has accepted the consequences and moved on past them, so I ask you to look over these." Meila put the file down in front of the judge.

He placed his glasses on his nose before flipping through the few pages that had been in the file then closed it. The judge looked up and asked that Mr. Perez step down. "This witness' testimony cannot be used in the case because no case was ever made against this man." The judge's eyes moved past Meila's head and to where Cody sat. "Counselor, I ask that you come better prepared tomorrow." He hit his gavel on the wood stand, adjourning the court until the next morning.

CHAPTER 61

Meila sat down at her desk and watched as JP was brought in. She smiled at him and then approached the judge's bench. "The last few days have been extremely boring for me, counselors. I don't see this case going anywhere." The judge leaned closer to the two of them. "I have more pressing matters that could happen in another courtroom, so this one needs to be solved by tomorrow night."

"But, Your Hon—" Cody started to object.

The judge put up his hand. "I was generous to give you that. I can have this case closed tonight if it were to my advantage. Don't waste any more of my time."

Cody's lips went into a straight line. Meila knew that he was frustrated. She nodded to the judge and moved back to the table. She knew that she had this case in the bag, mostly. She had proven that JP was innocent, which had been her job, but she was doubting herself.

She glanced over at Cody's table. He was speaking to the man that sat by him. By the expression on their two faces, they weren't talking about what they should have for lunch. It was something much more serious than that.

Meila looked over to JP and smiled. He gave her a quick smile but turned his attention to a guard on the left of them, forcing his eyes away from her. Meila looked down to his right arm. His orange jumpsuit stopped about halfway above his elbow. His arm did not have a deep orange band on it. How had he gotten rid of it so quickly?

It had been burned onto their skin. Something like that did not just simply disappear. Meila touched hers, remembering exactly what it looked like and how it defined her. She looked to his right wrist. It too was bare. That struck her as odd. Meila blinked a few times, trying to process this new information.

Meila looked back down at her notes, seeing if there was anything else that she needed to address before ending. Everything hadn't gone as smoothly as it could have. She had a couple of witnesses that didn't give her the information that she had been digging for, but Cody had a couple completely not show up.

She let her thoughts wander back to that day that JP escaped. She had seen flashes of it over the past few weeks. She closed her eyes and let the memory come. The morning had come, but something in her gut told her that something was up. She hadn't believed it at the time, but she wished that she would have. Something about Charlie had been off. He wasn't himself. He usually smiled or nodded to her and acknowledged her during meals, but he hadn't. He wouldn't even make eye contact with her. Meila shook her head. She needed more time to process this. She heard the judge's gavel being hit upon on the stand. Her eyes popped open. She looked over at Cody's table; she could tell that he was almost ready to begin.

She jumped out of her chair, interrupting him. "Your Honor, may we please have a recess?"

The judge looked shocked. "Counselor, we just barely started for the morning. Are you really sure that you need this?"

Meila nodded and let her body sink back into her chair. The judge hit his gavel on his desk, announcing that the court would proceed in a half an hour. Meila sighed, grateful for the chatter that started behind her. Meila opened her briefcase, pretending to be staring and finding something important. Instead, she let memories overtake her thoughts.

CHAPTER 52

Meila slammed her briefcase shut. *It wasn't a piece that she was missing. It was a person!*

Meila glanced around and saw many people looking at her. "I… I need a moment alone to collect my thoughts." Without looking back, she exited the conference room. Once out in the hall, she ran to her temporary office and sunk to the floor. It wasn't something that was causing all of these problems; it was someone. And not just anyone—JP.

Meila should have recognized his handwork. She finally did something that she thought she would never allow herself to do—go back to the day that he left them behind.

She had easily escaped her cell. That was a no-brainer from herself. She also recalled that no guards were on duty in her hall or near her hall. She had not found it strange at the time, but looking back, she saw a mistake. She had been framed for a crime, one that she did not remember committing. She knew that now. She had been more focused on getting out of the compound. If she would have looked harder, she would have seen that the man in the picture had been the one to help with the escape. JP must have known what both of them looked like before she came up here. How else did he know how to find her and to kill Charlie? Besides, she was supposed to be guarded at all times. She had not even seen a single guard on her floor the day of the first escape.

Next was the loud noise Charlie had made. She thought it may have been a guard that had gotten in their way, but it couldn't have been. JP had walked in front of Charlie. The entire time. It would have been too difficult for Charlie to get around JP before a guard had alerted others or when he could have hurt either one of them.

Then, having a delivery truck that day *instead* of the small car. The truck keys had been in the ignition. Meila knew that was more than just a coincidence. There was no way that a delivery man could forget those. She had heard the ringing when she had opened the door. No chance. They were set up.

Of course, there were other flaws in the plan, such as the bars in the empty room moving, no guards finding them sooner. Another big one dawned on Meila. Charlie had been shot. He hadn't really been himself that morning. Meila replayed that scene in her mind. He *hadn't* been himself.

Meila pushed herself away from the ground and wall, moving to her desk. She pulled out the pictures that had been copied for her, flipping through Charlie's file until she landed on an image that had been taken just before both of them were captured. His jumpsuit barely fit around his bulging arms.

Meila pulled up the pictures that Cody had gotten off of the security tape. The man with JP had most of the same features to Charlie's, but the overly large arms had not been there. In fact, he was a little bit shorter than Charlie. How could she have not picked up on that?

Meila leaned closer to the picture. Her mind must have been playing tricks on her. But she recognized the extra man; she supposedly had killed him.

Meila flicked closed Charlie's file and opened her own. She quickly read the article written on her. Nothing that she could pull from it, so she tossed it aside. Moving to the pictures, she found her mug shot staring back at her. She brushed her fingers along it. If she would have known what was going to happen by trusting JP, she never would have done it. Her brother was now gone. She had lived in hate for another ten months before escaping. But when she saw him again, she was more excited that she was free and had let her anger go. She flipped that picture, leaving the memories with it.

Moving on, she went through a handful more before she found the weapon—the pick. She was so anxious to escape that she hadn't seen it before. The pick that JP had used to open the door was the same one that had committed the crime. The first time she had seen it, it had been covered in blood.

She had escaped down their makeshift rope shortly after that, then she went to the truck. Meila analyzed each detail in her mind. She found the biggest issue. Charlie had been shot. When she had gotten to his side, he was covered in blood, but no one had been around them. If Meila would have been watching, she might have seen it happen. If they would have been in the president's car, she would have seen it. The truck had obscured too much of her vision to be able to see it. Now Charlie was dead. He wasn't coming back. She knew that, but she had a hard time accepting it.

Meila lifted her briefcase onto the table and pulled out what she had thought was an amazing invention: her small box. She pulled a paper clip off of the nearest file and used it to pop the top of the lid off, showing her the wires. She counted them and then closed her eyes, imagining her old one. She sagged in her chair. This one did not even work. Everything that JP had told her and was telling her was a lie. Leaving the useless item on the table, she stood. That's why JP hadn't been marked. He did not belong there. She should have seen it from the beginning. He had approached Meila and Charlie. He had been the source of all of their problems, yet he had gotten away unscathed.

Not anymore. Meila knew what she had to do.

She snapped her file closed. She knew whom she needed to talk to, and it wasn't going to be pretty.

CHAPTER 63

She picked up both of the files and her briefcase. She ran through the building until she could see the door of her old office. Meila checked her watch. The judge allowed her thirty minutes of recess. She had almost used ten of those.

She stepped up to her old office and rallied all the courage that she could. She had been worried she might have to do something like this, but she never imagined that day would be today. She pushed open the door to her main office. Marcus was at his desk, fiddling with a new gadget. "Marcus, I need to speak with Cody. Where is he at?"

Marcus just pointed to the conference room without looking up. Meila didn't even bother knocking. Everyone looked up, and conversations stopped when she entered the room. Cody looked ticked. He should be; she said some pretty rude things to him the other day. "You have no rig—"

Meila put a hand up, stopping his words. "I know that I don't, and I don't have time to apologize right now." She put her stuff down on the table. "I found some information that could put JP in jail and keep him there."

All eyes were on her now. "Aren't you fighting to keep him *out* of jail?"

Meila nodded. "Don't get used to me saying this, but I am on the wrong side of this fight." She pulled out the papers and spread

308

them out. "Now, if you want him to stay in jail, pull up a chair and get ready to listen."

Cody spoke before she continued. "And what do you expect in return? I know that you rarely work like this without a price. The man who is paying you will be put in jail."

"This information is more critical than money, and who better than me on your side to get him there?"

Cody thought for a moment. He nodded.

Meila felt a smile grow on her face. She finally was starting to heal.

* * * * *

Meila laid down her briefcase on the desk. JP looked up at her worriedly. "Is everything all right? You ran out of here like a bullet." He smiled at his joke.

Like a bullet is right. But instead of saying it out loud, Meila just nodded and sat down.

A few minutes later, the judge stepped in, requiring everyone to stand. After they had all sat down, Cody spoke. "Your Honor, may I please approach the bench."

The judge motioned that he may, and Cody started his way up there; Meila was not far behind. Cody had lowered his voice so that the rest of the audience couldn't hear them. "Your Honor, I was presented some information that would not only close this case but justify the actions of another one."

Meila looked at him in shock. *Justify another case?* He must be crazy. "I know that I already have shown all of my evidence and was going to close today, but it is vital that this information is not withheld," Cody explained.

The judge looked to Meila. "Do you have any objection to this, Agent Manning?"

"None, Your Honor."

"Very well. Prosecutor, please continue."

Meila returned to the table. JP looked at her expectantly. "What did you learn?"

"I guess that Mr. Lopez found some new evidence."

Meila watched as JP sat in silence for a moment. She wanted to call him out right there and then, but she knew how that would look to everyone who had attended court.

"Any idea what it is?" JP asked, catching Meila's attention again.

"We'll just have to wait and see," Meila responded. She then turned and watched Cody.

Cody pulled the files Meila had given to him out of his brief case. He flipped to the page that showed the pick. He set it aside and pulled a few other pages from his briefcase, some that Meila did not recognize. "Your Honor. As you are well aware, we are here in court to find if the man sitting with Agent Manning is innocent or guilty. I have found new evidence against him that he is guilty."

A murmur started around the room. The judge pounded his gravel and asked for silence before letting Cody move on. "I have been given a security tape that shows who helped Mr. Simmon escape, at least before he made it go dead. He tampered with the cameras, causing us to lose all of our feed." He held up a small screen, showing the judge the partial video. He then moved onto the pictures in a file. "These pictures pulled from a similar case will help you better understand why this man is guilty." He handed all these over to the judge. The clerk then stamped them, and then Cody continued. "Mr. Simmon was inside of the compound only a few days after the arrival of Agent Manning. He knew that she was there, and he knew her abilities. He also knew the abilities of Mr. Charlie Schren. In fact, Mr. Schren was murdered by the man sitting at that table."

There was a collective gasp around the room. Murmurs started up again, causing the judge to hit his gavel again. "Silence! Prosecutor, please explain this nonsense. This man is not on trial for murder. He is on trial for theft. Do you wish to switch the case?"

Before Cody could say a word, Meila jumped up. "Your Honor, I would like to switch the case."

"Counselor? This is very strange. I assumed that you would be against this, not for it."

Meila approached the bench, "Your Honor, I was there the day that Mr. Schren died. I know all of the details. I know that I am fighting for this man's life, but he needs to be put back where he belongs."

The judge sat there astounded. "Very well. Continue on."

"Of course, but will you please put an extra guard at the back door?" Cody requested.

With a flick of a wrist, a guard moved to the back of the room, blocking the exit way.

"As I was trying to point out earlier, Mr. Simmon is responsible for the death of Mr. Schren. They shared a jail cell. He did not murder him soon after he became associated with him, though. He needed crucial information that he knew that he could only get from one person." Cody pointed to Meila. "Agent Manning held that information. Mr. Simmon's informant made him aware of this, so he made sure that Mr. Schren's death was made to look like an accident.

"In his death report, it was written that Mr. Schren fell from a building, ending his life. But on a later look, it was verified that he was stabbed multiple times and shot. But as we heard in an earlier testimony, the guards were short a few men, but that hall didn't have a single prisoner on it. Mr. Simmon was found just a few hours later with a gun in his possession, along with this."

Cody held up the picture of the pick. "A man was killed using this pick. The person that was accused of this was framed. After checking the fingerprints, all that were on it were Mr. Simmon's."

Meila looked over at JP. His knuckles were white. His face was turning red with rage.

"Mr. Schren is not the main focus of this case, nor is his death."

Cody nodded. "I know that it seems irrelevant to the rest of the case. I understand that, Your Honor, but it will prove why Mr. Simmon should be behind bars, along with his informant."

The judge turned away from Cody, moving his attention to JP. Cody spoke before the judge could open his mouth. "Your Honor, I call Mr. J. P. Simmon to the stand," Cody announced.

JP was mad. Meila could tell that he was near boiling point. She was glad that he was forced away from her. The judge's head whipped back around, staring at Cody. He then moved to Meila, confusion written all over his face. "You have no objection to this?"

Meila shook her head no, trying to clear the image of an injured Charlie out of her mind.

"Very well."

JP slowly, grumpily, got up out of his chair and moved toward the witness stand. A guard took position behind him. Once he was under oath and sitting down, Cody started his interrogation. "Mr. Simmon, you were a cell partner with Mr. Schren for how long?"

"Just over three months."

"So you say that you knew him pretty well?"

"Yes. Well, as good as you can get to know a person in that amount of time."

Cody started to pace back and forth. "Did you know of Agent Manning before you met her at the compound?"

"No, sir, I did not."

One of the doors to the courtroom was thrown open, and Agent Walker walked in. He softly apologized to the guard standing there, moving past him and making his way towards Cody. Agent Walker held out a paper to him and leaned in closely to whisper something in Cody's ear. Meila tried to hear what was being said but couldn't make out any words. Cody nodded and took the paper, thanking Agent Walker. He then turned back to JP, continuing his questioning.

"Did you know anyone else inside of the compound besides these two?"

"No."

"Then may I ask how you had this in your possession?" Cody held up the pick.

JP looked around. "I…I picked it up off of one of the officers that came by my cell."

Cody stopped pacing and moved straight toward JP. "And that is where you are lying. You killed Charlie Schren with this exact pick. Then you framed the whole thing on Agent Manning!"

"I didn—" JP tried to interject.

"You killed him three days before you escaped. But you knew that Agent Manning would notice, so you asked for a friend to come in, a friend that looked very much like Mr. Schren. He had the same build and height. All that you had to do was put a number on him that was similar to Charlie's, which was easy with the help of the outside man or woman that you had."

JP just sat there in silence. His face turning a darker shade of red with every truth that was told. Cody didn't seem to care. He just continued on. "On the day that you escaped, you made sure that the look-alike was never close to Meila so that she couldn't tell the difference. You made sure that she was lowered down first, so that you could switch your friend and Charlie's dead body. You then took some fake blood and dumped it on him, making sure that it looked as if he had just died.

"You then threw him out of the second-story window, quickly following behind him and leaving before you could get caught."

JP just stood. "You can't prove any of this."

The guard that was standing behind him put a hand on JP's shoulder and pushed him down. Cody just moved back to his desk and held up a stack of papers. "I think that you would be incorrect on that statement."

The stack was given to the judge. The judge placed his glasses on the bridge of his nose and adjusted the papers so he could easily read them. He looked over everything and nodded. "This man is to be brought back to court where his sentence will be made final. I will review the new information that has been presented in court today. I will need Mr. Simmon to be kept here in a cell and under strict guard. In the meantime, I suggest that Mr. Simmon finds himself a very good lawyer if he wishes to see the outside world ever again."

The guard behind JP put him in handcuffs and moved him toward a door that would lead them downstairs. The judge moved to stand, but Cody stopped him. "Your Honor, I still have a few more things that I would like to say."

"Counselor, can't it wait for another day in court? I have had a long, tiring day."

Cody just gave him a small sympathetic smile and then replied. "I'm sorry, Your Honor, but no."

The judge plopped back down. "Very well, continue—and quickly, if you please."

"The man who acted in Mr. Schren's place after the murder had happened has been apprehended, and we have found evidence of who the outside person was." Cody turned around and pointed to someone on the back row. "Ms. Cassie Dephra!"

Meila gasped as she turned. Sure enough, Cassie was on the back row with a different hair color and cut.

Cassie stood and bolted for the door, but the guard stationed there forced her to stop her useless escape. Voices roared up behind Meila when she turned around, but Cody spoke over them. "I found this when I learned that she went to visit Mr. Simmon while he was being held in our temporary cells downstairs. She visited him often, and I found her looking at things that she did not have clearance for. She has been an accomplice to her father ever since she has worked here. She has passed classified information and stolen from the agency."

The chatter continued to grow and grow as Cassie was dragged to the front of the room. The judge pounded his gavel on the stand. "Order!" Once it had silenced down again, he continued, "I will see that the information that has been offered will be looked at and their final sentence will be determined. Is there anything else, counselor?"

"Just one more, sir." He moved around Cassie over to Meila's side. He pulled on Meila's arm, getting her to stand. "I ask that Agent Meila Manning is cleared of her court case that is to be held on June 2. She was put in the compound under false pretenses. She was not guilty of anything that would have sent her there. Besides, she is the agent that got us Old Man Manning. She also helped us apprehend Rodrigez and Mr. Simmon."

The judge looked to her and then back to Cody. "You believe that she really has changed?"

"Sir, I have watched her change over the last ten years. I can be the first to attest that she is not going to turn out like her father."

Cody moved back to his desk and handed a piece of paper to him. "I received this paper earlier today. It is a pardon from the governor. He has given Agent Meila Manning clearance."

The judge just sighed at the stacks of paper, not bothering to put his glasses on and examine them. "I will go over all of this information before truly determining what is going to happen, as long as there is no objection." The judge looked to Meila.

She just managed to shake her head. The judge gave her a satisfied smile and then dismissed the court. Meila walked over to Cody. "Why did you do that?"

"Not here. Let's go back up to the main office and talk about it."

Cody took Meila's elbow and pulled her to the elevator. Once they made their silent ride upstairs and to the main office, Cody spoke. "I didn't want to talk about it with others around. They didn't need to know all of the details anyway."

"Cody, I appreciate it, but if the judge looks at everything that I did *before* I joined the agency, then I won't be getting any of my rights back. Thanks for the offer, but for the longest time, I remember that you don't actually like me."

The door to the main office opened at that moment. April, Marcus, and Agent Walker walked in. "Way to go, you two. I don't think that the Simmons will be roaming the streets again anytime soon." April commented.

Meila smiled at April. She and April had always gotten along. How come she couldn't have this conversation with her instead?

"Thanks, April. I was just about to tell Meila about Charlie."

April's expression dropped. "Do you mind if we join you?"

Meila just looked at Cody. "What about Charlie?"

Cody just cleared his throat and moved to his desk. After a few moments, he pulled a note from his desk. "Charlie gave me this letter after the first mission that he went on. Do you remember the one that you followed him on, the one at the Old Mill?"

"Of course."

"He wrote this shortly before he left for it. He didn't think that he was coming back. He wanted to make sure that you were taken care of." Cody handed the letter to her.

Meila looked down at the note. "Why have you not given it to me before? You know, the day that I returned?"

Cody shrugged. "I hoped that if I held on to it, he would come back, just like every other time."

Meila understood that. She had spent a few hours in his apartment. Every time that she had heard someone in the hall, she expected him to walk through the door. He never did. She looked down at the note, it was written in Charlie's bold handwriting.

Cody,

If you are reading this, I must have passed on. We both knew that it would happen eventually. Our line of work promises that, I am sorry I left you behind, so please take care of our team. They really are the best.

If Meila is still there, please tell her that I love her and she can have my TV. She will understand.

Meila thought back to that happy day when they argued over his TV.

Cody, I have a file in my desk that has the name "Miny Schren" written on it. It is actually Meila's file. She does not know it, but we were watching her since before she met us. Make sure that she received those documents.

Please know that I am deeply sorry for leaving everyone behind and most likely in your care. This is one of the best teams that the agency has. Let them know that often.

I have enclosed a letter to everyone on the team, please make sure that they are delivered. And for Meila, please take care of her. She may not allow it but watch over her. She is still young and needs someone to train her. Please try and let her into your life. I know that she reminds you of your younger sister, but let her in.

Please read over this often. I hope that you never have to deliver the notes that I have written, but please know that I will be waiting for you on the other side.

Your brother,
Charlie Schren

PS: I have left some extra money in a safety deposit box in the bank next door. The box number is 273. I have left the key taped to the bottom of my desk. Use it wisely. The access card is in my desk. Cody, I have named you as a co-owner.

Meila put down the letter and held out her hand. "Where is my letter?"

Cody motioned to April. "I knew that you would not accept it coming from me, so I gave it to someone else that I knew you trusted."

April put the letter down on Meila's desk. She held it between her fingers, the last thing that she had from Charlie. She would read it once she got home or where she wasn't being watched. "Thank you." She placed the letter on her desk then stood and gave April a hug.

She nodded to Cody and then excused herself. She was going home to get over this exhausting day.

CHAPTER 64

Today was the day after court. Meila was still amazed that Cody had stood up for her. The two of them had never gotten along. Cody had always disliked her and pointed out everything that she had done wrong. He made fun of her often and made her feel insecure. Maybe it was time to give him another chance. She had spent a big chunk of her evening staring at the Miny Schren file that she had been given. She had found it chuck-full. Looking over the pages had brought back memories. She had learned that the agency had been watching her for about two years before she met Charlie. One of the last pages in it was a request that she be made part of their team. It was written the night that she had met Charlie.

Other documents showed the success that she made—names and numbers that she had found, cases that she solved. He even kept some of the letters, including those that told of her leaving him, the list and the quick background she had made for their last mission together. A few other odds and ends had been in the file as well, but they had been small notes. Most like the water can she had drawn up on a sticky note before busting into the office. Meila smiled as she looked back fondly on those memories of herself and Charlie.

As for the letter that she received from him, well, it asked her to give Cody a chance. He asked her to open up to the team, allow them to be a part of her life. He asked that she still think of him but find someone else to help, to move on and make someone else's life better, just as he had done with hers. She was determined to keep his promise. She was going to help someone else.

She pushed the door open to the main office. A woman at the desk in the front had asked to see her ID. Meila felt it was strange not turning the corner to her office and seeing Cassie's smiling face, but it was nice to know that the agency already had someone ready to fill her spot.

Agent Walker looked up when she walked in. He smiled and then waved her over. "Cody asked that you join him downstairs when you arrived. He has been given permission to listen in on the questioning of JP."

Meila nodded. "Thanks, Agent Walker. Are you coming down with me?"

He picked up some papers. "I am actually headed down to the lab, but I will go with you that far."

She put her bag and jacket on the peg she had been assigned then left with Agent Walker.

"So how have you been since learning yesterday's news?"

"I was excited to find out that my rights have been restored, although they never should have been stripped from me in the first place."

"And how about all of the other shocking news that you learned?"

"Well, I should have trusted my gut when it told me not to work with JP. But his plan made sense, so why wouldn't I trust him? As for Cassie, I didn't even see that one happening. I assumed that Cody could have been working with JP. You know, he has always hated me." Not to mention that he had snuck about Charlie's apartment a few times.

Agent Walker hit the button to call the elevator to their level. A beat passed before he responded. "I don't want to contradict you, but he never hated you."

"What?" Meila was astonished.

Agent Walker just shrugged. "Well, you should have seen how hard he fought to get you out of that place. You should have heard the relief in his voice when we got a call from you. I don't think that he ever hated you. I just think that he was mad, mad that you came into the office when you did. I knew him before you came."

Meila nodded. "I was told that Cody and Charlie were best friends, and I got in the way."

Agent Walker agreed. "Yes, but he also didn't have the natural talent that you did. He was jealous of you and how quickly you moved up."

Meila and Agent Walker stepped into the elevator. She had never thought of him being jealous. She never thought that he could possibly be jealous.

Agent Walker got off on the fourth floor and waved to her, wishing her good luck. Meila walked by herself down to the cells and questioning rooms that they had in the basement. She asked the attendant at the front desk to grab Cody. She nodded and then scurried off. Meila sat down in one of the arm chairs and stared at the modern art hung in the waiting room.

A minute later, Cody came around the corner. "Meila. Glad you're here! The investigators haven't gotten too far into the questioning. Come on."

She stood and moved toward him, but she did not follow him. "Cody, I know that I asked you this yesterday, but why? Why would you do this for me?"

He turned back. "Well, it is partially my job, but it is what Charlie would have wanted. He asked me to take care of you"

Meila's gaze turned cold.

"But you are old enough to do that on your own, but I would like for us to be at least friends, and friends don't let each other get down."

Meila let that process for a moment and then nodded. She had made a promise to Charlie that she would try to be kinder to Cody. Now was the perfect time to try.

Cody pushed the door open, allowing Meila to enter first. JP was sitting at the table in the middle of the room. An agent was in the interrogation room with him. Meila and Cody stood behind a one-way mirror. Cody signaled to a man that was with him. He stepped back in, and the interrogation pressed on. "Mr. Simmon, we might be able to reduce your sentence, but we need information from you first."

He just stared in between the two agents. "Fine," he began. "How much time will be taken off?"

The agent that had remained in the room shook his head. "That will be determined on how much information you can tell us, information that is useful."

JP steepled his fingers, thinking. "All right. What do you already know?"

"We already know how you got into the compound, but how did you get in the same jail cell as Charlie Schren? We have documents that a JP Simmon was never listed or even on the same floor as Mr. Charlie Schren."

JP smiled darkly. "You aren't the only type of agency that has people working for them in the strangest place."

The two agents exchanged glances. "Explain."

"Since you won't find any of them there anymore, I guess that I will. When I heard that Old Man Manning's daughter had lived, through my daughter of course, I did some digging myself. I found where he was and paid him a visit. He had, in fact, confirmed that she was alive and had sprung an interest in rejoining the family business. Old Man Manning confirmed that he hadn't told her about me.

"So I had some men sneak into the compound and get to work. I knew who Meila was the moment that she stepped into the cafeteria. She had the same air that her father had about him."

"Why did you wait to get close to them? And what information did she hold that you needed?"

JP leaned back into his seat. "I already had all of the information that I needed from her old man, but I am getting old. I was going to try and get her to switch over to my business. I knew that would never happen unless that big oaf was gone. I also knew the only way I would be getting close to her was through him.

"So I had my men run some interference. I was quickly moved to Mr. Schren's cell. Everything else after that was simple. My daughter even came and visited me after she had completed her part of the plan. I knew that my agent wouldn't be able to come in and look exactly like Mr. Schren, so I had a little drug used against her, a new one that I had been testing. I knew that if it didn't kill her, it would put her off for as long as I needed."

"How was it administered to her?"

JP smiled. "That part was difficult, but I put a larger dose into her lunch the day that those two inspections were made. Later in the week, I had some of my men slip it into the food and liquid that was taken to her cell. I knew that once she even had just a few drops of it, her vision would be off enough to use my man."

"What did you do with Mr. Schren once he was dead?"

"Oh, that was easy. I just made sure that some of my men would come and check my room. They know what happens to those that double-cross me."

"What about Old Man Manning? Weren't you worried he might double-cross you?"

JP shook his head. "He owed me a couple of favors."

The two agents shared a glance before turning back to JP. "Favors? I thought you wanted Miss Manning to join your team and leave his."

JP nodded. "The best way to do that is to pretend to earn the trust of your enemy. I made sure everything worked according to plan. This plan was set into motion years ago. I was the one who got my daughter the job here in the agency. It just so happened she dropped Meila's name a few times before the team looked into it. I was the one who sprung Old Man Manning from the cells under this building. We have been working together the last couple of years, trying to steer clear of cops." JP sat up taller. "Everything over the last ten years have gone according to *my* plan."

"Except for getting caught," one of the officers stated.

When JP didn't respond, the agent that was sitting made a note on his notepad. "One last piece of information we need to know before we can try and fight for your case."

JP motioned for them to continue.

"What was your connection to Meila Manning?"

"I met Meila in the compound. I found that she was still teachable. I knew that I could change her mind, but she didn't take it. Instead, she ran back."

The agent that Cody had signaled to leaned back against the wall. "What about before the compound?"

JP sat up taller. "I don't see how that could help my case."

"Mr. Simmon, we are trying to get the full story. We cannot help you if we don't have it."

JP nodded and leaned forward. "As I mentioned before, I was getting too old to get my business up and running. I needed some new people. I tried to get Meila when she was young, but she was too guarded. Every time I went to speak with her father, she was under constant guard. So I devised a plan. I first purchased a building with the money that my father-in-law, Mr. Miller, left me when he magically disappeared. He was an idiot anyway. He honestly believed that he was trying to help struggling families." JP chuckled.

"What about Meila?" one of the agents said, trying to keep JP on the right topic.

"Well, I tried to get to her while she worked at the agency, but that blonde goon stayed at her side all of the time. I tried to get Cassie to convince her to join me, but she failed. So I put plan B into the works. I planted a bug into Old Man Manning's ear that I have a place where he can send people to be forgotten. Then I played the waiting game."

Meila turned to Cody. "I think that I have heard enough. Can we please go?" Meila did not wish to hear about how naive she had been.

He just shook his head and then gestured back to what was happening in the room. "How did you know that he would send her up there?"

"I found Rodrigez listening in on my conversation with Old Man Manning. Between the two of them, I knew Meila would be on her way up to the compound. Rodrigez is a greedy snake. He can smell a mole a mile away. He just waited for the right moment to tell Manning. Then she was sent to me, and I tried to earn her trust. I worked through her friend to try and become her friend too.

I learned that he was the one that had been guarding her this entire time, so I got rid of him. If she would have listened to me, we would have overthrown this place months ago. She would be rich and free.

"When Mr. Miller was pronounced dead, his money was left to me. Well, it was actually left to my wife, but she passed away years ago. When I received the money, I found that my own business could grow and develop. That is why I needed Ms. Manning. She could help me run my business and take down her father."

"Our witness claims to have heard two gunshots right before you left the compound. Why was that?"

JP shrugged. "I had to sell the whole story to Miss Manning. If I ran up to the truck holding a gun in my hand, my whole plan would have been busted. But I also knew that Miss Manning wouldn't have believed that Charlie fell from one story up and passed away. I needed the situation to end how I wanted it to."

"It didn't look as if it worked out in your favor anyway," one of the agents pushed.

JP just sighed. "Is that everything?" he asked.

Meila looked back up at Cody. He grabbed her elbow and steered her out of the room. "*Now* we can go."

Meila was still speechless until they reached the elevator. Cody hit the button to their floor, and the door closed. "Did you know? Did you know JP was one of the men that my father wanted off the street?"

Cody shrugged. "We weren't sure until he went and visited your father. He saw him just a few hours after you had arrived there, you know." Cody looked away from her and stared at the silver doors. "I spoke with the judge this morning. He told me that JP is looking at thirty years or more. Every time he looks at JP's case, it just gets worse."

"I can't believe that I didn't see that he was lying to me."

Cody did not move his eyes from the doors. "We all make mistakes," Cody responded softly.

Meila nodded. "What about Cassie?"

"She was harder to crack, but I knew that she was plotting something when I found her snooping around your desk. She tried to brush it off, but I knew that something was up. I let her go that time, but I kept an eye on her. I didn't have to watch long, though. She was back poking around your desk about a week after I had found her the first time."

The elevator doors opened, and another few passengers climbed on, stopping Cody's retelling for now. When the doors opened to the seventh floor, Meila and Cody squeezed past the half-full elevator and moved toward the main office. After they entered, Cody pulled her into the kitchen. It was one of the only rooms that you could get relative privacy in their office.

"Cassie was watching security tapes and had some files under a false bottom in one of the drawers. I confronted her, and the next day, she disappeared."

"How did you know who she was?"

"Like I said in court, she visited this man, but she claimed that she had never met him. The next time that she went down to visit him, I sent Agent Walker down after her. He came back and told me that she was way too familiar with him. That helped me in the search too. Not very many people could be hired here without a reference. When I looked how she was hired, she had no paperwork. That was right around the time that I found her watching the security tapes."

Meila nodded in understanding. Cody stood and moved to the fridge, pulling out a water bottle. "I found out her real last name from a document I found online. She had done this fake ID at other places too, I guess." He opened the water bottle and brought it back to sit at the table. He was taking a sip of it when her next question came.

"What about JP? When I walked in to confront you yesterday, you were so confident. Why were you so sure that I would figure everything out?"

Cody closed his water bottle. "I knew that you would have found the truth out sooner or later, so I just found a few things that made me look like I had evidence that you would eventually produce."

"How did you know?"

Cody stood. "I didn't want to believe Charlie when you first arrived here. He told me that you were a smart girl and to never underestimate you. I did time and time again, but my gut told me not to this time. I just let you discover for yourself that you can do anything you set your mind to." He walked away from the table, stopping just before he stepped out of the room.

"Meila." He waited until she looked over at him. "We have another case that I think would interest you especially. Besides, the team could really use the expertise that only you can contribute."

Meila felt a smile grow on her face.

Over the two years, they had conquered her father, Rodrigez, JP, and Cassie. Whenever she had done something for her father, she had felt as if it only led to disappointment and heartache. At the agency, she noticed the smiles and the excitement of making the world a safer place. She finally felt victorious. She had conquered her hardships with the help of her team, and she was ready to do it again. She did not have to work alone anymore. She was wanted and needed.

Meila stood, following Cody out of the door, grateful to be a part of this team again.

EPILOGUE

Meila grabbed the arm of the teenage boy. "Please! Don't go!"

"You have no idea who I am or what I have been through! Leave me alone!"

"I will. I promise, but can I first have your name?"

He stared at her confusedly. "My name? Why? So you can find me later?"

Meila smiled. This reminded her so much of her and Charlie. "No. Here." She pulled out a card with her name on it. "I'm Meila. I know what you have been through and where you've been. Trust me." She smiled at him.

"Isaiah," he firmly said a few moments later.

"Well, Isaiah, I saw you leaving your house—"

"You followed me?"

Meila quickly shook her head. "No. We just happened to be going the same way. Anyway, I need you to answer a few questions for me, then you are free to go."

"Questions about what? You want to know my favorite color or something?"

Meila's felt her lips turn up higher. *He was so much like me when I was younger.* "No. I need you to tell me what you were supposed to tell—"

Isaiah's face split with surprise. "How do you know about any of that?"

"My team has been keeping an eye out on this part of the city. We almost have enough to put your aunt and uncle away, but you could do that for sure."

Isaiah seemed to contemplate this. "What do I get?"

"What your aunt and uncle could never offer you: freedom."

Isaiah started to pace on the roof. "Why did you give me this then?" holding up the card she had placed in his hand.

Meila walked toward him. "I'm giving you the advantage. If you want help after tonight, then me and my team will be there for you. But if not, you can disappear and never have to think of any of this again."

"Fine. I will come with you. Then and only then, will I decide what I'm going to do next."

Meila opened the door to the building. "All right." She motioned for him to precede her and guided him through the building.

ACKNOWLEDGMENTS

I want to thank my mom Linell who was my chief editor. She listened as I explained more about the book. She helped me through the many rough parts and dedicated so much of her time to help me with my dream. Thank you for reassuring me when I doubted. Thank you, Mom!

I also wanted to thank those who encouraged me once they learned about this book—my immediate family, cousins, aunts and uncles, friends, and coworkers. Thank you for pushing me forward. Thank you for being patient with me and believing in me.

This journey of having a book published has been amazing, and none of it would have been possible without Covenant Books. Thank you, Covenant Books, especially Adam and Ashley who answered my many questions and checked in with me to see how everything was coming along.

Last, one whom I am most eternally grateful to, is my Heavenly Father. Thank you for making me see more of my potential and go after it. Thank you for inspiring me day after day and never giving up on me.

Thank you again to everyone. I am truly blessed to have so many great people around me to lift me up in my hard times and to cheer me on when everything is going well.

ABOUT THE AUTHOR

Jakayla Twitchell was born and raised in Northern Utah. She is currently attending Weber State University. When not doing homework, she spends her time with her family, reading, and writing. She has a love of watching sports.

Jakayla loves Disney movies and music. She also enjoys playing games, but only if she wins!

CPSIA information can be obtained
at www.ICGtesting.com
Printed in the USA
BVHW080605220323
660849BV00006B/116

9 781685 264079